NO ONE
KNOWS
US
HERE

ALSO BY REBECCA KELLEY

Broken Homes & Gardens

NO ONE KNOWS US HERE

A NOVEL

REBECCA KELLEY

LAKE UNION
PUBLISHING

Text copyright © 2023 by Rebecca Kelley

Published by Lake Union Publishing, Seattle

www.apub.com

Amazon, the Amazon logo, and Lake Union Publishing are trademarks of Amazon.com, Inc., or its affiliates.

ISBN-13: 9781542038829
ISBN-10: 1542038820

Cover design by Eileen Carey

Printed in the United States of America

To my mom, who always believed I would be a writer

PART ONE

"Because I love you," he said.

That's when I did it. The knife was already in my hand. It was a boning knife he'd insisted on buying. A skinny six-inch blade with an extrasharp tip for gouging into joints. Scalpel sharp. I'd told him we didn't need it. He didn't like dealing with raw meat, all that cold skin and bone and gristle. Usually we made pasta. We made salads. Cheese plates. We didn't need a boning knife for any of that.

He insisted, though. He insisted on buying the whole set. Before meeting me, the man had nothing but IKEA knives, flimsy things made out of plastic and cheap metal.

The new knives were marvels of engineering, perfectly balanced. I had demonstrated in the store, perching the ten-inch chef's knife on my index finger. See how it hovers there, without dipping one way or the other? We inspected the edges. This was Japanese high-carbon stainless steel, I explained. I knew the whole sales pitch backward and forward. The edges were hand finished to nine-degree angles and then cooled with nitrogen. The handles were ergonomically designed, smooth in the palm. Feel that? He gripped the handle firmly, mimed chopping and slicing motions. He grinned and jutted the knife away from him, like he was winning a sword fight.

All he really needed was a good Santoku knife to get started. I *told* him that.

He bought them all. The paring knife, the serrated utility knife, the bread knife, two Santokus, the ten-inch chef's knife I'd balanced on my finger, the honing steel, the scissors, the magnetic strip we would install over the counter ourselves with the power drill. And the boning knife.

When he said he loved me, I plunged it straight into his throat.

CHAPTER 1

She came at the end of summer, when everything around us was on fire. The city suffocated under the dirty gauze of smoke. Ash fell like snow from the sky. Ash was everywhere that summer: on the hoods of cars, on the ferns in the park, caught in spiderwebs.

The forest fires surrounded our city on all sides. The early ones seemed far away, in British Columbia and Montana and California. If the wind blew just right, we could forget about them for a day or two; we could go on thinking everything was normal. But then the gorge burned, and the Coast Range. Farmland down in central Oregon. The Cascades. I lost track of them after a while, all of these fires.

People were walking around the city wearing face masks and carrying parasols to protect their outfits from the ashfall, like we were living in apocalyptic times, like we were the dad and that kid in *The Road*.

If I had known she was coming, I could have picked her up at the airport. I could have taken a day off work without pay or, at the very least, come home early. Or at the very, very least, I could have come home right after my shift instead of going out to drink at the Marathon with my friends. I didn't know, though. I wasn't expecting her, so I worked my whole shift.

The forests were burning and the sky was falling, but still we opened up shop on NW Twenty-Third Avenue, and still people streamed in and bought Le Creuset teakettles and WÜSTHOF knives and Zyliss salad spinners. It kind of made me feel better, like it was a good sign that we weren't nailing up boards to the windows and locking ourselves in fallout shelters. The people who came in were the same people who always came in. They weren't dressed for the apocalypse at all, save for the face masks. They were dressed in nice sundresses from J.Crew. They brushed the ash from their sleeves when they walked in, and then they bought their decorator tips and their toasters. Some of them set up wedding registries. When people are buying salad spinners, how bad could it be?

~

I walked home from the Marathon late. I couldn't smell the smoke in the dark. Either that or I'd gotten used to it. I couldn't see the smoke in the dark, either, except as an eerie haze around the streetlights. I could almost pretend it was an ordinary evening. The smoke had come and gone all summer, but the ash hadn't started falling until a few days ago. This is how it is now, I remember thinking. It will never be the same again.

My apartment was a rare three-bedroom place, not far from work, on a beautiful tree-lined street surrounded by much grander and more expensive houses and apartments. My apartment building was grand, too, or at least it had been at one time, with Corinthian columns and balconies in the front.

There were five of us crammed into that apartment. I had moved in almost a year ago with Steele. We were kind of going out at the time, and even though we weren't that serious, we decided to move in together anyway because the rent was cheap and it was within walking distance of La Cuisine, where we both worked. This was a long story that ended with us breaking up and both refusing to move out. He won a coin toss, and I moved into the closet—just big enough for a twin mattress on the floor. It was better than the alternative, which was for Steele and me to split the room in half, drawing a line down the middle like squabbling siblings.

Brooke and Melanie, a couple—married, I think—whose names appeared on our lease, had been there the longest. They lived in the middle room, hung dyed tapestries instead of curtains over their windows, and smelled like nag champa.

Then there was Mira.

Mira had her own room, the south bedroom. Sometimes she'd leave her door cracked open, and I would peek inside. Her room didn't seem to belong to the rest of the apartment, and neither did Mira, really. Her room had real furniture and an ivory wool rug that arrived in a huge, heavy roll from a store I'd never heard of. I looked it up online. The rug cost $1,500, and that was half off.

On that smoky summer evening I came home late, and the whole apartment was dark except for the kitchen, where two figures sat across from each other at the kitchen table. One was Mira, her black hair released from its usual updo and flowing down across the back of the chair. She was dressed up, in a tight black cocktail dress, though her feet were bare. She was laughing and drinking wine.

The other person was laughing and drinking wine, too. A friend of Mira's, I thought, though I'd never known Mira to invite a friend to our apartment. Not once in the year I'd lived there had she invited anyone over. I saw Mira only coming and going. She was the only person outside of TV doctors who looked sexy in scrubs. She wore them in jewel colors to set off her skin, her dark hair, and her almost black eyes. I'd often meant to ask her if she had them made for her by a tailor, sewn up to her exact measurements.

She would come back from dental school wearing scrubs and leave moments later in a fancy party dress. She had a rack of them—a genuine clothing rack on wheels. Sometimes, if our paths crossed, I would ask her where in Portland she was going in that satin ballgown, in those red-soled stilettos, and she would just laugh and say, "out and about" or "here and there."

When I closed the apartment door behind me, the two of them looked up, the blonde one swooping a curtain of hair away from her face in a practiced gesture that was designed to appear casual and sexy at the same time. "Heyyy!" she said to me in a gravelly, California way. "Surprise!"

It wasn't a friend of Mira's after all. It was my sister. I hadn't seen her since the funeral fifteen months ago. She'd been such a little kid then. She'd had braces. She'd worn a hair clip with a giant bow glued to it.

Now she was sitting across from my roommate, laughing and swishing her hair around. She smiled at me—a huge grin, her teeth smooth and straight and tinged dark from wine. Her eyes were sparkling and mischievous, like she'd pulled off some daring caper in a quirky crime comedy.

I didn't smile back—I couldn't smile back—because I was still taking it all in: my little sister, sitting in my apartment, miraculously all grown up. She was wearing an outfit I never would have dared to wear at her age—cutoff shorts and a white tank top over a black lacy bra. She had *cleavage*. When she jumped up to throw her arms around me, I could see that she had shot up in the months since I'd seen her last. She towered over me, pressed me against her new pillowy chest, making me feel like *I* was the younger one, a tiny scrap of a girl who could still wear clothes from the kids' section if I really wanted to.

Wendy collapsed back onto her chair and picked up her glass of wine—some huge Beaujolais glass—from the table and started swirling it around and taking big throaty gulps like she knew what she was doing, like she'd done it before.

That's when I marched up and took the glass from her. Wendy froze midlaugh.

I looked over at my roommate, the responsible adult in this situation. "She's *thirteen* years old, Mira!"

Mira's eyes went wide, taking Wendy in. She didn't look thirteen. I will grant her that. "Oh, shit, sorry."

Wendy narrowed her eyes at me. Even her eyes had matured. They were still big and gray-blue, but now they were rimmed with black eyeliner and mascara. It wasn't just that, though. They were wiser, somehow. Calculating. "Fourteen," she said. She plucked her glass out of my hands and raised her eyebrows.

I wanted to relent then, to sit down at the table and top off her glass of wine. Because until that moment I didn't really have a stance on underage drinking at all. It's legal in Europe, right? Children drink wine at dinner. It's just that the last time I'd seen her she was still a kid, an innocent little kid whose parents had both just died on her, and now she was swishing hair and swilling wine, and the crazy thing was it all seemed like yesterday—the phone call, the funeral, everything.

"I thought you'd be happy to see me," Wendy said. I couldn't read her expression. I couldn't read my own sister's expressions anymore, not after all these years.

I sat down at the head of the table and sighed. Mira set one of those gigantic wineglasses in front of me, and I poured myself some wine from the bottle on the table. Wendy took a sip from her glass, and I didn't stop her. Some role model I was. But really, after all she'd been through—we'd been through—a little wine wasn't going to do any further damage.

"How did you even get here?" I asked.

Wendy flashed her smile again. "Followed in Cleo's footsteps. Worked like a charm."

"Who the hell is Cleo?"

"Cleo from *The Island Keeper*?" She downed the rest of her wine in a few glugs, and again I didn't say anything. "Only our favorite book of all time?"

The way she said "our" broke my heart.

"My grandma signed me up for summer camp," Wendy explained. "It's like four hours from Sacramento, and she was going to drive me there herself, but then at the last minute she changed her mind—said it made more sense for me to fly there and have them pick me up. I made a few phone calls, Grandma dropped me off at the airport, and voilà! Here I am."

"You couldn't have just arranged a visit like a normal person."

Wendy laughed and poured herself more wine. "Face it, Rosemary. You never would have agreed to that."

Mira took this as her cue and stood up. "Listen, I've got to get going."

I looked up at the clock on the kitchen wall. It was midnight. "Where are you going at this hour?"

She smiled and raised a perfectly shaped black brow. "Oh, you know me. Cinderella off to the ball at the stroke of midnight."

"Cinderella has to *leave* the ball at the stroke of midnight," Wendy informed her, holding up a finger as if she were making a serious point. I realized then she was drunk. "Not *go* to the ball."

Mira picked up an overnight bag by the door. "You can crash in my room if you want," she said to Wendy. "Just three nights, though." Then she was gone.

I turned back to my sister. "So I guess you can stay here for three nights."

"Two weeks," she said.

I looked around the apartment and gestured to the living room. We didn't even have a couch—just your basic hodgepodge collection of rickety chairs, only one of which was upholstered. "There's nowhere for you to sleep," I said.

"Oh, we'll figure something out."

~

My job felt more pointless than usual. I paced around the maze of the store, Ms. PAC-MAN in slow motion, feather duster in hand. I dusted the ash from shelves, from the tops of boxes. Ash flew from the duster into the air, up our noses, into our lungs. Then it drifted back down again.

This is the kind of important work I was doing instead of hanging out with my little sister, my last remaining relative on earth, who had run away just to be with me.

A half hour before the end of my shift, I asked my manager if I could leave early. Rich was a gay guy in his early fifties. He always came to work wearing a suit and spit-polished black dress shoes, which we—the employees on the sales floor—found quirky and endearing. Even the store owner didn't dress up that nicely when he visited. "Go for it," Rich said. Then I asked if I could take the next two weeks off, claiming a family emergency. He shrugged. "Sure, I think we can survive without you." He didn't even bother to consult the shift calendar.

"Way to make me feel like I'm making a difference, Rich," I said.

"Enjoy your family emergency. See you in two weeks."

~

The ash settled down into the dirt, and the sky turned blue again. The city was beautiful, sparkling the way it did sometimes in the summer, when people visit and wonder how anyone ever leaves. I would show her a good time. It was the least I could do.

We ate blackberry pie and drank huckleberry milkshakes for dinner. Stayed up late watching movies and slept in as long as we wanted. When Mira came back from her trip, Wendy slept out on the balcony in a sleeping bag on an air mattress. During long summer afternoons, we did whatever we wanted: rode orange city bikes up and down bridges, sat in dark movie theaters, ate picnics in parks. We threw a party in the apartment. All my roommates and everyone I knew from work came and danced under the lights we'd strung across the ceiling.

On our last night, my little sister and I watched two old Hitchcock movies and grilled BOCA burgers and ears of corn on the hibachi grill out on the balcony. Charcoal smoke drifted up and dissipated into the evening sky. At three in the morning we were still sitting there, wrapped in quilts, looking over the treetops. It was quiet, no cars or people or even birds. The dead of night, as they say.

"Don't make me go back," Wendy said.

"You'll have to come visit again." I kept my tone light, as if I hadn't noticed the desperation in her plea. "Christmas, maybe."

"Mira's moving out next month. She told me."

"So?"

"You could move into her room. *We* could move into her room."

"My friend Margorie is supposed to move in. Maybe in a few years—"

"A few *years*?"

"I have a lot going on," I said. "I told you this. I'm studying for the LSATs. I've decided to apply to law schools. That's the plan. I'm up to my *ears* in student loans already." I laughed—a humorless bark of a laugh—and gestured to the direction of my bedroom. "I live in a *closet*, Wendy. I can barely take care of myself; I can't take care of a kid right now—"

"I'm not a kid. I'm your sister." Wendy was crying now. I pretended not to notice.

"I'll ask Rich for more shifts," I said. "I'll fly you here for Christmas. I'll work something out."

"You never even called." She looked so young then, the way I remembered her. She didn't bother to brush the tears from her cheeks.

"Maybe it will snow. We'll have a white Christmas."

"You liked me. You *used* to like me." The tears had stopped, and she wiped them off quickly with the back of her hand. When she looked over at me, her eyes seemed extra bright, the blue of her irises glowing. "We played Barbies for hours. You made them outfits. Built them houses under the dining room table. Gave them voices."

I picked up a skewer and prodded at the coals in the hibachi grill. A plume of white smoke curled from the coals like a ghost.

"It wasn't like you were just babysitting me. You were into it, right? Or maybe you're just a great actor."

"You should eat something." I unwrapped a BOCA burger that had been languishing in its cellophane sleeve all night and set it on the cold grill. She didn't eat it.

"Were you?" Wendy asked.

"Was I what?"

"Acting."

"Don't be stupid."

"So the minute you take off for college, I never hear from you again? And then our parents die and it's like, 'Have a nice life'?"

"It wasn't like that."

"What was it like, then? Explain it to me."

I had left her. That was true. I had left her deliberately and completely. Our mother, too. It was for her own good, I wanted to tell her. I had planned to leave years before I did, as a teenager. The only thing that got me through my teen years was the knowledge that one day they would end. After I graduated from high school, I would go off to college and never come back. I applied to colleges all over the country and a couple outside the country. I wanted to get as far away as possible. I didn't get any farther than Portland, Oregon. A small liberal arts college had not only accepted me but given me the most generous scholarship, so that was where I landed.

I hugged my mom and sister goodbye and vowed to never see them again. They would be better off without me. That was what I believed.

That first Thanksgiving, I didn't go home. I stayed in Portland in a special dorm for all the other stragglers, the exchange students and the kids who couldn't afford a plane ticket. After that it was easier. I made friends. I never went home again and discouraged my family from visiting. It was that simple.

It was Wendy's grandmother—my step-grandmother, I guess—who got a hold of me to tell me the news near the end of my junior year. I never asked how she tracked me down. My mother and stepfather had died in an accident, she said. I was sitting in the library, studying with a group of friends. Philosophy 312. Ethical Theories. I watched my classmates, their heads huddled together over books, while she talked. They'd driven straight off the edge of the mountain in broad daylight, she'd said. They were dead. I'm sorry, I remember telling her. You must have the wrong number. I ended the call, just like that.

"It wasn't about you," I said to Wendy after a moment. I took a few gulps of my wine, just to get it down. A dull pain throbbed behind my eyes.

"My parents just died! How was it not about me? Didn't I factor into it at all? Didn't you wonder, gee, what is my little sister going to do now?"

I shook my head and frowned. "What can I say? I'm a selfish bitch." The truth was, when Wendy's grandma called to tell me the news, I hadn't thought of Wendy at all. That was what a normal person would have done, right? Think of her little sister? To be fair, I hadn't thought much of myself, either. I had gone back to studying and focused on my notes. It was as if her words had entered my head but then immediately been erased.

The next day I got up and aced that test.

It hit me later that evening, when I was sitting around with a group of friends in their weird run-down house that was painted Pepto Bismol pink with brown trim. I was with Steele at that point, though it was fairly new at the time. We were passing around some disgusting drink—generic Kool-Aid and lower-shelf vodka—and at some point someone asked me what was wrong. I was just sitting there, practically catatonic, staring into space, glugging down that punch. I think my mom just died, I announced. I don't remember much after that. I don't even remember how I managed to make it to the funeral. Did I buy myself a plane ticket? Did one of my friends? It didn't seem like something I would have been capable of doing on my own.

Was I thinking of my twelve-year-old sister, wondering how she was doing or who was taking care of her? She didn't even cross my mind. Not back then.

"I *know* what it was about," Wendy said. "I know why you left and never came back." Her chair scraped across the balcony, closer to me. I could feel her wine-scented breath in my ear. Her eyes were huge, wild, scanning my face for a response.

My hands gripped the armrests in a flimsy attempt at steadying myself. I tried to keep my expression blank, neutral.

"I know what my dad did to you," she said, so softly I could almost believe I was hallucinating.

A shiver ran through me, though the air was still warm, at the tail end of summer. Even in the middle of the night. I pulled the blanket tight around my shoulders and let my eyelids sink down, the way they might in church, before a prayer.

"Wendy—"

"I know because he did it to me, too."

Everything went sideways, all at once. All the wine went straight to my head, and I felt drunker than I'd ever been. I tried to screw my eyes shut, clamp them closed, but it made everything worse, like I was seasick, lurching back and forth, this close to capsizing.

It was the worst moment of my life. Worse even than the phone call announcing my mother's death.

"You don't have to cry about it," Wendy said, and that's when I realized that tears were streaming down my cheeks, snot was leaking from my nose. "You had to have at least suspected—"

"He was your *father*," I managed to say at last. "Your own father." Fathers do bad things to their daughters all the time. I knew that. I just didn't think Jason would do that to Wendy. It honestly hadn't occurred to me. "I never would have left," I said. "You've got to believe me."

She shrugged, like she was over it now.

I pressed the heel of my hand to my forehead, trying to release the pressure forming behind my skull. "No, no, no," I muttered to myself. And then I yelled out onto the street, a wordless cry, so loudly a flock of birds in a nearby tree startled, flapped their wings, rustled the leaves, and shot out, one after the other, frenzied. Then they were gone, their dark figures receding into the distance.

"It's not like I blame you," Wendy said.

"But you should." I turned toward her, gripped her hands in mine, clasped her fingers.

"*He* did it," she said. "He did it to both of us."

"No," I cried out. I was hysterical by then. My entire face was wet, slick with tears.

"Calm down." Wendy tried to free her hands from mine, but I wouldn't let her. I held on tighter. I'd crush her fingers in mine before I let her go.

"I did this to you," I whispered. "Don't you see that? I never should have let this happen. This wasn't supposed to happen." I picked up another wine bottle from the balcony floor and unscrewed the lid. It was some sort of cheap rosé, as warm as the night air. Wine sloshed out of the bottle and into her cup, then mine, spilling over the rims and onto our fingers.

"I don't blame you for what he did," Wendy said, her voice raised. "I blame you for leaving."

"I thought you'd be happy." My voice came out small. "You, Mom, him. One perfect little family."

"Yeah, right. Like the wicked fairy."

"You remember that?" I opened my eyes wide at her, trying to focus on her face. It was getting blurrier and blurrier by then.

"You only told the story to me every night for two years straight."

"You were just a little kid."

There was once a beautiful young queen, it began. A beautiful young queen and her wicked little fairy. The wicked little fairy was a burden to the queen, tying her down. Every night the story would be a little different. The wicked fairy would do slightly different wicked things—funny things, outlandish things, little inventions to make Wendy laugh.

It always ended the same way. The queen would meet her handsome prince and they would have a beautiful baby princess and the wicked fairy would see how much happier the queen was, just the three of them. The wicked fairy would fly away, to join the other wicked fairies, so the three of them could live happily ever after.

It wasn't the most creative fairy tale. A mash-up of *Sleeping Beauty*, *Cinderella*, and *Where the Wild Things Are*.

Wendy leaned in. "What if the wicked fairy wasn't wicked after all?" she said. "What if she was a princess, too? What if the handsome prince was the wicked one? He was the one who needed to get banished to another kingdom, torn apart by dragons or something." Wendy gave a sad little smile. "That would have been a way better ending."

I could only nod. "You're right," I said.

The sky was lightening around the edges. Soon the sun would rise. I was due to drop Wendy off at the airport in three hours. We were silent for several minutes, watching the sky, listening to the sounds of the early morning. Leaves rustling. Cars in the distance, on other streets. "I could have stopped him," I said. Wendy's eyes were closed. Maybe she'd fallen asleep. The words rushed out of me then, a confession. "I could have stopped him, but I didn't. I didn't." I topped up my wine again, took a gulp. It didn't taste bad anymore. I'd grown used to it. I tilted my head up, imagining it, imagining my life without him in it, connecting the plot points of my life, how it would all add up. "Mom would still be alive." My voice cracked on the words. "They never would have driven over that cliff—"

Wendy's eyes opened. Her head rolled across the back of the chair so she could observe me. "You're drunk," she said.

"Think about it," I said. "If I'd done it—"

"Done *what*?"

"Killed him," I said. I had thought that was obvious.

Wendy let out a laugh, a single "Ha!"

"I could have done it. I was this close—" I was crying again. "Everything would be okay now—"

"You'd be in prison."

"Think about it. Think about it—some people deserve to die. Imagine if all the rapists, all the child abusers, all of them—imagine if they were just wiped off the face of the earth. The world would be a better place, right? I mean, I believe that. Sometimes, killing someone is the responsible thing to do. Sometimes, it—"

"No one asked you to kill my dad," Wendy interrupted. "I asked you to maybe shoot me a text every once in a while."

I stared down into my cup, swirled the rosy-pink wine around and around. It looked so beautiful in there, the dimming streetlights bouncing their amber hue off the liquid. It was so, so beautiful, a sunset in a glass. "I'll make it up to you, Windy-girl," I said. That was what I used to call her sometimes, when she was little. I don't know where it came from, or who started it—me or my mom. We both called her that. Our little Windy-girl.

"Let me live with you," she said.

I looked back into the apartment. Soon my roommates would be awake, puttering around the kitchen, setting the kettle to boil, eating cereal out of mismatched bowls. "I'd need a new place," I said. "A new job."

"You owe me," Wendy said, pleading. "Isn't that what you said?"

We locked eyes. Wendy tried to dab at my tears with the end of my blanket. She nodded slightly. A tentative smile formed on her lips. "You owe me," she repeated, until I could do nothing but bob my head up and down and tell her I'd give it a shot. At the very least, I'd try.

I promised her that.

CHAPTER 2

When I got a text from Mira while I was at work, I was surprised. I'd never gotten a text from her before. I didn't even know she had my number. She said she was having a going-away party that night, downtown. She asked me if I could come. I said I could. Good, she said. She gave me an address and a time. Then she said to dress up for the occasion. **Wear something of mine,** she wrote. **Anything you want.**

I thought it was strange, of course. I was also very curious. I had never seen Mira outside of our apartment. I'd never met any of her friends. Also, I'd always secretly wanted to try on her dresses.

The restaurant was way up on top of the old Meier & Frank Building downtown. I didn't typically frequent places like that. They were for other kinds of people. Rich people. Tourists. So this is what Mira was doing in all those satin gowns? Hanging out with her dental school friends at rooftop restaurants?

I took the elevator up and passed through a narrow hallway to the outdoor seating area. I walked with my shoulders back, swinging my hips like a model on the catwalk. It was how I felt wearing Mira's clothes. I'd taken one of her handbags, too. If only I could have fit into her shoes! My own black high heels, the ones I'd bought to wear to my mother's funeral, struck the only false note.

Outside the sky was getting dimmer, but the air was still warm. I'd expected to see revelers up there. Lights and dancing. Maybe some wild-and-crazy dentists hoisting Mira up on their shoulders. But the place was quiet. Couples stood along the glass railing, looking out at the city twinkling beyond. Some people sat on couches arranged under heat lamps. They were eating sushi.

I wondered if I had somehow arrived at the wrong rooftop restaurant. Maybe I'd mixed up the time or shown up on the wrong date. But then I saw Mira, sitting along the edge of the balcony, alone. I walked over and sat down across from her.

She smiled at me. "There you are."

I gestured to the other patrons. "Are these your friends?"

"No."

"So where is everybody?"

"I didn't invite anyone else," she said. "Only you." She took a sip of her drink as she looked me over. "That dress looks really good on you."

I looked down at myself. The dress was bright red and strapless. Short. Like something the bad girl wears to the prom in a teen comedy. "Thanks." I tried to smile, but I felt uneasy. If there wasn't a party, I couldn't think of any reason she would tell me to get dressed up and meet her on a rooftop. Was she trying to seduce me? After living together for so long, this seemed very unlikely.

Mira tapped a fingernail against the glass balcony railing. "Look at that," she said.

I looked. I saw the Fox Tower, the clock over Pioneer Square, the West Hills in the distance. The sky was twilight blue, about to fade to black. All the buildings sparkled as distant window squares flicked on, one by one.

Mira reached under the table. She seemed to be looking for something, riffling through her purse. The server came and Mira ordered for both of us, pointing at various items on the menu.

When the waitress walked away, Mira placed something in the middle of the table. It was a present, a wrapped box the size of a paperback book. "Open it," she said.

"For me?" The night was growing stranger and stranger.

Mira didn't say anything. She nodded at the gift sitting between us.

I took the package in my hands and turned it over. I untied the bow. It was a nice bow, a turquoise grosgrain ribbon. The paper was thick and brown like a paper sack, but it was speckled with white dots the size of fish eggs. Underneath the paper was a plain white box. Inside the box was a cell phone.

I wasn't sure how I was supposed to react. It didn't seem like an extravagant phone, or even a new one. It was basic and black. I didn't recognize the brand. "Thank you," I said, because I couldn't think of what else to say.

Mira was smiling at me, some secret, knowing smile. I smiled back, tentatively, unsure how to respond.

We were interrupted again by the server, who set down two martinis. Martinis. Of course Mira had ordered us martinis. I would have preferred something sweeter, less sophisticated. Something with a pineapple wedge and a sugar rim.

She picked up the phone out of the box like it was precious jewelry. She held it up for me to see. "This is your new life."

I must have flashed her a comically baffled look because she burst out laughing.

I laughed, too. So this *was* all just a joke. A very strange, not at all funny kind of joke. I wanted to tell her to spit it out. Obviously she had something important to say to me, some reason she had told me to put on her clothes and meet her on top of this building and open presents and drink these horrible, bitter martinis. The waitress walked by, and I raised my hand to get her attention. I ordered a lemon drop, with a sugared rim.

I pushed my martini across the table. "I can't drink this."

"An acquired taste, I suppose."

"I guess so."

"Listen, Rosemary. I'm trying to help you."

"Help me with what?"

"With Wendy."

I stiffened at the mention of my sister's name. "She'll be fine," I said.

"I hear you on the phone with her. She doesn't sound fine."

Wendy had been calling every night, asking for an update. I'm trying, I kept telling her. She didn't get how hard it was out here. My four-year plan to leave home and go to college had been just that: a four-year plan. When I graduated in June, I was in for a rude awakening. Surprise, surprise—a bachelor's degree in philosophy, even from a pretty good college, isn't exactly sought after in the job market. That had been a few months ago. It was no easier now than it was back then. I had dropped résumés off all over town. I wasn't being picky, either. I could work more than one shift. People did it all the time—worked several jobs to support a family. Our own mother had done it, until she met Jason. I applied to Trader Joe's. I applied to the Plaid Pantry. I wasn't even getting any interviews, let alone a job.

Listen, maybe we should wait, I had said on the phone just last night. Lawyers make good money. If Wendy could hang tight for three years—

Three years? Wendy had said. You promised.

I know, I know. It was just an idea. It wasn't as though I wanted out of my promise to my sister. It was more that I still had a hard time believing, back then, that I could make any difference. That I could make her life any better.

I'll find a way, Wendy had said the last time we talked. I hadn't taken it too seriously at the time. "She's a kid," I told Mira. "Whatever she's going through, she'll grow out of it."

"Didn't her *parents* die?"

I had made the mistake of confiding in Mira. She would come home late in her fancy dresses, kick off her heels. I'd make us tea, and we would sit and talk. Or rather, I would talk and she would listen. She was a good listener.

"I lost my parents, too." I could hear how pathetic I sounded.

"You don't want to help her?"

"What do you think I've been doing these last few weeks? I've sent my résumé all over town. I've asked Rich for more hours. Even a studio apartment is out of reach with what I'm making now."

"You're probably wondering how I afford all this stuff." Mira raised her arms up, as if she were supporting an invisible tray over her head. As if "all this stuff" included everything we saw around us—the martinis and the heat lamps and the glass railing and the city lights twinkling up into the hills, out beyond the river. "I'm trying to explain it to you."

"Okay," I said. "Explain it."

She leaned in closer to me. "You know what's in that phone? All my contacts. Very lucrative contacts. You know how many years it took me to build up that list? I'll tell you. Five years. My last year of college and four years of dental school. I've whittled it down for you. Sifted through the riffraff. The losers. The cheapskates. The disgusting *douchebags*—excuse me." She straightened up and cleared her throat. She waved her hand over the phone. "This is my gift to you. This is how you get out of Steele's closet. This is how you stop working retail"—she said "retail" with the same vehemence as she'd said "douchebags"—"and start figuring out what you want, how you really want to live."

I took a sip of the frothy, pale-yellow drink that had appeared on the table before me sometime during Mira's speech. It had arrived just in time. I needed something to do while I let all this information sink in. All the puzzle pieces were sliding into place—the dresses, the weekend trips. Mira seemed to be waiting for me to react, to say something. I couldn't come up with anything. I sucked at the sugared rim on the side of my glass and then took a big, icy gulp.

"You're a . . ." I let the sentence hang, hoping Mira would fill in the right words. Sugar baby? Escort? Working girl? Prostitute? Or maybe she was one of those people who wanted to reclaim a derogatory title. High-class whore?

"Yes." She looked relieved that I'd finally put two and two together. She sat back against her chair cushions and smiled at me. Audibly exhaled. "I am."

"I could never do that." My heart pounded in my ears. I was shocked. I was shocked but didn't want to be shocked. I wanted to be cool with it. I wanted to be the type of person who took this kind of information in stride. So I smiled at Mira. "I'm just not a people person."

She laughed. "You date, right?"

"That's not really the same thing."

"It's not so different, either. Weren't you hooking up with guys from Tinder and Bumble and Lookinglass after you and Steele split up?"

"I was on Tinder for maybe *five minutes*."

"Right," said Mira.

"It was just for fun. I'm not really looking for anything serious, anyway."

"You told me about some of these guys. They don't sound all that great, to be honest. Half the time they don't even buy you dinner first."

"I'm really not looking for—"

"I'm just saying, you don't have to settle for guys like that."

I tapped the phone that was lying between us in its nest of wrapping paper. "So these guys in here, they're all just amazing, drop-dead gorgeous guys? Is that what you're telling me?"

"I'm saying you couldn't do much worse than the guys you're dating now. You could actually do a lot better. These are professional guys, guys with money. They'll take you places, buy you things. They'll pay you more in one night than you make in two weeks working retail."

"Well, that's the whole problem, right? If they're so wonderful, why do they have to pay for it?"

"That's not the question you should be asking," Mira said. "The question you should be asking is, Why *not* get paid for it?"

Mira said it was all very simple. Nothing like what I was picturing. All her contacts were fully vetted. Classy guys, most of them businessmen from other towns, who wanted the girlfriend experience for the night. Oh, the "Girlfriend Experience" was a very common thing, Mira assured me. It had its own acronym: GFE. *The Girlfriend Experience* was even a movie starring Sasha Grey and a scripted TV show on Starz. This wasn't some sleazy affair. This was a "dress up and eat for free in fancy restaurants with educated businessmen" kind of situation! And if Mira put out after a date, it was in a hotel with robes and room service and fluffy white towels folded into swans.

"That's more than you can say for those Lookinglass dudes, right?" she asked me.

"It was *Tinder*—"

"Wasn't one guy a freshman in college?" Mira laughed, recalling a story I barely remembered myself. I didn't recollect telling her, though obviously I must have. "He took you to his dorm room and made his roommate get out of bed and sit out in the hall until you were done."

"I didn't *know* he lived in a dorm," I protested.

"And you did that for *free*, you know?" Mira wasn't looking at me when she said that. She directed her gaze up, behind my shoulder. Then she wet her lips and broke into a huge smile.

I turned around, but there was no one there. "Who were you looking at?" I asked her.

"No one."

"You were smiling at someone."

Mira pointed to a spot above my right shoulder, and I turned around again.

"It's a Glasseye," she said. "See? Just above that register area over there."

I saw the podium with a small register on it—a little station for the rooftop servers to plug in their orders. "I don't know what I'm supposed to be looking at."

"Under the eaves. It's like an eyeball."

I saw it then. It looked exactly like its name implied, a glass eye, the size of a ping-pong ball.

"They're just cameras," Mira explained. "If you're on Lookinglass, they recognize you."

"I'm not *on* Lookinglass."

"So don't worry about it."

"They can't see me?"

"Anyone can see you, I guess, if they're watching my feed, but they'll have no clue who you are, so it doesn't matter."

"Great."

"Someone is always standing around with their phone out, right? And then you walk by, and all of a sudden you're a part of whatever they're taking a picture of, whatever they happen to be recording at the time. It's no different than that."

It did seem different, though I couldn't articulate why.

"It's fun," she said. "I don't know. I'll probably close my account once I move."

I tried to busy myself with the food that had arrived on the table. I stirred wasabi into my soy sauce and grasped a maki roll with chopsticks. "Mira," I said when I'd swallowed it and washed it down with an ungraceful glug of water. "Thank you for the phone. Thank you for thinking of me. I just—I just don't think it will be necessary. I have a job. I have a place to live. I'm doing okay. Really."

"What about Wendy?"

"What about her?"

"She told me you were supposed to have custody of her. You flaked out."

"I was in *college*."

"So?"

"So I was in no position to take care of a little kid. I'm in no position now."

"But you could. If you tried."

I stood up quickly. The cloth napkin I had crumpled up on my lap fell to the floor. "Thanks for this." I waved my hand over the food, the drinks. No way was *I* paying for it. She was loaded. She was swimming in money. I was the one working retail and then getting lectured by a high-paid escort for not taking care of my little sister when I was still a kid myself. More or less.

CHAPTER 3

It was early October when I found out what Wendy had done. It was easy to remember because it was my birthday. All of us, all the house-mates—Steele, Brooke and Melanie, and Margorie, who had moved in when Mira moved out a couple of weeks earlier—were gathered around our kitchen table for the occasion. Margorie's boyfriend was there, too. He was new. A stocky, rockabilly type with oversize sideburns and a genuine vintage gas station attendant shirt with an embroidered name tag stitched to the breast. The name tag read LEROY, but that wasn't his name. I didn't remember his name. Skippy? Biff? Some other midcentury nickname that couldn't have been real.

Margorie had produced some of those cone-shaped party hats and made us all wear them. We were drinking room-temperature prosecco and eating cake.

The cake was in the middle of the table, twenty-three candles flickering and sparking. They were singing the birthday song and I was sitting there, that stupid paper cone hat on my head, when my phone, resting right in front of me, lit up and began to vibrate. The bluish light of the screen took over the room, and the singing stopped. Janet Moseby's name flashed on the screen. Wendy's grandmother.

I had an awful, sinking feeling, the way you do when you know you're about to hear bad news, something that will change everything.

"I need to take this." In one quick motion I grabbed the phone and exited the apartment in my stocking feet.

Halfway down the stairs, I put the phone to my ear, and Janet was already talking, her voice thin and trembly. "—don't know how to deal with her. She's getting Cs and Ds in all her classes, even English, her favorite. She was on the yearbook staff, writing articles, and she stopped going. It was a class, Rosemary, for credit, and she stopped going, so she'll get an F. My Jason never got a C in his life, and he did sports after school. That's what I keep telling Wendy, you've got to keep busy. You can't just bum around all day getting into trouble, you've got to keep yourself busy. Basketball, swimming, something—"

I sat at the bottom of the stairs in the lobby, a tight little corridor painted basement gray. One wall lined with a row of metal mailboxes. Beat-up bikes parked under the stairs.

"Janet," I interrupted. "I still don't know what's going on." And I didn't care what "her Jason" did to "keep busy."

Janet heaved a long, withering sigh. "She stabbed her own wrist."

This shocked me so much I let my hand drop from my ear to my lap. I stared at my phone, barely registering Janet's voice chirping out of it, a distant, robotic little voice, like something from a cartoon.

"—after school. I'm at work, I can't watch her every second of the day. That's what I mean about extracurricular activities. If she had been cheerleading or something, this wouldn't have happened."

I returned the phone to my ear and tried my best to focus on her words. This was what Wendy meant when she said she'd find a way. I hadn't taken it seriously, hadn't taken her seriously. The next time I had talked to her—two days ago—she had seemed calmer. I had told her she just needed to be patient. Something would turn up eventually.

"She drew a bath, a nice warm bath," Janet was saying. "A bubble bath. She used half a bottle until the bubbles were a foot thick. She read about this, you know. That you have to do it in a bathtub. She was smart about that. She got into the tub and brought some of the kitchen knives with her. She didn't know which one would work best, which one was sharpest. That's what she told me—she wanted options." I could hear a tremble in Janet's voice now. She was crying. For the first time during this conversation, I started to feel sorry for her.

"So she gets in the bath, and then she just stabs at her wrist with the knife. Shocked her so bad she couldn't do the other one. That's what you're supposed to do. 'I meant to do both wrists, Grandma,' she tells me." Now Janet was really crying.

"She's okay?" I asked. "She's . . . alive?"

I listened while she tried to contain herself. She blew her nose.

"She wrapped towels around her wrist as tight as she could and called 911 herself. She freaked out, is what she told me. Didn't expect to see all that blood. They called me at work. I rushed straight home, and they were taking her out on a stretcher. What a sight. And the bathroom—it's like a murder scene in there. I don't know if I'll ever get the blood out of the grout."

I closed my eyes and tried to steady my breathing. She wasn't trying to kill herself. I knew that. Or—I wanted to believe that. I should never have told her about law school. I had promised her. I had tried to find a new job, I really had. It's just that as every week went by without so much as an interview, it seemed less likely that anything would ever pan out, and frankly, it was hard for me to understand the urgency. The real threat—the Wicked Prince—was dead and gone. Our mother had perished with him. The worst that could happen had already happened.

"She wants to live with you," Janet was saying. "She said she needed you. I'm not sure why, she hardly knows you, what with you so much older—"

That got my attention. "I'm her sister."

"Her *half* sister."

Okay, I was beginning to see it, the urgency. "She grew up with me; she's known me her *entire life*—"

"I just don't know what to do, but what choice do I have?"

"I'll take her," I said. "I'll figure something out."

"What she needs is a stable environment. I'm not sure you understand what it's like, taking care of a child." Of course, just then a bunch of college kids had to come barreling down the stairs, whooping and hollering. I scooted over to let them pass, and they charged out the door and onto the street. I could hear Janet's disapproval over the line.

"You know, Jason never caused me a moment's trouble. People would say to me, they'd say being a mother was difficult, and I never understood them. It's a blessing, I would tell them. Every day is a blessing. But now I see what they mean. It's hard, dealing with a girl like this."

"She lost her parents, Janet. She's been through a lot." If she said one more word about her perfect darling Jason, I was going to lose it. "Let me talk to her."

"You know, Jason always said that Wendy—"

"I don't want to hear it!" I yelled. I held the phone away from my face, glaring at it. I was going to tell her everything. I wanted to tell her what her darling little Jason did—what he did to me, what he did to Wendy. I wanted to tell her how it was Jason who "took care" of me when my mom used to work night shifts, how he'd come into my bedroom at night and how I never uttered a word of it to my mom because I was sure it would kill her. I wanted to tell Janet the things Jason used to say to me, the things he whispered to me in his hot Listerine breath.

He killed her, he killed our mother! I wanted to yell to Janet about her beloved only son, even though I wasn't even sure I believed it myself.

I wanted to tell her. The words bubbled up and threatened to spill out, all at once, a hot, red gush. To stop myself, I hurtled my phone across the lobby. I yelled as it somersaulted around and around. It bounced off a wall and landed on the carpeted floor below. I could hear Janet's voice bleating out of the phone even as it was sailing through the air: "Rosemary, what on *earth*?"

~

I went back upstairs. The party was still going on, without me. I walked by them all, straight into the bedroom I used to share with Steele and back into the closet where I now lived. Somehow I thought my twenties would be different than this.

Standing on a precariously stacked pile of old textbooks, I managed to reach the highest shelf. That's where I kept the little box Mira had given me on the rooftop of the Meier & Frank Building. This box would change my life, she told me. I had left it on the table, but after Mira moved out, there it was, resting on my pillow. It was still wrapped in that polka-dotted paper, tied up in that turquoise grosgrain ribbon.

CHAPTER 4

On Saturday I wasn't nervous. I was excited. I was standing on the threshold of my new life, my better life. No longer would I be the kind of girl who would sleep with some loser on his narrow dorm bed, his ratty futon. No longer would I venture home to sleep on the floor of my ex-boyfriend's closet.

I was going to sleep with *men*, men who were grateful to be seen with me, who would buy me dinner and flowers and pay me $1,000. I would live in a luxury apartment and sleep in a real bed. Janet had sent Wendy to a rehabilitation center, and I called her there to tell her the news. She wasn't supposed to communicate with her family while she was in treatment, but I begged the woman at the front desk to make an exception. I'm doing it, I told Wendy. I'm getting you out of there. I felt triumphant in that moment, like I was breaking her out of a prison camp and not some sort of cushy residential treatment center her grandmother was paying for. I got her a plane ticket. This was happening.

Wendy had squealed with delight, and for a minute I could pretend it was normal, that she wasn't there for harming herself to get my attention and that, yes, it had worked, and now I was going to sell my body to fix the whole mess.

His name was Sebastian St. James. I'd never met anyone named Sebastian before, but I pictured someone dashing, dark haired, European. I created this little fantasy about Sebastian: his wife had urged him to call me. She was ill, too weak from some sort of debilitating illness to sleep with him anymore. She wanted him to be happy, to have some physical companionship while she wasted away on her death-bed. (I imagined her like a tragic figure from an old novel, like Beth in *Little Women* or Fantine in *Les Misérables*. Consumptive. Fevered brow. Beautiful and pale, wearing a sheer white gown, her hair spread out on her pillow.)

I was ready. In a simple ivory halter dress from Mira's collection, I felt invincible. She had left me her entire collection of dresses on the rolling rack with a note that read, "In case you change your mind." She wouldn't need them anymore. She had paid her dues. Attended dental school and moonlit as a highly paid escort, lived in a cute but crumbled-down apartment with four other people, and now she could go off and live the rest of her life, owing nothing to anyone. She was an inspiration.

Margorie had of course asked about the dresses when she moved into Mira's old room. I had crumpled up the note before she could see it and said maybe we could sell the dresses at a consignment shop, but neither of us did anything about it, and the rack of dresses just lived there in her room. Patiently waiting for me to come around.

As soon as my heels began clicking down the sidewalk at five fifteen in the afternoon, my mood shifted. I hadn't considered that to arrive in time for a six o'clock date (wasn't that awfully early for a glamorous date with a paid escort?), I'd have to leave before the sun had sunk behind the hills. I was click-clacking down the sidewalk in sky-high stilettos looking like—well, like a streetwalker.

My feet were killing me after three blocks, but I kept going. My makeup threatened to slide off my face. I would arrive at the hotel looking like a melted candle, my feet ground down to bloody stumps.

I thought about taking an Uber, but after laying out so much cash to get ready over the last five days, I had promised myself not to spend one more penny on this dubious "investment." Hair salon, waxing salon, nail salon. I had a legacy to maintain, Mira's legacy. She never left the house looking anything other than flawless.

The Valerie Hotel wasn't too far from my apartment—walking distance. I figured a nice fifteen-minute stroll would give me a chance to get into character. I would swan into that ritzy old hotel and toss my jacket to the coat girl, who would look at me with awe and admiration and stammer, "Thank you, miss!" when I slipped twenty dollars into her hand as a tip.

But obviously that was not going to happen, since I wasn't wearing a jacket in eighty-two-degree weather, and if I couldn't spare a few bucks to take an Uber, I definitely couldn't spare twenty bucks to tip a coat-check girl.

Instead of waltzing into the hotel, I slunk in, hoping no one would see me sneak into the lobby restroom. I assessed the damage in the mirror: I was a wreck. A complete mess. My face had bloomed an alarming shade of scarlet from the walk in the heat. Perspiration had dampened the tendrils of hair around my forehead. I took in several deep breaths, breathing in through my nose and out through my mouth like a woman in labor. I needed to calm down. If I could get my face back to a normal shade of pale, I could get through this.

A few minutes later, I'd pulled myself together and was sitting at a table in the restaurant waiting for Sebastian St. James to arrive. I had, as far as I could tell, the best seat in the house. From my corner on the upholstered bench, I could see out into the restaurant, watch the servers buzz around, spy on the other patrons.

I turned to look out the window. The sun had sunk down below the buildings, but it wasn't dark outside, not yet, and a strange light filtered in through the old windows. I could sit here all evening, watching them go by: the young couple with all the tattoos, pushing a baby in his stroller. The Thorns fans wearing crowns of roses, whooping their way to the stadium for a game. The homeless lady trundling her rickety old shopping cart down the sidewalk.

A throat cleared, and then I heard a man's voice saying my name.

I turned my head slowly toward the voice, a serene Mona Lisa smile on my face. *And you must be Sebastian St. James*, I had planned to say, raising my hand for him to kiss.

To my credit, my expression didn't so much as flicker, my Mona Lisa smile didn't show a whisper of a crack when I set eyes on him.

"Oh, there you are," I managed to say in a completely normal—perhaps even seductive—voice. Maybe I was going to be good at this. I was acting natural, I thought, under the circumstances.

Sebastian St. James took a seat across from me and extended his hand for me to shake. A strange gesture for greeting an escort in an expensive restaurant, I thought. But what did I know about these things.

He was blabbering about the menu. "Get whatever you want. Do you like oysters? The Caesar salad is good here. Very fresh." I was grateful for the blabbering. It gave me a chance to reassess the situation.

He wasn't a handsome man with a head of dignified salt-and-pepper hair. He wasn't wearing an ascot or war medals, either. I'd imagined him down to the strands of silver in his hair, and, as probably anyone might have guessed, I'd imagined him all wrong.

The man sitting across from me was older, yes. Midforties. But dignified and handsome he was not. *This* man was not mourning after a consumptive wife. If this man had a wife—no wedding ring, but that didn't necessarily mean anything—she was named Peggy and she decorated their house with framed LIVE. LAUGH. LOVE. artwork.

Sebastian St. James—the one sitting across from me—was tall and stocky. He'd probably been on the football team in high school. He probably thought being on the team would make girls fall all over him, and it probably hadn't worked. He had small, eager eyes and a huge smile crowded with teeth.

Talking to this guy was a piece of cake because he filled all the silences with banal observations, and all I had to do was agree.

"It's unseasonably hot in Portland for October."

"Oh, I know it."

"I wasn't prepared for the weather. Packed nothing but sweaters and hiking boots. I had to do a mall run to buy this shirt."

"Nice shirt." (I reached across the table and caressed the material with my fingers, as if it were the finest Egyptian cotton.)

"Oh, it's okay. A little bold for my taste."

It was pale-blue plaid. "Bold suits you."

I watched the tips of his ears turn crimson. I'd made him blush. It occurred to me that I was nailing this. I flipped my hair over my shoulder and leaned in so he could ogle my cleavage.

His Adam's apple contracted as he took a big gulp of his ice water.

I kept smiling and nodding, smiling and nodding. I kept drinking wine, too, and in that way, I made it through dinner. I made it through a dessert course, too. It was a five-layer vanilla cake with strawberry ganache, served on a large white platter decorated with a dark chocolate zigzag pattern. It looked like a piece of art, but I couldn't taste it. I might as well have been eating a Hostess cupcake.

Sebastian St. James drank Jack and Cokes. The more he drank, the surer of himself he became. I could tell by the way he threw his arm around the back of his chair, the way he pursed his lips and raised his eyebrows at me, that he thought he was hot stuff. "Damn, you're gorgeous."

"You're not so bad yourself," I said, because I thought that was probably what he wanted to hear.

About halfway through my cake, I put down my fork. Because after dessert—what then? I ordered a coffee. I could stay here all night, signaling the waiter for warm-up after warm-up. He had other plans. "Let's take this upstairs," he said.

Up in his room, he lifted a bottle of champagne from the ice bucket sitting on the narrow marble counter beneath a huge flat-screen television set. He poured us each a glass.

The room was elegant but fairly small—the bed took up almost the entire room. The room was warm, almost humid. It smelled the way old hotels do, even after they've been renovated and remodeled, like century-old cigarette smoke.

The money. I needed to ask for the money. I should have asked up front. Wasn't that one of the first rules of the game? Right up there with "don't give them your real name."

"I hope this is adequate," he said, handing me an envelope. "Jasmine's rates were reasonable—I stuck with that." I wasn't sure if I wanted to be known for my reasonable rates. I could say I was sure it was fine and tuck the envelope into my purse. Or I could stand there and count it, decide if all of this would be worth my while. I hesitated for a moment before peeking in the envelope. Without taking the bills out, I did a quick tally. Ten $100 bills. It took all my power not to bug my eyes out at it, even though I had been expecting it. The money was the whole point, after all. That would *almost* cover a deposit on a new place. I kept a straight face and nodded, tucking the envelope in my bag.

I drank my champagne in three gulps. "Let's do this," I said.

He sat on the edge of the bed. He was looking at me. I could see the top of his head, his thinning hair. It had turned ash with age. Not gray, not white, just this blank tone that left no indication of its former color. He just *sat* there on the edge of the bed, his back ramrod straight, his hands rubbing up and down his legs in excitement, like a trained dog who had been a very good boy and now deserved a bone. He was smiling a little to himself, his lips parted slightly. This was not a turn-on. But turning me on was not his job, was it? My job was to turn *him* on. Okay, I said to myself. Okay. I can do this.

I threw my shoulders back and stuck out my chest. The ivory dress fit me like a glove. It was so tight I didn't need to wear a bra underneath. I was wearing one anyway, a strapless lace number with matching underwear. I stood between his legs, so he had to look up at me. He did. His eyes were wide open, greedy.

He took my hands in his and tugged at them, pulling me down to my knees.

I knelt on the floor in front of him, but the room was so small that my feet hit the counter under the television set. I leaned back and removed my shoes, maintaining eye contact with him the entire time. My knees dug into the coarse wool rug. I wanted to ask Sebastian St. James for a pillow or a little folded-up towel to wedge beneath them, but I was afraid it would ruin the mood.

He didn't do anything. He didn't touch me. I was supposed to touch him. I was the professional, after all. I reached out to undo his belt buckle. It was cinched tightly around his waist. His belly bulged over the top of his pants. I had to yank a little harder than I had anticipated to loosen it, and once I had, I panicked, ripped it from the belt loops, and tossed it over to the side. An inelegant gesture, but one he seemed to like. He smiled, revealing all his teeth.

I unbuttoned his pants and pulled down the zipper. I kept expecting him to join in, to pull me up or run his fingers through my hair or push down my dress so he could grab me—but he seemed content to just sit there, to let me do everything.

Underneath the pants he was wearing white boxer shorts. I reached my hand through the slit in his underwear and pulled him out. He wasn't hard. His penis rested in my hand like a—like a hairless rodent. Like a mole, a pathetic, sightless little creature who spent most of his days underground in rotting trees, chewing on grubs with his spiky little teeth.

It occurred to me that I had made a tactical error. What I should have done was pull his pants off his body, then move up to unbutton his shirt. I should have saved the boxers for later, for much later. I could have talked him into unzipping my dress or unhooking my bra.

I shouldn't have gone straight for the slit in his boxers. He wasn't even hard. He just twitched in my hand. I didn't know what to do next. Or rather, I *did* know what to do next—I just didn't want to do it. I couldn't picture Mira doing what I was doing. I couldn't picture Mira, beautiful, glamorous Mira, up in this hotel with this man, even if he was named Sebastian St. James. Mira deserved better than this, I decided. Another dentist, maybe, someone a few years older. Maybe he could be a periodontist, or an orthodontist. She could send him referrals and they would fall in love and they would spend all their money on weekend trips to vineyards and helicopter rides over the Grand Canyon. That was the life I saw for Mira.

Sebastian St. James cupped the back of my head with his hand and pulled my face closer to the shuddering little hairless rodent in my hand and instinctively, I resisted. I could not put it in my mouth. If it so much as brushed against my lips, I would scream. Or throw up.

It wasn't a rough gesture, the way it could be sometimes, with some guys. But still, he pulled me in so close I could smell him, that intimate, animal part of him. I could feel the heat coming off him, the odor rippling off like waves. It's not that his smell was offensive, exactly. It just overwhelmed my nostrils, choked me.

I took my hand out of his pants and put it up to my forehead. I closed my eyes.

"You okay?" he asked. It didn't sound like he was too concerned.

I closed my eyes tighter. I did feel dizzy. I'd eaten too much, had too much to drink. "It's—it's kind of stuffy in here."

Fifteen more minutes. If I could pull off this performance for another fifteen minutes, I'd be done. Although I might need more than fifteen minutes. What if it took fifteen minutes for him to get it up? What if it took longer than that? I could be here all night. "Rosemary?" he was saying. His palm still cupped the back of my skull. I could feel his fingers raking through my hair. I had a sudden, panicky feeling that he might, at any moment, smash my face into his lap.

I twisted out of his hand and stood up so fast my vision blurred for a moment. I clamped my eyes shut. "I'm sorry," I said. "I'm not feeling too well."

What did I want more right now: $1,000, or to run out of this hotel in my bare feet, to run out of here and through the streets and back to my own apartment, my horrible, run-down apartment I shared with too many other people? I could be back in the kitchen making myself a pot of tea, drinking from a china cup and saucer, in twenty minutes. Or I could have $1,000. I could change my life. I could change my little sister's life. My poor abused little sister. I tried my best to picture her at her most pathetic, lying in the hospital with a bandage around her wrist, her face drained of blood. White-green skin, dark rings under her eyes.

I brushed imaginary dust from my dress. I collected my purse, removed the envelope full of cash, and set it on the counter. I cleared my throat. "Sorry I wasted your time."

I couldn't look Sebastian St. James in the eye, but I could tell that he was miffed. He didn't stand up. He didn't even tuck his penis back into his boxer shorts. It was still poking its sightless little head out, forlorn.

I picked my shoes up off the floor and darted out the door. I didn't want to wait for the elevator to pick me up in case Sebastian St. James decided to put himself back in his pants and run after me, so I took the emergency exit stairs instead. I ran down flight after flight and then, at the bottom, I burst out of the building and onto the street. The hotel was downtown, right by the MAX tracks, by the rats and the homeless camps, but the air felt fresh. I gulped it down like water, like I wanted to drink it. A weight I didn't know had been pressing down on me— the weight of pretending, of smiling and nodding and demurring and laughing at jokes I didn't think were the least bit funny—lifted off me then, and I felt so light I felt like I was flying.

CHAPTER 5

Time was running out. Twenty-eight days, Janet had told me. If I didn't have a place for Wendy when she got out . . . well, I had to find a place.

Nine days to go. I paced the floors of La Cuisine in a daze. A customer asked me where the trivets were, and I couldn't for the life of me remember what a trivet was. No image formed in my brain. "Trivet," I repeated. What on earth was a trivet? The entire concept escaped me. Steele popped up behind me, wielding three disks—a felt pad, a heat-resistant tile, and a square of composite bamboo. Trivets. Oh yeah.

I carried Mira's little black phone around with me wherever I went and checked it every day. I couldn't stomach contacting any of her johns, not after the disaster with Sebastian St. James, but if someone contacted me, I knew what I had to do. Do it for your sister, I tried telling myself. You promised her.

What would happen to Wendy? They'd send her to an orphanage. That was what she was, an orphan. A bona fide orphan. She'd have to sleep on a narrow iron bed alongside all the other wayward girls. Nights would be so cold she'd have to crack a sheet of ice in the washbasin every morning.

On my lunch break I checked Mira's phone. I had a new text message from an unknown sender. All of Mira's clients were programmed in. No one else had the number. That was what she'd told me. The message said he wanted to take me out to lunch, today.

Who is this? I texted back. Probably a pervert. A serial killer. I wondered if it mattered at this point. I just needed the money.

A moment later, a photograph appeared on my screen.

He wasn't old. Early thirties, maybe, thirty-five at the very oldest. Gray T-shirt, navy-blue hoodie with white strings. Cute in an awkward, offbeat kind of way. His fingers were raised in a wave. Something about the photograph gave me the impression that he'd taken the picture right then and sent it off. It didn't look calculated, as if he had taken a hundred photos and chosen the very best one.

I studied the picture carefully for a minute. **Where did you get this number?**

Doug.

Who's Doug?

I waited, staring at my screen. A few minutes ticked by, and then the phone vibrated. An image appeared. It looked like a professional photo, like a LinkedIn profile pic. Small eyes. A mouth crowded with teeth. It was Sebastian St. James.

I sat staring at that photo for a good minute. Doug. Of course his name was Doug.

Meet me for lunch, the guy in the hoodie texted.

I said sure. I also said it would cost him $200.

~

I made Margorie come with me. "Sit across the restaurant from us. Act like you don't know me."

"Obviously. I'll crouch behind a potted palm, maybe."

When we got to the restaurant, it was just past one o'clock. We stopped right outside the door. My stomach clenched. I let out a high, wobbly laugh. "Nerves," I said.

"Haven't you gone on a blind date before?" Margorie looked me over. She smoothed my hair with her hand and unbuttoned the top button of my shirt. "There. Gorgeous."

I went in first. I saw him right away, sitting at a two-top by the window. I recognized him by his navy hoodie with the white strings, by the mop of curly brown hair. Plus, he was the only person in the whole restaurant. He was leaning way back in his chair, his feet stretched out underneath the table, the way a teenager would sprawl out in front of the TV.

As soon as I sat down, he looked up at me. A slow grin spread over his face as he took me in. His eyes panned up and down my body. He nodded once. "I wasn't sure you'd show up."

"I wasn't sure I would, either." I noticed, then, a plain white envelope resting on top of the paper place mat. The envelope was puffed up slightly, a thin pillow. The money. I tapped my fingers on the table. Nervous habit. He wasn't one of Mira's contacts—so who was he? And he had offered to take me to lunch. *Lunch?* Why? Well, I had reasoned to myself earlier, what was the worst that could happen? He would offer me some humiliating job involving depraved acts I couldn't even imagine, and I would politely refuse. Anyway, it was just lunch. And $200.

The bells on the door jingled, and in walked Margorie. Quickly, I took the envelope and stuffed it in my bag. Out of the corner of my eye, I watched the hostess leading Margorie to a table at the back of the restaurant, about four tables away. I willed myself not to look over at her.

I'd chosen the restaurant myself. Thai Lotus, run by a husband-and-wife team. One or both of them were always around, and sometimes I saw their kids—a boy and a girl—in there, too, ringing up customers or just doing homework on one of the back tables. It was the wife who came over to our table to ask if we were ready to order.

He hadn't even opened the menu, but a stream of foreign words rushed out of my companion's mouth.

The owner acted neither surprised nor impressed that a white dude could speak Thai. They went back and forth, and he must have said something amusing because he got her to crack a little smile, and then they both laughed.

"Have you seen the movie *The Beach*?" he asked me once she'd slipped back to the kitchen.

"No."

"Thailand is nothing like that—not if you're doing it right." He talked at length about his travels there, the adventures he'd had, while I sipped at my Thai iced tea. I relaxed into my chair. This guy was normal, if a little on the self-involved side. What was it that Mira had said? These guys, they couldn't be that much worse than any of the other douchebags I'd been with, for free.

I sneaked a glance at Margorie. When I tilted my head slightly to see what she was up to, I couldn't help but observe that she wasn't trying to be subtle in the least. She had her entire body pivoted toward our table, and she was staring across the restaurant at us both. I attempted to signal her with my eyes: *What?* She bulged her eyes back at me. I didn't know what to make of it. I turned my attention back to my date, but I kept sensing Margorie's gaze on me.

Then my phone started buzzing. "Excuse me," I said. I pulled my bag onto my lap and reached in, trying to silence my phone. Margorie was sending me texts. I shot her another look. She looked like she was about to pee her pants from excitement.

I peered into my bag and tried to read my phone screen. OMG OMG OMG OMG OMG OMG, she'd written.

I was about to turn the whole thing off when the phone vibrated again in my hand. Another text: Do you KNOW who that IS?

I studied the man sitting across from me. At that moment, our food arrived, and I had another chance to shoot Margorie a warning glance. *What are you doing?* I mouthed to her.

I picked up my fork to spear a piece of tofu. "You never told me your name."

He had taken a bite of his lunch at that same moment, so he held his finger up while he chewed. He took a sip of water.

My phone buzzed again. I peeked into my bag to read the message on my phone's screen. THAT'S LEO GLASS!!!!!!!!!

"Leo," he said. "Leo Glass."

Maybe he was famous. An actor? An influencer? Maybe he was only Portland-famous, or famous in some way only Margorie would care about. Some sort of street artist or zine maker or pop-up restaurant chef.

Leo Glass was leaning forward, observing me with an intense gaze that threw me off guard. His eyes were blue, almost turquoise, but his pupils were so large—abnormally large, really—that his eyes appeared dark and alien rather than beautiful, the way you'd expect turquoise eyes to be. I couldn't return his gaze.

A few moments went by as we both dug into our food. It was spicy. I had to keep wiping my nose with my napkin. "Is it authentic?" I asked. "The food here?"

"It's decent," he said. "It's different." He began to enumerate the differences between Bangkok street food and American Thai restaurants. Men loved lecturing women, treating a date like an opportunity to deliver a little lesson, bestowing these gems on me like a favor.

"If you were to order *pad kra pao*, for example—"

"Why are we here?" I blurted out.

Leo sat back. His eyes narrowed, appraising me. Then he reached into his back pocket and pulled out what appeared to be a small, round mirror. Glass with a delicate silver edge. Real silver, not stainless steel or aluminum. Like old wedding china. He touched a finger to it, concentrating, and then he handed it to me.

I held the object in my hand. It was heavier than I expected, and more beautiful, but it wasn't a mirror after all. I peered into it and couldn't see anything, not even my reflection. Just blackness. "What is it?"

"It's a prototype." Leo tapped a finger to the object's surface, and it lit up with a picture as vivid as real life. It was a picture of me, sitting in the corner of the restaurant in the Valerie Hotel. I looked—well, I looked beautiful in that picture, like a woman in a painting, like if Edward Hopper and John Singer Sargent had collaborated to create this image of me sitting in that historic old hotel, with my pale skin and the soft ivory satin dress and the shimmering evening light that made my honey-brown hair look like spun gold. I had my face turned toward the window, and the soft gold rays of the setting sun illuminating my features. In this picture, I didn't look sweaty and overheated from that dreadful walk in the unseasonably warm weather—I looked youthful and alive. I was even smiling a little bit, as if I'd been transfixed by some private thought or memory, as if whatever I was looking at outside caused me a secret delight.

I wanted a copy of it, a physical copy. I wanted to frame it and stare at it, this version of myself that didn't really exist. The picture made me believe it could.

The image disappeared, faded to black. I handed the device back to Leo. "It's just a picture."

"Listen," he said, "I've been looking for someone like you for a long time."

"Someone like me? Like a prostitute?"

"NO! No." He chuckled. "God no. My business manager—Doug—showed me the picture. Bragging. I was intrigued. I wanted to meet you."

"Well. You met me." I stood up to leave, and Leo stood up, too, quickly pushing back his chair with an audible scrape across the floor.

"Come by my offices tomorrow." He handed me a business card. "Same time."

I took the card and slipped it into my bag without even looking at it. "Why?"

In the background I heard some shuffling and exaggerated coughing. Margorie was standing at the door. "Thank you!" she called out to the hostess. "Got to get back to work!" she said in an unnaturally loud voice. Our eyes met, briefly, and I gave her a quick nod.

"I want to make you an offer," Leo said.

"Like a job offer?"

He gave me a funny look. "Yes," he said. "Like a job offer."

Margorie was waiting for me at the end of the block. As I approached, she jumped up and down. She gestured frantically for me to hurry, to run toward her. I kept my typical brisk walking pace. When I reached her, she screamed in my ear. "Leo-fucking-Glass!"

"He certainly seems impressed with himself." I said it in a deadpan way, as if I could take him or leave him. "I think he wants to offer me a job."

Margorie bugged her eyes out. "Rosemary." She said my name in an exasperated way. "Do you know who Leo Glass *is*?"

"I'm sure you'll enlighten me." Even before she replied, my imagination was running wild. He was not like all the other douchebags I had dated. He was rich! And he wanted me for some mysterious job. He had said it was a *job*. He wanted to meet me at his office. This did not sound like a sex dungeon situation.

Margorie cleared her throat. She took out her phone and began reading from the screen: "Leo Glass. From Wikipedia, the people's encyclopedia." Margorie gave me a pointed look.

"He has a Wikipedia page?"

"Yes, he has a Wikipedia page." Margorie continued reading. No easy feat while we navigated our way down the sidewalk.

"Leo Jameson Glass is an American computer programmer and internet entrepreneur. He is the cofounder of

48

Lookinglass and operates as its chairman and chief executive officer.

"Glass launched Lookinglass with his cofounder, Jamila Heath-Jackson. The pair created Lookinglass from Heath-Jackson's dorm room at Reed College in Portland, Oregon. Heath-Jackson left the company before Lookinglass went public, leaving Glass at the helm.

"Glass has been nominated three times by *Town & Country* as one of the world's most eligible bachelors, and by *Forbes* as one of the world's most eligible billionaire bachelors."

She held up the screen to my face and scrolled down. "There is a *lot* more, too. Childhood, education, early career—it goes on and on."

We walked the next block in silence. "Holy shit," I said when we reached the doors of La Cuisine.

"Yeah," Margorie said. "That's what I was trying to tell you."

CHAPTER 6

The Lookinglass offices took up one narrow brick building downtown. The outside was unassuming—I'd walked by the building many times without noticing it wedged between an outdoor supply company and a French bakery/coffee shop. It wasn't labeled with a sign, just the Lookinglass logo, a stylized lowercase *g*.

The elevator opened up to a reception area on the second floor. Two hipsters, one male, the other female, sat at the front desk. Behind the desk was a living wall made from what looked like assorted varieties of moss and microferns. They invited me to wait for Leo on one of the modern couches in the waiting area, next to a fountain made out of recycled junkyard scraps.

There were no magazines on the tables, and I didn't want to bury my nose in my phone. I wanted to stay alert to my surroundings. I wondered if Leo was watching me as I sat waiting. A kind of test. I stared up at the walls, and dozens of Glasseyes stared back at me, unblinking, nestled along a shelf lined with potted plants.

I was dressed how I thought someone working at Lookinglass would dress. Blazer. Hair pulled back. If I'd had a fake pair of glasses, I would have worn them. I'd polished up my résumé and had it in my bag, just in case. Leo Glass had said he wanted to offer me a job. Maybe he'd seen something in me; maybe this could jump-start a whole new career in tech. Leo said he liked to work "on instinct." I'd read it in an interview. Maybe he had a gut instinct that I'd be an asset to his company.

In the back of my mind, I must have known it was too good to be true. That it wouldn't be this easy. Mira had handed me this new life as an escort, only for it to transition into some legit job in a successful tech company, after every other business in the entire Portland Metro area had overlooked me. Even Plaid Pantry.

Still (I reasoned with myself), why would he have invited me to his office? If he wanted a blow job or something, he would have booked a hotel room. And he had said "job offer." He had used those words, hadn't he? Wasn't it possible, then, that all of this could work out? That I could get a job and make enough money to take care of my little sister like I promised? Didn't we deserve a break, after everything we had been through?

I wouldn't waste it, this chance. I'd practiced my interview skills with Margorie, formulated answers for all the predictable ones: describe a work-related problem and how you solved it, name your greatest strength, talk about where you want to be five years from now.

The glass door separating the lobby from the rest of the building swung open, and a young guy about my age approached me, his hand extended.

"Rosemary, I presume?" he asked, with the supercilious air of an aging Hollywood starlet. He wore tortoiseshell glasses, skinny jeans, a New Order T-shirt, and a gigantic gray cashmere scarf that was wrapped around his neck a few times, one end tossed over his shoulder. The New Order T-shirt seemed like a good sign. My mother's favorite band.

I shook his hand, too stunned to do anything but nod.

"I'm Alejandro, and I'll be assisting you this morning—excuse me, this after*noon*. I'm *so* sorry to keep you waiting. Did you already check in? No—okay, just hand them your ID and—great. Thanks, Heidi, John. Okay, here's your guest pass. You can just wear it around your neck, like this; it has a retractable cord. You've got it. We swipe in and out of every door we pass through, like this, see?"

We each tapped our passes against the electronic pad next to the door. A green light flashed on the pad, and we exited the lobby. "Welcome to Lookinglass," Alejandro announced.

We stepped into a large open room furnished with midcentury modern furniture, ping-pong tables, another junkyard sculpture, and floor-to-ceiling bookshelves. "So this is just the general hangout area, a place to sit with your laptop and get stuff done if you want a change of pace, you know."

He took me to the other parts of the building, all three floors. We ended our tour in the break room, a light-filled space with high ceilings and exposed ductwork. "We have two flavors of kombucha on tap. Coffee—cold brew, regular drip, any type of espresso drink you might want. Do you want a latte? A cappuccino? I worked at Stumptown one summer. My barista skills are legit."

"Water's fine," I said. "Listen—I was supposed to meet Leo at one?"

Alejandro sat across from me. He gave me an impersonal smile. "It will be just a minute."

We were sitting there, me nursing water from a pint glass, Alejandro sipping an espresso out of a white Italian demitasse cup, when Leo burst through the door, his arms raised up in the "triumph" power pose. "Rosemary!" he bellowed. This was Leo Glass in his element. Cocky, sure of himself, parading around in his signature navy-blue hoodie. He owned twenty-six hoodies, each identical to the last. They were made to his specifications by a manufacturing company in Los Angeles. I had read that on his Wikipedia page.

Leo led me to his office. It wasn't like any office I'd ever seen. It was huge, bigger than the entire lobby downstairs. The ceiling went up two stories. Two levels of windows faced east onto the river, looking out at the bridges, at Mount Hood forming its neat white triangle in the distance. An entire office wall was made out of what appeared to be the side of a granite cliff, complete with a trickling waterfall. It looked like something you'd see in the middle of Yosemite. Or Disneyland.

"My climbing wall." Leo pointed up to ropes suspended from the ceiling, then at the pile of harnesses and rubber-soled climbing shoes in a basket at the foot of the rocks. "Do you climb?"

"No."

"I'll have to teach you sometime."

I followed him to a sitting area arranged in front of the windows—a grouping of modern-looking couches and chairs with ottomans surrounding a coffee table. On the coffee table sat an imposing, almost futuristic floral arrangement, a stark combination of white orchids and four-foot branches of curly willow.

"Can I get you something to drink?" Leo picked a crystal lowball glass up from a teak drink cart, which was stocked with crystal decanters of brown liquor, glasses, and an ice bucket, like we were on the set of *Mad Men*.

"I'm on my lunch break."

Leo gave me an intense, insistent look. "Please," he said. "Have a seat." I hesitated for a moment, then sat down.

Leo sat across from me and placed his elbows on his knees, resting his chin on his hands. "Let me ask you something. What makes a relationship work?" He leaned in, narrowing his eyes, like he really wanted to hear my response, like he was a talk-show host and I was his guest, the expert.

I wanted to give him the right answer. I wanted the job, whatever the job was. I felt like I needed to produce a response that would impress him, but my mind only spat out replies in magazine listicle format. Compatibility. Trust. Mutual respect. "That's the million-dollar question, right?" I said at last.

Leo raised his eyebrows, as if to say *yes*. "Everyone is looking for the right person. It's a basic human need, right? That connection. I built a business out of it, that need. No computer algorithm is going to find the perfect person, that perfect match. It's a fallacy."

"Your whole company is based on a lie?"

"It's the opposite of a lie. Lookinglass doesn't use an algorithm. It's not about ticking off boxes, matching up interests, blah blah blah."

"Lookinglass uses facial-recognition technology to allow users to observe each other in real time from the comfort of their own bedrooms." I was parroting the copy from the Lookinglass website. I had the whole thing memorized. "*Rear Window* for the lovelorn." My own little flourish.

"How did people find each other, before all this? They went to bars. They went to coffee shops. They'd sit there for hours nursing a warm beer, trying to summon up the nerve to talk to the girl sitting up at the bar, right? Now that same dude can keep an eye on girls in every bar with Glasseye compatibility, every coffee shop. He can sit at home in his tighty-whities creeping on fifty girls at once."

We exchanged amused smirks.

"You go to Starbucks, and strangers watch you," he went on. "You go to the same one every day, so does some guy, you get to talking in line one day—who knows, right? Anything could happen," Leo went on. "With Lookinglass, it's the same thing. The same exact thing. Some guy watches you, you watch him back. Maybe you start chatting. Maybe you meet up in real life. You just increase your odds is all."

"That's your idea of a relationship? Watching each other doing all their boring things through a screen?"

"What's *your* idea of a relationship?" Leo smiled at me like I was finally getting it, like I was answering the question he had brought me here to ask.

"I don't know. Having a real connection with someone? Knowing someone—everything about them—having them know everything about you, too. And choosing to be with them anyway."

"You're a romantic."

"Nah," I said. "What I described—it doesn't exist."

"What if I told you that wasn't what constituted a successful relationship? That it's not about knowing someone deep down, soul connections, hearts in your eyes, any of that fairy-tale stuff?"

"Tell me. What does make a successful relationship?" I smiled now. Easy, confident. I was killing this interview.

"It's making a decision. It's choosing someone, and them choosing you—and simply choosing each other again and again."

I nodded, taking it in. It made sense. It seemed to make sense. "So you're saying that Lookinglass—"

"This isn't about Lookinglass," Leo interrupted. "This is about you."

"Me?"

"I choose you."

Everything dropped out from under me then: this wasn't a job interview. Maybe Leo noticed something change in me, something flicker across my face, but I didn't think so. I'd dressed all wrong for the part. My blazer. The résumé tucked in my bag. I should have worn one of Mira's dresses. I should have curled my hair. When my voice came out, it sounded perfectly composed, no different than before. "And you choose me. Based on—what? A picture? One lunch?"

"That's what I'm telling you. It doesn't have to be *based on* anything. I decide, you decide, boom. That's it. That's all it takes. Look, I get it. It goes against every little fantasy you ever had about how this is supposed to go. And how does it work, on practical terms? I'd need to find someone who was on board, someone willing to test it out. That's when it occurred to me. I'm in a unique position to get exactly what I want. All the problems I usually have—I can make those disappear."

"You want to pay me to—what, exactly?"

"To be my girlfriend."

To my credit, I didn't show my disappointment. My posture was perfect, shoulders back. In an instant, I let it drift away, my entire fantasy of being a legitimate businesswoman, coming home to Wendy wearing a business suit, kicking off my sensible heels and flopping my briefcase on the kitchen counter. I was too stunned to think much beyond that, that absurd, deflated dream.

Leo walked over to his desk and held up a folder embossed with the Lookinglass logo. He returned to his seat across from me and slid the folder across the coffee table. Then he gestured for me to open it up and look inside.

I had seen job offers made like this on television and in movies, but never in real life. Offers slid over tables in folders, as if everything tucked within was too serious, too important to utter out loud.

Inside was nothing but a hot-pink Post-it with a number written on it in black ink.

I looked up at him, incredulous. "Twenty-five hundred dollars? A *month*?" I tossed the folder back on the table. It was barely more than I was making now, and I lived in a closet.

He lifted both hands up in a lazy shrug. "I'll be gone a lot."

"Not to be crass, but if I were hooking up with dudes like your pal Doug, I'd only need to do it three times a month to make that much. To make *more* than that."

"Well, sure," Leo said. "But if you take this offer, you won't have to."

All right. He had me there. But still. Twenty-five hundred dollars? "I need a job, Leo," I said. "A real job. I need a place to live, a place for my sister to live. I have *responsibilities*. Social services is hardly going to let me turn tricks out of my apartment." In that moment I was a triumphant young woman, refusing to be bought, standing up for what she believed she deserved.

I strode to the door and banged up against it, almost stumbling backward.

Leo was standing over me. He pulled the swipe card that was dangling over my neck and touched it to the pad by the door. A little green light turned on, and Leo opened the door. "I'll be in touch," he said.

CHAPTER 7

The next morning I stumbled out of my apartment, and there was Alejandro waiting for me on the sidewalk, a tall Starbucks cup in each hand. I had almost run into him in my rush to get out the door and make it to work on time. I stopped short, startled. "What are you doing here?"

"You're calling in sick today," Alejandro said. "I have something I need to show you." I stood on the sidewalk, deliberating. I had been kidding myself, thinking Leo Glass could be the answer to my problems. I had been planning on spending the day at work, messaging every contact in Mira's phone. One last desperate attempt to make good on my promise to Wendy. "Come on, Rosemary. It'll be worth it. Trust me." He held out one of the Starbucks cups to me.

Instinctively, I took it. I took a sip. It was a mocha with whipped cream, something I would never order. It tasted good, though, like a liquid candy bar. "You're lucky my housemate wasn't here with me. We usually walk to work together. What would I have told her if we'd walked out and seen you here?"

He shrugged. "I would have thought of something. Or you would have."

"Anyway, she's not here. She spent the night at her boyfriend's."

"So I guess it worked out."

"I guess it did."

"So . . . are you going to call or what?"

"Call who—Margorie?"

"Your work. Tell them you're not coming in."

"How long is this going to take?"

"Oh, not too long."

I shook my head, exasperated. Then I made the call.

"We can walk there from here," Alejandro said. "Actually, it's really close."

We walked down to Eighteenth Avenue, sipping our drinks. It was a beautiful fall day, cool and crisp. The sun lit up the trees—gold and crimson and tangerine. The leaves on the sidewalk made a colorful carpet under our feet. It was quieter in this part of the neighborhood, not so many restaurants and bars and shops—just parks and churches and schools and stately old mansions converted into law offices. And apartment buildings, too, old ones with columns and balconies and french doors, like my place but with fewer stoner college kids passing around bongs.

"This is it." Alejandro stopped in front of an old redbrick building, six stories high, wedged between an unobtrusive little coffee shop and another similar-looking building. I marveled again at the silence. We were only five blocks from the busy shopping and eating district where I lived and worked, but it felt like a different world. Maybe it was the trees. Their leaves filtered the noise.

In the lobby the walls were wallpapered, trimmed with lacquered walnut woodwork. The whole place felt empty, as if no one lived here—as if no one had lived here for some time. "What are we doing here?" I whispered. Alejandro didn't answer.

We took the stairs up to the fourth floor. The moment my foot traversed the threshold between the entryway and the living room, I knew: I had to live here. It felt like a crush, or maybe love. The living room was huge, filled with light. Gleaming hardwood floors, impossibly high ceilings. Old-fashioned divided-light windows.

The windows stretched almost from floor to ceiling, seven or eight feet high. The trees below, full and leafy, spanned the sidewalk up and down the entire block. I wanted to hear the leaves quaking, to smell that fall scent of smoke and earth and rain. "Do they open? These windows?" I was already unfastening the locks and hoisting up the wooden sash. It opened easily, or more easily than I imagined. The sash stayed up, too. The ropes and weights inside the window's architecture were in prime working condition.

I leaned out, bending at the waist, so most of my body was outside. If I fell, I'd land on top of the trees' soft, round domes. A breeze whipped past, blowing my hair, rustling the leaves. They looked like tiny fires, tiny fingers waving.

I swore I heard music—I *did* hear music. A string instrument, a violin. It wasn't a recording; it was someone practicing. I could tell by the arrangement—it sounded like half a song, like the accompanying part to something larger, grander. All by itself it was sad but haunting.

"Do you hear that?" I said to Alejandro.

He pulled me in by the cardigan. "If you fall out the window, Leo's going to have me fired."

I extracted myself from the window but left it open. The violin stopped. I stood there, hoping the player—a real violinist, I was sure of it, not some kid practicing for youth orchestra but a true musician—would start another song. I didn't know much about classical music, but I recognized talent and beauty when I heard it. The music didn't pick up again, but I began to sway. I lifted up my arms and waved them over my head the way a drunk or half-asleep person might bat at a fly, and I shuffled back and forth in a slow, languid dance. "Hey, Alejandro," I said. "Who am I?"

He widened his eyes in mock horror and shook his head. "You tell me."

I spun in wide circles over the floor. "I'm Victoria!"

Another dazed head shake from Alejandro.

"Like that New Order video. *The Temptation of Victoria.*"

Alejandro indulged me with a little laugh. "Never seen it."

I straightened up again. "Whose place is this?"

"It's yours," Alejandro said. "If you want it."

"So Leo—he'd just give me this apartment? Like as a part of my—uh, compensation package?"

Alejandro's lips formed a stiff, straight line. "You need a place to stay, right? For you and your sister? Will this do or not?"

I wanted this apartment more than I had wanted anything in a long, long time. I wanted it for my sister, to give her a second shot at a childhood, the childhood I'd never had. I could picture her having friends over, me wearing an apron, pulling a batch of cookies out of the oven. I would do that. I would do that for her. I *could* do that for her, if I lived here.

I wanted to fling my arms around Alejandro and dance him around the room. But I was getting ahead of myself. Showing all my cards. I narrowed my eyes and tried to come up with something critical to say about the place. "Let's see the kitchen," I said, all business.

"Six thousand," I announced after touring the rest of the apartment.

"What?"

"I want six thousand a month."

"Done," Alejandro answered. He responded so quickly that it made me feel stupid, as if I'd settled for much less than expected. He held out his hand, and I shook it.

CHAPTER 8

Three days after I moved into my new place, I locked myself out. I had woken up in my bed in my new room, the one at the end of the hall. So far, it was the only furnished room in the apartment. I had no dining room set, no couch. I didn't even have a chair. Over the next week I'd need to fill the apartment with rugs and paintings and furniture, to make it feel lived in, the kind of place a teenager could grow up in. I should have leaped out of bed and got cracking. That's what I told myself. Still, I lingered under the warmth of the covers. It was so difficult to get up without a schedule to adhere to, a clock to punch in the morning.

I had quit in a blaze of glory. I signed for the lease of the apartment before even agreeing to the terms of the job with Leo—of course I did—and then I marched straight over to La Cuisine and announced "I quit!" in that triumphant way people do in the movies. Maybe I expected everyone to cheer. No one even heard me. I had to track Rick down in his office, and he didn't seem that surprised or broken up about me leaving immediately. Don't you need two weeks' notice? I asked him. He said not to worry about it.

Margorie, at least, had delivered with an appropriate reaction. I was leaving, I told her down on the sales floor. I was moving up in the world, working for Lookinglass. It was true, I decided. More or less. She had yelped and screeched and then gripped me by the shoulders. Then she had frowned. She had asked what, exactly, I would be doing at Lookinglass. I hadn't hammered out the details, I answered breezily.

They were giving me time to move into my new place first. Margorie's frown deepened, and I quickly made up something about getting an advance on my first paycheck.

I could have told her the truth then, right at the beginning. Margorie, of all my friends, would have understood. She wouldn't have tried to talk me out of it, this whole sugar daddy arrangement. She might have even encouraged it. I didn't, though. I liked the lie better. The idea of it.

A quick shower revived me somewhat. Wearing nothing but a short, thin bathrobe and a towel wrapped around my head, I decided to throw in a load of laundry, just to feel productive. Ten thirty on a Tuesday. No one would be around hogging the machines. The apartment building was dead quiet.

When I returned from the basement with my empty laundry basket, my door was locked, my keys somewhere inside. I spent a few futile minutes jiggling the doorknob before admitting it was useless. I couldn't leave the apartment building with wet hair, barefoot, in a mini-robe. And even if I could leave, there was nowhere to go. It was raining outside, coming down in sheets.

I bent down at my waist, letting the towel fall into the laundry basket. My hair hung in wet strands.

Carl and Jessica, the apartment managers, lived on the first floor. I went back down there, pounded my fist against their door like a madwoman, and then rested my ear against it, listening. No one answered.

I couldn't think of anything to do but sit on the lower steps of the lobby and wait for them.

A good forty-five minutes ticked by, affording me more than enough time to take a thorough inventory of every architectural detail of the lobby, before someone finally walked in.

I stood up on the bottom step and adjusted my robe.

He looked familiar, like someone I already knew, someone I should recognize, a long-lost friend or an obscure celebrity. I supposed it was because we lived in the same building. We must have already crossed paths.

I couldn't help but notice that he was incredibly good-looking—good-looking in a tortured artist sort of way, with dark circles under his eyes and a fine line already forming between his eyebrows, though he was young. My age.

He walked right past me, almost brushing the satin sleeve of my robe, absorbed in his own thoughts. I had no choice but to follow him up the first flight of stairs and into the stairwell at the second floor. I thought of calling out to him but couldn't figure out what to say.

At the fourth floor—my floor—he exited the stairwell. In the hallway, he stopped in front of the door to the apartment next to mine and took out his keys.

"Hi," I said before he could disappear.

His head turned toward me in slow motion. At least that was how I remembered it, the way you tend to remember monumental events, like a car crash or the moment before death, when your entire life flashes before your eyes. There was something soothingly monochromatic about him. Gray T-shirt, darker gray sweater, like something a kindly grandfather might wear. Gray eyes. Nondescript brown hair, the color of dust.

He narrowed his eyes and looked me up and down, trying to assess my situation. The wet hair, the robe, the empty laundry basket. He reminded me of a grumbling detective in a noir film, trying to piece together the clues. "What happened here?" His voice was gray, too. Like gravel.

"I locked myself out. I, uh—" I tightened my robe around myself and wished my hair weren't wet. It was my best feature, full and shiny with golden highlights. Without it I was powerless.

He fiddled with the lock on his door. With a nod of his head, he gestured for me to follow him inside.

His living room was so dark he had to switch on a lamp. The entire west-facing wall of windows was covered with thick velvet curtains, which he pulled open with a flourish, revealing my familiar treetop view. I squinted as my eyes adjusted and took in his living room: bookshelves to the ceiling, tattered Persian rugs, oil landscapes in gilded frames, a music stand overflowing with sheet music. "Wow," I said. It was all so beautiful, but at the same time, odd. I couldn't match the apartment up with the man standing inside it.

He leaned against a bookshelf and stared at me again in that disconcerting way, like he was trying to figure me out.

"Rosemary, right?"

My mouth opened, but I didn't say anything.

"I met your friend Margorie," he explained. "The day you moved in."

I remembered now, Margorie telling me that she had met my next-door neighbor. She had said he was hot. Except that wasn't how she had put it, exactly. She had said *I* would think he was hot. I'd asked her what she'd meant by that, and she'd said he was skinny and sad.

Anyway, she wasn't wrong. I did find him hot.

"What about your sister?" he was asking me.

"What about my sister?" I narrowed my eyes at him.

"Your friend said she was moving in with you?"

"Yeah . . ." I shook my head, unsure where he was going with this line of questioning.

"She has a key, right?"

"Oh, *right*." I exhaled in relief. "She won't be here until next weekend. She's—" I shut my mouth, not sure what I planned to say next. "She's just a kid," I blurted out. "I'm taking care of her. I'm supposed to be taking care of her."

"Oh—wow."

"Margorie didn't tell me your name." I wasn't flirting; it was a matter-of-fact question, a very normal question I'd ask any neighbor I'd had the pleasure of meeting.

"Sam Ferguson."

"Sam," I repeated. "Nice name." It was a stupid thing to say.

"Thanks," he said in a sort of amused, deadpan way.

"Your apartment is just like mine," I told him. "In reverse."

"It's my aunt's. She's a patron of the arts." Sam gestured toward a music stand and an instrument case. The music stand was overloaded with books and loose sheets of music. On the floor next to it were more stacks: Bach, Walton, Bartók, Hindemith.

"That's you? The violin?"

"It's a *viola*," he said. This was obviously a mistake he had been correcting over and over his entire life.

"Sorry." God, he looked almost angry. "Do you play professionally or—"

"I'm a violist in the Oregon Symphony."

"You don't look like you'd play in the symphony."

"Oh yeah? What does someone who plays in the symphony look like?"

My hand waved in Sam's general direction. "Not like *that*."

He offered to lend me some clothes and left me in his room to change. His room was neat and spare, in contrast to the bohemian messiness of the rest of the place. These were his things, I guessed: a bed with a Pendleton wool blanket, a Danish Modern bookcase, another music stand.

The jeans and T-shirt he left for me were both too big, and not in a cute way. I knew this for sure when I checked myself out in the bathroom mirror—I looked like a prepubescent boy wearing his older brother's clothes. With my bathrobe back on over the whole ensemble, it looked better. Sort of like a smoking jacket, I figured. It gave my waist a little definition at least.

I found Sam making coffee in the kitchen. He placed a coffee mug in front of me at the small kitchen table. The mug had a cartoon of an old woman on it with a speech bubble coming out of her mouth. "I hate Mondays," she was saying.

"I don't have any cream," he said. "Or sugar."

"That's okay. I like it black," I lied.

He stared at me with a pensive expression. He really was very good-looking. Tortured hero in an indie movie. Too skinny, too sad to play the leading role in a Hollywood blockbuster. Like Margorie said, just my type. His right hand was twirling around and around, stirring his coffee into a whirlpool with a spoon.

"I thought you didn't have any cream or sugar."

"I don't."

"So what are you stirring into your coffee?"

Sam stopped stirring and stared into his cup. "Nothing."

We sat across from each other, not saying anything, for an awkward moment. "Your aunt—she just lets you live here? For free?"

"Nothing's free."

"You're really good, you know."

"Thanks," he said. I could tell what he was thinking: that my opinion didn't mean much, considering that, until a few moments ago, I hadn't known I was listening to a viola and not a violin. Sam sat up straighter in his chair. "You can hear me—through the windows?"

"It's an old building."

"Are they open now?"

"What?"

"Your windows."

"Why?"

"Yes or no."

I thought about it. The apartment had radiant heat, no thermostats to control the temperature. That meant I had slept every night with the bed pulled up under the window, so I could close my eyes and feel delicate drops of rain mist my face. "Yes."

Sam slammed his coffee mug on the table. "Follow me."

Back in Sam's bedroom, he unlatched the window and pushed up on the sash, letting in a chilly, rain-scented gust of air. He leaned out the window and looked down. And then he just climbed out. One minute he was in the room with me, the next he was outside, waving at me through the glass.

I stood staring at him for a second, disbelieving. Then I rushed over and looked down to see Sam standing on a crumbling old ledge of the building, not more than six inches wide. This was a Victorian building. That ledge had to have been more than a hundred years old. Our eyes met through the glass. We were facing each other, my hands pressed up to his. "What are you *doing*?"

He pointed in the direction of my apartment and began inching over there. "Meet me in the hallway," he said.

This guy was going to kill himself performing this Spiderman routine for me. "It's *raining*. We're four stories high."

When he disappeared from view, I leaned out his window and saw him making his way across the building like James Bond on a rescue mission.

I couldn't watch. I ran out of the bedroom and out of his apartment, making sure to prop his door open with a shoe. With my ear pressed to the outside of my apartment door, I listened. Thumps. Footsteps. Then my door opened and Sam walked through. He ran his fingers through his hair. His faded jeans were dotted with dark splatters of rain.

"That was really stupid," I said. "You could have killed yourself." I threw my arms around him then and held him tightly, resting my face against his chest. I wasn't sure what had come over me. I wasn't much of a hugger. The wool of his sweater scratched at my cheek. He smelled like something comfortable and worn, tucked away for years in a cedar chest. I'd chosen an awkward way to hug him, with his hands at his sides. I was pinning his arms to his torso, so he couldn't hug me back. Somehow he managed to free his hands from his pockets, and then he was patting me on the back, like, "Okay, lady, that's enough," so I let him go.

I offered to buy him lunch. It was the least I could do, to thank him. "I don't know—" he started.

"I *can't* do lunch," I blurted out, suddenly aware of the time. "Rain check?"

He frowned, but then he nodded once, curtly. "Rain check," he echoed, but I was already rushing back into my apartment, peeling off the robe as I flew down my hall and into my bedroom.

Two minutes later, I slipped a note under Sam's door on my way out: "Rain check," it said. "My place, seven o'clock." I drew the outline of a cloud around the words, and raindrops spilling out of the cloud.

~

I was ten minutes late to my noon appointment with Leo. He wanted to meet me, to go over the details of our arrangement. I didn't have time to figure out a ride or catch a bus, so I had run all the way there. I was panting with exertion by the time I checked into the Lookinglass offices.

Alejandro made me wait another ten minutes in the lobby, which was just as well. It gave me a chance to catch my breath. When he finally did come get me, he led me into a conference room. We were surrounded by glass—the windows faced east, with views of the river. We would have a view of the mountain, too, on a clear day. Today was not one of those days. A gauzy blanket of fog levitated over the river.

"Sorry I'm late," I said for the second time.

Alejandro's eyes traveled from my feet up to my face before he gestured for me to sit down at the end of a long conference table. I'd managed to throw on a proper top, to pull my hair up into a messy bun.

I gave him a level look in response.

But then Alejandro gave me a slight nod. A nod! "Typically, HR would take care of this kind of thing," he said, referring to a stack of paperwork he'd laid on the table between us. "Leo wants to deal with this personally."

"You look really good today." No response. "I really like that shirt." Alejandro was wearing what appeared to be a French sailor's shirt, the kind of garment I'd expect to see paired with those navy-blue high-waisted sailor pants. "Is it French?" I asked, when my compliment got no reaction. "It looks French."

Alejandro allowed himself an almost undetectable smile. "Yes, it is." With his left hand, he reached over and touched the sleeve of his right arm, as if to remind himself of the material, a trusty cotton cloth.

The doors of the conference room opened. "*Está bien*, Alejandro," Leo said. "I'll take it from here." Then he said something in rapid Spanish.

Alejandro nodded, mumbling *"Sí, sí, sí,"* and backed himself out of the room.

"All right." Leo shuffled through the papers Alejandro had arranged over the conference table. Then he looked up at me and blinked, as if noticing my presence for the first time. "How's the new place?"

"It's perfect," I said. "Thank you."

"I wanted to give you a chance to settle in," he said, "before we worked out all the boring stuff."

It was a huge red flag. I had signed the lease. I had moved in. *Then* he had me come over to hash out the details of my employment. I should never have gone along with it, this order of events. In hindsight, this was crystal clear. Back then, though, I wasn't oblivious so much as . . . desperate. Delusional, even, carried away in this vision of me and my new life. I was still, even at that moment, entertaining notions of me as a businesswoman, some young go-getter type with a real job and a nice place to live. Someone who could afford that apartment on her own and move her sister into the spare bedroom.

"Great," I said. "I mean—I'm ready. Looking forward to getting started."

Leo slid one sheet of paper across the table, and then another, until four pieces of paper were lined up in a row before me. "Everything is as we discussed. Sign here, here, and here when you've read it over."

A girlfriend contract. Seriously. I scanned the terms. A year-long contract, effective immediately. A nondisclosure clause: I couldn't talk about the arrangement, to anyone. To the outside world, we'd be a couple. A regular couple. No one would know. If they found out, he'd sue me. That was the gist of it. This was fine with me. I didn't want anyone to know about it, either.

I looked up from the pages. "Early termination clause?"

"It protects both of us," he said. "This whole thing"—Leo waved a hand over the contract—"is just a formality, really. It's perfectly straightforward: I want you to be my girlfriend. It needs to seem real. It needs to *be* real. After today, I don't want to talk about it, the arrangement. Kind of ruins the romance otherwise, you know?" Leo accompanied his statements with a roguish grin, as if he were only half-serious.

"I don't get it," I said. "You could go out with anyone. Actresses, models. You're rich, successful. Good-looking." I waved my hand in front of him. I had googled him, of course. He was a tech dude, not exactly a celebrity, but he had, in fact, been photographed at various events with models, or women who looked like models anyway. Long legs, high cheekbones. Never the same woman twice, and never anyone recognizable. The captions always failed to catch their names. "Leo Glass and his dinner companion," one might read.

"I don't *want* an actress or a model." Leo smiled calmly, as if he were explaining a very obvious point to a small child. "I want you."

"But why? Why me?" I was flattered, obviously, but I was still having a hard time believing that, out of all the available women in the world, I would be the one that Leo Glass decided he had to have.

"We've gone over this. It's a decision. It's really that simple. Finding someone, it doesn't have to be complicated. I'm attracted to you. You're attracted to me." I must have blushed because Leo gave me a little wink.

"You *said* I was good-looking." Okay, he got me there. "I'm a busy man—gone all the time, working nights. If you're busy, too, how is this thing ever going to work? That's where paying you comes in."

He made it sound very reasonable. He didn't want a model, an actress, or a professional escort. He wanted a shot to have a normal girlfriend. If he had to pay someone to act like a normal girlfriend, why not go for it? I looked back at the contract. "Maybe I should have a lawyer look this over."

"You're welcome to. I could have your first check deposited into your account as early as tonight, but if you're happy to wait—"

I leaned over the pages and squinted, like I was really studying it. "It says here we'll communicate using Lookinglass technology."

Leo reached into his pocket and produced a shiny round disk, a little silver compact, just like the one he had in the Thai restaurant. "I'll give you a Mirror."

It felt cool and smooth in my hands, heavier than I remembered. One side of the disk was silver, real, the patina of an old chalice. The other was darker. The screen, I guessed.

"Three years from now, everyone will have one," Leo said. "I can transfer all your data over if you'd like."

"My data?"

"Here, just hand me your phone."

Instinctually, I clutched my bag to my body. "That's okay," I said.

"It's really no problem. Let me show you. Enter your passcode." I found myself taking my phone out and entering the passcode.

Leo held out his palm to me, and I gave him my phone. After a moment he said, "There! Look at your Mirror."

The screen was much smaller than I was used to, a circle instead of a large rectangle, but there they were—all my apps, my photos, my contacts.

"Can I have my phone back?"

"The Mirror is a significant upgrade."

"But my phone—"

Leo frowned and handed it back. "I've already wiped the data from it."

"Leo—" I didn't know what to say. I had walked right into this, handed my phone over to him of my own accord.

"The Mirror can do everything your old device did and more. The processing power alone—"

I stared dubiously at the Mirror, the tiny round screen. "I can't watch a show on it."

"A laptop is better for viewing media anyway," Leo said. "Or use a tablet."

I turned the Mirror over and polished my fingerprints off on my jeans. It *was* beautiful, that silver. I noticed something else, then. My name was engraved into the silver. Beneath that, etched so finely I could barely make it out, was the Lookinglass logo. "Is this—is this like a tracking device or something?" I asked.

"It's not a *tracking device.*" He laughed, as if the idea were ludicrous. "It's synced up with Lookinglass, though. Double tap the screen."

I tapped it twice and it lit up. Two figures appeared in perfect resolution. Me and Leo, hunched over the conference table. I looked up from the screen and scanned the walls, the ceiling. On one wall, a shelf was lined with plants in white ceramic pots. Next to the pots, Glasseyes, their pupils pointed in every possible direction.

"I'm not on Lookinglass."

"You are now."

Leo explained that he had taken the liberty of registering me, using the photograph Sebastian St. Doug—as I now liked to call him—had sent him. It was that easy.

"Wait, so I can just take someone else's photo and sign them up to an app that's going to track every move they make? How is this legal? What about stalkers—"

"Of course not," Leo said. "We have very strict privacy controls."

"But—"

"*I* can do it. Thought I would save you the trouble. If you don't consent, I'll deactivate your account, no problem. That is what I'm asking for now."

"My consent? So you can monitor me on this thing?"

Leo tapped on the Lookinglass app and held the Mirror up for me to inspect. **Welcome to Lookinglass! You have one watcher**, a notification read. "It's really more of a convenience. We'll be each other's contacts. Use it to communicate with each other. It goes both ways. I'll follow you, you'll follow me."

"Maybe I don't want to be on Lookinglass. I don't want anyone watching me." I don't want *you* watching me, I almost said. At the same time, I was seriously considering it. Maybe it wasn't such a big deal. It made sense that the inventor of Lookinglass would want his employees to have accounts. When you work in clothing retail, you have to wear their clothes. It was like that. Sort of.

Leo shrugged, unconcerned. "So don't accept my offer."

"You'll be like the Wicked Witch in *The Wizard of Oz*," I remarked, "monitoring me through your crystal ball."

"You've seen the Glasseye stickers on store and restaurant windows, right? Glasseyes aren't a secret." I *had* started noticing them, ever since Mira brought it up. Some people even made a point to go into establishments with Glasseyes, so their followers could observe them there, holding up cute outfits, sipping coffees. I'd also seen "no Glasseye" stickers, like no smoking signs with a big eyeball instead of a cigarette. It was possible to avoid Glasseyes, then. They weren't everywhere. As Leo said, they weren't a secret. "People *buy* them," he was saying, "put them in their own homes—"

"I'm not doing that. Putting one in my place."

"I'm not asking you to."

"I'm serious. I can't be monitored in my own home."

"I get it. I don't have Glasseyes up in my place, either. I have six million watchers. You think I want them to see me dance around in my underwear?"

"If I agree to this, I need you to promise. There's my sister to think about. I can't have you watching me—us—with Glasseyes. If I so much as see one of those Glasseyes in my building, I'm out."

"Understood."

"Also, because of my sister—" I hesitated, worried I was pressing my luck. "She needs stability. I wouldn't be able to have you over; it wouldn't be good for her—"

"We'll meet at my place. Where we can have our privacy."

I smiled in relief, nodding. "Thanks. Thanks for understanding."

I bent over the contract, trying to concentrate. It was vague and legal-sounding. Nothing on it even outlined my duties. If I signed, I would be under contract for one year to work on a special project ("Hereinafter referred to as The Project") with Leo Glass. There was a noncompete clause: The Project would be my only employment. All the stuff about my complete discretion, never discussing The Project with anyone, even each other. All I had to do—on paper, anyway—was make myself available to Leo Glass, sometimes at a moment's notice. In return, I would get $6,000 deposited into my account at the first business day of every month. My rent (valued at $3,200) would also be taken care of.

Seeing the numbers made it seem real. *Six thousand dollars* a month, on top of rent? I could save a big chunk of it—most of it!—and divert it to a savings account. It sounded too good to be true. With the money I squirreled away, Wendy and I might even be able to stay in the apartment while I attended law school. After that I would have a legitimate job at a law firm. I'd be making my own money. Maybe that whole briefcase and business suit fantasy wasn't such a pipe dream after all.

I looked up from the pages to find Leo studying me.

"Well," he said. "What do you say?" Leo smiled and held out his hand for me to shake.

I looked into his eyes, disconcerted again by the shiny black beads of his pupils. He met my gaze and nodded, slightly, as if to say, *Go on. I dare you.*

My hand reached out, and we shook on it. His handshake was firm, almost bone-crushing.

Then I picked up the pen and signed.

CHAPTER 9

At seven o'clock, a knock sounded on my door, four steady raps. There was Sam, a bottle of wine in hand. He was wearing different clothes. The same jeans with a white T-shirt and different gray cardigan, all the buttons buttoned. Maybe he had changed his clothes because of something he had done earlier that day. Or maybe he'd changed them for me, chosen what he believed would impress me most.

I was still wearing his jeans.

"I like your jeans." He delivered this line in such a dry, matter-of-fact way, that I wasn't sure what to make of it.

"*Thank* you," I said. It came out sounding flirtatious. I wasn't supposed to be flirting with him. I was Leo Glass's girlfriend now, at least technically. Contractually? It still didn't seem real, not then. I had signed the contract. After I signed, Leo picked it up, flipped through the pages, and nodded as if to affirm that yes, everything was going according to plan. I wasn't sure what I was supposed to do next. Go over and start making out with him? Get down on my knees? I was just standing there, and Leo was already seated at the table, scanning something on a tablet. He looked up at me and then waved me away. I'll be in touch, he said.

Anyway, I wasn't flirting with my next-door neighbor. I was simply thanking him for rescuing me. Making him dinner was the least I could do. And it was *all* I would do. This was a very proper, neighborly transaction. That was what I had told myself as I was getting ready. Strictly reciprocal.

Sam gave me his noir-detective inspection, looking me up and down. To make a proper neighborly impression, I should have worn something sensible and matronly. Instead I was wearing a tight scoop-neck top that dipped a little too low. And his jeans. "You clean up nice," he said.

"You too." It made less sense when I said it.

I had decided to make waffles for dinner. I didn't have the equipment to make anything else. That was the downside of working at a kitchen store. I was the proud owner of dozens of specialty items and none of the basics.

We sat in the middle of the dining room, where a table should be. I spread a tablecloth on the floor and plugged the waffle iron into the room's only outlet. Steam billowed out of it in white clouds.

We drank through the entire bottle of wine and ate waffle after waffle. Sam went to his apartment to fetch another bottle, and I dimmed the lights on the crystal chandelier hanging over us. The light fractured around the room, like confetti.

I felt braver then, in the darkness. Drunker, too. We ran out of waffle batter. We ate through the stack of waffles. Then we were left sitting across from each other. I wanted to skip over this part: the getting-to-know-you part. I wanted to already know.

I wasn't thinking of the contract I had just signed, the apartment I had just moved into. I wasn't thinking of how this could ruin everything. I was just—doing what I wanted to do. As if it could be my last chance.

"Here's what we should do," I announced. "We should just tell each other everything right now. I'll tell you my deal, you tell me your deal."

"My deal?"

"Everyone has a deal."

Sam looked like he was thinking this over. He narrowed his eyes and stared into the corner of the room. Then he nodded. "You first."

I exhaled, closed my eyes, and started shaping the story in my mind. Then my eyelids lifted up like stage curtains. I gave my story the luster of a fairy tale, the sad fate of the two orphaned sisters and their beautiful young mother who had died at the hands of their wicked stepfather. *My* wicked stepfather, anyway.

You know how they died? I began. They drove off the road, off the side of a mountain, in broad daylight, like Thelma and Louise. I raised my hand in the air and flew it in an arc between us, in demonstration. Sam's eyes went huge.

Jason was driving, I went on. They left no skid marks—just disappeared over the edge.

My mother was young when she had me. Seventeen. Her mother—my grandmother—helped take care of me at first, but then she got sick. We were poor, living in a motel, and my mom was young and beautiful but tired. And very, very sad. I feel like I knew that, even as a little kid. I knew, too, that I was the one who was making her tired. I wasn't the easiest child.

Everything changed when my poor, innocent mother met Jason with his wavy hair and tan skin and his Listerine breath and his nylon jogging shorts. Jason was the love of my mother's life. *My* dad was just some loser she knew from high school who took off for college and was never seen again.

With Jason, she was happy. We moved out of that hotel. We moved into a real house. He was a good dad, too, at first. So I tried to be good, too. To be the perfect daughter. I was terrified of ruining it, of breaking the spell. Terrified that Jason would leave and we'd be penniless and my mom would get that vacant look in her eyes again. When Wendy was born, I was glad. I was *thrilled*. It meant he was in it for good. That everything would be perfect.

It was perfect, for a while, I told Sam. But—I stared straight into Sam's eyes when I said this next part—I hated him.

Sam held my gaze. He didn't blink.

I took in a deep breath. I felt myself unspooling. I wanted to tell him everything.

I told him about the first time it happened. I was twelve. Jason had been under a lot of stress around that time. He worked longer hours, came home grumpy, though he always seemed to have a smile for my mom and Wendy. That night, the first time, my mom was gone for the evening and left Jason in charge of the bedtime routine. Wendy was four years old, already sound asleep. When Jason told me to pick out a book and he would read it to me, I was excited. Pleased, maybe, that he was smiling at me, paying attention to me. I chose a classic, *Where the Wild Things Are*. He had bought it for me, back when he was first wooing my mom and I was just some stupid little kid, five or six years old. He sat next to me on the bed and read to me, just like he used to. He was a good reader. Very expressive. He took his time, acted out all the monsters' voices.

I had never told anyone this story before. I felt detached from it, almost, like the whole thing had happened to someone else a long, long time ago. I kept going.

Jason reached the final page and closed the book. He told me to lie back on my bed, so I did, with my arms down at my sides. He pulled the covers up to my chin, folding down the edge. He tightened the sheets over me and tucked them under the mattress, like he was making the bed with me still in it. I could barely move, pinned down by the sheets. When he was finished, he leaned his face in next to mine. Snug as a bug in a rug, he whispered into my ear.

Then he smoothed the sheets with his hand, slowly, the way you'd smooth the sheets on a perfectly made bed to get out all the wrinkles. He ran his hands over and over the sheets, over me, my body. His hands gathered speed and his breath quickened, and I shut my eyes tight and then it was over. He kissed me on the forehead. Then on the lips, lingering. I stayed still, pinned down like a mounted butterfly. His breath blew hot against my neck when he spoke again, his parting words: Love you. Night-night.

The next time my mom had to go away, I asked if Jason was going to tuck me in again. She said he loved me. He *loved* tucking me in. He had told her that himself. I could tell she was happy about it. It made her happy. For years I thought of it that way, that "tucking me in" was what it was called, this elaborate ritual of flattening down the sheets with me straitjacketed beneath them.

That was the beginning, how it started. It got worse, as these things do. I didn't say this to Sam because when I stopped talking, I looked over at him and he was still taking me in with those gray, mournful eyes.

"I'm so sorry," Sam said.

I topped off both of our glasses. Our teeth were stained with wine. The story wasn't over yet. I wanted to keep going. I would tell the whole thing, all the way through. I would unburden myself from this story, and then I would be ready for my new life as Leo Glass's paid girlfriend.

I never told my mom, I told Sam. The next morning, after that first time, do you know what I did? I got up and acted like nothing was wrong. I went up to Jason and kissed him on the cheek while he was shoveling Cheerios into his mouth. I said, "Good morning, Daddy!" I had never kissed him on the cheek in my life. I rarely called him Daddy. I don't know why I did it, but my mom looked so happy when I did. So I kept doing it.

My stepfather's nighttime visits went on until I was fifteen years old. Jason was laid up in bed after knee surgery following a mountain bike accident. He had to keep off it for two weeks, lying in bed with his leg raised up on pillows. He was out of it half the time, dozing off and on all day. Our mom didn't come home until well after dinner, and Wendy was just a little kid, so I was supposed to check on him when I got home from school—ask him if he needed me to heat up any food, refill his water jug, stuff like that.

He had a whole shelf filled with orange bottles—pain medication, antibiotics, sleep meds, and some over-the-counter stuff, too. I started pilfering from the bottles—a pill here, another pill there. After a few days I had a couple of dozen. I put them in a zipper bag and crushed them with the rolling pin in the kitchen.

I read up on it, and it turns out it's difficult to overdose on Vicodin, or sleep medication, or antibiotics. All three together, though? Maybe it would work. I could stir it into his morning coffee. This was another chore that fell to me during his convalescence. He drank his coffee black with eleven packets of Sweet'N Low. Eleven! It was a brew so strong and so sweet that he would never notice the addition of twenty-four assorted pills mixed in there, too.

He'd drink it, fall asleep, and then his organs would begin to shut down. If he puked it up, or caught on and called the doctor, he wouldn't die. He needed to drink his whole cup of coffee in the morning and be alone all day while my mom worked and Wendy and I were in school. We'd come home from school and it would be done. I would take the coffee cup and wash it on the sanitary cycle in the dishwasher. If they did an autopsy or screened his blood or something after he died, they'd find nothing more than the pills lined up on his bedside table and a revolting amount of Sweet'N Low. It would be ruled an accidental overdose. Case closed.

I carried that baggie of powder with me every day for a week. Every morning I brewed his coffee. I poured it into his cup and added each packet of sweetener. After I'd stirred in the final packet, I would take the baggie out of its hiding place, a zippered pencil bag buried at the bottom of my school backpack. All I would have to do is open it up, sift the contents into the cup like poison snow.

I couldn't do it, in the end. Too many variables. What if he drank half of it and didn't die? What if he called 911 and the police came and they tested the coffee and realized I'd poisoned him?

I couldn't kill him, but I could end it, all those silent little visits to my room in the middle of the night.

My mom asked me to bring him his dinner. It was steak. When I brought the tray in, he was lying in bed in a grubby old T-shirt and nylon athletic shorts. The whole room had that stale locker room smell. Old socks and sweat and bologna sandwiches. He didn't even look up when I set the tray down. Didn't bother to say so much as thank you. But he noticed when I took the steak knife to his throat. He noticed when I pressed the tip against his skin.

I wasn't trying to hurt him. I was just trying to scare him. And Jason did look scared, at least in that first moment. His eyes bulged out in surprise, and I saw the flash of fear. He might not have feared the steak knife so much as the idea that the jig was up, that I was going to go to my mom or maybe even the police. It only lasted a second, that frightened rabbit look. Then he scoffed. Do it, he told me. When I didn't do it, didn't plunge that knife straight through his neck, he laughed. He told me to quit messing around with the silverware and let him eat his dinner in peace.

I gripped the knife tighter, so tight I could see the whites of my knuckles. I told him he was never going to come into my room again. I told him if he did, I'd kill him. I dropped the knife so it clattered on the tray, and I walked out. He never touched me again.

A lone blueberry languished on my plate, drowning in its own blood. I popped it in my mouth and it burst, sweet and mealy. "You know what I can't stop thinking about?" I said to Sam.

Sam shook his head. His eyes had grown a bit wider now. I was scaring him off. Good. Maybe that was for the best.

"I keep thinking that if I'd had the guts back then to do it—to finish him off—everything would be different now. All those years, I thought if I just left, everything would be okay. Maybe *I* wouldn't be okay, but they would be okay. I really believed that. But now—" For the first time since I started telling my tragic little tale, my voice faltered.

"Now my mom is dead and my little sister—" I could only shake my head, unable to complete the sentence.

"Hey," Sam said, and he reached for my hands. We sat, facing each other, so close our foreheads almost touched. Our four hands clasped together. "Hey," he said again, softly. "You're doing a good thing here, taking care of your sister."

"But it's too late! If I'd taken care of things sooner—"

"We wouldn't be here right now," he said. "We never would have met."

"That would probably be better," I said. "For you, I mean."

"I don't think so," he said. "I don't believe that."

I almost leaned in and kissed him. Almost. I shut my eyes tightly and thought of my sister. The apartment. My new job. Leo. I stood up, too quickly, overturning my wineglass on the tablecloth. I felt the blood rush to my head. My vision went dark for a second. I had to close my eyes and take in a gulp of air. Maybe I had had more to drink than I'd realized. "You should probably go."

I put my hand to my forehead, trying to gain my composure.

"You okay?" He placed his hands on both sides of my arms, as if to steady me. Then, with one finger, he brushed a strand of my hair from my forehead, tucked it behind my ear.

We looked straight into each other's eyes. Not many people had such perfectly gray eyes. Usually it was just a trick of the light, and when you inspected them up close, you realized they were really an ambiguous shade of blue or green. Sam's were gray. Purely gray. There was no other color to describe them.

I thought he might kiss me. I thought of what it would be like to go to bed with him. His face listed toward mine and I angled my body closer to his, so the edges of our clothes were touching, and it seemed like in a moment we'd be wrapping ourselves up in each other, but then something shifted. I felt him inching back.

He squeezed my arms gently. "It's getting late."

I lifted my hand to his cheek. There was something sort of romantic and tragic about it, like a tearful goodbye at the train depot, when the soldier goes off to war and the wife has to wave to him from the platform, a brave smile on her face that crumples the minute the train rumbles out of the station.

"Thanks for the waffles," he said. And then he left.

CHAPTER 10

I couldn't get to sleep after Sam went home. I was drunk, maybe, but also strangely energized from telling him everything, the whole story leading up to this current predicament I found myself in. It was like shedding an extra skin. I kept jumping out of bed and pacing back and forth across the floor. It took all my willpower to stop myself from going over there and throwing myself on him, one last wild act before buckling down and becoming Leo Glass's paid girlfriend and the perfect older sister/mother figure to Wendy.

That thought sobered me, a little. Mother figure. I was too young for all this, I kept thinking. But when my mom was twenty-three, I was in kindergarten and she was already married to Jason. She did it. I could do it. I would do it.

I buried myself under my covers with my laptop and passed out sometime around three o'clock watching videos on YouTube.

The next morning I was still restless. I cleaned my whole apartment. When there was nothing left to do, I went back to my room and sat on my bed, my back against the wall. I could hear him playing. I closed my eyes to listen, to make out the melody. It was something familiar, something I had heard before, though I didn't know where. A haunting melody that made me think of impending winter, of early nights, of raindrops on windowpanes. Or maybe I'd taken the landscape around me and superimposed this music over it, assigned it as the soundtrack to the life I was living, right now.

I sat there and listened, my eyes closed, until he finished. The music stopped. The walls were so thin that I could hear him set his instrument back in its case, his footsteps padding around his room.

When I was sure he was finished practicing, not just taking a little break between pieces, I stood up. I didn't check to see if my hair and clothes looked all right. I didn't even put on shoes. I simply walked over to his place, and I knocked.

No one came to the door, and after waiting for what seemed like five minutes, I knocked again, louder this time. Footsteps thudded across the floor.

He opened the door. He didn't look surprised to see me. He didn't look especially happy to see me, either.

"We had an agreement." I pointed an accusing finger in Sam's face. "I tell you my deal, you tell me yours."

"I know."

"So tell me your deal."

"Maybe I don't have a deal." His face had no expression at all. His voice no inflection.

"I said a lot of things last night. Outlandish things. I was drunk."

"Okay." He was just standing there. Now he looked—just slightly— amused. I barely could detect the shift in his expression, but it was there. A minuscule glint in his eye, a perceptible lift of the corners of his mouth. This infuriated me.

"I meant it, everything I said." My voice was too loud, the words coming out too fast. "I wish I'd killed him. If I had to do it over again— if anyone tried to hurt me again, tried to hurt my sister, I wouldn't hesitate. I'd kill him so fast he wouldn't know what hit him. If you have a *problem* with that—" I stopped myself short, listening to myself. I was breathing hard, in and out of my nose.

"I don't have a problem with it," he said, completely poker-faced. For a few seconds, we just stood there, staring at each other. A standoff.

Then he hooked his fingers through the belt loops of my jeans and drew me inside, shutting the door with his foot.

He pulled me closer to him, until our bodies were almost but not quite pressed against each other, and smiled his sad little smile, and before I knew what I was doing, my hands were reaching for his face, and then I was pouncing, lurching forward, smashing my mouth onto his.

He didn't kiss me back, and I stopped myself, pulling away from him, mortified. I'd been up almost all last night, unable to sleep, my head spinning, thinking about him, running over and over the conversation. I'd told him my deal, I'd confessed to murder—to attempted murder, anyway—and he . . . well, he had probably gone home, straight to bed. While I lay awake, thinking about our bodies lying there, not one foot apart, separated by our apartment walls, by wooden beams and plaster and wires, he wasn't thinking about me at all.

My hands were still cupping the back of his head. I was breathing loudly, like I'd just run a mile. I could hear him breathing, too. He looked me straight in the eyes and smiled with just one side of his face. "You are crazy, you know that?" His tone was affectionate, as if he had just realized this about me, as if I hadn't been warning him all along. He leaned down and kissed me, and I kissed him back, and our arms circled around each other, and I felt like I was in a movie, the end of a movie. Swelling orchestra, cheering crowd, curtains swishing closed over the screen.

We made out in a ridiculous way, our hands all over each other. When we finally broke apart, we were both out of breath. Sam ran his hands through my hair. I put my hand to his cheek. Our faces collided together again, and we stumbled back, into his bedroom, onto his bed. We pulled each other's clothes off, and his fingers felt rough and calloused on my soft skin. Within moments he was on top of me and I was wrapping my legs around him, holding on to him, tightly, like I was afraid to let him go. He liked it, my desperation. I could tell. He felt the same way, like he couldn't get enough of me, like he was already afraid of losing me.

Only after our breathing quieted down did I notice the rain. Not a gentle pitter-patter but pounding rain, thrashing against the windows.

It was the middle of the day, but the room was so dark I could barely make out the contours of Sam's face. "I know what your deal is." My voice came out hoarse, as if unused to speaking.

"Oh yeah?"

I was nestled in the crook of his arm, so I couldn't see his face. "There are articles about you. Videos."

Sam propped himself up to look at me. "You were spying on me?" He didn't sound upset.

"I was up half the night. I needed something to pass the time."

"And what did you learn?"

"You were in a band," I said, and Sam's head rested back on his pillow. He closed his eyes, listening, like I was telling him a bedtime story. "You had a brother."

Before he joined the symphony, he was in a band with his twin brother and two other musicians, Imogene Wu and Timothy Karr. I'd never heard of them, but they had quite a following. Ferguson, they were called, an alt-rock ensemble of classically trained string players.

Last night, after Sam left, I huddled under my covers and watched their videos on my laptop, studying them. There they were, on a hillside, the Golden Gate Bridge in the background. In another, they sawed away on strange, body-less instruments in what appeared to be an abandoned warehouse. Four videos altogether. In every one of them, Sam faded into the background, his hair falling over his face. It was his identical twin brother, T. J., who was the leader, the star, staring directly into the camera, stomping his feet, raising his violin bow into the air. He looked just like Sam, but harder. Wilder.

"That was a long time ago."

"Not that long ago." I waited in case Sam wanted to stop me, but he didn't. His body was relaxed beside mine, his breath steady and slow now, his hand caressing my shoulder. "I'm sorry about your brother," I said.

"So am I."

"You don't have to talk about it."

"I know." But then he told me anyway. He told me about growing up in a narrow Queen Anne house, right in the Mission District in San Francisco. Outside grew a giant cork oak tree that Sam and T. J. used to spend hours playing in. They could climb out their bedroom window straight into the tree's branches. Sam's first memory was falling out of the tree. He was three or four and landed on the sidewalk, broke his arm. Spent the rest of the summer in a cast. He remembered the feeling of it, how it itched. The white, shriveled skin underneath the plaster.

"Years later I find out it never happened," he said. "I never broke my arm. I never even fell out of that tree."

"What do you mean?"

Sam looked up at the ceiling, and I studied his face in profile. His long, straight nose. "It came up one year. I must have been fifteen, sixteen years old. I was talking about it, about breaking my arm, and my mom goes, 'That wasn't you. That was your brother.'"

I'd heard that before, I said. Twins, they have that connection.

"So when I found him—he was in the bathtub, his face underwater—"

I brushed my hands over his face as if to wipe away his tears, although he wasn't crying. "I know. I know." I'd read about T. J.'s addiction problem, their last concert in Sweden, the overdose. I kissed Sam so he wouldn't have to tell me all his sad stories, and he kissed me back, and then we had sex again, slower this time. When we were done, the rain had stopped and it was quiet in the room.

∼

We stayed in bed until dark.

We lay on our sides, facing each other, our foreheads touching, murmuring stupid things, things only the two of us thought were funny, things only the two of us would understand. We agreed we were starving, that we needed to get up, to nourish ourselves. We discussed ordering a pizza and dismissed the idea as impractical. Someone would have to buzz the pizza guy in. Someone would have to open the door. It all seemed like too much effort, just for a bit of sustenance.

We needed to go to the store for provisions, stock up for days or weeks or months. We could prepare like we were alpine backpackers or astronauts. We could eat out of foil packets of freeze-dried food. We could drink Tang.

We made the difficult decision to venture out, to tear our bodies apart, to climb out from the warmth of the bed, to pull our clothes back on. It was a terrible feeling, to pull chilled, rumpled clothes onto warm skin.

In the elevator, we kissed. We stepped out of the building and onto the sidewalk, holding hands. And right then, I froze. I dropped his hand and shoved mine into my coat pockets. I looked up and down the street. It was still raining, but just a little bit. More like very aggressive mist than actual raindrops. The street was empty. Not one car was coming in either direction. I exhaled.

What was I thinking, waltzing out of my apartment building, my neighbor's hand in mine? He'd been in a band—a "classically trained alt-rock ensemble." He could have fans, paparazzi. Autograph hounds. They would take our picture. I'd show up on the gossip pages of the newspaper, and then it would all be over for me.

"What's wrong?" Sam asked me.

"Nothing." I looked over at him. His eyes were narrowed in concern. "I felt paranoid all of a sudden. Like I was being watched." I laughed, to show him that I knew I was being nonsensical. "Have you ever felt like that?"

"No."

I looked around again, up and down the street. I inspected the outside of our building. When I determined that it was safe, I linked my arm through his. I could explain that better than hand-holding, if it came to that. "Let's go," I said. "Stock up on provisions and never leave the apartment again."

In Fred Meyer, we wound our way through the kitchen goods aisle, and Sam picked up a four-quart stockpot. My housewarming present, he told me, so we could make pasta sometime. It was just Revere Ware, nothing fancy like we sold at La Cuisine. We carried it around the store, filling it with lettuce and garlic bulbs and a lemon and wedges of cheese.

We ate doughnuts straight from the case and wrote the item numbers down so we could pay for them later. This made me feel self-righteous, for a brief moment. See, I told myself. This proves that I am a good person. An honest person who wouldn't even steal a doughnut.

I forgot about Leo. I forgot about the Glasseyes. We were in the checkout line when our eyes met, mine and Sam's, and a tiny jolt of electricity buzzed through me. Sam was smiling, and his eyes were shooting sparks, and for a moment I let myself think it was all because of me, that I'd awakened him somehow, given him a reason to feel alive. I knew I should stop this line of thinking because, god! How narcissistic could I possibly get? But it seemed true. After all, he did the same for me. I'd never felt the way I felt right then, standing in the checkout line at Fred Meyer, and when he leaned in to kiss me, I let him. I couldn't help myself.

～

We spread a blanket down on the threadbare Persian rug in his living room and ate bowls of pasta sitting cross-legged on the floor, surrounded by his aunt's oil paintings and velvet curtains and flickering beeswax candles. We drank our wine from Czech crystal. We ripped the baguette apart with our hands and dipped it in olive oil. I told him I always ate like this, on the floor. When I used to babysit Wendy, that was what we'd do.

"What if it's a mistake?" I asked Sam. It could be a huge mistake, letting my sister move in with me. I was afraid, I admitted. Afraid of making everything worse. She hated her grandmother, sure, but her grandmother was at least a proper adult. I wasn't ready for this level of responsibility. I wasn't cut out for it.

Sam said all the right things. He said I didn't need to be a proper adult. I didn't need to know what I was doing. All my sister wanted was to be with me.

We kissed then and I thought: We could grow old here. Me, Sam, and Wendy. We could open up the walls between these two apartments and stay here forever. It could be a happy ending for all of us, finding each other after losing so much. Sam could play the viola while spaghetti sauce simmered on the stove. And then—

I stopped myself from taking it any further, even in my head. I couldn't believe how stupid the fantasy was. I had just met this guy. We hardly knew each other.

It seemed like we did, though. It seemed like we knew each other better than anyone.

~

When we finished eating, we each picked up a candlestick and wandered around his dark apartment, inspecting the paintings, the treasures from his aunt's travels. Masks from Borneo. Lace from Venice. Painted plates from Mexico.

"What's in here?" I asked, my hand on the doorknob of the second bedroom, the one next to Sam's. I didn't expect the knob to turn, but it did.

"Just my aunt's things."

I flicked on the light. The closet overflowed with clothes, fancy dresses and costumes that spanned the styles from the last three decades. A dress form in the corner wore what appeared to be a late nineteenth-century riding costume. Paintings—abstract ones, different from the landscapes and still lifes in the rest of the apartment—leaned against one wall.

"I never come in here," Sam said.

I lifted a black shag wig from its Styrofoam head and placed it over Sam's hair. I laughed so hard tears leaked out of my eyes and streamed down my cheeks. "You look like a member of KISS," I said.

I picked up a lamp and looked around for a socket to plug it in. The cord was old, covered in cloth, but I stuck it in a socket, pulled the little chain by the bulb, and the bulb glowed with light. "It works!" I exclaimed needlessly, and directed the light to Sam, his expression still somber beneath that black wig.

"We shouldn't touch anything," he said, watching me riffle through a hatbox filled with silk gloves and clunky old costume jewelry. But then, a few minutes later, he held up a gold dress. "Try this on."

The dress was shiny gold, in a scratchy woven fabric, like something a Barbie doll would wear. It came with a matching bolero jacket. I stood up and stripped down to my underwear and pulled it on, turning so Sam could zip me up in the back. "How do I look?"

He crowned me with a wig of cascading blonde curls. "Beautiful," he said, and though I must have looked like I'd wandered off the set of an eighties soap opera, he seemed serious, like he meant it, and I tilted my head up so he could kiss me.

"We should go out. Like this," I said. It was perfect. We could go wherever we wanted. I drew a mustache over Sam's lip with an old eyeliner pencil I retrieved from an ancient makeup box and covered his eyes with oversize rhinestone sunglasses. A feathered mask obscured the entire top half of my face. "No one will recognize us. No one will know who we are."

We went out to somewhere with thumping music, so loud we couldn't talk, with a disco ball spinning, sending flashes of light over the dance floor. If there were Glasseyes, I didn't see them, but I didn't care. They couldn't find me here, not in the gold dress, not with the blonde wig and the mask. Not with the rhinestone glasses and evil villain mustache. They were playing old songs, songs from the 1990s, my mother's favorite dance songs. New Order and The Cure and OMD. We spun around on the dance floor, twirling around and around, and I closed my eyes and let him spin me in the middle of this crowd, all these people who didn't know who we were and would never be able to describe us.

We made out in the taxi on our way home. In the elevator, Sam tried to pull off my wig. I said no, not yet. As soon as we stumbled inside, we ripped off the wigs, the clothes, our disguises. We fell onto the blanket we'd left in the middle of the living room floor. Bread crumbs pressed into our skin.

I wanted it to stay dark forever. I wanted the night to go on and on. Once the sun came up, it would all be over. We'd have to clean up and fold up the blankets, and nothing would be the same. I couldn't ask him to wait for me—just wait, right here, freeze!—while I ran off with a billionaire.

As long as it was still dark outside, we could stay together. It would be a good time for the world to end. Right now. A zombie apocalypse, a plague. Something that made us—no, *required* us to—stay here, nail boards over the windows and hunker down until the crisis resolved. We could grow old in here. I knew we could.

"Sam?" I wanted to see if he was still awake. When he didn't answer, I poked him with my finger. I shook him by the shoulders.

He turned toward me, placed a hand on my hip.

"I can't believe we just met," I said.

"I know."

"I feel like we've known each other forever."

"Me too."

We must have known each other in a past life, I told him. When you meet someone and feel that connection, like you know them and you've always known them, it's because you do know them. You've known them for centuries. Like your souls are linked by threads, crisscrossed over millennia.

Sam blinked at me. "You believe that?"

"A lot of cultures believe in it. In reincarnation."

"Do *you* believe it?"

I wanted to believe it, I told him. I wanted to believe it the way I wanted to believe in a lot of things, like Santa Claus.

He never believed in Santa Claus. His parents didn't approve of lying to children, he told me, his voice fading, his eyelids drooping back closed.

I was glad, I decided, as I sank into sleep. Glad I'd been given the choice to believe in a magical man who lived at the North Pole and made toys with elves and rode in a sleigh with reindeer. What was the alternative? To believe in nothing? That Santa Claus was just some old dead saint? I'd rather believe in something beautiful, something greater than reality.

~

In the morning we bathed together in Sam's claw-foot tub. Sam sat behind me, brushing my hair, careful not to drop it in the bubbles. We didn't talk much, still bleary from sleep. We sipped coffee out of china teacups we'd found in a box in the extra bedroom.

"Finished," he said, and I pulled my hair to the top of my head, twisting it around itself until it stuck together in a bun. I leaned back, resting against his chest, and he closed his arms around me, and my eyelids drifted down.

A terrible sound sent me jolting upright. Water splashed out of the tub and onto the tile floor. The sound of shattering glass, like a car crash, like a rock hurled through a window.

"What the—" Sam began to lift himself out of the tub, but I whirled around and stopped him, pressing him back down. The water churned as I propelled myself out of the tub, wrapping myself in the nearest piece of cloth, some sad old towel dangling from a hook. "It's nothing," I said. "It's me—it's my phone."

The glass was still shattering, in a loop. The Mirror's ringtone, coming from the bottom of my handbag on the floor of Sam's bedroom.

When I got to the Mirror, it was glowing. I tapped the screen, and Alejandro's voice emerged from the device. He'd sent me five messages, he said. Where *was* I?

A minute later, I returned to the bathroom. I was already dressed. Sam was still in the bath, leaning back, his face lifted, as if he were inspecting the ceiling. I knew this would be it, the end. I tried my best to sound normal, but I didn't succeed. I sounded like a bad actor in a play. "I have to go," I told him. "Work emergency."

"See you tonight?" He gave me a strange look I couldn't read, and I went over to him. I bent down and kissed him hard on the mouth.

CHAPTER 11

Fifteen minutes later, I was standing on the curb outside my building. A black SUV pulled up next to me, and I got in the passenger seat. "A little advance notice would have been nice," I said.

"Good morning to you, too," said Alejandro. He pulled out into the street and drove south, toward Burnside.

"My sister is coming this weekend. I can't have random people driving up in black SUVs and whisking me off at the spur of the moment like this."

Alejandro was wearing sunglasses despite the gloomy weather. The rain clouds hung heavily over the hills and into the city. With both hands on the steering wheel, he shrugged. "I *did* tell you. I told you I'd need to run some errands with you the last time I saw you. And I texted you yesterday. And this morning."

I turned my head to watch the buildings blur by. What Alejandro said was true. I hadn't exactly been keeping on top of my messages.

"Did you bring everything I told you to bring?" Alejandro asked.

"Yes," I said to the scenery out the window.

"Your driver's license and birth certificate? Social security card?"

"I *told* you I brought everything."

"Just checking."

We spent the next hour at the passport office on Hawthorne. Leo wanted me to apply for a passport, Alejandro explained, in case he decided to take me on one of his trips. This cheered me up somewhat, imagining where he would take me. I had visions of walking over stone bridges in Kyoto, or along the Seine. Climbing the Matterhorn. Drinking tea from a samovar.

"I've never really been anywhere," I said.

After the passport office, Alejandro said we had one more stop. My stomach felt hollow. I hadn't eaten anything this morning. I felt a pang, then, for Sam.

We took another ten-minute drive, and then Alejandro parked in front of a new-looking brick office building. "Here we are," he said.

"Where?"

Alejandro didn't answer. I followed him into the building, and we waited by a bank of elevators. "Are you going to tell me what we're doing here?" I asked.

We rode the elevator down to the basement and stepped out into a long corridor. The walls were yellow. I hated it when people painted basement walls yellow, as if that would trick anyone into forgetting that they were underground, surrounded by nothing but dirt and tree roots and darkness.

Alejandro beckoned me to follow him down the hall, and then we entered one of the offices. The door was labeled RIVERCROSS WELLNESS CLINIC. Only one other person was there, a middle-aged woman sitting in the corner. She was reading *Sunset* magazine. It was quiet in here, eerily quiet. The only sound was coming from a large fish tank, an electric hum and the gurgling of bubbles.

"Just a quick checkup." Alejandro sounded a little embarrassed when he said it, like he knew it was weird but was trying his best to act like it wasn't.

"A checkup?" I bugged my eyes out at Alejandro. "Like a physical?"

"Leo just—" Alejandro looked like he was struggling to come up with the right words for this. "You've just got to go along with this, Rosemary, okay? This is it."

I laughed. "I don't have to go along with anything."

"You do if you want this job."

"Well, maybe I don't." I stood before him, my hands on my hips. I wondered, then, what Alejandro knew about The Project.

"If you want to back out, Rosemary, now's the time to do it," Alejandro said to me. "Just return that deposit we made into your bank account. No harm, no foul. You can just walk away."

I thought of the apartment. I thought of all the furniture I ordered the very day I moved in. I ordered it all in a rush, thinking of Wendy walking into that apartment with the huge double-hung windows, the new velvet couch, the side tables. The wool rugs, the brand-new bed, the dining set with the chairs and buffet. Her eyes would light up, and she would smile and twirl around the way I had twirled around when I first saw the place and knew I had to live there. I had to do whatever it took to make it happen.

"Okay," I said after a beat or two, and Alejandro visibly relaxed. He may have even smiled at me, almost. "Let's get this over with."

He told me to check in at the front desk. He would wait for me out here. For that I was grateful. It could have been worse. Alejandro could have escorted me into the exam room and watched the whole thing, dictating notes into his Mirror for Leo.

After about ten minutes, a nurse called my name. She was wearing magenta scrubs and a coordinating head wrap in a bright tropical pattern.

"Good luck," Alejandro said to me as I stood up. I just shook my head at him.

It seemed like any normal doctor's appointment. Maybe that's all this was, I thought. Just some regular checkup. Maybe Leo liked to make sure all his employees are nice and healthy. Maybe this was a perk of the job. Yeah. That's what I tried to tell myself. The nurse jotted down my height and weight, took my blood pressure. All the usual stuff. She was very friendly. She led me to an examination room and told me to change into a hospital gown with the opening at the front. She said she'd be back in a few minutes.

I sat on the end of the exam table, waiting. The walls of the room were painted dusty rose. Along the ceiling was one of those wallpaper runners in a rose pattern. It was all very eighties.

The nurse came back in, shutting the door behind her. She looked over the form I'd filled out in the waiting room. "So, it looks like you have some family history of breast cancer?"

"My mom's mom," I said.

She tapped that answer into the computer. "How's she doing now?"

"She died."

"I'm sorry to hear that. Any other members of your family with a history of breast cancer?"

"No."

"Your mom, she's doing fine?"

"She's dead, too. But she didn't have breast cancer. She was killed in a car accident."

She didn't say she was sorry to hear that, but she did look sorry. She opened her eyes wide at me and shook her head sadly before turning back to her computer and typing into it.

"How many sexual partners in the last year?"

I hesitated before answering. I wondered how much of this was going into a report Leo was going to read. I wondered what the right answer was. Maybe I could say thirty, and Leo would think that number was too high. Maybe he'd let me go, and I could keep the $6,000.

"Two," I answered. Steele and Sam, I figured. They were the only ones worth mentioning, anyway.

She raised her eyebrows slightly, as if she doubted that answer very much, and then she dutifully plugged the number into her computer. She asked a few more questions and then instructed me to wait for the doctor.

I waited, swinging my feet, debating whether to put my socks back on. My feet were freezing. I should paint my toenails, I mused. I hadn't done anything to them since right before that ill-fated date with Sebastian St. James. I'd gotten a professional pedicure, just for him. What a waste.

I must have been sitting there for fifteen minutes before hearing a soft knock on the door. I sat up straight and tightened the hospital gown around me.

The doctor was a man. He looked young, for a doctor. Maybe he was one of Leo's buddies. I could see that. Some childhood friend, maybe. Some bro from college. He had a lot of hair—thick, brown hair that cascaded out of his head and flowed back in waves. It was probably his pride and joy. I could picture him taking a comb out of the back pocket of too-tight jeans and smoothing back the strands, admiring himself in the mirror.

The moment I saw him, I knew I couldn't go through with this. A chill ran through my whole body. At the same time, my pulse quickened. I swallowed and tried to take in a deep breath to control myself. Instead I just sucked in the air wrong. I felt like I was going to choke on my own spit. I curled into myself, coughed into the crook of my arm.

"Hello, hello!" he said in a jolly way, as if he was delighted to see me sitting there on his exam table. He ignored my coughing fit.

I looked up at him and cleared my throat. "I'm sorry." I coughed again, more out of nervousness than necessity. "I'd like to request a woman doctor."

He smiled and rolled a chair over to the foot of the exam table and patted my leg. "Don't you worry," he said. "I have a lot of experience with these exams."

"I didn't say I was *worried*." I was more confident now. I had rights, after all. I didn't have to do this. I could walk out if I wanted to. "I *said* I wanted a female doctor."

He kept that smile pasted on his face. "I'm afraid we can't help you there," he said. "This is a private practice. *My* private practice."

"Oh." I didn't know what to do. I could leave. I should leave. I didn't have to put up with this. "I've never had a male doctor before," I said, biding my time.

"I promise I'll be gentle." He rested a warm hand on my knee.

I shuddered. Sometimes it was difficult for me to know what was reasonable or not. I had a friend in college who claimed to look forward to her gynecology appointments. She had a handsome doctor—he could play a doctor on TV, she had said—and one time after the exam he'd told her that everything looked beautiful down there. She took it as some sort of high compliment. He would know, she'd told me.

Maybe I was the messed-up one. Maybe when you weren't like me, having some dude rooting around in your uterus was no big deal. Maybe it was easy to lie back and open up. Just like that.

Was it so unreasonable, what Leo was asking of me? He just wanted me to get a clean bill of health. That was all. I chose this, I kept repeating to myself. This is just part of the job.

I asked the doctor what he planned to do to me.

"Just a standard pelvic exam," he said. "Pregnancy test. The full STD panel. We'll take a urine and blood sample before you go. And then in a couple of days, you can come back for that IUD fitting."

I put a foot in each stirrup on either side of the exam table and lay down on my back. IUD fitting? Sure. Sure, I could get an IUD. Why not.

The doctor placed his hands on the insides of my calves. His hands felt warm against my cold skin.

"You've got to relax," he said, trying to open up my legs. They were locked together at the knees.

I couldn't move. I felt paralyzed, lying back on the table, like I was twelve years old again, trapped under the sheets pulled tight over my body and tucked over the mattress, so tight I could barely breathe. Jason's hands ironing out the wrinkles, running over me, back and forth, back and forth.

Tears brimmed out of my eyes and flowed into my ears. I squeezed my eyes, tightly, pushing more tears out. I had to stop. "I can't," I said.

"Just breathe." He had a soothing voice. Not very deep, but not nasally, either. Neutral. A nice, neutral voice. "Look above you. At the ceiling."

I opened my eyes. It took a minute for my vision to adjust. I focused on the ceiling. It, too, was painted dusty rose. I imagined the doctor hiring a painting company to do the whole office and telling them to paint it a color ladies would like. This is what they came up with: dusty rose.

On the ceiling, right above my head, was a small white sign, about the size of a playing card. On it was the word BREATHE, written out in fancy calligraphy with a purple pen.

I breathed, and the doctor spread open my legs.

"Scoot down a bit, toward me. Yes. That's good."

I stared at the BREATHE sign, and I breathed my way through the entire exam. I heard him snap on his gloves. He squeezed some lube onto his fingers and slid them into me. With one hand inside and the other on my abdomen, he pressed, palpating each organ in turn. Certainly the doctor could see, just peering into my body like this, everything I had been up to these last couple of days. He would tell Leo all about it. They would probably get together over microbrews and talk about it. I'd had sex, and not with Leo Glass.

I'd had sex more than once. First in Sam's bed. Once more before we got up in search of sustenance. Again afterward, on the floor. And again last night—or this morning, before dawn, when we were both half-asleep, and we reached for each other. Sam was behind me; I could feel him against me. He kissed the back of my neck and pushed down my underwear . . .

"*That's* better," the doctor said. "Nice and relaxed. I'm just going to insert the speculum—"

All the muscles in my body clenched back up.

"Whoa there," the doctor said, chuckling softly. "As you were."

I felt a cold steel finger pinch my cervix, and for a moment my vision went white from the pain. But it was only a moment. He slid the speculum out and dropped it onto a tray. The speculum looked like a metal duck head, covered in slime and blood.

The doctor patted my legs and said, "All done."

~

"Take me home," I told Alejandro, who was waiting for me in the parking lot. He started the car up right away, without saying a word. I wouldn't have tolerated even one more errand, and he knew it. If he suggested so much as a quick detour to a drive-through Starbucks, I would have revolted. Unfastened my seat belt, opened the door, and jumped out of the moving car and rolled into the street, where I would be smashed flat in seconds.

We drove in silence through the streets. I grew angrier and angrier with each passing mile.

Most of all, I was angry at myself. Why didn't I just leave? No one tied me down to that exam table. I should have laughed in their faces. I should have walked away. Then I thought of my sister, my promise to her. It had been easier back when I believed I was the wicked fairy. When I believed everyone was better off without me. I couldn't fly away anymore.

"Did you ever have to dissect a frog in school?" I asked Alejandro, breaking the silence.

I wasn't looking at him, but I could sense his head moving toward me, then back to the road ahead. "Sure," Alejandro said.

"They pass out these frogs, lay them out on a piece of butcher paper, and they're just lying there, flat on their backs, their frog legs flopped wide open. And then—you remember what we had to do? We had to take a scalpel and cut out a little window. And then you could peel the skin back and look inside at all the organs. Those giant flaps of lungs and the tiny little heart. We pinned the skin down, pinned it to the table, to get a better look. We looked inside and we made *drawings*." I looked over at Alejandro then. He was still staring straight ahead, a parody of the perfect driver, both hands on the wheel. "That's what it was like in there. Like a frog pinned to the table. But at least the frogs were dead before we sliced them open."

Alejandro's head whipped around to face me then. I'd shocked him. "It's an *analogy*," I said, waving my hand at his face.

We were silent again for a minute before I started up again. "I have to ask," I said. "Is this a big part of your job—accompanying ladies to the wellness clinic?"

Alejandro narrowed his eyes at the road. After a moment he let out an indulgent little laugh. "Oh, Rosemary," he said.

"You've got to find this unusual."

"It's not my job to ask questions," he said.

"Blood sample, urine sample. Cervical cells scraped out. I can't wait to see what's next."

He dropped me off in front of my apartment, even offered to escort me up.

"No!" I slammed the door and walked away.

The car remained idling in the street. The engine hummed, and I could sense it, its presence. Drive away, I willed it. Just go. I heard the mechanical whir of the window lowering.

"Rosemary!"

I considered pretending I hadn't heard Alejandro calling after me. He called again, tapped on the horn.

I whirled around. "What? What now?"

Alejandro crooked his finger, beckoning me back to the car.

I leaned in, resting my arms on the open window. *"What?"*

Alejandro lowered his voice, forcing me to stick my head back inside the car. "Just be careful, Rosemary. Okay?"

Before I could respond or even register what, exactly, Alejandro was trying to tell me, he stepped on the gas, causing me to stumble back onto the sidewalk.

As soon as I got inside, I undressed and stepped into the shower. I wanted to scrub my skin raw, sterilize myself with chemicals, but I was too tired to do anything but stand under the water.

Be careful, he'd said. Be careful.

I tapped the handle to make the water hotter. Be careful of what? Did Alejandro know something? Was he trying to tell me he knew, that he had been hiding out in the shrubbery outside my building, training Glasseyes in Fred Meyer on me and Sam as we walked around the store filling up my new stockpot with garlic and cheese?

He couldn't know. If he did, why be cryptic about it? Just tell me it was over. Tell Leo, have him fire me for breach of contract.

I turned the water hotter, as hot as it would go. The drops pelted my skin. I closed my eyes and turned around slowly, like a pig on a rotisserie.

Be careful, he'd said. Or maybe it was "take care," just something you say when you're saying goodbye. Take care. That wasn't such an odd thing to say at all.

Suddenly my vision went dark, and my foot slipped on the floor of the enameled bathtub. My hands reached for the shower curtain to catch my fall, and then I was steady again, breathing quickly, my eyes screwed shut. I'd almost fainted. As fast as I could, I turned the handles until the water stopped.

Dripping onto the tile floor, I held my arms out in front of me. They were red and puffy. All the blood had rushed to the surface. I could see it pulsing, right below the skin.

CHAPTER 12

I went through several versions of the breakup text before settling on something simple, something that left no room for a false interpretation: Sam, I'm sorry. I have to end this thing between us. I held my breath and pressed send before I could change my mind.

And that was it. I'd done it.

I stared at the screen for just a second. Then I blocked Sam's number.

Tight white dress. Red lipstick. Oversize sunglasses. Hair loose, straight down my back. I looked like a different person. Exactly the kind of person I needed to be.

Downstairs I waited for my car to arrive. I had him drive me all over town, like I was Julia Roberts in *Pretty Woman* shopping up and down Rodeo Drive and telling those snobby saleswomen they'd made a big mistake. Huge.

I bought a painting at Anthropologie for $598. It was called *Three Lines* and looked like a kid had scribbled all over a blank canvas with a thick black Sharpie, but it was huge and framed in gold and I needed it to hang over my charcoal-gray couch.

I bought a handwoven, fair trade–certified pouf ($143) and a wheeled midcentury bar cart ($299) from West Elm.

I bought four gallons of paint at the hardware store at $50 a gallon.

I bought a huge antique brass lamp that shot up from the ground and arched overhead. I don't remember where I bought it or how much it cost. Everything went on my card. I would worry about it later.

Then I went back home. I flopped down on my new couch and rested my feet on my new handwoven, fair trade–certified pouf. The lamp shone down on me like a spotlight. It was dark outside, though it was only five o'clock in the afternoon. Quiet, too. The city muted. No sirens or the clanking of shopping carts down below. Not even the sad, mournful tones of the viola interrupted the cold, perfect silence.

I tried calling Wendy, but no one answered. I called Margorie, too, perking up the moment I heard her voice and deflating again as soon as I realized I'd only reached her voice mail.

I was alone. I padded into the kitchen, filled a gigantic Beaujolais wineglass to the top with red wine, and sat back under my spotlight. I tried summoning up the triumphant feelings of earlier in the day. It had all been so very romantic, hadn't it? A whirlwind romance, destined to end. Sam would be heartbroken. That was understandable. But maybe . . . maybe our brief but ill-fated connection had been good for him. Maybe I'd taught him that happiness was still possible. Maybe he would go on to meet someone new. He would look back at the time we spent together, that one long, beautiful night, and he would thank me.

My wineglass felt light in my hand. It was empty. I set it on the hardwood floor and sank back into my couch cushions.

No, I didn't like that little story. How about this? He'd be angry. Understandably angry. But then—then he'd realize it was all for the best. That I'd given him a reason to live again. He would play the viola more beautifully than ever, with more soul. He would travel the world, win some sort of international prize. He would credit me for everything. He'd never love again. Not after what we'd experienced, together.

I sat on my new couch and looked out over the trees. I tried to make myself cry. I needed to cry, to feel like I was mourning what could have been. I couldn't seem to will myself to produce tears, so I just sat there, staring.

An idea—a perfectly formed idea—sprang into my head: I would paint! I'd bought all the supplies. Drop cloths, brushes, rollers. I would start in the dining room. That peachy color had to go.

Three hours later, I stood back and admired my work. I was good. If this sugar-baby gig with Leo didn't pan out, I should offer my services as a professional painter. The color was perfect, a muted gray, a Northwest winter sky.

In the kitchen I ate three peanut butter and honey sandwiches in a row before getting back to work. Wendy's room was next. She had asked for something beachy, so I settled on aquamarine, a shade called Balmy Sea.

With my music blaring, I painted. I painted until my arms felt sore and limp, until my head was light from paint fumes.

When I heard the knocking on my front door, I kept on painting. When I heard the pounding on the wall, the wall between Sam's bedroom and my bedroom, I turned the music up as loud as my little speaker would go.

Someone was calling my name. I put down my paint roller and leaned out the open window. Sam was doing the same thing, twenty feet away. "I'm coming over," he said.

Then there was Sam, standing in my doorway. He gave me a hard look and ran his hands through his hair. He looked so tortured and sexy that I almost gave in and flung my arms around him. Just kidding, I wanted to say.

That was why seeing him was a bad idea. It would have been so much easier if he had simply read my breakup text and accepted it, first thing.

"What the fuck, Rosemary?"

"I'm painting." I was barefoot, still wearing the tight white dress, only now the dress was splattered in gray and aquamarine. Paint had dried and crusted on my skin, in my hair.

"So this is it, huh?" Sam held up his phone and shook his head. He read my message out loud in a monotone voice: "Sam, I'm sorry. I have to end this thing between us." He tucked the phone in his back pocket and then shook his head again, as if to say, *really?*

"It's not like we were together," I said. "It's not like we're . . . breaking up."

Sam shook his head and squinted at the same time. He was disgusted with me, or angry. Probably both. He looked . . . really good.

My eyes squeezed shut. It would be easier if I didn't have to look at him making those damaged hero faces at me.

"I'm *very* serious." Then I opened my eyes.

We looked at each other, and I tried to keep my gaze very neutral and steady. His mouth was set in a firm line, and his eyes darted all over my face. And then, as if by sudden mutual agreement, we lunged for each other. He kissed me so hard I couldn't breathe, and we crashed up against the wall, knocking over a little console table I'd bought. The vase I'd arranged on top of it tottered and then fell, smashing into a thousand pieces. When it crashed to the floor I didn't even flinch. Sam's hands were under my dress, pushing it up. I repositioned myself, allowing him to remove my underwear, while I raced to undo the buttons of his jeans.

We kept kissing, hard, our teeth clicking together. I liked it, the urgency of it. This would be our last time. He seemed to sense it, too. It seemed like only yesterday we'd had slow-motion sex on the blanket spread out over the Persian rug, gazing into each other's eyes in the flickering flames of the candles, our naked skin bathed in an orange glow. That *was* yesterday. Now we were clawing at each other, smashing faces against each other, rolling around on the floor like animals.

When it was over, we lay panting on my faux-fur rug in the middle of my bedroom floor. That was where we had ended up on our way to the bed. His head was buried in the crook of my shoulder. His breath warmed my neck. My fingers traveled lazily through his hair, slightly damp with sweat.

Gently, I rolled him off me and tried to sit back up, tugging at my dress. My eyes scanned the room in search of my underwear before I remembered casting it aside in the entryway.

"You'd better go now." I smoothed my hair with my hands and sat up straighter.

He was still buttoning up his jeans. He froze, trying to make sense of the words that had just left my mouth.

He reached out to touch me, but I scooted back to the edge of the rug. I was crouching down, ready to bolt out of there if I had to.

"Rosemary—" His voice sounded tired. Defeated. I could tell he was trying to formulate a response and coming up with nothing.

"I can't be with you," I said. "I have a boyfriend."

Sam's eyes blinked once. Twice. "What do you mean?"

"I mean, I have a boyfriend."

His eyes opened wide for a moment, then went back to normal. "Since when?"

"Sam—"

"Who is he?" Then, a second later: "Break up with him."

"I can't."

"You can't? Or you won't?"

"It's complicated."

"You're telling me that whatever you have with him is better than this?" He gestured to me and back to him. Cue a flashback of our whole romance, starting with meeting on the stairs and ending a few moments ago when we were rolling around on this faux-fur rug and he was murmuring my name into my ear and I was digging my fingernails into his back. "You're in love with him?"

I didn't say anything.

"What about the zombie apocalypse? All that stuff about our *souls*." His expression was mutating before my eyes, getting chillier by the second. Good. That was how it needed to be. He could hate me if it made things easier.

"I didn't mean any of it," I said. "Everything I said last night was just"—my hand fluttered through the air—"pillow talk."

CHAPTER 13

I'd expected my sister to look different when I met her at the airport. She'd be thinner, paler. No spark left in her eyes. Something like that.

If anything, Wendy looked healthier than ever, an all-American teenage girl in tight jeans and an off-the-shoulder sweatshirt that revealed a lacy black bra strap. She squealed through my tour around the apartment. Here's where we'll have parties, and here's where we'll sit down for breakfast, and here's where we'll eat Thanksgiving dinner. We'll have to invite everyone, she said, and I laughed and said, Who's everyone? and she laughed, too. In her mind, we already had dozens of mutual friends, people who would attend our parties, sit around our table for Thanksgiving, bring us presents to display under a ten-foot Christmas tree.

I sat on her bed and watched her unpack. She didn't have much. An oversize suitcase that must have been her grandmother's, a big duffel bag, and a rolling carry-on. She pulled her clothes from her suitcase and stuffed them into the built-in dresser drawers.

"Remember this?" She tossed a framed photograph in my direction. It landed faceup on her bed.

It was one of those old-timey sepia photographs, of me and Wendy. I was a teenager, a senior in high school, Wendy a little girl about nine or ten. We both wore lacy high-collared shirts and long, dark, heavy skirts that swept the floor. I sat ramrod straight on a high-backed cane chair, and Wendy stood behind me, a hand on my shoulder. We wore hard, unsmiling expressions, our chins tilted up. We weren't orphans then, but the picture made it look like we saw it coming, our grim future. "Of course I remember."

"Remember how I stayed home sick?"

"Mom had a class."

"Dad was away, on a business trip or something. You said you'd stay home with me."

"But you weren't sick." We smiled at each other. My mom didn't want to let me miss school to take care of my little sister. Usually she'd stay home herself, but she was taking classes until late in the evening, trying to get her bachelor's degree. She had a test that day, something she couldn't miss. I said I didn't mind missing school. I didn't. As soon as our mother's car pulled out of the driveway, Wendy perked up. She brushed her hair and styled it in two tight braids. I fake-scolded her, and she told me she needed a "mental health day." Ha! She'd been a funny little kid.

We went out to breakfast at Denny's and then drove up to Virginia City, a tiny little mining town way up in the foothills of the Sierras, the kind of town you'd visit on school field trips to learn about the old Wild West. It had wooden sidewalks, jangly old-time casinos called things like Bucket of Blood and the Mark Twain Saloon, and tourist attractions—fudge shops, ice cream parlors, old-fashioned photo studios.

We walked up and down the sidewalks, wandering into shops and dinky museums. I stuck a few quarters in a slot machine and won fifteen dollars. Quarters jangled into the metal trough, and we gathered them up with our hands, looking around, afraid we'd get caught. We ran out whooping with laughter and used the winnings to pay for the old-timey photo.

"We got home like a minute before Mom pulled up into the driveway. We jumped onto the couch and turned on the TV, trying to act all casual."

I laughed. "You think she bought it?"

"Who knows. She was in a good mood. She made us her special lasagna for dinner."

"God, you do remember everything."

"Best day ever. Best day of my entire *life*."

"It was a pretty good day."

"You know what we should do?" Wendy asked. "Make that lasagna. And we should eat it in the living room, watching the same movie we watched that night."

"What did we watch?"

"You don't remember?"

I closed my eyes, trying to recall every detail of the night. The lasagna our mom made, with the béchamel sauce instead of a marinara sauce. Sitting in front of the TV to eat it, something we never did when Jason was around. And the movie—"*Dirty Dancing*," I said.

"Yes!"

"Mom thought it was inappropriate."

"But you talked her into it. Like I said: best—day—ever."

I didn't have a recipe—I'm not sure our mother did, either—but I figured I could make it from memory. We went to the store to buy the noodles and the spinach and the fresh tomatoes. Everything out of season. We bought two pints of Ben and Jerry's, too, and popcorn for the movie.

We chopped vegetables and whipped up a perfectly smooth béchamel, and everything seemed worth it then. I'd done it. Sure, it had required some sacrifice and I'd sold my soul and would probably never find love again—but look at my little sister! A month ago she was suicidal or, at the very least, pretending to be suicidal, which was not all that much better. And now she was laughing and we were putting a lasagna in the oven and getting ready to stream *Dirty Dancing*.

I hadn't watched *Dirty Dancing* since that night with my mom and Wendy, but there had been a time when it was my favorite movie, probably because it had been my mom's favorite movie when she was growing up. I knew all the lines, could sing along to every song. I could probably even re-create half the dances.

Wendy and I were on the couch, the smell of the lasagna wafting from the kitchen into the living room, reminding us of our mom, our beautiful young mom. We were leaning against each other, arm to arm, as the opening credits flashed across the screen over couples in fedoras and headbands gyrating in jerky slow motion to "Be My Baby" by the Ronettes.

And then the jarring sound of shattering glass rang through the apartment.

"I have to get this." I jumped off the couch, scampered off to the dining room, and answered the call.

"Hello?" I almost whispered, staring at Leo's face in the Mirror.

"Hey, babe. Miss me?"

All the air whooshed out of the room at the sound of his voice. After what I hoped was a barely perceptible pause, I spoke. "So much."

"We have reservations at eight. Wear something nice. I'll come pick you up."

God, why now. Why *right now*. What would I do with Wendy? I couldn't leave her alone. Not on the first night. She was a troubled youth. A suicide risk!

All that flashed through my mind in about half a second. "Can't wait," I said to Leo Glass. Part of me still couldn't believe I was doing this. I looked over at Wendy.

Maybe Margorie could come over and watch *Dirty Dancing* with my sister. She picked up but said she couldn't do it, not tonight. She was out with her boyfriend. They had tickets for a show—in Seattle.

I had half a mind to ask Sam. He wouldn't be home anyway. It was Saturday night; he would have a performance. I felt relieved then, knowing it was impossible. It would be difficult to come up with a worse idea than asking Sam to babysit so I could dress up like Melania Trump and go out with my new billionaire boyfriend.

"Who was it?" Wendy asked when I walked back into the living room. She had paused the movie for me.

"That was work," I said. "Something urgent came up. I have to go—uh, go deal with it." This sounded fake, even to me.

"What came up?"

"I set the timer for the lasagna. When it's bubbly and browned on the top, you can take it out. Don't forget to turn off the oven."

"You're seriously leaving."

I put on a desperate, pleading expression that I hoped would communicate how sorry I was, for everything. Then I disappeared to my room to get ready.

I came out wearing a tight dress and lipstick and high heels, and Wendy just stared at me. Her mouth fell open. Whether this was actual shock or fake shock, designed to make me feel even worse than I already did, I couldn't say. "Some emergency," she said.

"It's a work event." Maybe she'd fall for this. "Important people are there. Investors. I just need to"—I racked my brain, trying to think of why anyone would possibly call upon me to deal with a team of important investors—"to smooth things over."

Wendy sank deeper into the couch cushions and glared at the frozen dancers on the television screen.

"We can do this whole thing tomorrow night. Lasagna's good the next day. It's *better*—the flavors have time to meld."

"Tomorrow's Sunday."

"So?"

"It's a school night." She would be starting at Lincoln High School on Monday. It was all arranged. Her grandmother had signed whatever needed to be signed, filled out all the forms. All I had to do was make sure she actually went.

The Mirror pulsed in my handbag. Leo was waiting for me downstairs.

~

The car dropped us off on a darkened street on the South Park Blocks, right on the edge of the university campus. "Where's the restaurant?" I asked.

"We're not going to a restaurant."

"We had reservations at eight. You said—"

"I canceled them."

I took in a deep breath, to calm myself. This is my job. It's only a job. I recalled what Mira had said, about all the douchebags I'd slept with of my own accord: And you did that for free, you know? Is that what she had said? She was right. This was no different. This was better! Leo was a successful, good-looking (in his tech-nerd way) man. I could do this.

Leo took my hand, and we walked into a stairwell on the side of a parking garage built inside an old brick building, an old warehouse, maybe, that had been converted. Following a stranger—a near stranger—into a dark parking garage at night—this was a stupid thing to do. If I got murdered here, I would have no one to blame but myself.

We approached a metal door with no handle. Leo tapped a combination into a keypad on the side. The door slid open, revealing what appeared to be some sort of freight elevator.

"I know what you're thinking," Leo said.

I was thinking I was going to die. Right here, tonight, in this parking garage.

"You're thinking I'd have a more state-of-the-art security system. Retinal scanning or something." Leo took my hand and led me into the elevator. I took in deep, slow breaths through my nose, trying to calm down. "Totally unnecessary," he went on as the doors closed us inside the steel cell. "No one even knows I live here."

"You *live* here? In a parking garage?" I let out a high-pitched, nervous little laugh. I was overreacting. He wasn't taking me to a murder dungeon; he was taking me home. Of course. This is my job. This is my job.

The doors of the elevator opened to a hallway with exposed redbrick walls, like the outside of the building. At the end of the hallway stood a console table with an outsize floral arrangement on top—orchids and curly willow, just like the bouquet I'd seen in the Lookinglass offices.

"Here we are," Leo said, pulling open a door made out of planks of old lumber.

We stepped into a cavernous loft that filled the entire third floor of the building. Streetlights outside the factory windows that spanned the west-facing wall cast an eerie blueish light in the apartment. Leo said, *"Hola,* Consuela. *Iluminación ambiental, por favor."* The lights all around the apartment began to shimmer. A lamp on an end table by the couch, the futuristic chandelier made out of driftwood and iron over the dining table, the undercabinet lighting in the kitchen. The light was dim at first, the barest flicker, and slowly grew brighter until the apartment was just barely illuminated.

"Consuela?" I said.

"Just something I'm working on. She's teaching me Spanish."

"I thought you already spoke Spanish," I said. "And Thai."

I looked around, half expecting an android to come marching out from a trapdoor somewhere, some sexy human robot with full lips and gigantic breasts. Leo laughed, as if he could read my thoughts. A disturbing notion entered my head, a notion I tried to stamp out as soon as it bubbled up: maybe he *could* read my thoughts.

Leo led me to the seating area, two long couches arranged in an L shape with an end table at the apex and a low, square coffee table in the middle. Again I was reminded of the Lookinglass offices. Wood and metal and low modern furniture. Sparse and clean, with just a few offbeat pieces to elevate the decor above a hotel lobby.

Leo yawned. "God," he said. "Sorry. Jet lag." The worst part was, he had to leave again in the morning, he said. Ghent this time. He should have expedited my passport; I could have joined him.

We weren't supposed to talk about the arrangement. I knew that. I opened my mouth to say something to Leo and then thought better of it. "What?" he asked.

"It's nothing."

"You can tell me."

"It's just—I'd love to go to Europe with you sometime."

"I'd love to take you."

"I'd need some advance notice is all. My sister, she's sort of fragile, and—"

Leo didn't appear to be listening. He was tinkering around, filling up an electric kettle and flipping the switch. From a cabinet, he found two mugs and set them on the counter. The whole kitchen would seem like something out of a science fiction space novel if it weren't for the mirror hanging over that shiny black stove. Who would hang a mirror over the stove? One of those midcentury mirrors, a round face surrounded by long, sharp metal spikes, like a cold winter sun.

I knew exactly who would hang a mirror over the stove: someone who either never cooked or never had to clean up after himself if he did.

Leo was making us tea. This was not the wild night of debauchery I had feared. I could fake a headache or a sore throat, slip out early. An image of my sister, her wrist spurting a fountain of blood, wouldn't stop rattling through my mind. Yes, her suicide attempt had been a cry for help. But what if she cried for help again?

Sam could go over and check on her. He could climb out the window and work his way along the ledge like he did last time, peek into the window and make sure Wendy was all right—that she was, at the very least, alive.

I stood up and walked over to one of the windows looking out onto the Park Blocks. "You can see the Schnitz from here," I said. Sam would still be there, onstage. So he wouldn't be able to check on Wendy after all. Anyway, I'd unceremoniously dumped him and then deleted his number. Great. Really excellent planning on my part.

"Turn around," Leo said.

I turned to find Leo on the couch, two cups of tea steaming on the coffee table in front of him. He was sitting up straight, like a kid sitting in the front row of the class, the teacher's pet.

"Yes?"

"I want to look at you."

I stood up straighter. I felt nervous all of a sudden. Stage fright. I tried to smile. "No one's watching, are they?"

"Just me."

"I mean—" I glanced up at the ceiling, with its exposed ductwork and thick wooden beams. "Like surveillance cameras? Glasseyes?"

"You think I'm filming myself?" He said it as if the very idea were preposterous. "Why would I do that?" Leo took a tentative sip of his tea and set his mug back on the table. Then he stretched his arms up over his head and rose to standing. He walked over and circled around me, slowly. He stopped in front of me and we stood face-to-face, only a few inches between us.

He was tall. I knew it, but now I could feel it, too, him towering over me. I tilted my head up to meet his eyes.

Perhaps he was waiting for me to make the first move. I could do that. I'd done this so many times, with other guys.

Sometimes you just have to go for it—jump right in. I took a deep breath for courage and then went straight for his crotch. My hand kneaded the front of his pants, searching for him, but somehow I managed only to grab a handful of fabric.

"Whoa!" Leo stumbled backward, his hands raised up, his eyes opened wide. He looked—he looked scared. And maybe—angry? "What are you *doing*?"

"I'm—" I froze, searching for words. "I thought—"

"What?" He patted himself down, trying to smooth himself out. "I'm sorry."

Leo raked his fingers through his curls. "No, *I'm* sorry," he said. "I don't know what—"

"It's okay." My voice was smooth and sweet. He was shy; I could work with that. I turned around and lifted my hair up. "Can you help me with this?"

Leo unzipped the back of my dress so slowly I could hear the zipper, its metal teeth loosening. He slipped the straps from my shoulders and lowered the dress down, past my hips, and then he held it there so I could step out of it, one leg at a time.

He draped the dress over the arm of the couch and sat back down. "You can keep going," he said.

Underneath the dress, what I had on was all wrong: the same basic black bra I always wore. Black cotton underwear. I'd gotten dressed so quickly, I hadn't had time to dig out my fancy lingerie. At least the bra and underwear matched. At the last minute, I'd yanked on some sheer nylons. It was cold outside, and I hadn't known where Leo was planning to take me.

I didn't know how to take off a pair of nylons seductively. I just took them off the only way I knew how: pushing the waistband down past my hips and pulling them off at the feet by the toe.

My feet looked like they belonged to a senior citizen. The polished cement floor was hard and cold under my bare feet. These were inhospitable conditions for a striptease.

When I straightened back up, Leo was still appraising me.

The nylons had pressed angry rivets into my flesh, a rippled dent from my belly button on down, a ring around my waist. My body was washed in an eerie bluish light. I stood backlit against the windows. Maybe I didn't look so bad. It was like stripping down in a cave.

I waited for a moment—for him to give me direction, maybe, or for some primal instinct of my own to kick in. Nothing happened. So

I put a hand to my waist, jutted my hip out, and narrowed my eyes at Leo Glass. After a moment, I switched position, jutting my hip in the opposite direction. "You like what you see?" The words sounded insincere. Not seductive in the least.

"Keep going," he said, eyeing my bra.

I reached behind me to unhook the clasps. My eyes stayed glued to his face. This should have felt raw and intimate. It was more like a grade school staring contest, daring the other not to blink first. It was difficult to remove my bra under this kind of scrutiny. My fingers felt clumsy, twisted behind my back, tugging at the material. The hooks wouldn't release from the eyes. I was about to pull the whole thing down to my waist when, at last, I managed to unclasp the thing. I smiled to cover up what must have looked like a pained expression.

With one arm, I held the cups of the bra to my body. With the other hand, I nudged one strap off my shoulder, then the other. The bra dropped to the floor, and I stood there awkwardly, unsure of what to do with my hands.

"Come here," he said.

I walked up to him, crisscrossing my legs and swinging my hips like a model on a catwalk, and sat down next to him on the couch. He inhaled sharply through his nose and shook his head briskly, as if to wake himself.

My hands reached toward him to caress his arms. I scooted closer to him, expecting him to make a move, to wrap his arms around me, to kiss me. He didn't do anything. Maybe he wanted me to do it. Maybe that was why he had hired a girlfriend—because he didn't know how to do these kinds of things. I leaned in and kissed him gently on the lips. He didn't respond, and I tried again, more forcefully this time, parting his lips with the tip of my tongue.

Leo placed his hand on my leg. His hand felt hot and soft. I met his eyes. He tightened his grip around my thigh. "Hey." His voice was low. I kept expecting his hand to travel farther up my thigh, but it didn't.

"Hey yourself." I gave him what I hoped was the right kind of smile, something between shy and seductive.

"Close your eyes," he said.

I closed my eyes. I felt his hand leave my thigh and move to my face. He ran a finger along my jawline. I waited. I waited for him to pull me toward him, to kiss me. Instead I felt his fingers on my eyelids. He tugged at the end of my false lashes and then, one after the other, he ripped them off. Quickly, like they were Band-Aids. It was a strange sensation, feeling each eyelid break suction with the eyeball. *Pop.* When I opened my eyes, they felt lighter, empty and strange.

If this had been a regular date—if it had been Steele instead of Leo—I would have yelled at him. Maybe, if I felt like making a statement, I would have slapped him across the face. It wasn't Steele, though, so I just sat there, waiting for some kind of explanation.

Leo smiled at me. "That's better."

I wanted to yell at him and storm out. Instead I smiled at him. Instead I said, "Thank you."

"Let's go to bed," Leo said.

In his bedroom, he handed me a stack of clothes. "You can get ready in there." He gestured to the bathroom. The bathroom was huge and modern, everything clean and glistening. Nothing was out on the countertop or in the shower. Not one toothbrush or bottle of shampoo. I tried to open the drawer under the sink, but it didn't open; it was a false drawer. I tried the cupboard next. Inside was a rattan basket filled with rolled-up towels. That was it.

I changed into the clothes Leo had given me. A pair of his sweatpants and one of his T-shirts. They hung off me. When I raised my arms, my breasts peeked out through the sleeves. I rinsed my mouth out with water and washed my face. In the mirror, my reflection stared back at me with wide, scared eyes. A young, frightened girl. Maybe that was what he was into.

When I got to Leo's bed, he was already asleep, lying on his side, his mouth slack. I debated with myself for a moment. I could put my clothes back on, rush out. It wasn't even that late. Wendy and I could watch *Dirty Dancing* and eat the lasagna. It would be like old times, like a slumber party.

I decided to stay. Slowly, careful not to rouse Leo, I lifted the covers on the other side of the bed. I slipped in beside him and lay on my back, unable to sleep. Unable to even close my eyes. I texted Wendy several times, but she never answered. I didn't know what to do. I briefly considered calling the police, asking them to do a wellness check. I quickly thought better of it—how would that look, on my very first night? What on earth would I say? She was fine. I had to believe she was fine.

Hours later, when it was still dark outside, I found myself alone in Leo's bed. I must have fallen asleep because I didn't remember hearing him get up. His side of the bed was already made. "Leo?" My voice bounced off the cement walls. My bare feet felt cold on the ground.

The loft looked eerie in the dark, illuminated by distant streetlights, the furniture casting shadows over the polished concrete floors. I felt along the base of the lamp on an end table and couldn't find a switch. There was no switch near the bulb, either, or along the cord, which disappeared through the table and plugged into an outlet underneath the couch. I searched the whole loft and couldn't find one light that worked. The walls didn't have light switches.

The sky shifted from black to a dull gray. A sunrise without the sun, like so many Portland dawns.

My clothes had disappeared, and so had my shoes. My handbag was resting on a bench—like a minimalist wooden box—near the door. Leo wouldn't respond to my calls through the Mirror, leaving me no choice but to rummage around the loft like a madwoman for my clothes.

His entire apartment felt empty, unlived in. No jars of dull pencils or stray coins under the cushions. It occurred to me, as I ran around the loft scrambling for my things, that he might be watching me, that this might all be some sort of weird experiment, but during my very thorough search of his apartment, I didn't run across one Glasseye. Of course, a camera could be almost invisible. It could fit in the tip of a pen, in a woman's earring.

Finally I gave up and threw one of Leo's navy-blue hoodies on over the T-shirt, planning to go outside in my bare feet, but I couldn't leave the apartment; the door refused to open. I was locked inside. The door had no latch, no knob. It was one of those rustic barn doors made out of slats of weathered wood. It slid open—or it was supposed to slide open—on heavy iron tracks. I pressed my hands against the door and tried with all my strength to push it open, but it wouldn't budge.

I tried again to use my weight to force the door to move along its track, but it refused. Kicking didn't help. Nor did pounding my fists against it. I screamed for someone to let me out, to help me.

"Leo," I cried into the voice messaging system on the Mirror. "Let me out. You have to let me out." He wouldn't pick up. Where did he say he was going—Brussels? I closed my eyes, trying to remember if he had told me when he planned to leave, when he planned to arrive. He was going to be gone for weeks. I could die in here.

"*Hola*, Consuela," I said, squeezing my eyes shut, trying to recall my high school Spanish. "*El puerto—la puerta por favor?* Please open the door? *Abierto.*" Nothing happened.

Thoughts rushed into my head, one after the other: I could call somebody. I could call the police. The fire department. They'd bring a trampoline and force me to jump out the window and onto the street. A crowd would gather. I would probably make the evening news.

What if the windows didn't open, either? I rushed over to the bank of windows that looked down onto a narrow street below. They were old factory-style windows made of iron and wavy glass, spanning floor to ceiling. Some of them had awning openings. With a little finagling, I managed to turn the latch on one of them and push open the sash. A gust of air entered the apartment, and I gulped it in as if I'd emerged from underwater. Mist landed on my skin. The sounds on the street grew louder, and this comforted me. My mind took me to dark places, to the people who jumped from buildings during disasters, choosing to die from the fall instead of the fire. Don't be dramatic, I scolded myself.

I shot off a text to Wendy, telling her I was still hung up with this work thing. All the texts from last night lined up in a row. All of them unread. Then I waited, willing myself not to picture the worst. She wouldn't do it again, I reasoned. Not after just moving here. Not her first night. She was just upset, I decided. Teaching me a lesson.

There was nothing to eat in the apartment. I knew that already. The cupboards contained only the barest kitchen essentials—cheap stuff. A rich guy like Leo could have all the latest gadgets. Triple-clad pans and high-speed blenders and Italian espresso machines. The refrigerator was completely empty and sparkling clean, as if he had never used it, not even to store a bottle of ketchup.

This would be an interesting way to kill me, if that was what Leo was doing. Watching me wither away through some secret hidden cameras. The windows opened, I reminded myself. I could jump first.

A human body can go for weeks without food but only a few days without water. If the water was shut off, then I'd know for sure he was trying to kill me. At the sink, my hand reached out slowly, approaching the faucet. It didn't have a handle, but I'd washed my face the night before in the bathroom. The water had worked then. When my fingers reached the faucet, water poured out in a gush, and I almost collapsed with relief. I tilted my head into the sink and opened my mouth, drinking in sloppy gulps.

I would wait until three in the afternoon. That would give the police or the fire department or whoever was going to pry me out of this building plenty of time before the sun went down, before darkness set in. There was no way I could stay another night here, in the dark, by myself, with no food. And my sister. She needed me.

I didn't have to wait that long. At ten in the morning, the now-familiar sound of breaking glass echoed through the loft. Leo was calling me from Belgium. He was sorry he hadn't been able to reach me earlier.

He sounded so normal on the other end of the line, so apologetic. I wondered if this was a test of some kind. I wondered if I had passed it. I had been planning to yell at him, to curse, to quit on the spot.

"It's okay," I said. "I'm fine."

"My poor baby." Then Leo directed me to look at a slat of wood on the door, near the edge, a darker hue than the rest. All I had to do was press it.

The door looked like it was two hundred years old, like it belonged to a railway station from the old Wild West, but when I ran my hand along the darker slat and pressed with my fingertips, the slat rose from the surface of the door, creating a handle. When I pulled it, the door slid easily along the metal tracks.

My clothes and shoes were in the bench by the door, he explained. That bench that looked like a minimalist box. It opened up. He had rested my handbag on top so I would know.

Before we said goodbye, Leo lowered his voice. "I miss you already."

I don't remember if I answered, or if I did, what I said. I was already out the door.

~

At first I thought Wendy had fallen asleep on the couch. She could have watched the movie without me, shed a couple of tears, drifted off to sleep under the soft blanket I kept artfully draped over the back of my new couch. She must be exhausted, after all. Her whole life had been uprooted. She was going to start a new school, a new life. She was fourteen. She needed her beauty rest.

I tiptoed up to her, planning on clicking off the light and covering her with another quilt just in case, and I saw she was *not* asleep. She was passed out.

A bottle of wine—an entire bottle—lay empty on the floor. She'd spilled wine on my new rug, leaving a dark burgundy stain against the cream-colored knots of wool. I knew when I bought that thing that something like this would happen. I knew it. I picked up the bottle and set it down loudly on the coffee table. The glass made a satisfying thwack against the wood. Wendy didn't budge.

She was facedown on the couch, her blonde hair loose and cascading in every direction. I brushed her hair away from the upholstery with my hands. If she had thrown up on it, spilled wine, if she had so much as dropped a crumb on it, I'd kill her.

Only then did it occur to me to check to see if she'd already died. Quickly, I held two fingers against the side of her neck. Her skin was warm. Her pulse thrummed under my fingertips.

I went back to being upset about my couch.

"Wendy." I shook her shoulders. What was the protocol in this situation? Maybe you were supposed to let them sleep it off. Or maybe it was the opposite—you were supposed to keep them awake. Make them coffee and feed them toast.

A groan escaped from her, a pitiful bleat.

Did she really drink an entire bottle of wine by herself? I examined the label. I had bought the bottle last week—I definitely hadn't opened it myself. The foil had been torn off haphazardly, as if she'd hacked at it with a butter knife or peeled it off with her fingernails.

An unpleasant odor—the lasagna, undoubtedly petrified into a charred stone in the oven—wafted through the air.

"Wake up, Wendy."

This time she rolled over, shielding her eyes with her arm. She groaned again.

"So this is how it's going to be? I can't leave you alone without you self-destructing?"

"You left," she said in a slurred, mumbly voice. "On my first night."

"We're not going over this again. I have a real job now." I tried not to flinch at my own words. "That's how we can afford this place. How we can afford to be together."

"I'm going to be sick."

"The bathroom!" I stabbed my finger in the direction of the hall-way. "Go!"

When she came back out, she looked better. She had pulled her hair up into a messy bun and splashed some water on her face. The hair around her temples was still wet.

I was kneeling down on the rug, trying to blot out the red wine stain. I'd poured white wine over it—requiring me to open another bottle—and was blotting away at it with a dishrag. While I blotted, I had composed a little speech for Wendy, a speech about respect and boundaries and authority and only being fourteen years old and dam-aging brain cells.

She plopped herself back on the couch and wrapped the blanket around her head, clasping it under her chin. She looked so forlorn and pathetic, like a little pioneer child abandoned on the side of the road because they'd needed to lighten the load of the covered wagon mak-ing its trek out west. "Are you going to send me back now?" Wendy asked me.

Her soft voice, her pathetic little abandoned orphan routine—this should have sent arrows straight through my heart. I searched deep inside of myself for some of those sisterly feelings we'd shared last night. I couldn't feel them. It was impossible for me to believe that this girl sitting here, with the blanket tucked around her, those doleful eyes, was the same girl who used to follow me around. She used to wear my clothes, even when they were way too big. I indulged her. I was a good older sister. I had this boyfriend, junior year of high school. Duncan

Kline. I used to let Wendy hang around with us. For several weeks, we were like the three amigos. Two sixteen-year-olds and an eight-year-old, going out to the movies, drinking hot chocolate in coffee shops, drawing gigantic sidewalk murals up and down the driveway.

He broke up with me because of it. He wanted a girlfriend, not a full-time babysitting gig, he told me. I hadn't thought of it that way. I'd thought we were having fun, the three of us. When I broke the news to Wendy, she shook her head sadly. You're too good for him, she told me. I remember that she said it like that, wise beyond her years. I had to laugh. *We're* too good for him, I agreed.

The hungover teenager on the couch was the same little girl, I told myself. My little sister. It still seemed impossible to believe. I sighed theatrically. "I owe you, remember?" I said to her.

"I could have my grandma come get me." A tear trickled out of the corner of one eye. She was really milking it. "Get out of your hair."

"You're not leaving," I said, my voice firm. "No one's leaving anyone again. Got it?" I kept dabbing the rug with the cloth. That was the secret to getting stains out. Never rub. Dab. Dab, dab, dab, dabdabdabdab.

"I'll clean that up," Wendy offered.

"That's okay. The stain's almost out." It wasn't true. The blemish remained visible on the carpet, though it was more a bruised gray than dark burgundy now. I could dab for hours and it would still be there, a dirty shadow. I exhaled. "Once it dries, no one will ever notice it."

CHAPTER 14

"How's the new job?" Steele asked me. We—Steele, Margorie, this guy William we used to work with, the old gang—were sitting at a back booth in a dark bar, the kind of place that would have been clouded over in smoke when that was still allowed. The booths were old and ripped, the tables sticky with years of sugary cocktails.

"The new job?"

"How is it working for Leo Glass?" Margorie added.

"It's fun," I said. "Challenging." Over the last two months, I'd seen Leo only a handful of times. He'd be in town for a night or maybe two, or he would fly me somewhere to visit him. Business trips, I told Wendy.

Most of the time I was home, with nothing to do. Every morning I got up, got dressed, and walked out the door with Wendy. She went to school, I pretended to go to work like a laid-off Japanese businessman.

Wendy and I were careful around each other, ever since that first night. On our best behavior. I spent afternoons baking cookies or laminating dough or frosting cupcakes, which I would set out on a plate, awaiting Wendy's return from school. This was what a loving sister would do, I thought, and I imagined her coming home, her eyes widening in delight at the treats. We would eat cookies, dipping them in glasses of cold milk, and she would tell me about the cute boy she sat behind in biology class.

This never happened as I hoped it would. She met up with friends, stopping for ice cream or bubble teas on the way home. She would have a cookie later, after dinner, she would announce. Then she would join friends for dinner, or maybe I would have a "business meeting" to attend.

I kept baking anyway. The more complicated and time-consuming the recipe, the better. After a day or two, I would wrap everything up and put it in the freezer.

I'd spent Christmas in Hawaii with Leo, while Wendy visited her grandmother. She wanted to go to Hawaii with me. We should be together on Christmas, she insisted. Conveniently enough for me, her grandmother had already made arrangements for Wendy to spend the school break with her, so I didn't have to talk my way out of it.

Leo had business, in Hawaii, over Christmas? Yes. He met with some businessmen from China—he worked late into the night. With my days to myself, I lounged on the beach and at the pool and on the hotel balcony with its postcard-perfect view, the ten-foot turquoise waves framed by swaying palms.

We had separate hotel rooms. He didn't want to bother me, with his hectic schedule, coming in and out at all hours, he said. Every evening I sat on the balcony and taught myself how to play chords and pluck out melodies on a ukulele I found in the hotel gift shop. After a week I could play three songs: "Somewhere over the Rainbow," "Ring of Fire," and "Riptide."

In that booth with my friends, I was saved from elaborating on my new career when the server arrived with baskets of fries.

We ordered round after round. Margorie and I went to the restroom together, locking ourselves in the grimy little cell. We took turns peeing, and then I watched as she reapplied her makeup. Margorie had had the same hairstyle ever since I'd met her, baby bangs straight across her forehead. She always wore liquid black eyeliner, winged. She was reapplying it in the mirror, darkening the lines, flicking it out at the end. "Now you," she said, and I turned to face her. The liquid liner felt cold on my eyelids. She blew on them, gently, to dry them. Her breath smelled like alcohol and limes.

"Check it out," she said, and I looked at my reflection in the mirror.

"Nice," I said.

"Steele certainly seems to think so."

"We're just friends."

"Hmm."

"Actually . . . I'm seeing someone."

"That guy who lives down the hall?" Something must have passed over my face. "I knew it," Margorie said, delighted with herself. "I told you he was your type. All brooding and artistic. He's like a musician or something, right? A violin player?"

"Violist," I corrected automatically, further piquing Margorie's interest.

"Violist, huh," she said.

"I only know because I can hear him play." The last thing I needed was for Margorie to figure out who he was, that he was famous, at least a little bit. This seemed like something Margorie would find very interesting. I feared it was written all over my face, the whole story, or that I'd spill it all at once, the way we'd met, the whole love-at-first-sight, star-crossed-lovers situation. The way I memorized his schedule so I wouldn't run into him in the halls, waiting to hear him start practicing before I slipped out to go to the store, darting back in right when he finished hours later.

For the most part, I had managed to avoid him. It would be easier, I reasoned, for both of us. We could just forget it ever happened. It was overkill, I knew. We could be grown-ups about it. Sleep together and then end it and then say hi to each other if we happened to collide by the mailboxes in the lobby. Exchange pleasantries. Maybe one day—why not?—become friends again.

I couldn't do it, though. I didn't feel capable of it, not after spilling my guts to him, then ending it the way I did. Not after everything. I ran into him only once. Wendy and I did. We were leaving the apartment to go somewhere, and he was leaving his apartment at the same exact time. It was bound to happen. Our eyes met, and both of us just stared at each other for what seemed like an eternity. I broke the awkward silence and said hello. And then we all began moving to the stairway, descending. We didn't have to say anything to each other after all. We were spared by Wendy. I know you, she said to Sam. He smiled cryptically and said he didn't think she did. You look so familiar, she insisted. We all exited the building, and I mumbled that it was nice to see him, and then we parted ways. Ten steps down the sidewalk, Wendy turned. Hey! she yelled. Sam turned around, and we looked at each other again. Ferguson! she exclaimed in triumph. He gave an embarrassed little smile and turned back around. I knew I recognized him, she said to me. Did you realize we live right next door to him? Isn't that amazing?

I didn't realize, I said. I had no idea.

"No," I said to Margorie. "Not him. Someone else."

"You know what would look good on you?" Margorie rooted around in her bag and produced a tube of highlighter, a palette of eye shadow. She began applying various powders and gels to my skin as I talked. I told her about my new boyfriend. His name was . . . Seth. He was a computer guy. I had met him in San Francisco, when I was there a couple of months ago, on a business trip. It was true I had been to San Francisco, to visit Leo. He flew me in for the day. We ate lunch in Chinatown and walked in and out of the shops. He bought me a fan and a porcelain spoon. Then he sent me off, back to the airport, and I was home in time to watch *Saturday Night Live* with Wendy.

Seth was a nice guy, I told Margorie. A little controlling, perhaps. He liked me to wear certain clothes, to do my makeup in a certain way.

Margorie snorted a laugh at that. Someone was pounding on the door.

"Just a minute!" Margorie yelled.

"We should leave," I said.

"So what's wrong with him?"

"What makes you think something is wrong with him?"

"He's controlling," Margorie reminded me.

"Yes, and—okay." I laughed nervously.

"Try not to move your face."

I told her the rest, barely moving my mouth while Margorie dabbed at my skin. I told her how Leo—"Seth"—wouldn't sleep with me. He seemed attracted to me. Very attracted to me. I didn't know what was wrong with him.

What I didn't say was that I didn't know what was wrong with me. If I was supposed to be doing something, if Leo expected something I wasn't giving him. If *I* wasn't doing it for him, he could find someone who would. Maybe sex wasn't what he wanted—but then why had he sent me to that shady doctor? I had even gone *back* to the doctor so he could cram an IUD into my uterus. It just didn't make any sense for Leo to go to all this trouble, to pay all this money, just to keep me hanging around my apartment baking cookies all day. Two months had gone by, and we had only been on a handful of dates. It was easy. *Too* easy. I wanted to count myself as the luckiest woman in the world, but I didn't feel lucky. I felt like I was always waiting for the other shoe to drop.

"Maybe he's a virgin," Margorie said.

"He had a girlfriend," I told her. "A very serious girlfriend. Six years. She was beautiful, too. I saw a picture."

"He showed you a picture of his ex-girlfriend?"

I had done my due diligence and learned all I could about Leo Glass and his love life. According to my research, he'd had only one long-term girlfriend, and that had been back in college. He met Jamila Heath-Jackson at Reed College their freshman year. They dated all through college and two years after that. They lived together, they founded Lookinglass together, and then—poof. They parted ways. She cut ties with Lookinglass for "an undisclosed cash settlement," according to one online source.

The internet didn't have much to say about Jamila Heath-Jackson after that. I found only one image of her online—a picture of her and Leo from their college days.

They had been featured in *WIRED* magazine, a Q and A about some new software they'd invented together, the facial-recognition technology they would eventually put to work in Lookinglass. In the picture, they were sitting on her dorm bed, "where it all started." They both sat cross-legged, facing each other. A laptop on each of their laps. Their heads turned to the photographer. They were smiling.

I had studied the picture carefully, examining it for clues. Leo was surprisingly unchanged since his sophomore year in college. A little skinnier, maybe. At the same time, his cheeks were plumper. His hair was longer, dark curls springing out every which way. His eyes were the same, all-pupil, wide open.

And *Jamila*. She was beautiful.

She was very tall—even seated, it was obvious, just by the length of her limbs and neck. She was cool and bohemian, with her natural hair, the artfully tied headband around her hairline, perfectly faded jeans and halter top. She was also some sort of genius, the first Black woman to win the Turing Award when she was barely out of college.

Leo had been with this woman for six years—practically a lifetime when you're young.

"What are you doing to my face?" I craned my head to look at myself in the mirror, but Margorie wouldn't let me.

"Maybe he's impotent?"

"He's *not* impotent." I said this with such emphasis that Margorie let out a laugh like a squawk.

Since that awkward striptease on our first date, I had been unsure how to proceed with Leo. He didn't like for me to be too forward. He didn't like me to take the lead. We would kiss sometimes, and he would seem into it—*really* into it, breathing hard, pressing his body against mine, squeezing my breasts over my clothes—and then he would break away, scoot back, straightening out his clothes like we were two teenagers making out in the basement, afraid of getting caught by our parents. That's enough of *that*, he would say.

"Abstaining for religious reasons?"

The knocks on the door grew more persistent. "All right, all right!" Margorie yelled. "I'm pretty much finished." She whirled me around so I could check out my reflection. I looked like a caricature of myself, with chiseled cheeks and painted-on brows and iridescent highlights all over.

"Beautiful," I said.

We stumbled out of the restroom and found Steele and William playing pool. After their first game, Margorie and I joined them, and we drank more and raised our voices and knocked the balls around the table with our cue sticks, inventing new rules as we went along.

When fast songs came on, we danced. I flung my arms around Steele's shoulders and he whirled me around, and we laughed, and I remembered those first days with him, when I thought we might actually make it. We had been a terrible couple. I knew he wanted me to go home with him, and if I kept drinking like this, maybe I would. I didn't miss him, but he was familiar. I remembered what it was like, to just be normal, to actually have fun. With Leo, I might be on a tropical island or eating in a Michelin-starred restaurant, but it didn't seem fun at all. It seemed like a job, a job I wasn't very good at.

I closed my eyes, raised my hands over my head, and danced to the music. When I felt a tug on my arm, I whipped around, smiling, thinking it was Margorie or William or Steele.

"Come with me." It was Alejandro.

My smile disappeared. I felt temporarily displaced, the way you do when you wake up in a strange bed and can't remember what time it is or where you are or how you got there. "What are you doing here?"

"You're making a fool of yourself."

"I'm out with my friends. I'm allowed to go out with my friends."

"Don't you have a little sister you're supposed to be taking care of?"

"She's at a sleepover—" I started to say and then stopped myself. I didn't have to explain anything to him.

"Don't make a scene." Alejandro had to yell above the din of the band, but the song ended and the last word echoed out over the dance floor.

"Who's this?" Margorie asked, looping her arm through mine.

"Just a friend," I said.

The music started up again, and I was grateful for it, grateful for the noise that rendered us incapable of further communication.

"I have to go," I shouted to Margorie. "Work emergency."

"It's Saturday night."

I mouthed the word *sorry* as I followed Alejandro out the door and onto the sidewalk.

"What the hell?" I yelled at him as soon as we were outside. The bar was on a busy street. Cars rushed by. We were lit by streetlights.

"You think I want to be your goddamn babysitter?"

"So I'm not allowed to go out now? I'm not allowed to have a good time—"

"You can do whatever the fuck you want. Just don't do it where there are Glasseyes all over the place. Don't make Leo call me from Copenhagen and—"

"Amsterdam."

"He doesn't like seeing you like this." Alejandro looked embarrassed now, like he did the day after my appointment. Like he didn't want to be the one to deliver this news.

"Like what?" I put my hands on my hips. I knew what he meant.

"Drunk." He waved his hand over my face, my clothes. They were ordinary clothes, the kind of clothes you put on when you want to have a good time. Tight top. Short little skirt. "The whole look," he said vaguely.

"I'm not drunk," I said. "I'm not *that* drunk."

"All right," Alejandro said. He bulged his eyes at me. His expression said, *Please, Rosemary.* "Do what you want."

"Fine," I said. "Let's go." It was too late to return to the bar anyway. Nothing I could tell Margorie would sound the least bit believable. I followed Alejandro to the black SUV.

I didn't hear from Leo for almost two weeks.

CHAPTER 15

For two whole weeks, I paced around my apartment, convinced I'd blown it. Failed whatever crazy test Leo was administering on me. I waited. I waited to receive a phone call, an official notice in the mail, something, telling me it was all over, that Wendy and I needed to pack our bags and vacate the premises. I didn't know what I was going to do. I had nowhere to go. Even if I could get my La Cuisine job back, I wouldn't be able to afford another place. Not even a dingy studio apartment in Gresham.

And what would happen to Wendy? I couldn't just move across town, pull her out of her school, and put her in another one. She was finally settling in, making friends. She had joined the yearbook staff.

When he finally called, it was the middle of January, the dead of winter. "I'm back in town," he announced cheerfully, as if nothing had happened. He was home, he said, and not for just a few days. For good. Or at least for a good while. He was sick of living out of a suitcase. He would be delegating. Scaling back.

He wanted me to meet him at his place, tonight. "Everything is going to be different now," he said, which is how I got the idea that things were going to change—that tonight was the night. I took extra care in getting ready, like it was our first date, like I was up for anything. I wasn't nervous or scared. I was relieved. Maybe he had just been stressed out all this time. Too *busy* to have sex with his paid girlfriend? Maybe. I was grasping at straws.

In his brick-lined hallway above the parking garage, I shook the rain from my coat. I'd bought the too-large raincoat at the William Temple House my freshman year of college. Forest green and covered in pockets and zippers, the coat was more suitable for a park ranger than a high-class escort, so I stuffed it in the corner, behind the console table. Underneath I had on a short, tight silvery dress.

The door rolled open on its heavy casters before I had a chance to knock. "You're here." Leo clasped both of my hands and pulled me in.

He looked handsome. Well rested for a change, no dark circles under his eyes. The curls on his head a little overgrown, softer and shinier than usual.

"I thought we were dressing up," I said.

He was wearing his signature navy-blue hoodie, a white T-shirt, and charcoal-gray sweatpants. Granted, they appeared to be expensive sweatpants. "I *said* it was a special occasion."

"Okaaay."

"It's a surprise."

"What's the occasion?"

"Patience." Leo enfolded me in his arms and kissed me, slowly. He ran both of his hands down my back, resting them on my behind. Then his hands wandered down, pulled up the edges of my dress. His fingers caressed the backs of my bare thighs and traveled up higher. I was prepared. I was wearing expensive underwear. I did this thing when I was with Leo. I committed to my role. My various mantras scrolled through my head. *I am choosing this, this is my job, I couldn't do much worse than all the other douchebags*, etc. I wasn't into him, but I wasn't repulsed by him, either. I was pretending to be into him. Exactly as I had agreed to do.

Then Leo stopped himself. He removed his hands from under my dress and stepped back from me. He lifted up his palms, like he was surrendering, showing he was unarmed. "That goes for me, too. *Patience.*"

On the dining room table sat a white garment box, unwrapped, illuminated by the chandelier above. "I have something for you," he said, lifting it from the table and handing it to me ceremoniously. It was heavier than I'd expected.

This was it—I had a feeling. Inside this box was his fetish, revealed after all this time. Some leather bondage gear. A schoolgirl costume. Something. Something so outlandish, my imagination was incapable of anticipating it.

I laid the box back down on the table. Remember why you're doing this: Wendy. Whatever it is, you can handle it, the pep talk continued. Two and a half months down. Nine and a half to go. You can put up with anything for nine and a half months. Remember your training, I reminded myself. I'd been running over my lines in the mirror, complete with facial expressions.

Sex dungeon? No, Leo. I'm not shocked at all. (Eyebrows lifted, eyes wide open in innocence.)

You're a furry? Really? I love animals. I donated to PETA one year, in college.

Golden showers? Cleveland steamers? (I had grimaced in the mirror—I couldn't help it—and then quickly rearranged my features, creating a mask of smiling acceptance.) Let me spread out some water-resistant drop cloths.

Whatever was in the box, I was going to look excited to see it. I was going to look absolutely delighted.

One, two, three—in a flourish, I lifted the lid, like a magician performing a magic trick.

"Agh!" I shouted. Then I laughed, in an attempt to disguise my outburst as a screech of joy. "Are you serious?"

Leo's pupils dilated a fraction. I recovered.

"Are you *serious*?" I said again. "Because I *love* it."

We both looked down at the contents of the box. It was a pair of charcoal-gray sweatpants. A white T-shirt. And a navy-blue hoodie. All in my size.

~

Leo made me go back into his bedroom to change. I unzipped the dress and then didn't know what to do with it. I decided to hang it in his closet. The silver dress dangled among an army of navy-blue hoodies. Cinderella at a ball of nerdy software developers.

Leo was waiting for me in the kitchen. He looked at me with approval. He clapped his hands together so loudly they sounded like the crack of a whip. I jumped. "Yes!" Leo raised both palms up in the air so I could give him a double high five. "Everything fit? I had to guess at your size."

"It's perfect," I said. "Very comfortable."

The kitchen island was piled high with groceries: flour, eggs, tomatoes, garlic, lettuce. He waved over everything like a game show host. "Okay," he said. "So have you guessed it yet?"

"Guessed what yet?" I smiled at him coyly, playing along, like I was having the time of my life. I hadn't prepared for this. Whatever it was, I had no clue.

"Guessed the surprise."

"Give me a hint."

"All right, all right." Leo rearranged the groceries on the island, pairing the flour with the eggs and some other items: baker's chocolate, butter, and sugar.

"You want to make . . . brownies?"

"We're going to make a cake," Leo said. "A birthday cake."

"It's your *birthday*?" I should have known this. I should have read it on his Wikipedia page, written it down, put a note in my calendar. Alejandro should have told me. Surely Alejandro knew.

"Don't worry about it. I usually don't even celebrate. This year is different." He paused and gave me a meaningful look. "It's like I told you—I'm tired of all this traveling. New York, San Francisco. Room service every night. It gets old. It's a new decade. I want to do things differently."

"Your thirtieth," I said. "That's a big deal."

"I spent my twenties building my business. And it was great. No complaints. But I want more now."

"Right." I was nodding, smiling, like I knew where he was headed with this line of conversation, but then he was looking back at me with this expectant raise of his eyebrows, like he wanted me to respond, and I didn't know what to say. "So this sweat suit"—I gestured to my ensemble of cozy knitwear—"and the chocolate cake . . ."

"It starts tonight. It's my birthday, and this is how I want to spend it: with you." Leo reached out to caress my cheek, but his hand hovered just inches away from my face, as if I were a statue he was afraid to break. He let his hand fall back to his side. "I want to spend it with you—here, at home, like a normal couple."

I shook my head, as if I was having trouble believing his confession but was nonetheless thrilled to hear it.

"It's all I could think about, every time I was away—being with you. Not for a night, not for a ride to the airport. For real."

"I want that, too," I murmured.

He smiled then. "Really?"

"Of course."

"Good. Because I've cleared my schedule. I don't have to be anywhere for at least a month. I mean, I'll still go to the office. I still have to run the place." He laughed self-deprecatingly. "But no more trips for a while. We can get to know one another. Hang out."

"I'd love that." I tried not to think about what this would mean. This was how I did it—how I saved my little sister. It wasn't working down in the coal mines, it was "hanging out" with Leo Glass! I was lucky. Very, very lucky.

For an awkward moment we just stood there, unsure what to do next. We seemed to have reached an agreement.

"We'll start tonight. First we'll make my favorite dinner and chocolate cake for dessert. My mom gave me the recipes, the ones she used to use when I was a kid."

If a real boyfriend had just announced that on the occasion of his thirtieth birthday, we were going to wear matching sweat suits and re-create his childhood favorites using his mother's recipes, I would be eyeing the emergency exits about now. But I was getting paid for this.

"Let's do it."

~

Two hours later we stood over the kitchen island, marveling at our creation. The cake was lopsided, covered in thick swirls of chocolate icing. I'd done the best I could with the equipment we had at hand. Leo lacked the little luxuries of an accomplished home baker. We'd measured out the flour with a teacup, whipped the egg whites into stiff peaks with a cheap wire whisk. We'd baked each layer in a different-size pan and trimmed the edges of the larger one with one of Leo's flimsy IKEA steak knives.

I started to enjoy myself. This was fun. This could be fun.

You should get a few basics, I had told him. Especially if we're going to do a lot of cooking together.

He'd liked that.

I'll get whatever you want, he'd said.

Take this knife, for example, I'd said. See this? See how shiny it is? It was stamped out of a sheet of metal. A real knife is made out of forged steel. The metal runs all the way through it. Look at this knife—the blade is just glued into the plastic handle.

It's junk, he admitted.

We'd worked well together, though. Better than I had expected. You never know how you'll get along with someone in the kitchen.

"We did this." Leo was smiling down at our cake with the goofiest grin on his face, like he couldn't believe how well it had turned out.

I put my hand on his right forearm. "You put some real muscle into that whisking."

He leaned across the island to kiss me.

My eyes fluttered closed, but then the kiss was over and Leo was cutting the cake with a butter knife.

"Well," I asked, "as good as Mom used to make?"

Leo ate his piece in what seemed like a few bites.

I took one tentative nibble. We hadn't eaten dinner. I hadn't eaten anything since breakfast. The frosting stuck to the roof of my mouth. The cake itself was dry, disintegrating on my tongue. I chewed and chewed, opening the cupboards in search of a cup. With a glass of water, I washed it down. "Delicious."

"I've got to show my mom," he said.

Before I could say "show your mom what?" Leo pivoted around to face the stove. He looked at his own reflection in the mirror above the cooktop and grinned. It was a wide grin, spanning ear to ear. I could see every one of his teeth in his reflection. Narrow teeth, spaced ever so slightly apart. Little white fence posts. "*Hola*, Consuela," Leo said. "*Llama mamá.*" Nothing happened, leaving me to wonder if Leo had lost it, grinning into the mirror at an imaginary friend.

"*Corrección.*" Consuela's voice echoed out into the apartment. Her accent seemed pure. Authentic. "*Llama a mamá. No olvides la preposición.*"

"*Gracias*, Consuela," Leo said. "*Llama a mamá, por favor.*" Then to me: "We're releasing a beta version of Consuela next year. A household assistant who teaches Spanish. What do you think?"

It didn't seem like he actually wanted my opinion. A ringtone sounded out as we waited for his mother to pick up on the other side.

"I mean—Consuela?" I whispered. "Isn't that a little . . ." I wasn't sure how to phrase my objections. I settled on "culturally insensitive."

146

Leo opened his eyes wide, as if this thought were brand new and surprising. "Why would it be insensitive?"

He was making me spell it out. "She's basically a maid who speaks Spanish? It's a stereotype—"

"You think all Spanish speakers work as maids?"

"That's the opposite of what I'm saying—"

"And what's wrong with being a maid? It's important work—"

"Hellooo!" Another voice trilled out into the kitchen.

On the edge of the mirror, Leo's reflection shrank down to a small bubble, and another face took its place, a woman's face. At first all we could see was her nose and lips. The lips opened up in a huge smile. White tiles of teeth, just like Leo's. "Happy birthday!" she trilled, and then she sat back so I could make out her whole face.

She was older than my mother had been by at least twenty years, but that was no surprise. My mom, if she'd been alive today, would be forty. Ten years older than Leo. Like her son, Leo's mom had dark curly hair and piercing blue eyes. Unlike Leo, she wore glasses.

Leo lifted the cake from the counter and positioned it in front of the mirror. "We used your recipe, Ma."

It all happened so quickly, I didn't have time to react. If I had, I would have tiptoed out before Leo had a chance to pull me in by the arm. Within seconds we were cheek to cheek, huddled in front of the mirror.

"Ma," he said, "meet Rosemary. Rosemary, my mother, Christine."

"Call me Chris," his mom said. "I've heard so much about you."

My mouth stretched open in the imitation of a smile. Breezy and natural was what I was going for. I looked like a wild animal baring its fangs at an approaching enemy. "Hi!" I managed to squeak out. Speaking helped my facial muscles fall back into place. My expression softened into something a little more pleasant.

Christine told me she couldn't wait to meet me in person, that I had made her son so happy these last few months.

"Wow." My cheeks turned pink. It wasn't a bad thing. Blushing made me appear youthful and shy, just the way a young woman should act upon meeting her boyfriend's mom for the first time. That's what I told myself anyway.

"You even dress the same," she said. "You're made for each other."

Leo kissed me on the cheek. "We're just chilling for the weekend," he said. "Best birthday present I could ask for."

Once the call ended, Leo turned to face me, his eyes bright. He held up both hands in the air again for me to slap. He was very into high fives. We slapped palms. *Whoo!* he said, as if talking to his mother had injected him with adrenaline.

I wanted to scold him, to tell him it wasn't cool to spring his mother on me like that. I needed time to prepare, to think about putting my best face forward. I had a general rule about wearing matching outfits when meeting a boyfriend's parents for the first time, especially when the outfit involved a navy-blue hoodie.

"She seems nice," I said once we had settled over on his couch.

"The best."

"Look, Leo—"

He held up his hands. "I know, I know. I should have given you a heads-up." I relaxed. Exactly. He got it. "But this is what we talked about, right? A few months go by, and we tell everyone we're together. You've been at Lookinglass long enough now, we just fell for each other, started dating, blah blah blah. I told my mom all about you. And now I can meet your friends, your family. Your sister—"

"No!"

Leo stopped talking and widened his eyes. "We discussed this—" he said.

"No, Leo." I was breaking one of his rules—never talk about The Project. I didn't care. "Not my sister." I paused, not sure how far I was willing to take this. "Not my friends, either." I braced myself for his reaction.

His eyes narrowed at me, and he shook his head slowly, like a disappointed parent. "Rosemary." His voice was steady. Calm. "This is supposed to look like a normal—"

I placed a hand on his arm. "I just want to keep you to myself. Is that so wrong?"

Leo muttered something I couldn't understand.

"Can I be completely honest with you, Leo?" My voice soft. Vulnerable.

"Of course." Leo sat up straighter, held both of my hands in his.

"I want my sister to be proud of me, you know? She thinks I got this great job at Lookinglass, that I can afford my amazing apartment all on my own. . . . I can't tell her that I started dating my boss." This was pretty good. Leo was nodding. He bought it. Maybe because it was the truth. "And my friends. Most of them are from work—from my old job." I lowered my eyes. "I guess I just wanted them to think I'd moved on, done something with my life. If they saw us together—"

"I get it," Leo said. "I do."

I flashed Leo my most seductive smile and caressed his cheek with my hand. "I knew you would."

We kissed. It was a soft kiss. I pulled back, and we looked at each other. He kissed me again, harder. Objectively speaking, he was a good kisser. Confident. Lips firm, tongue insistent. Not sloppy. It wasn't as if I enjoyed kissing him—but the person I was pretending to be had no complaints.

I grabbed a fistful of his hoodie and pulled him closer to me, and then I reached under his clothes. The skin on his back was warm, and softer than I had expected. He moaned and sent a string of kisses down my neck. I threw my head back to give him better access.

My fingers ran along the edge of his waistband.

"You're so beautiful," he murmured, pushing me back into the cushions.

He was on top of me, pressing against me. He wanted me. This was obvious. I tried to pull down his sweatpants, but our bodies were fused together too tightly. The pants wouldn't budge more than an inch. Finally, it was happening. After all this time doubting my ability to perform this job to Leo's satisfaction, I got overzealous.

I reached under the waistband and grabbed hold of his butt.

He reared back. He sat on his haunches on the couch and stared down at me. He was making no effort to disguise his erection, visible through the material of his knitted loungewear.

"What are you *doing*?" he said.

I didn't know what to say to that.

"That's not what I want," he said. He was angry. *Angry.*

"Leo, I—I'm sorry."

"That's not what this is about."

"I thought you wanted me to be your girlfriend, I thought—"

"That's right," he said. "A girlfriend. Not a slut." He had his Mirror out. He tapped something into it. "Alejandro will be here in a few minutes."

"What?"

"He'll pick you up. Just wait on the sidewalk outside the building."

I raised myself up on my elbows to look at Leo. He was all business. "But—"

"That way you don't have to call a cab or take the bus." Leo was standing over me now, offering me his hand and hoisting me to my feet. "Come on, you don't want to keep him waiting."

He ushered me out the door and into the elevator so fast I didn't have time to retrieve my coat from the hallway, so I had to stand on the street corner wearing my good high-heeled shoes and the sweat suit.

A slut. He'd called me a *slut*. It would be insulting if it weren't so baffling. He knew what I was doing, out on that date with Sebastian St. Doug. He knew who I was, right from the start.

It was still raining—cold, flat drops. I zipped up the sweatshirt and pulled the hood over my head, scanning the street for Alejandro. The black SUV pulled up a moment later.

I jumped in the passenger seat and pulled back my hood.

The car idled in the middle of the street. I whipped my head around to face Alejandro. *"What?"*

He was staring at me, his eyes growing wider by the second. His eyes traveled up and down the length of my body, from the shoes to my sweatshirt.

Then he laughed. His laugh came out loud and long, like a howl. He pounded the steering wheel. "Oh my god!" he screamed.

"You're holding up traffic."

Alejandro glanced up to check the rearview mirror. No one was waiting behind us.

"I'm *sorry*." Alejandro wiped tears from his cheeks and sucked in a breath of air, as if trying to control himself. "I mean, what the hell, Rosemary?"

I set my jaw, tried to look angry. I wanted to command him to drive, drive me straight back to my apartment and never utter another word to anyone about this, ever. Instead I found myself almost cracking a smile. "Shut up."

"So are you planning on explaining this?"

"Just drive, okay?"

Alejandro put his foot on the gas pedal and began navigating through the narrow downtown streets.

We were both silent for a minute. It was a tense silence, a silence begging to be filled. "It was a training exercise," I said at last. "You know, because I'm going to be his personal assistant."

"Uh-huh."

"He wanted me to get in character. See what life is like as Leo Glass, you know? He probably made you wear this when you were training, right?" I turned to look at Alejandro, an innocent expression on my face, as if this were a perfectly reasonable explanation.

Alejandro only shook his head back and forth. He wasn't laughing anymore, as if he were struck, suddenly, with the gravity of my predicament. I almost expected him to warn me then. Say something like, You need to get out. You need to change your name and skip town or, at the very least, file a restraining order. He left you on the sidewalk wearing a replica of his clothes. This has gone too far already, and it has barely even begun.

He didn't say any of that, though. He said, "You couldn't *pay* me to wear that."

~

Leo called me the very next day, as if nothing out of the ordinary had occurred the night before. He said he had a few more of his mother's recipes for us to re-create. We could start with her famous banana muffins and move on to her signature marinara sauce, handed down from some long-lost Italian foremother. The secret ingredient was nutmeg.

CHAPTER 16

It rained every day, on and on. Leaves fell from the trees and into the storm drains. The streets turned to raging rivers. Then everything froze into ice. Every day I read weather-related horror stories: Homeless man found dead behind a rhododendron bush under layers of blankets and frost. Two women fell to their deaths after abandoning their car on a frozen highway, setting off for home over the ice and tumbling off the overpass. A family of four drove the wrong way on a back road on Mount Hood. No one ever saw them again.

Inside my apartment, the radiators churned with hot water. I still had to crack my bedroom windows open every night, just to avoid roasting to death.

I was gone more often, spending time with Leo. "Getting to know each other," as he put it. This meant cooking lessons. I had been getting into it. I spent my free time combing through cookbooks and reading recipe blogs. I made out lists of ingredients and, if I had nothing else to do (and, let's face it, I usually didn't), I would go all over town hunting something down. Pomegranate syrup. Tamarind paste. Fenugreek leaves.

Someone was probably keeping track of me as I traveled around town, by foot or train or car. This gave me a perverse form of satisfaction because I was doing exactly what I was supposed to be doing. If I visited a store with the Glasseye sticker on the window, I would linger extralong, wandering up and down the aisles. Angling my body so it would be sure to catch the features of my face.

Wendy and I never seemed to be home at the same time. I would come back from Leo's and find empty containers in the sink. Lasagna and curries I carefully packaged up, labeled, and stashed in the freezer. The cookies and multigrain muffins. She was eating them, sharing them with her friends. I saw evidence of this—plates and cups and crumbs on the coffee table. So we weren't having slumber parties and staying up all night talking. She was a teenager. She needed time to herself, time with her friends.

The dirty dishes, the crumbs on the coffee table, the empty containers in the sink—this made me feel like I was doing a good job. This was what a loving mother would do, right? Bake things? Make a bunch of meals with cooking instructions included: transfer to a 9 × 13-inch pan. Bake in a preheated oven at 375 degrees until cheese is browned and filling is bubbling. Cool for fifteen minutes before serving.

I missed the February deadline to take the LSAT. I had no excuse. Those first couple of months with Leo, when he was always gone, I had nothing to do but study, and I hadn't done it. I had still been adjusting, and I had other things to worry about. I could take it in June. I wouldn't be able to start law school fall term anyway. I'd still be here, with Leo, until the beginning of November. Nine months to go.

~

Leo called me late one morning. "Dress up," he said. "You can wear those eyelashes if you want."

"For lunch?"

"I'm taking you somewhere nice."

"I thought you hated that stuff. Makeup and fancy clothes."

"I don't hate it."

Okay. I could wear one of Mira's dresses, but I didn't have a coat to go with it. I'd forgotten mine at Leo's on his birthday. I'd been bundling up in sweaters and hoodies for the last month. I had asked Leo to look for it in the corner of his hallway where I left it, but the next time I went over there, he informed me that he had thrown it away. I was annoyed, but I let it go. He was paying me good money. I could afford to buy another coat. I could probably get a pretty decent one at Goodwill. Those credit card bills and student loans weren't going to pay themselves.

~

We had lunch at a nice restaurant in my neighborhood. In one of the few long-sleeved numbers Mira had left me, a tight red velvet dress with a plunging neckline, I was overdressed. Everyone else was wearing snow boots and fleece.

"You look beautiful," Leo said, sitting across the table from me and reaching for my hand. I smiled back. It was a role, I told myself. Just play your part, and you get to keep the job.

Because the weather was so awful—frigid rain, threatening to freeze into snow—Leo had his driver wait for us while we ate. We climbed in the back seat, and Leo tapped the window, signaling the driver to proceed. "I want to make one more stop," Leo said. A minute later, we were pulling into the La Cuisine parking lot at the back of the store.

Suddenly I understood it—I understood it all, why Leo had wanted me to dress up.

"Why are we here?"

"Surprise!" Leo said, a huge grin spreading across his face. "You're always saying I need to upgrade my kitchen equipment."

My heart was beating too quickly. Underneath the thick fabric of my dress, I was sweating. "You did this on purpose."

"What?" Wide-eyed innocence.

"Had me get all dressed up."

"I *like* seeing you all dressed up."

"No, you don't."

155

"I like seeing you in a variety of ways."

The look on Leo's face was difficult to interpret. He looked . . . sincere. His expression was eager, as if he aimed to please. Maybe he thought I'd enjoy going back to my old workplace, swanning around in a velvet gown in the middle of the afternoon. It was possible. And it was true—I had told him he needed better kitchen equipment, especially if he wanted us to cook more of our own meals.

I went inside. What else could I do? It seems stupid now. I could have left the car and just walked away. I could have walked away, and Leo might have yelled after me, but what more could he have done? I could have walked away and never talked to Leo again. It didn't seem like a choice at the time. It seemed inevitable, like I was destined to walk through that door. To buy all those knives. That knife.

On the sales floor, Steele found us comparing blenders. "Can I help you find—oh—" In a split second, he took it all in. The low-cut velvet dress, the cleavage, Leo at my side, his arm around my shoulders. "Hi, Rosemary."

"Hey." I tried to meet his gaze but found myself lowering my eyes, like I was some blushing courtesan.

"We're going to need pretty much everything," Leo said to Steele. Leo either didn't notice my discomfort or had chosen to ignore it. "Top of the line."

As Steele walked Leo through the pros and cons of each blender model, I surveilled the store. We didn't have a great vantage point from where we stood; I wasn't sure whether Margorie was here or not. Please don't be here, I silently pleaded. She might have taken the day off. Or maybe she was out for lunch. That would be convenient.

They settled on the Vitamix. Steele told us he'd leave it for us behind the counter when we were ready to check out. "Thanks," I muttered.

Leo wanted me to show him the knives myself, but we needed someone to open up the display case with a key. He went to find someone and returned with . . . Margorie. I felt heat rise up my face, all the way up to my ears.

Margorie approached the case, her keys jingling in an exaggerated way. She acted like she didn't recognize me, or like she didn't know me at all. And god. She was right. She didn't know me.

Or she did know. She knew everything the minute I—dressed in a tight velvet dress—waltzed into the store with the man I said was my boss. She knew then that there was no boyfriend in San Francisco. Only this.

"My girlfriend wants to give me the sales pitch," he said to Margorie as she twisted the key in the lock and opened up the case. "She used to work here."

"She knows that," I said to Leo. I tried to catch Margorie's eye, but she wasn't looking at me. I sensed something behind her ice-cold expression. Fury? Yes, that was definitely what I was picking up from her—it came off her in waves. So I'd lied. I'd lied only for my own vanity, so she'd think I'd made something of myself. I wanted her to admire and respect me—was that so difficult for her to understand? It didn't affect her, anyway! Why be so judgmental? This was why I didn't want to tell her the truth in the first place.

All that ran through my head. Meanwhile, she'd walked away, leaving me to talk knives with Leo Glass. It wasn't difficult. I knew the sales pitch backward and forward.

"The edges are hand finished to nine-degree angles and then cooled with nitrogen," I told him in a monotone voice. "The handles are ergonomically designed, smooth in the palm. Feel that?" I placed a ten-inch chef's knife in his hand, and he gripped the handle firmly, mimed chopping and slicing motions. He grinned and jutted the knife away from him, like he was winning a sword fight.

"All you really need to get started is a good Santoku knife," I said, but Leo reached for the one with the long, narrow blade.

"I want this one."

I tried to talk him out of it. What did we need a boning knife for, anyway? A skinny six-inch blade with an extrasharp tip for gouging into joints. Scalpel sharp. You don't like dealing with raw meat, I reminded him. All that cold skin and bone and gristle. He wanted to make pasta. Salads. Cheese plates. We didn't need a boning knife for any of that.

He didn't listen. He got them all. The paring knife, the serrated utility knife, the bread knife, two Santokus, the ten-inch chef's knife I'd balanced on my finger, the honing steel, the scissors, the magnetic strip we would install over the counter ourselves with the power drill. And the boning knife—he got that, too.

Everyone in the store pitched in, carrying boxes up to the counter, wrapping up glasses and placing them in boxes. They laughed and chatted and high-fived each other, buzzing around us like bees. I stood there, in my dress, and tried to disappear.

~

"You're upset," he said when we were in the back seat of the car, driving away.

I was fuming. If someone drew a cartoon version of me in this moment, there would be smoke billowing out of my ears. "You humiliated me."

His eyes widened as big as they could go. "Humiliated? What?"

"Did you think I'd like parading around my old workplace dressed like this? You *told* me to dress up."

"We were going to lunch. It was a nice restaurant."

"No one else was dressed up. No one is *ever* dressed up."

"You look beautiful."

I glared at him.

"I thought you'd enjoy it," Leo said. "We've been having fun lately, right? Cooking? The cake for my birthday. We made marinara from scratch. Remember?"

158

"It was last week."

"And I couldn't even slice a tomato with my knives—I pressed down and just squished it." Leo petted my hair. "You're cold." He jabbed at some buttons and tilted the vents toward me. Heat streamed in. Outside, the streets were slick with rain, and the sky was dark. It was the middle of the day, but it felt like the end. I closed my eyes. I was exhausted all of a sudden. I wanted to go home, get out of this awful dress, and crawl under the covers.

Wendy would be home in a couple of hours. I could tell her I was taking the rest of the day off. We could watch a movie. She was used to me "working from home" now. I had a flexible schedule, I had told her. She didn't seem to pay much attention one way or the other. All those weeks I'd spent faking going to the office had been pointless.

"Tomatoes are out of season in the middle of the winter anyway," I said to Leo.

"The point is my knives suck. You told me that."

I smiled a little.

"There," he said. "That's better."

My Mirror was vibrating. I opened my bag, trying to read the caller information on the screen, but I couldn't get a proper look.

"Answer it," Leo said.

I fished the device from my bag. "It's Wendy's school." He nodded and I accepted the call.

"Hey." It was Wendy's voice at the end of the line, soft and far away. She was calling from the nurse's office, she told me. Could I pick her up?

"What's going on? Are you okay?"

"Just come pick me up."

Leo was already rapping on the glass between us and the driver.

We arrived at the school moments later, in record time. I thanked Leo for dropping me off, but he got out with me, escorting me across the parking lot, and I didn't know how to stop him, how to make him go back to his car and drive away. I can take it from here, was all I could manage. Don't be silly, he had replied.

Wendy was sitting on the exam table in the nurse's office, looking like the waifish orphan she was. Stringy ash-blonde hair. Dark circles of kohl around her eyes. Layer after layer of clothing: ripped-up tights over another pair of tights, black skirt, a moth-eaten sweater, a scarf. She was sipping juice from a juice box, her legs stretched out in front of her like a little kid. "Hey," she said.

"She gave us quite a scare." The nurse was young, younger than I expected a school nurse to be, with aggressively straightened blonde hair and periwinkle scrubs. "She needs rest, hydration." She turned to Wendy. "And don't skip breakfast next time."

"Excuse me." Leo's voice sounded deep and commanding, a little too loud for the room. "Is someone going to explain what, exactly, happened here?"

The nurse dropped her eyelids and then cleared her throat. "She lost consciousness in class—"

"What?" I turned to my sister.

"I fainted," Wendy said. "That's all. I was sitting up on my desk—we all were—watching this slideshow in health class. It was disgusting. A live birth. A human birth. The woman, she had her legs spread open, and she just kept opening, getting wider and wider. You could see the top of the head, the hair on the baby's head, all slick with blood and this goo, and—"

"They let you watch that?" It didn't seem like something kids should be watching in school.

"And I just—I don't know. Blacked out, I guess."

"She fell flat onto the floor," the nurse added. "Just—clunk."

"I forgot to eat breakfast this morning. Low blood sugar."

"Take it easy the rest of the day," the nurse said. "Get plenty of fluids."

"We'll take good care of her," Leo said.

Only then did Wendy seem to take notice of him there, with me standing beside him. Me in a tight red dress and matching lipstick. Leo in his jeans and hoodie. "This is my boyfriend." I tried to smile, but it probably wasn't working. "Leo."

This wasn't supposed to happen. These two worlds weren't supposed to collide. I had been doing such a great job, up until then. She had no clue. She thought I was a respectable person, with a respectable job. That was my dream, anyway. My delusion. I wanted to be angry with Leo. This was a violation of our agreement. Or—it should have been. I should have seen to that. Anyway, this was a special circumstance. He was helping. He had driven me here.

I didn't know how she reacted because I couldn't meet her eyes.

"Can I have a word?" the nurse said to me.

I glanced at Wendy. She was sucking on the straw of her juice box. The box folded in on itself.

"I'll take care of her," Leo said.

"No!" I yelped. It came out too quickly, and the nurse shot me a cautious glance. "I mean—"

Leo was already helping Wendy off the table. "We'll wait for you in the car."

"Rosemary." Wendy said my name in a tiny little voice.

"It's okay." I tried to nod reassuringly. What was I thinking, in that moment? Did I have my little sister's best interests in mind, her well-being, when I let Leo take her out to the parking lot? Obviously not. I was only thinking that I needed to get through this, that I needed to seem normal, like an appropriate guardian. If I acted like I was worried about my putative boyfriend taking Wendy out to the parking lot, well—what then? The nurse might make a few phone calls, a social worker would come over to inspect us, and . . . I didn't know. I didn't know what would happen.

The nurse was talking to me, trying to tell me about Wendy, but I couldn't listen. My eyes kept darting toward the door. "Could be stress," she was saying. "Eating disorders aren't uncommon at this age. Drugs."

My head snapped back in the direction of the nurse. "Drugs?"

"Follow up with her pediatrician. That's all I'm saying—"

"She's not on drugs."

"If you have a minute, I can give you some referrals."

I told her I didn't have a minute. I had to go. My sister had been through a lot. She'd lost both her parents. She was adjusting. I couldn't just leave her alone out there—

The nurse gave me an inquisitive look. "She's not alone. She's with your boyfriend." When I didn't respond, she put a hand on my arm. "Miss Moseby—"

Moseby was Wendy's last name. Her dad's name. "Rabourne," I corrected her.

"Miss Rabourne—are you all right?"

The name meant nothing to her. It wouldn't have, back then. Rosemary Rabourne wasn't a household name. Rosemary Rabourne was no one anyone had ever heard of. Not yet. "I've got to go."

We took Wendy home in the black SUV. She sat between me and Leo in the back seat.

"Thanks for everything," I said when the SUV pulled up in front of my building.

"It was my pleasure." He got out of the car and held out his hand for Wendy.

"I'm fine," she said, but she took his hand and allowed him to help her step out of the vehicle.

The elevator was closed for repairs, so we had to take the stairs. She had to stop and rest after just one flight. Her face was pale, with rings forming under her eyes.

"Take it slow," I said.

"May I?" Leo asked, and then he gathered her in his arms and carried her the rest of the way. He lifted her up like she was nothing, like she was air. I followed behind them, and Wendy looked over Leo's shoulder. Her eyes opened as wide as they would go, as if to ask me what the hell was happening, why the hell I was letting this happen.

Later I wondered why she had put up with it. She hadn't signed a contract. She hadn't known who he was—at least, I assumed she didn't—and if she had, would it have mattered? She could have told him to screw off. She could have screamed at him to get the fuck out of our apartment. When I went back over this moment, in the months that followed, this was how I explained it: Wendy sensed it, the fear in me. I must have been giving her a look, a warning. Just play along with this. Pretend everything is normal, everything is okay, and maybe one day, it actually will be.

We were used to pretending. We were used to playing along. To waiting it out.

Leo deposited Wendy in her room, on her bed, still unmade from this morning. "Thanks," she said with the restrained politeness children reserve for older relatives.

"Anything else we can bring you?" Leo asked. "Ginger ale, crackers—"

"I think I just need to rest," Wendy said, giving me a meaningful look.

Leo and I backed out of her room, shutting the door behind us.

I offered him a cup of coffee, and he accepted. He'd leave after he finished drinking it. That was the idea. When he set his empty cup in the sink, I said I had better go check on her, but instead of making a move to go, to leave me alone with my sister, he followed me down the hall. He watched as I knocked softly on her door and cracked it open. Wendy was in her bed, the covers pulled up over her. Fast asleep.

I pulled her door closed and opened my mouth to thank him, to usher him out of the apartment, but at the same moment my lips parted, he bent down to kiss me. He kissed me harder than he had before, pressing me against Wendy's door. When he stopped to take a breath, I held a finger to his lips. *"Shh,"* I said.

I meant that we shouldn't be kissing, not leaning against my sister's door, not in the hallway, not at all, but he took my hand and led me down the hall.

We went into my room, and he picked back up where he left off, kissing me, tearing off his hoodie. I'd given him all those chances, worn all that fancy lingerie, run my hands all over him in his loft, on our trip to Hawaii, on those weekends he flew in for just a few hours, just to see me, and now—*now* was when he wanted to do this? Here, in my apartment, with my sister sleeping down the hall?

"Leo—" I started. I didn't know what to do. If I'd pushed him off me, if I'd yelled out, *No, not here*, he would have stopped, but I didn't push him off me, and I didn't yell anything. I didn't say anything.

It seemed easier, I guessed. This was my job, I reminded myself as he unzipped my dress, as he slid my underwear past my hips and down my legs. I chose this.

I lay there, on my bed, on top of all the covers, and he stood over me. He pulled his T-shirt over his head. He unbuttoned his jeans with one hand, yanking at the fly, and then his jeans were off, and his underwear. Dark-gray boxer briefs. I could see that he was ready, that this was going to happen. We were going to do this.

I tried to become her. The person who wasn't me, but the girl who wanted this, who admired and respected Leo and felt turned on by his body. He had a nice body. Very toned and tanned all over, with no tan lines. Computer geeks spend their time locked up in basements, stooped over their monitors. They should have stringy arms, no muscles. I widened my eyes, as if in appreciation of his sculpted physique.

Then he was on top of me. He was kissing me. He was breathing hard and moaning, and I had to keep putting my fingers to his lips, hushing him.

I didn't want to wake up my sister. That was true. It was also true that Sam was on the other side of this wall. He could be lying in his bed. He could be listening to everything.

Leo was staring down at me, his curls brushing against my forehead. I closed my eyes. He moved faster, and I knew he was close, and then he let out a final groan, slapping the wall with his hand.

"Shh," I whispered, though he wasn't listening. He rolled off me, panting. The skin on his face was flushed, prickled with beads of sweat.

He stayed until the sky grew dark, and he ordered us food—cartons and cartons of noodles and soups and curries and rice. We sat around the dining room table—Leo, Wendy, and I—scooping mounds of food onto our plates. "Eat," Leo told Wendy, and he watched as she lifted noodles from the carton with a pair of bamboo chopsticks.

"You must be busy," I said to Leo after dinner, after Wendy had gone back to her room, but he assured me he wasn't busy at all. He would spend the night, he said, if that was all right. It wasn't all right, but I couldn't figure out a way to express it without ruining everything, so he stayed. That night in bed, he didn't reach for me again. We lay next to each other without touching, like we usually did.

"I'm sorry," Leo said to me in the dark, long after we'd turned out the lights.

"Sorry for what?"

"We shouldn't have done that. It wasn't right," he said. "It wasn't the right time."

I lay there, staring up at the ceiling, trying to formulate a response. After a few moments his breathing deepened, so I didn't say anything.

The next morning I woke up alone in my bed, but I could hear the cranking sounds of water flowing through pipes. I tiptoed down the hall and pressed my ear to the bathroom door, listening to the water flowing from the faucet and into the sink.

What if he stayed here? What if he just—moved in? This wasn't the arrangement. This wasn't part of the plan. I had told him I needed space, Wendy needed space.

In the hall, I came up with a plan, with the words I'd use to get him to leave. The door of the bathroom opened and Wendy stepped out, and we both jumped, startled.

Is he gone? she mouthed, tipping her head toward my door. She looked so small, like a child, all wrapped up in some old flannel pajamas and a well-worn fleece bathrobe.

I held up a finger—wait—and crept into the living room, the dining room, the kitchen. "He's gone," I said, my voice in a whisper, as if I half expected him to spring out of a closet.

"What the fuck was that?" Wendy whispered back, angry. She looked terrible, her hair tangled and matted on one side, the eyeliner she hadn't removed flaking over her lids and sinking into the creases of her skin.

"He's my boyfriend." I said it at a normal volume level, in a steady voice. At least I tried to deliver the line naturally.

I must have failed—she must have sensed a slight hesitation between the "my" and the "boyfriend" because she shook her head. "That's not what he is."

"He won't be back here. That was a—that won't happen again. I promise. Okay?"

"Your boyfriend won't ever come here? Won't stay the night?"

"That's what I'm telling you." My sister's expression told me she didn't believe me. "I promise you, Wendy," I said to her. I gave her what I hoped was a reassuring smile. The smile of someone who knew exactly what she was doing. "It will never happen again."

CHAPTER 17

It started to snow. Gently at first, melting at first contact. Now it was falling in tufts as big as cherry blossoms, gathering on branches, blanketing the streets.

I kept meaning to talk to Wendy, to invite myself into her room for a little heart-to-heart chat, but I put it off. She might be sleeping in there. The nurse said she needed rest. Maybe I should talk to someone first, a professional. A doctor.

I wouldn't talk to her, I decided, not today. I would simply be there for her, make her some lunch, bring it to her on a tray. When I emerged from the kitchen with the tray piled with cheese and crackers and slices of apple and carrots, Wendy was standing in the entryway, all bundled up, her boots and coat on. She held up a hand in a wave. "I'm going to Hannah's," she said.

"You're supposed to be resting," I said. "It's snowing."

"She has snow tires."

"It's supposed to get worse, isn't it?" We both looked out the window as if to confirm the weather report. Yep. Snow was falling down, thicker than ever. The window was a blur of white.

"I'm spending the night." Wendy opened the door then, letting in a blast of cooler air from the hallway.

I wanted to run after her, but I wasn't dressed for it. I still hadn't bought a new coat, and I couldn't find my shoes. I ran out into the hallway in my socks, following Wendy down the stairs. "Wendy, wait, I wanted to talk to you about something."

She was running, flying down the stairs, and I was chasing after her yelling, "We don't leave each other, no one is leaving!" And then we were in the lobby.

"Wendy—"

"Bye!" She slammed through the apartment doors. I hesitated for a moment before I shot after her, onto the street. Wendy scrambled into the passenger side of Hannah's car. It was a compact SUV, with a rack on top for skis. It did look like the type of car that would have snow tires. Hannah didn't seem like someone who enjoyed skiing. Maybe it was her parents' car.

I'd met Hannah a few times, but only briefly. She was older than Wendy, already driving. When I asked Wendy why an older kid would want to hang out with a freshman, Wendy took offense, acting as if I had disparaged her entire personality, so I dropped it. Sometimes Hannah would give Wendy a ride home from school, and the two of them would rush in and disappear into Wendy's room for hours at a time.

She was very unusual-looking, with huge brown eyes set in a tiny, heart-shaped face under a messy mound of tangled dark hair piled on top of her head in a deliberately unkempt way. She was tiny, tinier than I was, always bundled in endless layers. Tights and a skirt and knee-high slouch socks. A tank top and an oversize flannel shirt, with a cardigan *and* a denim jacket and a scarf that wrapped around and around the top half of her torso.

I knocked on the driver's-side window, and Hannah rolled it down halfway. "Hey, Rosemary." Hannah blinked her anime eyes at me. They seemed to occupy most of her face. She was like a kid from one of those velvet paintings from the 1970s. Her face was unreal, a doll's face. The high cheekbones, hollow underneath. Black eyeliner, perfectly applied, and long, long lashes.

"You're sure it's okay for Wendy to stay over?" I asked Hannah.

"Rosemary." That was Wendy.

"It's cool," Hannah said. "I'll take good care of her." She gave me an ironic little smirk and raised the window without waiting for me to respond. The SUV rumbled down the street, a billowy cloud of exhaust trailing behind. They didn't hear me yelling after them, my voice thin and shrill in the snowy silence.

I shivered, rubbing my bare arms. My toes throbbed from the chill of the sidewalk. The snow was coming down in soft clusters. At the entryway, I pulled at the door to go back inside, but I'd locked myself out. "Damnit, Wendy," I said out loud.

I pressed the button next to the label reading APARTMENT MANAGER, hoping to summon Carl or Jessica. Nothing happened. My finger hovered over the button next to S. FERGUSON, but I didn't press it. Maybe I *should* freeze out here. Burrow under some bush and wait for death. I sighed and then, with a quick jabbing motion, pushed the button by Sam's name. I stood in the snow, waiting, for what seemed like ages. Then I heard it, his voice. A little hoarse, deeper than normal, like he was recovering from a cold. "Hello?"

Even through the tinned, crackly sound of the intercom, his voice sounded real, like he was right next to me again, not separated by any walls. Just one word sent me on this split-second flashback of every moment we had spent together. Sitting on my floor eating waffles, telling him everything, throwing myself on him in the hallway, stumbling down to his room, tearing each other's clothes off . . . This must be what it's like when you die, I thought. When your life flashes before your eyes.

He said hello again before I snapped out of it.

"It's Rosemary!" I yelled into the speaker. "I'm locked out—"

The buzzer sounded. I took the stairs instead of the elevator, to give myself time.

When I reached my floor, Sam was waiting in his doorway. He was smiling an amused little smile. I thought again about past lives, about being destined to meet someone. Maybe this was the pattern our two souls couldn't escape, with me getting locked out and him letting me back in, over and over, across lifetimes. "Thanks for letting me in." I had to concentrate to keep my voice sounding normal. I was afraid it might come out trembling—or worse, as a sob. "My sister ran off."

Sam opened his door all the way and leaned against the doorframe. He looked good. He didn't look sad or angry. I realized then that I'd feared exactly that, all this time. That I'd see the heartbreak written all over his face. He didn't look heartbroken. He looked perfectly fine. "Ran off?" He raised his eyebrows.

I went over to him. The snow had formed a crust on the bottoms of my socks and then melted. I wrapped my arms around myself to keep my body from shivering. Briefly—very briefly—I entertained a fantasy that Sam, inspired by my pathetic performance, would wrap me up in blankets, gather me into his arms, and carry me to his bed.

Sam looked back inside his apartment, and I followed his gaze.

My eye caught a glimpse of something—someone, a shadow moving across the floor inside his apartment. "I've caught you at a bad time," I said.

A voice rang out from inside his apartment. A woman's voice. "Sam? You have any sugar?" She came into view then, a willowy woman with waist-length hair, jet black. "Oh, hi!" she said, noticing me in the hallway.

"Hey." I couldn't even try to smile. Imogene Wu—the cellist/vocalist from Ferguson, Sam's old band. I recognized her instantly. I'd watched their videos enough. Over and over, some nights. She looked different in real life. Younger, maybe, like an ordinary person instead of the wild, hair-swinging personality she exuded onstage.

"I just have packets," Sam said to Imogene. "They're in the drawer next to the silverware."

"Ta," she said, faking a British accent. She wiggled her fingers at me in a wave and headed back into the kitchen.

"Anyway," I said, "thanks."

"Hey—" Sam started, but I darted over to my apartment and slipped inside before he could finish whatever he was going to say.

Thank god I'd left my door unlocked. I went inside, shut the door, and leaned against it, my eyes shut tight.

In dry socks and with a throw blanket draped over my shoulders, I set the kettle to boil. Someone was knocking on my door. "Just open the door, Rosemary."

I swung the door open midknock. "Yes?" I said in an overly polite manner.

"Can I come in?" Sam asked.

I let him in, and we sat on opposite sides of my couch. Sam slung an arm behind the back of the couch and raised both eyebrows. He looked familiar and unfamiliar at the same time. His hair was the same rumpled mess, that same gray cardigan he had worn that first night, the night we made waffles. It was his expression that felt off-kilter. Like he was challenging me. "He's not here?" Sam asked.

"Who?"

"Your boyfriend." His head pivoted around in an exaggerated way, as if he expected Leo to pop up from behind a plant or crawl out from under a table.

"No," I said carefully. "He's not here."

"That's too bad."

"Why's that?"

"I wanted to meet him."

"You wanted to meet him," I repeated stupidly.

Sam nodded.

"You're saying you want to meet my—my *boyfriend*?"

"I'd love to," Sam said.

"He's not here."

"So you said."

"You don't think I *have* a boyfriend." He hadn't heard me, through the walls. Me and Leo. Thank god.

"It doesn't *seem* like you have a boyfriend. He's never *around*."

I had to suppress a smile then. He'd been watching me, too.

"And what about you?" I asked. "You and . . . Emmeline Wu? How's that working out?"

"Imogene," Sam corrected. "She's from my old band."

"I know that."

"She's visiting." Sam was staring out into the living room. "She was my brother's girlfriend."

"Oh," I said. "Really?" This made sense, then. Sam and Imogene, they had been in a band together. They had that bond. They had both loved T. J., they shared that sadness, and—

"We did hook up a few times," Sam announced, without changing his expression. "After T. J. died."

I squeezed a decorative pillow to my abdomen, just for something to do with my hands. "Huh," I said, trying hard not to picture it. In trying not to picture it, I *was* picturing it, the two of them having sex. She would be on top, whipping her hair all over the place. I squeezed my eyes shut and then opened them again, too wide. All of a sudden I started to cry. Tears streamed down my cheeks. I wiped my face with my hands, but the tears wouldn't stop.

"Rosemary." The hard expression on Sam's face was gone, and he tried to scoot closer to me, but I held up my hands.

"God," I said. "It's none of my business, anyway. And you deserve to be happy. Maybe not with Imogene"—I made a vague gesture in the direction of Sam's apartment—"but someone. Someone else." Sam opened his mouth to respond, but I interrupted him. "I'm sorry." I tried to smile and wiped my face again. "This isn't about you." I was aware of how unconvincing this sounded, though it was true, more or less. "It's my sister. Something's wrong with her. Two dead parents, that suicide attempt. And now—I don't know."

Sam reached out his hand to touch my shoulder but then seemed to think better of it, letting it fall against the back of the couch again. "She seems like a normal enough kid to me." His mouth opened and then shut again, as if he were debating whether or not to add something.

"What?" I asked.

"Nothing. I mean—it's not exactly relevant."

"Just say it—whatever it is."

"It's just—they're Ferguson fans, actually. Wendy and Hannah."

I laughed. "I know."

"They follow us on social media. I've run into her a few times. You know, in the halls."

I straightened up, struck with an idea. "You should talk to her—talk to Wendy."

"Me?"

"She likes you, right? She's your number one fan."

"I wouldn't go that—"

"You've been through this, with your brother."

"You think she's an *addict*?" Sam's eyes narrowed in concern. I could tell what he was thinking—he was thinking that I was officially losing it. Going off the rails. Again.

"Wendy fainted. In school. She just—dropped straight down onto the floor for no apparent reason whatsoever." I threw up my hands. Just take her out to coffee, have a little conversation, I begged him. She would listen to him; I was sure of it. Sam was nodding, considering it. After everything I'd put him through. If I scooted closer, he would put his arms around me. If I kissed him, he would kiss me back. It would be that easy. And then, what? We would have sex here in my living room while Imogene Wu and her stupid fake British accent drank coffee on the other side of the wall, and then I would come to my senses and have to leave him all over again, and he would hate me even more than he probably already did, and he would refuse to help my sister, and I would be left worse off than before, and all of this would have been for nothing.

The sound of breaking glass rang through the apartment, startling both of us.

"I've got to go," I told Sam. "I have to answer that."

Sam gave me a worried look. I was already pulling him off the couch, scooting him out the door. The sound of shattering glass continued. It seemed to be getting louder, glass breaking over and over again on a loop.

With Sam unceremoniously pushed into the hallway, I ran to the Mirror and touched my finger to the screen. Leo's face stared back at me. He wouldn't make it back in this storm, he told me. He was going to wait it out. "Sorry I had to rush off this morning," he said. He had flown up to Seattle. It was snowing there, too, he said. A whiteout.

"I'll miss you," I cooed. He liked that kind of talk. Then I hated myself that I could do it, snap into my role that quickly, like some sort of sex robot.

"You all set with supplies?"

"Supplies?"

"You'll need food, enough food for a week. Bottled water in case the plumbing stops working."

"I live two blocks from Fred Meyer."

"I don't want you going out in this." He was talking like we were in the middle of a blizzard, as if I'd wander out and not be able to find my way home. Like I'd have to dig myself a snow cave and pee on my own hands to stave off frostbite.

"If I need anything, I can always go out and—"

"If you need anything, Alejandro will bring it to you."

"Okay." I rolled my eyes at him.

"There's no sense in risking it. There's no need."

I didn't venture outside the rest of the day. Not because Leo had told me not to, but because I didn't feel like it. I enjoyed it, the novelty of it, of sitting on my couch and watching the snow fall outside the window, landing on the treetops, coating the branches. Down below, children were making snowmen on the sidewalks. An elderly couple glided down the middle of the street on skis.

I texted Wendy to see how she was feeling, and by way of reply she texted me a photo series of her and Hannah, the two of them frolicking in the snow in a city park. They made a snowman, dressed him in one of their scarves, and posed with him between them. They were laughing. They were having a great time. She posted the last picture on social media with the caption SNOW!!! followed by a series of snowflake emojis.

That night I pressed my ear against my bedroom wall. I kept my ear there for a long time. If I closed my eyes and concentrated, I could hear footsteps padding back and forth across the floorboards. I could hear Sam and Imogene laughing and talking, but I couldn't make out any words.

~

The next morning the snow was still falling, but slowly, gently. The streets below had been refreshed with another layer of white. I wanted to go out in it. I'd throw a snowball and look up at the frosted branches and feel the snow crunching under my feet. This type of snowstorm, in Portland, happened once every five years, at the most. Once every decade. Everything shut down—the schools, the offices, half the shops and restaurants.

Wendy was going to stay with Hannah until the roads cleared. I asked about her parents, if they were okay with this. Was Wendy feeling okay? She had just fainted in school. Didn't she want to come home? She said she was fine. This was exactly what she needed, actually. A forced vacation.

I didn't *need* to leave the apartment. It just looked so beautiful out there. Besides, I needed milk.

I bundled up in wool sweaters and scarves and a thick stocking hat with a pom-pom on the top. My feet were swaddled in thick socks and stuffed into my rain boots.

Outside the streets were quiet. I felt like a character in a story, like a tiny figure in a snow globe, with flakes whirling around me. I held out my mittened hand to capture the snowflakes and inspected them. Perfect six-sided snowflakes. All these winters in Portland, I'd never seen one; the snow was usually too loose, too wet, falling to the ground in clumps.

At Fred Meyer people scurried around with carts loaded with supplies. The vegetable bins had been scooped almost clean. Delivery trucks hadn't been able to get in, I overheard someone say. Shipments full of kale and lettuce were shriveling and turning to slime somewhere out there, in the cold.

In my basket I collected some carrots and a potato, a carton of milk, a loaf of bread. I wandered up and down the aisles, picking up items that appealed to me. A jar of peanut butter. A pint of ice cream. A box of Grape-Nuts, Wendy's favorite cereal. She soaked them in skim milk and sprinkled them with packets of artificial sweetener. She must have inherited that from her father, that love of fake sugar. I grimaced and shook my head, erasing the thought from my mind. Wendy was nothing like her father.

As soon as I stepped back in my apartment, I knew something was wrong. It wasn't obvious, not right away. The Mirror, which I'd left behind on the dining room table, was glowing. It wasn't lit up, exactly, or blinking. It was charged with a very subtle, eerie light, like those glow-in-the-dark stars kids stick to their bedroom ceilings.

"Sorry," I said into it, knowing Leo was there, connected through it somehow, waiting. "I accidentally left it at home."

"I told you not to leave."

We stared into our Mirrors, at each other. "I thought you were joking."

"You don't have a coat."

"Seriously?"

"When I say not to go out, I mean—"

"I didn't sign up for this." I was furious.

Leo's face revealed nothing. His features remained frozen in place for so long I wondered if a glitch had occurred, if the transmission had stopped, freezing his image like a pause button. Then his eyebrows came together, slowly. He let out a breath. "Stay safe," he said, his voice a robotic monotone. "Anything could happen out there." Then the screen faded to black.

CHAPTER 18

I didn't leave the apartment for four days. I didn't call Alejandro and ask him to deliver me supplies; I made do with what I had on hand. Crackers and cereal and buttered spaghetti noodles. Wendy remained at Hannah's. She was fine, doing much better. That fainting spell was a fluke. A human head emerging from a woman's body, all red and slick with mucus. It was horrifying. No wonder she'd passed out, just at the sight of it.

"How are you doing?" Wendy asked me one night. I had called her, just to hear her voice. Just to hear anyone's voice. I must have sounded sad, or deranged. I said I was doing fine, and she said maybe she should come back. We could drink hot chocolate and watch movies. Unexpectedly, hot tears burbled from my eyes and spilled down my cheeks. No, no, I insisted, keeping my voice bright. Normal. I didn't want them out on the roads, not in these conditions. Cars were veering off the streets, people were abandoning their vehicles on highway overpasses and braving their way home by foot. Stay there, I told her. Where you'll be safe.

I was bored out of my mind, pacing the floors of my apartment, pressing my ear to the wall between my room and Sam's, hoping—or desperately *not* hoping—to hear him. Him and Imogene. I heard only one set of footsteps, the usual set of footsteps. Sam padding down the hall and into his room. Sam—only Sam—practicing the viola. Imogene was gone, I decided. Long gone.

During those days, Leo didn't call again. I imagined him staring into his Mirror, waiting for me to wander by a Glasseye.

On the fifth day, the snow began to melt into dirty piles of slush piled up on the sides of the streets. I got dressed in warm clothes and considered leaving. Just a quick run to the store, maybe a coffee. The danger was over.

I was standing in the entryway, but I didn't leave. I was hovering at the threshold. Something was keeping me from stepping over it. Leo would call. He'd send me a message: you are permitted to leave. I wanted to laugh at myself. What was I doing, letting a man tell me when I could and could not leave my own apartment? I could leave. I could walk out. I *should* walk out. I didn't have to do anything he said. I didn't have to follow any of his rules.

That was where I was—glued to the floor in the entryway of my apartment—when someone knocked on the door. No one knocked on the door unless they already lived in the building—you had to be buzzed in. I threw the door open to find a young man standing before me. He presented me with a large, flat garment box with a ribbon tied around it. "Special delivery," he said.

He looked like Alejandro. Perfectly coifed black hair, check. Nerd-cool glasses, check. Dark-wash skinny jeans, check. He wasn't Alejandro, though. He was taller, for one, with long fingers and smooth, well-manicured fingernails. His face was narrower, too. His nose long and thin, his eyes golden instead of dark brown. Someone had taken Alejandro and stretched him out.

"Who are you?"

"Me?" the guy said. He didn't talk like Alejandro. Nervous, unsure of himself. "I'm supposed to give this to you." He tried to hand the box to me again, but I didn't make a move to unburden him. I stood halfway out the door, inspecting him.

"You didn't answer my question."

"Oh—right." He laughed, a weak little chuckle. He really was nervous. "I'm Teddy? I'm Leo Glass's assistant. He told me to deliver this package to you. He wants to see you, tonight."

179

"Where's Alejandro?"

"Alejandro is—" Teddy swallowed. His Adam's apple bobbed up and down. "I'm replacing Alejandro."

"*What?*" Teddy opened his mouth to explain further, but I waved my hand in front of his face. "What happened to Alejandro?"

"I just started yesterday, so—"

I held a finger up, silencing him. Then I took out my Mirror to message Alejandro. When I clicked on my Lookinglass contacts, I was used to seeing two there. Leo and Alejandro. But where Alejandro's profile picture—the top half of his face, from the thick-rimmed glasses on up—used to be, a new one appeared in its place. Teddy.

I took the box out of his hands. "Listen, Teddy, you're not supposed to come up here. This is off limits, okay?"

"Downstairs was open, so I just thought—"

"I won't tell anyone, okay? Just don't do it again."

I took the box from Teddy and closed the door. If it was another Leo Glass–themed jogging outfit, I would freak out. The box felt heavier than a sweat suit, though.

I set the package on the dining room table and pulled off the bow. Inside the box was the most beautiful coat I'd ever seen in real life. A black double-breasted trench coat in a soft, almost shiny cashmere wool. It fit perfectly. I traipsed through the apartment with it on, feeling the softness of the fabric. In my bedroom, I admired myself in my full-length mirror, turning around, posing. I looked like a movie star playing a glamorous detective.

~

"Thanks for the coat," I said when I arrived at Leo's apartment that evening. I paced back and forth in front of him and spun around once, modeling it. I wouldn't mention the four days imprisoned in my apartment, all alone. I had had a lot of time to think, those last four days.

The question I kept mulling over was the same one I had been asking all along: Was it worth it? I had voluntarily signed my life over to this guy who watched me with Glasseyes, who trashed my coat, who told me to stay in my apartment, or else. Or else what? What was he going to do? I didn't know what I was afraid of, back then. I just know that even after the snow had melted, I hadn't walked out that door.

I don't want to think I stayed because of a coat, a brand-new cashmere wool trench. As soon as I put it on, I knew I would do anything Leo asked me to do. Sitting in an apartment for four days, had it really been so bad? He had been worried about me was all. Worried about my safety. If someone wanted to pay me to sit out a snowstorm in a beautiful apartment, I could do that. In the meantime, that apartment was a safe haven for my sister. She needed that more than ever right now. It was a way out, a way forward. The only way out and forward. I didn't see any other way but to lie in that bed I had made for myself.

And I really did love the coat.

"Beautiful," Leo said. He placed a hand on each of my shoulders and looked me up and down. "Looks like it fits."

"It's perfect." It wasn't exactly practical. It didn't have to be, though.

Leo bent his head down as if to kiss me, but then it looked like he thought better of it. He stared at me and I stared back, straight into the black pools of his pupils. We stood like that, eyes locked, for an uncomfortable length of time, but I didn't let my gaze falter. "Are you ready to take this to the next level?" Leo asked me.

I didn't know what he was talking about, but I said I was. I was ready for anything.

~

Leo wanted me to make him dinner. "Let's go out," I said. "I've been cooped up for the last four days."

"I've already bought the ingredients," he told me. "Follow the recipe." He said something in Spanish to Consuela, and a recipe—handwritten in cursive on a vintage recipe card labeled FROM THE KITCHEN OF *Christine*—appeared on the mirror over his stove.

After I breaded and fried slices of eggplant, after I layered them in the baking dish with sauce and cheese, after we sat down at Leo's table and ate everything I'd made, everything I'd made while Leo sat on a stool and watched, after we'd finished our glasses of wine and little dishes of gelato for dessert, Leo said he had a surprise for me. He disappeared into his room and emerged a few moments later in a charcoal-gray suit.

His hand slipped into the suit jacket and came out with the Mirror. On the screen, a barcode. "Surprise," he said.

I shook my head. "What is it?"

"Symphony tickets."

"Symphony tickets." To my credit, my voice didn't catch on the words.

"Taking it to the next level," Leo said. "That's what we agreed on, right?"

"Right."

I kept my arm threaded through his and matched his pace as we crossed the street. Hard, dirty patches of snow remained on the grass of the Park Blocks. The concert hall blinked before us. The whole building twinkled with lights, beckoning us. "What are they playing tonight?" I asked in a steady voice.

"Brahms. The Academic Festival Overture."

"Brahms," I repeated in a whimsical way, as if to imply a greater connection to the music than I actually had, as if the very idea of a night listening to Brahms enchanted me.

The walk to the concert hall took all of a minute, maybe two. In those two minutes, my mind clicked through all the possibilities, starting with the worst-case scenario. Worst-case scenario, he knew about me and Sam, and he was taking me to the symphony to taunt me, to taunt us. He planned to disgrace us both.

But, I reasoned with myself, I'd ended things with Sam *months* ago. If Leo knew, wouldn't he have tested me back then?

Second-worst scenario: He wasn't *sure* about me and Sam, but he wanted to take me to the symphony as some sort of test. He wanted to see how much I'd reveal, or what secrets I'd keep close to my chest.

Best-case scenario: We were going to the symphony because it struck him as a fine idea. Something fun to do on a night out. A real date. That was what he wanted—just to go out like a regular couple. Well, that was exactly what we were doing.

We had excellent seats, right in the front row of the mezzanine. Flipping through the program, I made a decision. I started back at the beginning of the program, this time turning the pages slowly, as if I were studying each one. Near the end were the bios. Strings first. There were a lot of violin players. Violas would be next. Sure enough, there was the principal viola chair. Then two other guys. Then a woman. Then Sam.

In his picture, he was staring intently at the camera. His hair looked shorter and neater than I was used to seeing it, as if he'd had it styled for this photo shoot. He was wearing a tuxedo and holding the viola, the neck just visible in the bottom of the frame.

It both did and didn't look like Sam. I could stay silent. If Leo mentioned it later—insisted that he knew something, that he knew everything—I would have plausible deniability.

Or I could get ahead of him. "That's my neighbor." I pointed at Sam's picture and smiled over at Leo. We looked up on the stage, where the musicians were sitting, tuning their instruments, and I pointed him out to Leo. "There he is."

Leo frowned and took the program from my hands. "He studied under Magdalene Heiss. She's a big deal."

I searched his face for any hint that he knew something, or that he was testing me. I couldn't find one.

"He was in this band called Ferguson." This information was straight from the program. "Do you know them?"

"I might have heard them on NPR or something."

"Wendy is a big fan, actually."

Again I studied Leo's face. He looked . . . mildly interested. That was it. I started to relax in my chair. Maybe this was all a coincidence. Nothing more. Going to the symphony was a perfectly ordinary activity, especially when you lived right across the street from the concert hall. Leo probably went all the time. He probably had season tickets.

Leo snaked his arm around my shoulders and kissed my temple. "Here we go," he whispered as the lights dimmed and a spotlight appeared in the center of the stage. A bald man in a tuxedo made some announcements about special events going on over the summer, about musicians already on the docket for next year's program. Behind him, a lowercase letter *g* appeared on a screen I hadn't realized was there, and then the man was saying, "As you may already know, these endeavors are made possible thanks to our partnership with Lookinglass. Lookinglass's CEO, Leo Glass, has long been a generous sponsor to the symphony. Tonight marks the first night of what we hope quickly becomes a global phenomenon."

I turned to Leo, who squeezed my shoulder. The bald man in the tuxedo was going on about how the entire concert hall was now crawling with Glasseyes, little cameras perched on every rafter, catching the action onstage from every possible angle. Through Lookinglass, watchers all over the world would be able to tune in to every performance. What a wonderful way for the "less fortunate" to participate in the arts, to immerse themselves in the world of music. The bald guy was really patting himself on the back there, bragging how as an organization, they were pioneers of this cutting-edge innovation, music for the people, and Lookinglass was instrumental in that—excuse the pun.

The picture on the screen switched to Leo. To Leo and me, larger than life. Leo was smiling and waving, revealing all of his evenly tiled teeth. I was there, cowering next to him, my eyes wide and scared, like someone emerging from captivity. The audience was applauding, and Leo whispered into my ear, "Smile," and I widened my lips into the semblance of a smile. He kissed my temple again and, finally, the screen flashed back to the musicians on the stage.

As I watched the musicians play, I tried not to focus on Sam, tried not to pick him out of the sea of faces on the stage. I closed my eyes and tried to hear him, just him, a dark little voice in the background, harmonizing with the higher, brasher voices of the violins. He must have seen me there, up on the screen, seen Leo Glass kissing my temple, squeezing my shoulder. Seen my mouth open wide in that jack-o'-lantern grin.

The after-party—of course there was an after-party—took place in a room that rivaled the concert hall in elegance. A big, open space with shiny floors and gold and crystal chandeliers. Waiters circulated with trays of hors d'oeuvres and glasses of champagne. I grabbed a glass off a tray as a waiter passed by and began drinking at once, finishing it in three greedy gulps.

None of the musicians appeared to be here. Maybe they weren't coming. Leo and I were the youngest people in attendance by about thirty years. The crowd was a sea of gray hair and sequined gowns and dark suits.

Then they arrived, all together. The musicians—only about a dozen of them, not the whole orchestra—stood together in a semicircle around the conductor, who raised his baton. They lifted their instruments, the baton went down, and they began to play.

I recognized this one, too. It was a part of Sam's repertoire. A lively piece, one that got everyone smiling and clapping and migrating toward the source of the music so they could be a part of it, a part of something amazing, an encore just for us.

Sam was there. He was tapping his foot to the beat, dipping his head, his hair messed up and flopping like it did in all the Ferguson videos.

Leo was concentrating on the music, his head bobbing in time with the beat. Was it my imagination, or was he focusing on Sam in particular? Leo bent down and whispered in my ear, "He's good, isn't he?"

Before I could open my mouth to answer, Leo started making his way to the bar on the other side of the room. I followed him mutely. I second-guessed myself again. Maybe he had no idea. I just needed to play it cool.

At the bar, Leo presented me with a dry martini. When I sipped, alcohol fumes bubbled up my nose. A good stiff drink. Okay. That was how I was going to get through this.

I turned around with my drink, but Leo was no longer by my side. No, he was ten feet in front of me, an animated look on his face, talking to someone. Through the crowd, I couldn't see who it was, but I knew. I knew before I sidled up next to him and saw with my own eyes. He was talking to Sam.

I linked my arm through Leo's and gave Sam a cool smile. "Hello," I said, interrupting their conversation. I hadn't heard anything either of them were saying. I'd decided to jump in, the way you needed to jump into an ice-cold pool, all at once.

I extended my hand for Sam to shake. He had to shift his viola to his other side to offer me his hand. We locked eyes, and I gave him a steely stare as we shook. I prayed that he'd get it, this silent communication. "I'm Rosemary," I said. "We've met a few times. You're my next-door neighbor."

"Of course," Sam said.

In that moment when our hands were touching, I could feel something between us, like an electric shock. He felt it, too, I could tell. He recovered, though. "Leo was just telling me that."

"My sister, Wendy, is a big fan," I said.

"It's always nice to meet a Ferguson fan. It's not like there are that many of them."

Leo chuckled at this. He asked Sam about Magdalene Heiss, the teacher. "I saw her perform once, in Vienna. She is remarkable."

"Excuse me." I slid my arm out of Leo's and dipped my head in a demure way, the lady's method of announcing she needed to retire to the restroom.

I slipped into the crowd. I walked slowly at first, moving my hips back and forth like a model on the catwalk, in case Leo was watching. When I got out of their eyesight, I sped up, pushing past waiters and the gray-haired ladies. My heart was pounding in my throat, and my vision dimmed. I was still holding the martini glass in my hand. It was empty. I set it on a small table I passed by on my way out of the main room and into a long hallway. It was quieter in there. My footsteps echoed down the polished stone floors.

The restroom was large, one of those old-fashioned lounges with a seating area complete with makeup tables and upholstered chairs. It was empty, and for that I was grateful. I bent over, resting my hands on my knees, and breathed in and out rapidly. I was hyperventilating. I was wheezing, the air stuck in my throat. I closed my eyes and tried to focus. Breathe, I told myself. Breathe.

Just hours before, I had told Leo Glass I was up for anything. He made me sit inside my apartment for four days for my own personal safety, I had convinced myself. Threw away my old coat because I deserved a beautiful new one. And he took me to the symphony because he loves classical music. Sure. Maybe.

After a moment, I stood back up and smoothed out the skirt of my dress. A woman entered the restroom and beelined straight toward the stalls. I examined myself in the mirror and adjusted my hair. I looked fairly decent, my face flushed but not terribly so. I reapplied my lipstick and gave myself an approving nod.

I strode out confidently and ran straight into Sam. A pair of old ladies were walking toward us. Two of Sam's orchestra pals, a man and a woman, were whispering together on the other side of the hall, next to the men's restroom.

Sam gripped me by the arms, and for a second I thought he might start shaking me, but he let go with a heavy sigh, as if he didn't know what had come over him. "*Jesus*, Rosemary." He didn't sound angry. Just—exasperated.

"I didn't know we were coming here tonight. If I had, I'd—" I wasn't sure why I was explaining this to him.

"Leo Glass?" He shook his head in disbelief. "Leo *Glass?*"

"I should have told you," I said in a hushed voice.

The couple near the men's restroom were looking at us now. Anyone could walk by and see us arguing out here. Leo could see us. He was probably watching us right now.

"*He's* your boyfriend? *That's* the guy—"

"Keep your voice down." My eyes darted around again. The couple across the hall weren't looking at us anymore, but they weren't engrossed in each other, either. The woman who had entered the restroom came back out. I waited until she was out of earshot before continuing. "We can't talk here," I said, my voice low and urgent. "He could be watching."

Sam looked up and down the hallway. "Let him watch."

I looked around, too, casting my eyes along the walls, up to the high, tiled ceiling. "With Glasseyes," I whispered.

"So what?" Sam said. "We're just talking."

It didn't make any sense. I couldn't pin anything down. If I told him Leo asked me to wear a fancy dress and buy kitchen equipment with him at La Cuisine, if I said he carried Wendy up the stairs and stayed the night when he promised to never set foot in my apartment, if I told him I had locked myself inside for four days just because Leo said so—I would sound pathetic.

"He fired someone," I blurted out. "All of a sudden, for no reason, replaced him with someone else."

"What are you saying?"

"I think something might have happened to him," I said, "to Alejandro." I hadn't thought that until the moment I said it, but now I wondered if it might be true. He just disappeared, with no warning, and someone who looked just like him popped up in his place. It was a message, I realized. Leo was trying to tell me something: I was replaceable. And he was probably watching me at that moment, while I stood in the hallway engaged in an intense conversation with Sam.

Sam placed his hands on my arms again, gently this time. He stared into my eyes, as if trying to divine the truth, a coded message. He probably thought I was a battered woman. I was acting like that, a little off-kilter. The reality was, Leo hadn't done anything. He hadn't even touched me—not since that one time—let alone abused me. He was harmless.

"*Rosemary*—"

"I'm fine, Sam. Truly. And Leo is a really nice guy. I—I should have told you it was him."

He wasn't buying this. I glanced over his shoulder across the hall. The other two musicians were straining to listen. Their conversation had stopped. They were leaning against the wall, their heads cocked toward us.

He lowered his voice so deep I had to strain to hear him. I leaned in toward his lips. "If you're in trouble. If he's *hurting* you—"

"I can take care of myself."

Sam stepped back and folded his arms in front of him. He inspected me with narrowed eyes. "All right." He frowned and nodded his head. "All right."

I straightened up and stared back. The standoff lasted so long I began to worry that we would be here all night, frozen in our spots, neither of us backing down.

"I talked to your sister, by the way," Sam said at last. "Like you asked."

This surprised me. "When? She hasn't been home since before the storm."

"I messaged her. She says you have nothing to worry about. She has lost a little weight, but it's because she's gone vegan. She didn't want to tell you."

It took me a few moments to process this. Then I laughed. I laughed so loudly I could hear it bounce off the polished stone walls. "Vegan?" Sam looked confused. "No, I mean, this is great. I thought she was on *drugs*." Leave it to a teenager to make a major dietary change without telling anyone. She probably had a protein deficiency. She was low on her B vitamins. I needed to get some vegan cookbooks. We could make nutritious meals together, coconut curries and black bean tacos. I'd fatten her up with guacamole and cashew cream. It would be easy.

"You still need to talk to her. She has a lot going on."

"Thanks, Sam." I grinned and clapped him on the shoulder, like he was an old pal, and I pretended to ignore the expression on his face. Once again I became aware of how this must look, the two of us standing in the hallway together. "Well, it was nice seeing you again, Sam," I said in a normal—or possibly much louder than normal—voice. I straightened up and threw my shoulders back, and his hands fell down to his sides. I pivoted and walked away at a brisk pace, my heels click-clacking on the floors. The walk seemed interminable, my footsteps louder than gunshots.

~

Back in the main hall, I spotted Leo conversing with a short, round man in a tuxedo. I strode up to him purposefully. "Let's go," I said to Leo. Leo had given me a warning. A series of warnings: he was watching, and I was replaceable. At that moment, I didn't know what I thought he was capable of, but I definitely thought he was capable of something.

That if I didn't do exactly what he wanted, exactly how he wanted, that harm would come to me somehow. That I'd disappear.

"Rosemary, I'd like you to meet—"

"I'm not feeling well. I need to get out of here."

"Of course." Leo made his apologies to the round man and led me out the door.

We walked back to his loft in silence. In the kitchen, he offered me some ginger ale, a few crackers.

"I feel fine," I said.

He narrowed his eyes at me, and I came up next to him, fiddling with his bow tie. I offered him what I hope was a seductive smile. "The next level. Isn't that what you said?" I slipped the tuxedo jacket off his shoulders and it crumpled to the ground.

Leo held up a warning hand. "Why are you doing this?"

"I'm in this," I said. "I want you to know that." My fingers began working on loosening his bow tie. He didn't stop me. I worked on the buttons of his shirt.

"Remember what I said, when we first met?" he asked.

"You said a lot of things," I murmured.

"About what makes a relationship work."

"It's a choice."

"Right." He gave me a hard look again. I unbuckled his belt, and his eyelids fluttered closed. "I love you," he said, head tilted up to the ceiling. Then his head snapped back upright and he looked straight at me. "Tell me you love me."

I exhaled slowly, playing along. I'd figured him out, what he wanted, what I needed to do. He wanted to do this right, he had said. He wanted to have a girlfriend, to fall in love. It was almost sweet, in a twisted kind of way. Love wasn't about compatibility or common goals. It wasn't a feeling. Wasn't that what he'd said? It was a choice. Also, it was my job.

My eyes met his, and I tried to imbue mine with passion, with feeling. "Yes," I said.

As soon as the word left my lips, Leo hoisted me up into a fireman's carry and strode purposefully into his bedroom, where he tossed me onto his bed—a maneuver that worked better in romance novels than real life. My body bounced on the mattress, and my arms shot out to steady myself. "Sorry," Leo said.

I just laughed, rose up to my knees, and reached behind myself to unzip my dress. Midzip, I paused.

"What?" Leo's eyes darted across my face. His curls seemed to jut out in every direction. "What is it?"

"They aren't watching us, are they?" I whispered. My eyes traveled to the ceiling, as if I might detect some secret Glasseye hidden behind a light bulb, jabbed into a crack in the ceiling.

"We've been over this," he said, but his voice was affectionate. "Look." He took his Mirror from his back pocket and tapped on the Lookinglass icon. "Here's my feed."

Inside the round screen was another circle, like a frame. Inside the frame it was blank, pure white.

"And here's you," he said, tapping over to my profile. Blank as well.

"No one's watching," he said, tucking the Mirror back in his pocket. He leaned in to plant kisses up and down my neck, so close I could smell him, that strange, almost antiseptic scent he had, like a hospital. Like a public bathroom with the CLOSED FOR CLEANING sign propped in the doorway.

He stood up next to the bed, forcing me to look up at him. I reached out to touch him, but he stepped backward, still maintaining eye contact. Then he undressed, one piece at a time. First the tie. He finished loosening the knot I'd started, yanked the material from around his neck, and hurled it to the corner of the room. Then the shirt. He undid the rest of the buttons and then ripped the shirt off in a flourish, revealing that surprisingly tanned and muscled chest of his. I wondered, idly, if he visited tanning beds. Did people still go to tanning beds? It was dangerous, wasn't it? Overexposure to UV rays and all that . . .

He stepped out of his pants and stood before me, waiting. I nodded once, like I was a boss issuing a demand. "Do it," that nod said.

In one very deft movement, he freed himself from his underwear, and then he stood before me completely naked. I was lucky, I supposed. If I was going to get paid to sleep with someone, I'd much rather be paid to sleep with a young, ripped billionaire than some Hugh Hefner type.

Leo knelt on the floor before me. I wrapped my legs around him and ran my hands through his hair. I leaned in to kiss him.

"Say it," he said when we broke apart.

So I said it. I didn't say the words out loud, but I met his eyes and mouthed them with my lips, slowly. I'd never said those words to any guy before. I'd only said them to my own mother. I knew the last time I said them, too. The last day I ever saw her, the day I left home.

He groaned and buried his face in my neck. Then he pushed me back onto the bed, so I was lying with my feet hanging over the edge, and he pulled my underwear off, tossing it over his shoulder. He leaped back on top of me. Within seconds, he was inside me.

"Are you okay?" Leo had stopped moving. He was poised on top of me, raising himself up by the arms, looking down at me. He looked different from this angle, his curls dangling down.

My body lay still beneath him. I'd been lying there, unmoving. A dead starfish. "Yes," I said. And then, as if to explain my behavior, I added, "I'm just nervous." I was having a hard time keeping my head in the game. I had to remind myself that it wasn't me. It was the person pretending to be in love with Leo Glass.

He kissed me on the forehead and then on the lips. When I kissed him back, he started to move again.

I responded with a little moan. You love him, I told myself. My eyelids fluttered closed. It wasn't working. My hands roamed up and down Leo's back. He had a good body. I could work with that. Pretend he's Sam, the little voice inside my head told me. My body tensed up at that suggestion, causing Leo to stop again. *Okay, okay*—my mind buzzed, desperately searching for a way through this. *Pretend he's Steele.*

Fine. I could do that. Steele and I, we'd had some good times together. I hadn't had to fake anything with him. Usually we were both drunk. He had his own brand of charm. Pretend you're running your hand over Steele's back. Pretend you're kissing Steele on the mouth. Pretend Steele is flipping you over to position you on top, that his hands are reaching up, that his fingers are the ones squeezing—

Leo shouted when he finished. His hands released my breasts, and his arms fell down to the mattress, spread out wide. I looked down at him, studied his face. His eyes were closed, his head lolled back, a huge smile still lingering on his lips.

I lifted myself off him and was about to excuse myself to the bathroom, but he pulled me next to him, into the crook of his arm. He ran a finger down my body, from my shoulder, down my side, up over my hip. I resisted the temptation to swat his hand away. Instead, I made another move to leave, but as soon as I started to roll away, he clasped my hip with his whole hand. "Stay another minute." He kissed me on the mouth, like we had all the time in the world.

"I need to—"

"*Shh.* Just for a minute." Leo petted my hair, talking. He told me about how love had eluded him, all these years. That was exactly how he put it: "Love has eluded me." He planted a kiss on my head, his lips getting tangled up with my hair. "The thing is—what people don't realize—is how hard it is for someone like me to meet people. Women, I mean."

"I have a hard time believing that," I managed to say. I ran my hand over his bare chest. It was completely bare—no hair at all. I wondered if he shaved it, or if he was naturally hairless, like one of those cats.

"Women these days," he went on, "they have lives of their own. Careers. As they should! I'm not going to stop them. More power to them, you know."

I said I did know.

"But it's difficult. I have a career, they have a career—when do you ever see each other? When do you have time to fall in love?"

"I know." My eyelids closed. I felt gross. Our bodies fused together with some sticky substance. Cold liquid dripped out between my legs. It was going to dry there, glue me shut. "You told me this, remember?"

"I know, I know," Leo was saying. "But that's what got me thinking—how I came up with this whole thing. What if I just eliminated that obstacle—"

"What obstacle?"

"The woman's career." Oh. Of course. That. "What if we didn't have to worry about that? We could give this thing a real shot. No one really tries anymore—have you noticed that? They just move on from one person to the next. What if we agreed to stick it out for a year? What would happen then?"

"I don't know," I murmured. If I couldn't get up and take a shower, maybe I could fall asleep.

Leo laughed and, in one swift movement, rolled on top of me, wedging one of his legs between mine. He kissed me on my mouth and then peppered my neck with little kisses. They felt like nibbles, creating the sensation of being devoured by tiny mandibles, of bugs crawling on my skin. Leo was writhing over me, and I felt him getting hard again. Surely it was too soon for that—

"We fell in love," he said into my ear, his voice thick and urgent. "That's what happened."

~

On my car ride home, my Mirror began to pulse. I took it out of my purse and tapped on its screen. You have 1,835 new watchers, the notification read. I jolted upright, startled, convinced for a moment that he'd tricked me somehow, that I'd just put on a sex show for 1,835 strangers. I scanned through my recent activity, unsure of what I was even looking for. I never used Lookinglass aside from the messaging feature, when Leo wanted to communicate with me. I'd never even filled out my profile.

A few moments tapping around set my mind at ease. My new watchers seemed to fall into two camps. Most of them had names like Dvorjackie and Symphonee_Love. Music lovers. Or they went by something like Geeklord or Daemon Demon. Programming nerds, Leo Glass acolytes.

They had seen me at the symphony. That was all. I could handle that.

CHAPTER 19

It was the first sunny day we'd had in months. With the light hitting the windows, suddenly the grime of winter became visible. Dust and fingerprints. It surprised me, this filth. We'd hardly been around lately. I'd been spending so much time with Leo, and Wendy was busy at school and hanging out with Hannah. My poor apartment had the neglected look of a school shuttered for summer vacation.

I tied an actual apron around my waist and bustled around, dusting surfaces with an old T-shirt. I watered my Christmas cactus. All its blooms were gone now. The desiccated blossoms gathered in the dustpan. Light as air, bright red faded to rust. I crushed one to powder in my hands and tasted it with the tip of my tongue. It tasted like nothing at all.

After all that rushing around tidying, sweeping, dusting, washing, and polishing, the apartment felt stifling. The radiators clinked off and on, off and on, and there was no way to stop them from pumping out heat. I stood on a dining room chair and fiddled with the top window sashes, jiggling them loose from their frames. Soon I had them open from both the top and bottom. The stale air flew out, and a fresh breeze rushed in.

Spring cleaning and airing out the house. These seemed like such old-fashioned, wholesome things to do. I put my hands on my hips and surveyed my surroundings, like a proud housewife. I would bake cookies, I decided. Something vegan. Wendy would come home from school, greeted by their freshly baked aroma. We would sit here in our immaculate, well-kept home, we would eat vegan cookies, and she would tell me all about her day—all her little triumphs and troubles and fears.

I really should be doing this every day. What kind of sister was I?

With the windows open, I could hear the viola. It wasn't classical music. Something new. Whatever it was, it reminded me of the Ferguson stuff. Sam was composing something, maybe? Working on some new material? Good. He was moving on, as he should. That was what I wanted for Sam. At least, that was what I *would* want for Sam, if I were a selfless person.

I was still standing in the middle of the apartment in my proud housewife pose when I felt something whoosh over my head so fast it rustled my hair. I screamed and ran for cover under the dining room table. Through the legs of a chair, I watched as a bird darted back and forth through the living room and dining room, back and forth, up and down. It was panicked, its wings flapping furiously.

Finally the bird landed, balancing itself on the light fixture dangling from the living room ceiling. I stared up at it and debated whether or not I should crawl out from under the table. What if I did, and the bird flew at me? I didn't know what kind of bird it was. It wasn't a vulture or a crow—just a small, brown bird. I didn't know enough about birds to know if it was the kind that would attack me. I didn't want to crawl out from under the table only to have it dive at me, pecking my eyes out and ripping off my clothes with its angry beak.

A memory. I was about twelve, Wendy four. We were outside, making forts in the sagebrush. We'd found the perfect place, a clearing of bitterbrush we covered with more sticks and branches until we formed a little cave we could crawl into. We covered the floor with an old blanket and spent hours playing out there, pretending we lived there. We'll run away, I told Wendy. At that age, it was all I wanted to do—get out.

It didn't occur to me that you needed to run farther than your own backyard to escape.

One day Jason called to us from the driveway while we were crouched down in our fort. I laid Wendy down on the dusty blanket. *Shh,* I whispered. Let's pretend we're asleep. Wendy closed her eyes tightly and made fake snoring sounds.

Girls! Jason yelled, adamant this time.

We climbed out of the fort and scrambled up to the driveway to see what he wanted, and he was standing there, his hands cupped together. He told us to come to him, and he opened up his palms, slowly, until we could see what he had hidden inside. A tiny cottontail bunny, with two perfect ears, a quivering nose, and a soft fluff of a tail.

You can pet him, Jason said. We each took a turn, petting the animal with careful fingers. Its whole body was trembling. We could feel it pulsing under our fingertips.

He's scared, Jason told us. He hid the bunny back inside his cupped palms. And now he's going to die.

We screamed in unison. No, no! Don't kill it! We thought he was going to crush the bunny with his bare hands.

Jason laughed. He had a deep, booming kind of laugh. I'm not going to kill it. He's already dead, he said. It's our human scent. His mother won't let him back home. He won't survive the night.

That haunted me for a long time. We killed it. We killed this helpless, trembling little creature with our human scent.

I crawled out from under the dining room table and into the kitchen, searching for something I could use to capture the bird. A dish towel? A colander? I settled on a stainless steel mixing bowl. Bowl in hand, I crept back into the living room. The bird had moved during my absence and was waiting for me on the coffee table, perched on a stack of books.

The plan was murky at best. Contain the bird by throwing the bowl on top of him and call animal control. Have a professional deal with it, an ornithologist. Someone in a khaki safari suit would arrive with a net and sort this out for me. Or perhaps I could fill the bowl with bait—sunflower seeds or worms or bread crumbs—and the bird would hop inside, allowing itself to be transported out the window where it could fly free.

As soon as I got within two feet of my feathered friend, he charged straight toward me. I screamed and held the bowl up to my face, but then somehow I lost my balance, stumbled backward. I landed on the floor with a thud, and the bowl went skittering off to the side. The bird took off again, zigzagging over my head, wings whirring.

"Stop!" I yelled to it. My screams were met with a shrill, almost sad little squawk and the furious flapping of wings. "Please, stop!"

Someone was pounding on the door and yelling my name.

It was Sam.

"Help!" I screamed.

The doorknob rattled. "Let me in."

I ran to the door and crouched down, while the bird flew overhead like a bomber pilot.

Sam rushed in. "Where is he?"

"Over there." The bird had taken Sam's arrival as an invitation to settle down. It had landed, tucked back its wings. I could see his chest vibrating, his heart beating a million beats a minute. "On the lamp."

Sam's narrowed eyes surveyed the scene. Then he looked back at me. "I thought he was attacking you."

"He was."

"I mean—" I had successfully avoided Sam for more than a month, since that night at the symphony.

He had changed, shed some layers in the warmer weather, like a snake. Hair a little shorter. Barefoot, in a soft gray T-shirt and faded jeans. They were the jeans he'd let me wear, way back when. I could tell by the way they were worn at the knees.

"It's just a bird," I said unnecessarily.

"I can see that."

The bird watched as Sam approached him. It may have been my imagination, but the bird's heart began to beat more slowly the closer Sam got. Sam reached out his arm, toward the bird, and the bird didn't fly away. He watched Sam with trusting, unblinking eyes.

"What are you going to do?" I whispered, tiptoeing behind Sam.

"I'm going to let him out."

And then, like the kid in *My Side of the Mountain*, Sam extended his index finger to the bird. The bird cocked his head and then climbed aboard like a man stepping onto a train.

Slowly, Sam walked, the bird perched on his finger, over to the window. He stepped onto the chair I had left there, reached his hand out the open window, and made a quick shooing motion.

The bird took off, flapped his wings rapidly, testing them out. We watched until he disappeared from view.

"He'll probably die out there," I said. "They'll smell you on him. Your human scent."

"He'll be fine."

"You don't know that."

"Where's Wendy?" he said.

"It's the middle of the afternoon. She's at school."

"It's Saturday."

"Oh." A wave of concern washed over Sam's face. I laughed nervously, trying to come up with something. "I forgot," I said. "She's—she has a study group. A group project *for* school."

"Okay."

Our eyes met for a moment. Sam looked as if he were about to say something but had decided against it. He started toward the door.

"Are you going somewhere?" he asked. We'd reached the entryway. He saw my suitcase, the one I'd just brought up from basement storage.

"France," I said, because it was the truth, and I didn't have the wherewithal to come up with a convincing lie.

"France, huh?" He was shaking his head, as if he couldn't imagine why anyone would want to go there.

"Thanks for rescuing me," I said. "Again."

Sam's lips parted, then closed again. Then he started speaking, the words coming out in a rush, a *what the hell* expression on his face. "Listen, Leo Glass—he's not who you think he is. Have you read about the working conditions in his factories in China? Who knows how many international labor laws he's— And then there are the environmental issues. Privacy violations." Sam ran his fingers through his hair. His words picked up speed. "You know he's selling *surveillance packages* to unstable governments. They're already using Glasseyes to arrest dissenters in Singapore. You *have* to have read about this . . ." He stopped, midstream, pausing for air.

"Wow," I said. "You've really done your research."

"This isn't some top-secret information; it's practically common knowledge. God, Rosemary, just google him."

"You're making him sound much worse than he is. When he found out about those factory conditions he—" I remembered reading something about this, but couldn't quite recall how the situation resolved. "He's trying to change that," I concluded. "And he just donated like a million dollars or something to—"

"I can't believe you're with this guy. I can't believe you're *voluntarily* with this guy. Whatever arrangement you have with him—"

"It's not an 'arrangement.' He's my boyfriend." I put my hand to my forehead and squeezed my eyes closed for a moment. I didn't know what to do or what I wanted. Looking back, it seems like what I wanted was for Sam to rescue me. He saw me, he saw me flapping my wings and banging my head against the glass, he was telling me this, but I wasn't listening. Maybe I wanted him to save me, to swoop me up and into his arms and tell me he would take care of everything. But why would he? We were just neighbors. We had spent what amounted to two days together.

"I know he's not your boyfriend." Sam rested a hand on my shoulder and gave me a sad, knowing look. I wondered what he would do if I collapsed onto his chest, or if I smashed my lips onto his. I wanted to. I wanted to let him whisk me away from all this. I could feel the heat from his hand radiate down through the fabric of my shirt and onto my skin.

Sam inched closer to me. "Because I know you." He was staring at me with an intense focus I'd never seen in him before. "And I know what you want."

I stopped breathing, and in one split second, a wild fantasy spooled out of my head—that I'd tell him everything, that he'd say he understood, and he would tell me how to fix it, this mess I was in. Or he would just fix it for me, the way he climbed out his window and walked along that ledge to open my door, or ushered that bird out into the spring sky. He would fix it, and I would be grateful, and we would fall into each other's arms and live happily ever after.

All this came to me in the space between breaths. When I did inhale, it sounded like a gasp.

"Why would you be with someone like him?" Sam was asking me. "Money?" I shook my head, but he went on as if I hadn't responded at all. "Whatever it was, you could have just been *honest* about it—"

I stepped back, and his hand fell from my shoulder, the spell broken. I laughed. "You can't be serious."

"Just give me one logical reason why you'd be with Leo Glass of all people, and I'll shut up about this."

"So you're saying I'm so desperate for money, right?" I managed to deliver this line in the most disdainful tone possible, despite the fact that he had guessed everything exactly right. "But I should have just *told* you about it. You. A one-night stand. A guy who lives for free in his aunt's apartment."

Sam didn't flinch. "I could have helped you."

"*Why?* Why on earth would you do that?"

"It wasn't just a one-night stand," he said. "That's not what that was."

"It was for me," I lied, but I couldn't look at him while I said it. I told him he had better go, let me finish packing.

For a moment, he didn't respond. He just stood there, assessing me, like he was planning his next cutting line, some barb that would change my mind, that would change everything. I stood there, too, my hands on my hips. Finally Sam shook his head. "Well, have a great trip," he said at last, in a monotone. "Bon voyage."

CHAPTER 20

France didn't agree with me. It started before we even arrived. As soon as the jet lifted up over the Seattle airport, a pressure built up inside my head, so sudden and alarming that I had to squeeze my eyes shut and breathe my way through it, gripping the armrests. The cabin trembled and the engines roared, and the pain swelled so intensely that I couldn't believe everyone else wasn't experiencing it, too. Maybe something was wrong with the plane; maybe they'd gotten the cabin pressure all wrong and we were going to die. They would drop the oxygen masks, and we would struggle to suck air into our lungs, but then it would be too late and the whole thing would burst with us inside and we would splinter off, spin through the air, break into millions of pieces—luggage and flotation devices and plastic cups and airline magazines and us, too, human parts. We'd rain over everything, fall onto earth, unrecognizable. Dust.

That was how bad it felt, like impending death, and I unscrewed my eyes to see how the others were taking it. I expected to see everyone holding their heads, crying out in misery, telling their loved ones this is it, I love you, goodbye.

No one was doing any of those things. The woman across the aisle was taking a sip of the complimentary champagne they'd poured us before takeoff. The couple in front of her were thumbing through a book, reading it in tandem, agreeing with a nod when to turn the page.

And Leo, next to me, was chewing gum. "What's wrong?" he asked, observing me with both hands to my temples, as if I were holding the pieces of my face together. I could smell the peppermint on his breath.

Once we reached cruising altitude, the pressure subsided, leaving in its place a dull nausea. I placed the sleeping mask over my eyes and buried myself under the airline blanket for the next ten hours of the flight.

~

We arrived in France in the morning, and Leo told me to stay up, to adjust to the time change, but I couldn't. In the hotel room I pulled shut all the curtains without bothering to take in the view. The bed was very high up, a princess and the pea bed, piled with heavy embroidered blankets. Underneath were cool white sheets. I climbed inside and slept and slept.

When I woke up it was night, and I was alone. The room was dark, but I could make out the outline of shapes. My body was a limp rag, worn out and frayed at the ends. *I'm in Paris, France.* These were the words I played over in my mind, a little pep talk. *Paris, France!* Behind the curtains, *Paris, France,* twinkled before me, an unmistakable landscape, with the Eiffel Tower lit up, glowing yellow. I opened a window, letting in a gust of cold city air. Still, I craned my head out and glanced up and down the street. I had no idea was time it was. The street was quiet.

Back inside, with the lamp on, I saw what I was wearing: a pair of gray sweatpants and a white T-shirt. No bra. I had no memory of changing, of getting changed into this getup.

I stayed in bed for three days, drifting in and out of sleep. I wasn't feeling well, I couldn't adjust to the time change. On the third day, Leo said we were going south. The sea air would do me good. I was like a character in a Victorian novel. I wondered if I was dying. That was what it felt like. My symptoms were mysterious. Sensitivity to light, severe fatigue, headache. A doctor had visited me in the Paris hotel. He said I had a cold.

It didn't feel like a cold. It would be embarrassing, really, to suffer so much from a cold, or to die from a cold.

Leo drove us down himself. I'd never seen him drive before. When we arrived at our destination, he installed us in a hotel, and once again I slipped under the covers and slept.

~

A rash began to form on my arms. Little red dots. They traveled up my arms to my chest, my cheeks. Wendy texted me from Portland. She was spending spring break with Hannah. How's FRANCE? she asked me. I sent her a picture of me with my prickly cheeks, my limp hair. She wrote back: That bad, huh?

If I died now, what was the point? Everything would have been for nothing. Wendy would go back to her grandmother or wind up in foster care. She wouldn't last a month. She would run away, end up on the streets. Sam would find someone else. My whole life had led me here, to this crumbling little town on the edge of the Old World.

One morning in the new hotel, I woke up to the sound of pounding on the door. A key turned in the lock. Two maids entered, pushing their cleaning cart. They spoke to each other in animated voices. It wasn't French but some other language.

I sat up in bed and cleared my throat, and the two women jumped. They spoke in French to me then, apologizing. I didn't catch each word, but I got the basic gist of what they were saying: we're sorry, please excuse us, we will come back later.

"Désolée," I said. They were already backing the cart from the door. I wanted to explain to them why I was still in bed at this hour. I didn't know what hour it was, exactly. The afternoon.

I couldn't say what day it was, how long we had been here. Leo had booked himself a separate room. He checked on me sometimes, asked me if I needed to see another doctor. What I needed, I told him, was quiet. I needed to sleep it off, whatever it was.

From the balcony I could see the sea, a gray line across the horizon. The sky above was not all the way blue. Everything was bleached out.

After the maids left, I decided I should get up. Take a shower, get dressed, find Leo. I didn't feel any better than before. Maybe I'd just gotten used to it. This was how I would be now, groggy and achy and half-alive.

I riffled through the contents of my suitcase but couldn't find anything I wanted to change into, so I climbed back into bed with the Mirror and looked up how to say "I am sick" in French. *Je suis malade.* I clicked on the microphone and listened to it, over and over. I practiced forming the words in my mouth. When the maids returned, I could tell them what was wrong with me, and they would understand.

I spoke the words into the Mirror, to see if it would understand, and it suggested a video for me to watch. "Je Suis Malade" was the name of a song, a very famous song by Lara Fabian. I watched the video—a live performance, with a pianist and orchestra—all the way through. I didn't understand anything she said other than *"Je suis malade,"* but I understood that something was tearing away at her, wearing her down. She was getting sicker and sicker—she didn't know if she would survive this, whatever it was. She was heartbroken and furious. I could feel it in her voice, see it on her face. At the end, the audience erupted into applause, and Lara Fabian stood there, stunned, as if she had lived her pain all over again during the song and hadn't yet emerged from it. Like she didn't remember she was onstage at all.

I fell back asleep and dreamed of my stepfather, Jason, holding that cottontail bunny in his cupped hands. Of Wendy and me running to him, screaming, "Don't crush it! Don't crush it!" But as soon as we reached him, he smashed his hands together, twisting them back and forth. We screamed louder, but then he opened up his hands and it flew out. Not the bunny—a bird. A little brown bird. It shot straight out of Jason's open hands and flapped its wings. The sound of its wings whirred in my ear so loud I shot up in my bed.

~

My eyes adjusted to the light. The room was different, not the darkened tomb I'd fallen asleep in. A frigid sea breeze billowed the curtains out into the room.

"You're awake."

I jumped at the sound of his voice, unsure where it was coming from. Then Leo stepped in from the balcony. He came up to me, placed his hand on my forehead. "Your fever seems to have broken," he said.

I didn't know I'd had a fever.

"Feeling better?"

I nodded and sank back into the cushions. I did feel better, I decided. "What time is it?" I squinted and peered out the window, but I had no idea. It wasn't nighttime. The sky was hazy white. I wasn't sure how long I'd slept, if it was still the same day or the next.

"Almost four," Leo said. "I came to get you. You have an appointment downstairs."

"An appointment?"

"You'll feel better afterward."

Leo said I didn't need to get dressed; I could head straight downstairs wearing what I was wearing now. What I'd been wearing for days. He let me go to the bathroom. I needed to brush my teeth. I needed to go home. I'd feel better as soon as I touched American soil again, I was sure of it. I wondered if I was allergic to France.

It was funny, I mused, how the best part of this job was actually the worst. I'd *wanted* to go to France. I'd wanted to see the world. Just not with Leo.

All this faking was wearing on me.

I had this friend in college who could speak two languages fluently, Korean and English. He majored in international relations, so everybody always asked him if he wanted to be a translator. He said no. That was one job he would never do, no matter how desperate. It was dangerous, he explained, to spend all day saying someone else's words. You'd lose a part of yourself.

He didn't believe in donating blood, either, I remembered, for similar reasons.

That was how it felt, I decided as I brushed my teeth. Like I didn't know who I was anymore. Always playing a part. That was what ailed me. I was weakening by the minute. It had only caught up to me, making my voice hoarse, my skin break out in angry red bumps. My body was rebelling against me. I was aging out of my role.

Leo was pounding on the door. "Time to go," he said.

~

The appointment was downstairs, in the basement of the hotel. He left me in the hands of four Frenchwomen in white outfits, like nurse uniforms. They led me to a windowless room and undressed me like I was a child and submerged me in a warm bath. The bath made me drowsy again. My mind wandered off, and my body stayed there, in the basement of this French hotel, while the women attended to me. Scrubbed me and washed me. Took me out, dried me off, waxed me. Sat me in a chair and combed out my hair. Took out scissors and snipped, snipped, snipped.

They picked at my skin and then made me lie with cold compresses on my face. The cold compresses came off, and one of them held a mirror to my face. "Very bad," one of the women said. "Very bad."

I knew my skin was bad. If I spoke French, I would tell them it was an allergic reaction. I was allergic to their country. *"Je suis malade,"* I said, and they nodded. They knew that.

After consulting each other in rapid French, they settled on a plan for my broken-out face. They applied creams and lotions. Dabbed on something with what looked like a long-handled paintbrush. Patted my skin with a foam pad. They stepped back, satisfied with their work.

They twirled my seat around and showed me myself in the mirror. They had cut five inches from my hair and hidden my red rash under layers and layers of makeup, so when I emerged I looked better—even beautiful, maybe—but less like myself than ever.

CHAPTER 21

We walked down cobblestone streets. My legs felt unsteady after spending so many days in bed. "You look good," Leo said to me, propping me up by the arm. "I'm glad you're better now."

I wondered what he had been doing all this time, but I didn't ask him.

We arrived at the restaurant, a quintessentially French place on a steep hill, with tables outside, tilting. It was too cold to sit outside, but we sat outside anyway. The streets were empty. All the other restaurants were shuttered, closed for the season. I sat on an uncomfortable wooden bistro chair and pulled my cashmere trench around me. Leo gestured for the waiter and ordered us wine.

He told me he would bring me here in the summertime. I tried to picture it then. Throngs of tourists walking on the promenade below our hotel balcony. Spending days lying topless on sun-bleached rocks, nights sitting outside in cafés. Summer seemed so far away from this moment.

~

Back in my room, we stood on the balcony and looked out at the sea. The moon was out, reflecting on the water. We could hear two young men below, arguing about something.

The wind rippled my dress, a halter sundress unsuited to the season. I should have left my coat on. Leo came up behind me and wrapped his arms around me. "I'm glad you're feeling better now."

I didn't feel better, though. Not really.

"I love you so much." He kissed my neck and I closed my eyes. I tried to relax into him but only managed to stand stick straight in his arms, gazing out at the water. He whirled me around and gripped my arms.

I knew what he wanted, but I didn't say it back. I didn't, not every time. It was too much. Usually I could distract him. Kiss him. Go down on him. I tried that now, reaching for his belt buckle. I wasn't feeling up to it; it was the last thing I wanted to do. The second-to-last thing.

This time it didn't work. He grabbed my face. "Say you love me, too."

I focused on the space in between his eyebrows. This gave me a very sincere look of concentration. Complete focus. "I feel the same way," I said.

"Say it."

I had to say it. "I . . . love . . . you." My voice might have been a little robotic. He didn't notice. He led me back into the room, leaving the doors to the balcony open, letting in the moonlight.

He unzipped his hoodie and tossed it to the floor in a dramatic fashion that, in normal circumstances, would have made me laugh.

"I'm still not feeling one hundred percent—"

"You're doing so much better." He pulled me to him and kissed me. After we broke apart, he said, "*So* much better."

I gave into it, letting him kiss me again. We stumbled around and crashed onto the bed. He liked it like this. Theatrical, action-packed lovemaking, like we were characters in a movie.

He fell asleep naked in my bed, leaving me only a small triangle of space. I curled up and tried to sleep, but I couldn't seem to drift off.

I must have finally fallen asleep because when I opened my eyes, it was morning, with sunlight streaming in through the open windows. Leo was gone. I stretched my arms and legs out to fill the entire bed. For the first time since we'd arrived in France, I felt good. I was alone.

Maybe he'd disappeared on some adventure and I would have the day to myself. Now that I was feeling better, I could go out, explore the town. I smiled as I imagined this, me traipsing over the cobblestones carrying a wicker basket filled with baguettes and carrots with their tops still on.

"Looks like you're on the mend," Leo said from across the room, startling me. He walked toward me, dripping wet, a very small towel wrapped around his waist.

"I didn't hear the shower running," I said, making very little effort to keep the disappointment out of my voice.

"I was in the bath. Are you almost ready?"

"Ready for what?"

"Breakfast."

"I'm not really hungry—"

A knock on the door. "Here they are." Still wearing only a towel, Leo opened the door, and I quickly pulled up a sheet to cover my naked body. A man wheeled in a cart cluttered with dishes covered in silver domes and a silver coffee service. He nodded demurely to me as he passed. Leo directed him to the balcony, and the man made quick work setting the table with a white cloth and fine china plates. He left the tray with the covered dishes next to the table.

The man went away, and Leo invited me out to the balcony with a flourish of his arm, like a game show host.

"I wasn't *dressed*."

"Well, put on some clothes!" Leo exclaimed, sailing over my point entirely.

"I said I wasn't hungry."

Leo wasn't listening. He riffled through my suitcase and threw items to me, one at a time. Underwear, sweatpants, T-shirt, hoodie. "You should really unpack your suitcase into the dresser," he said. "It makes staying in a hotel much more comfortable."

Leo pulled on his clothes, and we met out on the balcony, wearing our matching outfits.

"It's freezing out here."

Leo chuckled as he poured coffee into a cup. I topped it off with cream and took a sip. I must have smiled at that first delicious taste because Leo said, "*That's* better."

After the first cup, I lifted my head and surveyed the view. A weak sun shone out through tattered strips of clouds. In the distance, seagulls circled around fish that had washed up on shore overnight.

Leo lifted the dome off the largest dish. "This looks so good," he said.

I didn't turn to look. "I don't have much of an appetite."

We sat in silence for several minutes while I tried to block out the sounds of his chewing.

"Rosemary," Leo said, and I turned to him.

"Open the next one, the one closest to you."

"I'll eat something at lunch," I said. "I promise." I was trying very hard not to snap at him.

"Just open it."

Leo was smiling at me, leaning forward in his seat.

My hand hovered over the silver dome.

"Lift it up," he said, and I did.

Under the dome, resting on the fine bone china, lay a ring. A platinum ring with an oval diamond in an east-west setting.

My eyes went round and terrified as I watched Leo pick up the ring from the plate, push aside the cart, and kneel before me. He took my left hand in his.

"What is this?" My voice came out rushed, panicked.

Leo wore a look of great solemnity. "Rosemary," he intoned.

"What's going on?" I tried to stand up to leave, but my hand was still in Leo's, and he gripped it more firmly, pulling me back down on the wooden chair.

"Don't ruin it," Leo muttered, sotto voce.

I relaxed then, understanding. The confessions of love, the proposal, none of it was real. This was just part of it—part of the game Leo and I were playing. Part of what Leo was paying for. He didn't want the girlfriend experience—he wanted the fiancée experience. I could deliver.

"Oh my god!" I exclaimed, in a high, nervous squeal.

"Rosemary," Leo began again. "These last few months with you have been . . ." He delivered a whole proposal speech. He said these last few months had opened his eyes to a whole new way of living, that he wanted to keep living just like this, that I made him so happy and he thought he could make me happy, too. He said he'd take care of me, of me and Wendy, that we would never have to worry about anything ever again. We'd tie the knot, have babies, buy a house, grow old together— the whole shebang.

"Wow," I said at the end of it. "I had no idea you felt this way." This reaction had the benefit of being 100 percent sincere.

"Since the moment I laid eyes on you—on that picture of you—I knew I had to have you," he said. "I wanted you to be my wife. Please. Say yes."

It all sounded so real, I almost had to admire him for it. It seemed crazy, how far he was willing to take this little game of ours. When you had all the money in the world, this was the kind of thing you could do. Hire a young woman to have sex with you, to pretend to love you, to agree to marry you.

I didn't think about what would happen in seven months, when the contract was supposed to end. I didn't think of me or my life or my future. I couldn't envision any sort of normal life for myself. Law school and Sam playing the viola while Wendy and I danced around the apartment. I had lost sight of that the way I had lost sight of why I had entered into the agreement in the first place, for Wendy. Because I promised Wendy. At that point, I was just following along, doing whatever Leo wanted me to do. I had stopped counting down a long time ago.

He slipped the ring on my finger, and I held up my hand to admire it. The diamond was so large that it spanned the width of my finger.

"Is it real?" I joked. It looked weird on my hand. My nails looked beautiful, though, thanks to my whole spa treatment the day before.

"Say yes," Leo said, and he gathered both of my hands in his and squeezed, as if he feared I'd say no and dash all of his dreams.

"Yes." I injected the word with as much feeling as I could possibly muster.

~

That night, in the bathroom, I changed into a nightgown Leo had given me. He'd bought it in Paris, he said. It was beautiful, made of white silk. More like a slip than a nightgown, with a lacy bodice and a skirt that swept down to the floor. Not Leo's style at all. This fact might have clued me in, sent a little tremor of warning through me. I didn't question it. I just put it on and stepped out into the hotel room, where Leo was waiting on my bed.

"Lie down," Leo said, patting the space beside him. He had the covers thrown back, so I lay down next to him, on my side, resting a hand on his chest.

"On your back."

I rolled onto my back and lay with my arms at my sides.

"Good," he said. "Just like that." He leaned over and petted my hair, smoothing it around me on the pillow. "That's right," he said. "You can close your eyes. Just relax."

I was tired, still not recovered from that mysterious illness, my France allergy. It felt so good to lie back on those feather pillows, feeling the chilly breeze waft in from the balcony. His fingers traced the contours of my face. I felt him moving down the bed, positioning himself between my legs, and still, I didn't move. I was half-asleep. If I fell asleep—or pretended to fall asleep—he would stop. I wasn't up for this. Not tonight.

His hands pushed the nightgown up over my hips, and I groaned like I was in pain.

"*Shh,*" he said. "It's okay. Just lie back and relax."

It was impossible to relax, but I was tired. When he tugged at my underwear, I let him. I even lifted my hips off the bed and let him slip it down, dragging it down my legs.

He spread my legs apart, and I could feel his hot breath. I waited to feel his tongue on me, but that didn't happen. He touched me with a finger. Tentatively at first, like he was pressing a lump of dough to see if it had risen enough. He inserted a finger into me, and I took in a sharp breath, and he said, "It's okay," and I tried to relax.

He stayed like that for a while, his finger inside me, exploring. This was not something that turned me on, particularly. Or at all. I wasn't sure how it could be doing anything for him, either, but I just let him do it. I considered faking an orgasm to get him to stop.

Finally, unable to stand it anymore, I raised myself on my elbows. "Come up here," I said.

I peered down at the top of Leo's head. His finger deep inside me. "Not now," he said. He withdrew his hand, and I sank back onto the pillows. I closed my eyes and tried to summon that pretend version of me, the one who wanted this. I couldn't find her anywhere. It would be better if I could just drift away entirely, float out and away from myself, like I used to do when I was little, with Jason. I couldn't seem to do that, either. This was me. This was all happening to *me*. My body temperature dropped, and I thought maybe I was going to be sick.

A moment before I almost pushed him away from me, Leo announced that he would be right back and disappeared into the bathroom. I sat up, pulling the nightgown down over my hips. I wasn't going to lie there spread-eagle, exposed.

He returned, a white towel draped over one shoulder. "Now where were we?" Leo assumed his previous pose and dragged me by the legs back down into a supine position on the bed. He pushed the material of my nightgown back up over my hips. "Just a minute—don't move." He reached over to turn on a lamp on the bedside table. I shut my eyes.

"Leo, why don't we—" I murmured. My voice sounded very faint and far away, like it was echoing down a well.

"*Shh.* Just lie back. Close your eyes. Yes. Like that."

I felt his lips and tongue on me, for just a minute. When his fingers found me again, he muttered, as if to himself, "That's better."

"Leo—"

"This will be easier if you relax," he said.

"Easier? What are you—" I don't know if I said that out loud or if it was just something that went through my head, right before it happened.

"Just lie back!"

I did as I was told, shutting my eyes tight while he touched me. Once again I felt his finger deep inside me. Moving around, tickling my cervix.

The next part happened all at once. The finger came out and then something else went in—something cold and metallic.

"You're going to feel a pinch," Leo said.

And then I screamed.

PART TWO

After that time I *didn't* murder my stepfather, I thought about it a lot. I thought of how to get away with it. When other girls my age were fantasizing about weekend parties and boys and college applications, I was thinking about all the ways I could do it. I'd run over scenarios and weigh their pros and cons during class when I should have been learning how to graph a parabola or write a villanelle.

Drown him, push him from a great height. Shoot him, stab him, poison him, light the house on fire. Cut the brakes. There were so many ways to do it, but only three ways to get away with it. That's what I figured.

Make it look like an accident.

Make it look like self-defense.

Never get caught.

I didn't kill him, but I felt like I could, if it came to that again. It comforted me, knowing what was possible.

CHAPTER 22

The moment before I passed out, a sharp pain pierced me from somewhere deep inside. It was a raw, jangled-nerve kind of pain that radiated through my entire body like electricity. Then everything went black. I couldn't have been out for more than a moment or two, because when I opened my eyes, the first thing I saw was Leo blinking down at me, holding something aloft in one hand. A pair of tweezers. And in the tweezers' grip, a small plastic *T*, smaller and finer than a rosary cross, slick with a film of poppy-red blood.

I remember what Leo said then. He said it wasn't supposed to hurt. You were supposed to be able to reach right up there and pull that IUD out by the strings.

For a minute I could only blink at him.

He thought it would be simple. He'd read about it; he knew what he was doing. He thought he'd save me a trip to the doctor. I hated the doctor. He knew that. He still felt bad about that, making me go.

We were getting married, Leo reminded me. We were going to spend the rest of our lives together. We could have a baby now. Once I felt better.

At first I couldn't focus on his words, what had just happened to me. I just lay there, inert on the bed. His voice sounded warped and distant, as if I were listening from somewhere very far away, dark and underwater.

Sensations began returning, like I was floating upward, ready to break back to the surface. I sat up, gasping, clutching at my throat, trying to breathe. In that moment, all my symptoms from earlier returned.

My head pounded. Hot pinpricks of pain erupted from my cheeks. It was my hives, my rash, whatever it was. They were returning. Little fireworks, warped sparks of light, flashed before my eyes. I squeezed them shut. "I want to go home," I said.

~

The trip back was a blur. We flew to Seattle first class from Paris, but then we had to take a small commuter plane back to Portland. Leo had said something about a private jet, but I refused that outright. There was no way I would spend even a few hours trapped in a private airplane with him.

The commuter plane was loud and flew close to the mountaintops. In the window seat, Leo faced forward, his eyes closed. The pilot made an announcement: if we looked now, we could see Mount Saint Helens.

I craned over Leo to look. We were flying low to the ground, and I could peer directly into the volcano. A plume of smoke feathered out of it. I could stare straight into its blue basin, a bowl with cracked edges. The whole ancient mountain glowed white, sparkled with snow. It glowed so bright it hurt my eyes, but I kept staring as we flew over it. It felt magical, seeing it like this. Once-in-a-lifetime, even. From the city it was difficult to see. When it became visible, its rounded dome emerging behind the buildings, it was a surprise. Oh, there it is, where it's always been, where it's been all this time, obscured by clouds and mist. I watched until it receded from view, and then I sat back in my seat, closing my eyes tightly and gripping the armrests like someone afraid of flying.

And then, that was it—the last moments of our flight as the plane descended into Portland.

Leo appeared to be asleep, so I said his name and he murmured "Hmm?" without opening his eyes.

"I'm ending this," I told him. "I never want to see you again."

He acted so contrite after the IUD incident; he must have seen this coming. I'd hoped he would make it easy on me—realize he had gone too far, screwed things up. Best-case scenario, he'd simply admit defeat and let me go.

His eyes opened. He turned to me with an expression I'd never seen on his face before. Surprised confusion. Desperation, maybe. "Why would you do that?" he asked. "If you really loved me?" His hand lifted up to caress my cheek.

At first I could only stare back, my mouth half-open in shock. I reached up and removed his hand from my face. "I don't," I said.

His eyebrows came together, as if he were trying to perform a complex mathematical equation in his head. "You lied?"

I studied Leo carefully. He appeared to be sincere. Of course, he could be acting. Or he could actually believe his own words. *Or* he could be a sociopath. "I was being paid," I explained, my voice neutral. Kind, even. I would give him the benefit of the doubt. "That's what you paid me to do, right? It wasn't lying. It was pretending."

His pupils seemed to vibrate, opening and closing. A vein on his forehead emerged, and his skin went from tan to pink. I didn't flinch, but I prepared myself for—I didn't know what. He wouldn't slap me, not on a public airplane, not in front of all these people, but he looked like he wanted to. His nostrils flared, and that vein bulged from his skin with such force that I swear I could see his blood pumping through it.

It was a sight to see, Leo's face. His anger was alive; it had an energy of its own. It was so thick I could feel it; I could smell it, sharp and metallic. I watched in horror, not knowing what Leo would do, what he would say.

Then, as quickly as it had begun, it faded, his anger. His pupils returned to their normal size, beetle-black orbs. His vein sank back into his forehead, as if it had never been there at all. He frowned. This frown was a calculated frown, a performance of a frown. "*I* wasn't pretending," he said, and he didn't sound hurt or particularly upset by this admission. "Anyway, you can't leave until November. You signed a contract."

I exhaled, letting go of the air I'd been holding in for the last terrible minute. I realized my hands were still gripping the armrests. I let them go. When I spoke, I sounded calm. Reasonable. "Both you and I know that contract isn't legally binding. You can't *make* someone be your girlfriend."

"I know that." He sounded calm and reasonable, too. "And that's why the contract didn't say anything about making you be my girlfriend. What it *said* was that you agreed to provide your services in exchange for a salary and reduced rent."

"Okay—"

Leo rattled off something about the contract, back payment, an early termination clause.

"I don't care." I tried to think. I couldn't remember how much money I had in my bank account. I had meant to spend as little as possible. Save up so at the end of the contract we would have a cushion. We could stay in the apartment until I got into law school. Once I did that, we'd get by on student loans.

But then I had to go on that spending spree, right from the beginning. Student loans, credit card bills—I didn't know how much money I had. I did know it wouldn't be enough. I didn't care. I would figure something out. I always did.

The flight attendant walked up and down the aisle with a plastic garbage bag. Leo held up a finger to detain her, and then he made a big show of digging around in the pocket in front of his seat. He produced a crumpled-up napkin and an empty foil peanuts packet, which he tossed into the bag. "Thank you," he said to the flight attendant, flashing her a bright smile, revealing all his teeth. Like a jackal, I thought.

"Thank you, Mr. Glass, for flying with us today." She had a bit of an accent, a southern drawl. She knew who he was. Of course she did.

After she left, Leo turned back to me. This time his face was wide-open innocence. Round eyes and raised eyebrows. "Aren't you worried they'll take Wendy away from you?" I stiffened, but he acted like he didn't notice. "You won't be able to afford that apartment. You'll have no place to go."

"I'll figure it out."

"You don't have legal custody," he said, as if it had just occurred to him. "Just temporary guardianship."

"So?" This was true. Had I mentioned it to Leo? I might have. We used to talk, the way boyfriends and girlfriends do. It wasn't all bad. It wasn't all acting. Still, this didn't seem like the kind of thing I would share with him, even after sex, while we lay naked under Belgian linen sheets in his king-size bed.

"So they'll take her away from you."

"Why would they do that?" I asked carefully.

"How much do you know about Hannah Westover?"

"What?" Of all the things I thought Leo might say to convince me to stay, I hadn't been expecting *that*. "What about her? She's just a girl from Wendy's school." I tried to remember when I'd told Leo about Hannah. I'd definitely never told him her last name. Hannah Westover. I hadn't even *known* Hannah's last name.

"She's not a girl," Leo said. "And she doesn't go to school."

The plane was plummeting down to earth. We were almost home. Ever since we left the South of France, I'd been telling myself something, over and over again. I'd been telling myself: As soon as we get back to Portland, it will be over. It will all be over, and everything will be fine.

Leo went on. "Wendy's friend, the one she's been spending all her time with? The one you let her stay with for a whole week while you jetted off to France? She's an adult. She's twenty years old."

I knew Hannah was older—she could drive after all. I assumed she was sixteen, tops. She was so tiny. She could pass as a seventh grader. "So what?" I responded, but my voice sounded small. Twenty years old. Hannah was *twenty*? She was closer to my age than Wendy's! Why would a twenty-year-old want to hang out with a fourteen-year-old? How did they even meet? It didn't make any sense. Unless she was— what? Some sort of child abuser? A sex trafficker? My mind was running wild, and Leo was still talking.

229

"It's no wonder they're friends. They've both been in treatment for attempting suicide . . . What's Wendy's grandmother going to say when she learns about that? That you left Wendy with an unstable twenty-year-old—"

"She was staying with Hannah's *parents*—" I cut myself off. Did Hannah even have parents? I didn't know. It had seemed like a reasonable thing to assume, that your sister's friends had parents. That your sister's friends were not full-grown adults with places of their own. That your sister was not spending spring break unsupervised with a deviant criminal.

"Is that what Wendy told you?" Leo's eyes went huge. "Because if that's what she told you, she was lying." Had Wendy lied? I'd offered to call Hannah's parents, to speak with them on the phone to make sure they didn't mind having Wendy spend spring break with them. Wendy said she would die of embarrassment if I did that. I never called.

She hadn't lied. Not exactly. She just left out quite a few details.

The wheels of the plane hit the runway at what seemed like full speed. We bounced on the asphalt, and the aircraft juddered before righting itself, screeching to a halt.

I felt sick. A different kind of ailment this time. Like I was going to throw up. I riffled through the pocket in front of me, searching for the sickness bag. I unfolded it and held my face over it, heaving, but nothing came out.

"Ladies and gentlemen," the flight attendant announced. It was the same one who had collected our trash, the one with the slow southern drawl. "Welcome to Portland, Oregon. The local time is 2:47 p.m. The temperature is fifty-six degrees Fahrenheit."

"How do you know all this?" I asked Leo.

Leo unfastened his seat belt and pulled out his backpack from under the seat in front of him, as if nothing were out of the ordinary, as if this were the end of any other trip. "I like to keep an eye on things," he said.

CHAPTER 23

At the airport, my suitcase arrived first. Leo retrieved it from the conveyor belt and extended the handle for me. When he craned his neck to look for his own bag, I slipped away. Just—slipped out the door and into a taxi. "Drive!" I commanded, ducking down in the back seat like I had just robbed a bank.

Once we pulled onto the highway, I sat back up. I felt silly. Leo wouldn't follow me. He loved me, or he thought he loved me. Maybe I should sit him down, have a rational conversation with him. I had misunderstood the rules of the game—that was all. Maybe we could just have a normal breakup, like any other couple.

No. That didn't seem possible. That had never been possible.

"Where are you headed?" the driver asked, and I realized I hadn't given him a destination. I couldn't go home; Leo could find me there. I couldn't get Wendy; I didn't know where she was. I couldn't call her or text her. Leo was watching. Listening. Anything I did, he would know. My hands were trembling. "I don't know," I said. "Just drive."

I needed to stay calm. Figure out what I was dealing with, exactly, so I could formulate a plan.

~

I went back home. I didn't know where else to go. Anywhere I went, he'd follow. He'd know. Wendy wasn't there. I knew she wasn't there, but I walked through each room anyway, calling her name. I sent her a text and told her I was back, that I had returned a couple of days earlier than expected. Come home, the text said. Leo could be reading it, but I didn't know what else to do. We'd figure it out when she returned. Put on disguises and escape through some back door, some secret passageway.

Something felt off about the apartment. Maybe it was the fact that it was clean. I'd tidied up before I left, but it seemed . . . cleaner than before, somehow. Every surface polished to a shine. The recycling bins emptied.

In the kitchen, I dumped the contents of my purse onto the counter. There was the Mirror, shining, smudged with my fingerprints. I picked it up and opened my Lookinglass account.

You have 10,540 watchers.

My fingers stabbed at the various prompts, trying to make my way around it. Because I watched only one person—Leo—my feed was quiet. Nothing appeared on the screen.

Finally I found what I was looking for: Delete account.

Are you sure you want to close your Lookinglass account?

Yes.

We'll miss you! All your preferences and settings will be saved.

There was no way out of this, no way to erase myself from it forever. I wondered if it would do me any good, deleting my account. Surely Leo had planned for this, had found a way to watch me anyway.

He could have bugged the Mirror; he could be tracing my calls, tracking my moves, spying on me through the camera. I wasn't going to take any chances. I set a pot of water to boil on the stove. While it heated, I recorded a new outgoing message for my voice mail: "You've reached the voice mail of Rosemary Rabourne. Don't bother leaving a message. I am no longer able to make or receive calls. If you want to talk to me, try to find me."

If the Mirror had a battery, I couldn't find it. It wouldn't open up. I placed the silver disk on my John Boos cutting board. Then I smashed it with my chrome meat tenderizer. Flat on one side, for poultry. Ridged on the other side, for beef. I'd never used it before. I pounded and pounded, using all my strength, grunting each time the mallet made contact. When I finished, I was breathing hard. My hands were clenched so tightly around the handle, the whites of my knuckles were visible. The silver exterior of the Mirror had suffered a few dents. On the other side, the screen was still intact. There wasn't a scratch on it. I dropped it into the pot of boiling water and watched for a few minutes.

I felt better. I was fixing things. I just needed to wait for Wendy to come home. That was all I could do. I tried not to panic, thinking of everything that could go wrong, that had already gone wrong. I tried not to think of her, my little fourteen-year-old sister, with her weird twenty-year-old "friend." I tried not to think of the fact that I had no idea where she was, but Leo did. Leo did. My body slumped down into a chair by the kitchen table.

The shriek of the fire alarm woke me. I must have drifted off. The Mirror was black and smoking at the bottom of a dry pan, releasing a horrid, noxious smoke. I leaped up to switch off the burner and pry open the window. I stared into the pot, the heat scalding my face. Now I couldn't call anyone, and no one could call me. Now I would never get a hold of my sister. I hadn't exactly thought this through.

"Wendy!" I yelled out once again, this time in exasperation. I wondered if she and Hannah had been hanging out here while I was away. That would explain the slight sense of unease, the impression that items had shifted in my absence. A ninth grader and a twenty-year-old. Why would a twenty-year-old become best friends with a freshman in high school? Maybe she was some sort of predator. Maybe they were having a twisted love affair. If Hannah had been a guy, I'd be freaking out even more than I already was. This would certainly be a crime. Wouldn't it? Another wave of guilt washed over me. I'd let her hang out with Hannah, spend the night. I had never called Hannah's parents. But that was normal. I had convinced myself it was normal. What would a diligent parent do, run background checks on everyone who wanted to hang out with their kid? Yes. That was probably exactly what they would do.

I had told her. I had told my sister I wasn't equipped to do this, that I would be terrible at this. I had told her from the very beginning, when we were kids. The wicked fairy had to fly away, find her kind. That was how the story went. Everyone was happier without her there, getting into mischief, up to no good. She ruined everything she touched.

In the space of a minute I convinced myself that something had happened, that Wendy and Hannah had been hanging out here, that they had thrown a party. Maybe things had spun out of control. Maybe someone had passed out from drinking or worse—drugs. Someone overdosed here in the apartment. The girls didn't know what to do. They got scared. They cleaned up all the evidence—the syringes and bottles and cigarettes—so no one would ever suspect a thing. They hid the body in a suitcase and managed to get it into Hannah's car, and now they were on the run.

If a party had been going on here, Sam would have heard it.

I pounded on his door, heavy thumps. He didn't come to the door, and I pounded again, defeated. My fist rested there, on his door, mid-pound. I pressed my forehead against the painted wood and squeezed my eyes shut. I was so tired. I'd flown across an ocean to get back here, and nothing had improved. Tears welled up behind my eyes. I could feel the pressure, a dull throbbing.

On the other side of the door, footsteps approached. I heard Sam muttering "okay, *okay*." When the door opened, I stumbled forward, almost falling inside.

His expression mutated from annoyed to incredulous in an instant. "Rosemary?"

I was so happy to see him there. His faded jeans, his rumpled T-shirt, his uncombed hair. That sweater he always wore, the gray cardigan. The tears that had been welling up spilled over, gushed down my cheeks, and I laughed, swiping at them with the back of my hand. I didn't know why I was crying.

His eyes roved over me in alarm, taking in my appearance. My skin must still be dull and speckled with red welts, my eyes bloodshot and wild. "Jesus, Rosemary." His arms went around me, and he pulled me close. I stiffened at first, but only because I was so surprised. I thought he hated me. I thought he was through with me. My head settled against his chest, and my eyes closed. For that moment—and that was all it was, not even a minute—I could breathe in his wool-and-cedar scent and pretend everything was like it had been before.

It was Sam who pulled back first. His thumbs swiped away the last of my tears. His fingers brushed back the stray strands of hair from my face. "You cut your hair." He said it as if it were the saddest thing in the world.

He hugged me again. "What did he *do* to you? Where's Wendy?"

My eyes met Sam's, and I held my finger up to my lips. Then I carefully surveyed the ceiling of the landing where we stood. I didn't see any Glasseyes, but maybe Leo wasn't using those to track me after all. They could hide cameras anywhere these days, in the electrical sockets, in the tip of a pen.

That's when I saw it. I wasn't imagining it. It wasn't even particularly well hidden. A Glasseye, nestled on the light fixture on the wall right above the elevator. I froze, trying to come up with a plan. It couldn't have been here for long, that Glasseye. I would have seen it. Teddy must have put it there, I decided. That day he delivered my coat.

In one decisive movement, I grabbed Sam by the hand and tugged, leading him out of his apartment and into the stairwell. I kept my finger to my lips as we ascended the stairs. The door to the rooftop said EMERGENCY EXIT ONLY, and for a second I hesitated. Then I pushed down the lever and braced myself for lights to flash, alarms to sound. Nothing happened, and we stepped onto the roof of the building.

In the distance, clouds gathered in layers of gray and violet. A troubled, stormy sky. Wind whipped my hair into my face, splattered us with drops of rain.

"He's watching," I said. "Listening. Not just me—Wendy, too. Her friend, Hannah. Maybe you—I don't know. I don't know."

Sam didn't say anything.

"He can't hear us up here," I said, though I didn't know. Maybe he could. Maybe he'd installed some sort of tracking device under my skin without me noticing.

"You have to tell me what's going on," Sam said.

"Wendy—I'm trying to find her. Was she here? Did you see her? Hear her, maybe?"

He shook his head, slowly. "I thought she was staying with her friend."

"She was." My voice cracked. "I thought she was."

"Rosemary," he said, "start from the beginning."

"You'll hate me."

He gave me a crooked little smile. "Tell me anyway."

I exhaled loudly, a skittering, choked-up sigh. Then I told him.

I told him everything. I told him about Mira and her phone, and Sebastian St. Doug, and how I met Leo Glass. I told him about Leo Glass's offer, how it seemed like the answer to all my problems. I told him how then I met him, Sam, and I fell in love with him. I used those words—"I fell in love with you"—and the look on Sam's face was so heartbroken I almost couldn't keep going, but I kept going. I told him about the doctor's appointment and how Leo wanted me to choose him, to tell him I loved him. And how I did it, I told him, but only because I thought it was a part of it, a part of this strange job of being Leo Glass's girlfriend.

My story edged closer to the present, to this moment on the roof. I told him about France, how I'd fallen ill, but then Leo had proposed and given me a huge diamond ring. "Look at this thing," I told Sam, and I held up my hand to show him the enormous rock on my finger. My hands had swollen during the flight. It wouldn't come off. I told Sam the end, or what I viewed as the end, when Leo had pulled my IUD out of me with a pair of tweezers.

My body felt light from the relief of it, for shedding this story I'd been dragging around for the last five months. A gust of wind could carry me off, into the clouds. I imagined my symptoms disappearing before his eyes, the rash fading, my hair regrowing, the color to my skin returning. My fingers would shrink down to their normal size, and the diamond ring would fall off my finger, bounce off the roof, and disappear down a storm drain.

Sam didn't say anything, not at first. He saw me shiver, and he pulled off his sweater so he could drape it over my shoulders. I tightened it around me by the sleeves like a cape. He placed an arm around me and pulled me close, and we both looked out at the city below. We could see farther than I had expected, from way up here. The buildings downtown, the river below, the bridges, the mountains. Raindrops pelted down on us. It was a slow, fat rain. Sporadic. Minutes between drops.

We turned toward each other, and my hair flew out from behind me, into Sam's face. Our eyes locked, and then a look of resolve settled onto Sam's features. He leaned in, and I thought he was going to kiss me, but he only brought me in for another embrace. We stood like that, holding each other, my head against his chest, for what felt like a long time.

"Call the police," Sam said into my ear. The wind almost carried his words away, but I heard them.

I leaned back to look at Sam, our arms still around each other, and I let out a sad, desperate laugh. "What would I even say? Everything I did—pretending to be his girlfriend for money and the apartment—I agreed to it." Sam looked like he was about to protest, so I amended: "Most of it."

"What he did to you—with the IUD. It's assault. And Wendy—what if he did something to her?"

My mouth fell open in alarm. "You think he did something to her?"

"That's what you said." He shook me by the shoulders. "We need to *do* something."

"I don't know—"

"You can't talk to him again."

"I *know*."

"You can't see him again. You know what you need to do." Sam's eyes were dark and wild. He was gripping me by the arms. "End it."

I could only shake my head. "I tried," I told him. "It didn't work."

I told Sam I needed to go back down to wait for Wendy. Sam wanted me to wait at his place, but I said no, it was too risky. Leo could be watching. "If he sees me at your place . . ." I let the sentence dangle.

"Let him watch," Sam said. "What's he going to do about it?"

Our voices echoed in the stairway, an industrial cement chamber that didn't feel like it belonged to the quaint, old-fashioned architecture of the rest of the building. My body reacted to his words before my mind or mouth could catch up. It started to tremble. First my hands quivered. My legs followed, weak and boneless. My teeth chattered, too.

Sam had to hold me up. "I'm going to call a doctor."

"I'm okay." I breathed in and tried to steady myself. I offered him a reassuring smile. "Just jet-lagged is all. I haven't slept in—I don't know. Twenty hours or something."

"Then you should get some sleep."

"I need to find Wendy."

"How about this." Sam's voice was measured. "I'll go look for Wendy while you rest. Just close your eyes for a few minutes."

"I should look for her. I'm the one who lost her."

"But he's tracking you, right? He's following you?" We knew that for sure, Sam explained to me carefully. Leo could be following him, too, but we didn't know that. So it made sense. It made sense for Sam to look for her. The best thing I could do was wait, in case she returned on her own. Right?

I thought it over. Then I nodded.

Sam exited the stairwell first, at my insistence.

For a few minutes, I waited. My heart was beating too quickly; I couldn't catch my breath. Finally I did it—opened the stairwell door and stepped out. The Glasseye tracked my moves as I traversed the hall and entered my apartment. I could feel it, the way you can sense a person staring from across the room. I'd disabled my account, but it was tracking me anyway. Glasseyes followed everyone, I reminded myself, but if my account was disabled, it wouldn't know who I was. It wouldn't send notification to my watchers, my 10,540 watchers. Ten thousand, five hundred, thirty-nine strangers and Leo Glass.

At least, that was what they said. That was how it was supposed to work.

Wendy still wasn't home. I hadn't expected her to be, though I had hoped. In my bedroom, I opened my laptop and considered contacting her some other way—email, instant message, or something. He could be monitoring all of it. It was better not to risk it.

My body sank back onto my pillows. My own bed. I shed layers, the limp clothes I'd been wearing for too long, through airplanes and airports. Everything would be better if I could just get some sleep, if I could just think straight. Outside, the sky was darkening. It was almost night. I could close my eyes and rest, and when I woke up, I would know what to do.

Almost instantly I felt myself giving in, my body shutting down, my mind going dark and blank, and it was such a relief to be back home, to be back in my own bed. Everything was going to be better in the morning.

CHAPTER 24

I woke up to distant voices, to laughter, to clattering pots and pans. Wendy! I sat up straight in bed and looked around for something to put on. As I padded down the hallway, the laughter grew louder. A voice came from the kitchen, a deep, male voice, and for a moment I let myself think it was Sam, because wouldn't that be perfect?

Wendy sat at the head of the dining room table. Before her lay plates of food, some of it hot, the steam rising up from them in lazy swirls. Dozens of pancakes, a bowl of fresh blueberries, wedges of cantaloupe. She wasn't eating any of it, but she held a fork in one hand.

I was so relieved to see her that I gave a little gasp. My arms opened, and I wanted to lunge toward her, hold on to her, make sure she was really there, but something stopped me.

"You're up!" she said in a falsely bright tone. Her eyes inspected me, taking in my appearance, which couldn't have improved much even after a long, turbulent sleep. "Are you *okay*?"

As if responding to a stage cue, Leo stepped out from the kitchen bearing a plate of fried eggs. He'd fried up a whole dozen and arranged them in a neat design, like the overlapping slices of apple on a tarte Tatin. My first thought was how odd that was, this geometric egg arrangement. Each egg a uniform circle, the bright-orange yolks quivering in the center. I'd never seen anything like it. My second thought was that Leo Glass was the one holding the plate, standing in my kitchen, trying to feed my sister.

"Hungry?" Leo said.

I froze. Wendy was staring at me, waiting for direction. I could have yelled at him. I could have told Wendy to call the police. I didn't do either of those things. Maybe I should have. Maybe if I had, things wouldn't have ended the way they did.

Instead, I did what I had been doing for the last five months. I played along. I sat down next to my sister and raised my eyes to Leo. "Starving." I helped myself to three pancakes and an egg. "Aren't you having any, Wendy?"

She placed a hand on her stomach. "I already had breakfast."

"When did you get home?"

Wendy glanced quickly at Leo, then back at me. "Hannah dropped me off last night. You were out like a light." She spoke in a crisp, formal style that wasn't like her at all. No trace of that vocal fry.

I wanted to communicate to her somehow that I knew what I was doing. That this was the way to handle Leo Glass. It seemed to me then that if I could just get through that breakfast, he would leave. I could play nice and get him out the door. I didn't want him there, in my apartment, where he didn't belong. He wasn't supposed to be there. I wanted Wendy to know that. I wanted her to know I had tried. I had tried to keep him away from her, all this time.

Leo sat across from me, his eyes darting back and forth between me and Wendy. He speared a cube of cantaloupe with his fork and took a dainty bite.

"This is certainly a surprise," I said to him now.

"Thought I'd check up on you," he said.

We appraised each other from across the table.

"We'll eat breakfast," I said. "And then you need to leave."

Leo dabbed at his face with the edge of a cloth napkin. He raised his eyebrows at me. "*I* need to leave? It seems to me that I pay for this place."

"It's over, Leo. I told you that." I tried again to pull the ring from my finger, but it still wouldn't budge past my knuckle.

"Oh my god," Wendy said at the sight of the ring. She didn't sound excited. She sounded terrified.

"I asked your sister to marry me." Leo smiled broadly and placed a hand on Wendy's shoulder, and that's when I stood up, quickly, scraping the chair across the hardwood floor so fast it toppled over, crashing to the floor.

"Get your hand off my sister and get out of here. Now."

"Or what?"

Suddenly all my jangled nerves—the fear, the anger—smoothed over. When I answered Leo, my voice was low and steady. Sam had been right. I just needed a good night's sleep to clear my head. Everything seemed very clear to me then, sunlight through a polished window. After all these months, I knew exactly what I needed to do. Wasn't this what Sam had been telling me? Leo was a bad person. It wasn't just me and Wendy anymore, either. What about those factory workers in China? What about the environment? I could fix everything. I just needed the courage to follow through with it.

A weight lifted from me then. I felt lighter, better. Better than I'd felt for days, weeks. Months. I could make everything all right.

I may have even smiled at him. That was how I remembered it. I smiled and I said, "Or I'll kill you."

"Rosemary—" my sister started.

"Go to your room," I told my sister. When she opened her mouth to protest, I shot out, "Now!" and she jumped up and scampered away like a startled cat.

Across the table, Leo stood up, slowly, his hands raised.

"You shouldn't have come over. That was our agreement."

I braced myself for his reaction. Surprise, hurt, anger—whatever it was, I would deal with it.

Instead he bowed his head in contrition. "I know," he said. "I'm sorry. I tried calling but—"

"You won't be able to reach me. Not anymore."

"You disappeared from the airport. I was worried."

"I'm fine now."

"One more dinner. That's all I'm asking. I screwed up. I'm admitting that. I got carried away—"

"I don't think so."

I walked him to the entryway and was about to usher him out the door when he tried again. "I'll make it worth your while," he said, dropping his voice several decibels. "Even if you don't forgive me—and I wouldn't blame you, seriously—I want to make it up to you."

"You *can't*." Our eyes met. Silently, I pleaded with him: Let me go. Let me go. Let me go. If he knew what was good for him, he'd let me go.

I knew he understood. I could feel him debating with himself, and for a sliver of a moment I thought maybe that was how it would end. He would smile forlornly and give me a little kiss on the cheek and slip out of here, out of my life. That would be that. It was his choice.

He was *this close* to letting me go. I was sure of it. Then he let out a great sigh and said, "Just one more dinner. For old times' sake."

"Leo—"

"I'll even give you a severance package. You'll be able to stay here as long as you want, take care of your sister. No strings."

"Why would you do that?"

"I care about you. I love you. You know that."

"Okay," I said. "Okay, I'll do it. One more dinner. And then you'll let me go."

"Yes," he said. "I promise."

"I'm holding you to it." I looked straight at him. I wanted him to know I wasn't afraid of him anymore. I'd been through this before, after all.

"Wear that white dress," he said on his way down the stairs. An afterthought.

"What white dress?" Even though I knew exactly the one he was talking about.

"The one you were wearing in the picture," he said.

CHAPTER 25

I didn't need to wear the dress. I didn't need to please him anymore, or cater to his whims. I did it because I was going to uphold my end of the bargain. A professional to the end.

I was giving Leo Glass one more chance. One more chance to make this right. He could give me a severance package and get out of my life. If he left me and my sister alone, disappeared from my peripheral vision, faded into the background, never so much as spoke to me again, then it was over. I was a reasonable person, a forgiving person.

I took extra care with everything, the way I had my very first night before meeting Sebastian St. Doug at the Valerie Hotel. I curled my hair with the big-barreled curling iron. With makeup, I concealed the dark circles under my eyes, the vestiges of the red bumps traveling up my neck and cheeks. With lipstick on—the same shade I wore that night—I looked better than I'd looked for days. At least in low lighting.

Last, the ivory dress. It was ivory, not white. Leo didn't know the difference. Pure silk satin. The nicest dress in Mira's collection. I zipped it up the back and checked myself out in the full-length mirror on my bedroom door. The dress hung looser than it did almost half a year ago. I inflated my lungs with air, puffed up my chest to fill out the bodice. Then I exhaled all at once, like a deflating balloon. It didn't matter if the dress fit right anymore. This was the last time I'd ever wear it. After tonight I would take the whole pile of glittery gowns and burn them in a metal trash can on the rooftop. Something spectacular, a pagan ritual.

At seven o'clock, I stepped out into the living room with my cashmere coat slung over my arm. My sister was curled up on the couch, her neck craned over her phone. The tiny heels of my shoes made clicking sounds over the hardwood, and Wendy looked up. Her eyes roved over my outfit, the curled hair, the makeup. Her whole face transformed into a caricature of horror—wide-open eyes, dropped jaw. "Don't tell me you're going out with him."

I swiped her phone from her hands and made a show about turning it off. I opened it up and removed the SIM card, just in case. "Don't talk to anyone. Don't go online."

"What are you doing?"

"You don't know who Hannah really is," I warned her. "You don't know what she wants."

"She's my best friend. She wouldn't—"

"I hope you're right." I set the dismembered phone back on the coffee table.

"Where are you going?" Panic rose in her voice.

"I have everything under control."

"He just showed up here this morning," she said in a rush. "I let him in. I didn't know what to do."

"You don't have anything to worry about." I perched myself on the edge of the couch next to my sister, careful not to wrinkle my dress. "I'm going to fix everything."

"Fix everything," Wendy repeated.

She didn't get it. I softened my voice, placed a comforting hand on her shoulder. "Do you trust me?" Her eyes met mine. This girl, this frightened girl on my couch, was the only thing I had left. She was the kid who used to follow me around, dress in my clothes. My little sister. She loved me. She was nodding. She trusted me.

"Windy-girl," I said, calling her by her old name, her forgotten name. "Leo's not going to bother us anymore. Remember what I told you?"

Wendy shook her head, bewildered.

"I told you I could have saved you," I prompted in a placating tone. "I *should* have saved you all those years ago, but I didn't, and I'm sorry. I'm so sorry, but I'm going to make it up to you."

"What are you talking about?" she whispered.

"Remember—about your dad? How I could have stopped him? Everything would be different now. He wouldn't have hurt you. Mom would still be alive." Her face crumpled in confusion. I reached out and smoothed her hair with my hand. "Don't you worry, Windy-girl. I'm going to take care of everything."

~

In the landing outside my apartment, I checked the door, making sure it was locked. Sam was leaving his place at the same time. He was wearing his tuxedo and carrying his instrument case. "Rosemary—" he started, but I silenced him by widening my eyes and shaking my head. My eyes roved up and fixated on the Glasseye perched over the elevator.

Sam followed my gaze, and when he saw the Glasseye, his expression hardened. "Give me your shoe," he said, setting down his viola case.

I didn't question it. I slipped off one of my high-heeled shoes. Sam aimed at the Glasseye and threw the shoe, and both came down, bouncing once or twice on the floor. I scrambled over to my shoe and put it back on. The Glasseye rolled on the carpet before stopping with its pupil trained on the ceiling. Sam stood over it, frowning. Then he leaned down and waved. "Bye-bye, Leo," he said, right before smashing his heel down hard. I heard it crunch. A sickening sound, like a car crash.

He looked back up at me as if nothing had happened. "I found Wendy last night," he said. "We ran into each other in the lobby."

"Why didn't you tell me?"

The line between his eyes deepened. "Rosemary," he said. "I did."

"What?"

His face clouded over in concern. "I woke you up. We talked for maybe five minutes."

I had no memory of this.

He studied me carefully, registering the ivory dress, the hair, the lipstick. "What's going on?"

"One last dinner, and then it's over."

I could tell he wanted to grip me by the arms, shake some sense into me, but he didn't touch me. "You can't go back to him," he said. "You know that."

"I'm *not*. I'm ending it. Just like we discussed."

"You can end it on the phone."

"I destroyed my phone."

"You know what I mean."

"He came to my apartment," I said. I brushed past him and headed down the stairs. Sam's footsteps followed close behind.

"What—when?"

"This morning," I said over my shoulder as I descended the stairs. "Wendy let him in. I told him I'd meet him tonight. It was the only way to get him out."

"So don't show up. What's he going to do?"

I no longer heard Sam's footsteps. I stopped, on the landing between floors, and turned around to find him right behind me.

"Don't go," he said. "I don't want you to go."

We stood like that, frozen in the stairwell, until someone brushed past us, two residents, teenage boys in jogging gear. They stomped down the stairs, continuing the conversation they'd been having, their dialogue punctuated with "dudes" and "whoas."

I had to move in closer to Sam when they whizzed by, and he circled his arms around me. After the two guys had clambered all the way down and exited the building, his arms were still around me, holding me tightly. "Don't go," he repeated.

I brushed his hair with my hand, and then I tilted up my chin and kissed him—a long, sad kiss. Like a goodbye.

A lump formed in my throat, and my nose began to tingle. I pulled away and started back down the stairs ahead of him, so he wouldn't see me cry. He called my name, but I kept going, running out of the building and onto the street.

~

I was calm all the way over to Leo's. I walked, just like I did that first night with Sebastian St. Doug. That night had been warm, unseasonably warm. Tonight was different. Cool, the air heavy and smelling of salt and ozone. Storm clouds billowed overhead, but it wasn't raining. I walked from my apartment to Leo's, my high-heeled shoes clicking on the sidewalk.

I walked with my back straight, like I was being watched, like I was a character in a movie, the main character. The beautiful woman who knows exactly what she wants and exactly how she's going to get it. My hair swished across my back.

I walked down dark streets, past people huddled in tents they'd pitched on the sidewalks, over tattered plastic bags and abandoned shoes. Past all the beautiful downtown stores with headless mannequins in the windows, mannequins wearing designer clothes and dangling $4,000 handbags on the crooks of their arms. Store windows with displays of wool blankets in Native American designs, thick leather boots with steel toes, something a logger might wear at the end of the nineteenth century. The stores were all closed, the windows only partially lit. Everything looked different now, in the night.

By the time I got to Leo's place, my feet were killing me. I'd forgotten this part, how I'd walked and walked, how my feet had swollen up, rubbed the skin from the sides of my toes. It was only right, though, to do everything exactly the same way, as if I needed to follow these steps carefully, not making any mistakes, in order to reverse the spell.

~

As I rode the elevator up to the top floor of Leo's building, my predominant feeling was relief. This was the end. One more dinner. I would give him an opportunity to make good on his promise, give me a severance package and let me go. I didn't even want the severance package! I just needed him to set me free. Leo would plead with me to stay with him, offer me more money, a bigger apartment. Whatever it was, I wouldn't take it. I didn't want anything from him anymore.

I felt almost noble about it. I was someone who couldn't be bought. Not anymore. I would live on the streets before accepting another dime from Leo Glass. This idea no longer terrified me; it emboldened me. In the length of that elevator trip, visions swept through my mind of Wendy and me carrying our worldly goods in satchels tied to sticks. We'd jump on and off trains, camp in the woods on beds of pine needles. We'd find our tribe—other drifters, philosophers and scientists who could teach Wendy everything they knew. It wouldn't be the life I had planned, but it would be a good life, an adventurous, dangerous life—and isn't that what we really wanted after all? Not to be safe, snuggled in our little houses with a mortgage and high-speed internet, but to be in danger, living closer to the edge. We needed to creep closer to that edge to feel anything, to feel *alive*—

The doors to the elevator opened, and I stepped out into the hallway. The floral arrangement on the console table at the end of the hall had been changed since the last time I saw it. Tree branches with delicate bright-green leaves, barely unfurled. Unopened buds. The twigs arched up high over the clear glass vase in every direction, stark and beautiful in their own naked way.

The loft door was open, but no lights were on. "Leo?" I stood there in the darkness, waiting.

"*Hola*, Consuela," Leo said from somewhere inside the loft. My head pivoted around, straining to follow the vibrations of his voice.

After a stream of Spanish, the light fixture above the kitchen island burst on, like a spotlight, illuminating Leo standing behind it, his hands spread open wide, like Jesus presenting the last supper. His hands gestured to platters of food, all slick and glossy under the island lights. Pasta piled on a platter, swirled like a nest of worms, covered in what looked like specks of red pepper and sautéed mushrooms and kalamata olives. A composed salad of tomato and cucumber and basil. A loaf of crusty white bread on a wooden cutting board, butter in a dish. Leo's mouth stretched open, revealing those white tiles of teeth. "Surprise," he said.

"You made all this yourself?" I *was* surprised, just a little.

"The bread's from the bakery," Leo said modestly. "Can I pour you a glass of wine?" He reached for a corkscrew and began uncorking the bottle he had set next to the food.

"Sure," I said. "Why not."

He poured us each a glass, and we toasted across the island, catching each other's eye as our glasses clinked together.

"To us," he said.

I didn't say anything. I just drank. The last drink I'll share with Leo Glass. That was how I was going to get through the evening. Each bite, each sip was a celebration. Each bite one bite closer to the end. A couple of hours of eating pasta and buttered bread and sipping what I am sure was very, very good wine, and it would all be over. One way or another.

When I smiled back at Leo, it was genuine. "Everything looks delicious."

Getting through dinner was easy. I could say whatever I wanted; it didn't matter if Leo found it amusing or not. I talked about a lot of things. He could listen to *me* for a change. "You don't know the first thing about me, do you?" I mused, pouring myself another glass of wine. Our plates were empty by then. We'd eaten up all the pasta, the salad. Very tasty, I'd admitted to Leo after the first few tentative bites. He said I'd taught him well. "Did you know I used to live in a motel?"

"No," Leo said. "I didn't know that."

I told him about the motel we lived in, one of those pay-by-the-week places, a bona fide motor hotel, with fake shutters outside and heavy blackout drapes on all the windows, an ancient electric heater on one wall. When you turned it on you could see the little wires inside glowing, and it smelled the way I imagined a doll held over a flame would smell, like charred hair and rubber.

I told him the whole story, my twenty-one-year-old mother working graveyard shift while I slept in a sleeping bag in the motel office, a little room behind the front desk.

When I finished, I had to suck in a deep breath to keep myself from tearing up. I hadn't thought about that little scrap of my early childhood in years. Leo would have no idea why the memory made me want to blubber like a little kid. It wasn't because it was rough, living in a motel, sleeping in the office with the night manager. It was because I missed it; I missed that time before everything changed. Before Jason, before Wendy. When it was just the two of us, my mother and me, before anything bad had happened.

I shook my head briskly, the way you do when you want to wake up from a bad dream. "I think I'm still jet-lagged." I yawned for effect. "I should probably head out."

"We haven't had dessert." Leo gathered our plates and carried them over to the dishwasher. I followed behind him with our glasses. They were delicate, German crystal, so I took them to the sink to wash them by hand.

Later, in the days to follow, the months to follow, I would wonder about this moment, this decision to wash the crystal. Leo had a state-of-the-art dishwasher, silent and thorough. I could have left the glasses to the dishwasher, or to Leo. What did I care if they were ruined? I could have thrown them both to the ground, let them shatter down onto the cement floors of the loft, little shards tinkling and chiming and skittering across the floor, under the furniture. Then I could have marched out triumphantly, and my life would have veered off from there, on some unknown course.

But I insisted on washing the glasses. Stood over that sink and scrubbed at them with a soapy cloth. I felt him step behind me. I smelled him, a milky-minty odor, the vestiges of toothpaste and hair gel.

His hands clenched my hips. "You don't have to do that," he whispered into my ear.

Every muscle in my body stiffened, but I didn't push him away. The water rushed over each glass, and the suds swirled down the drain.

His fingers traveled to the hem of my dress. He inched the hem up and pressed himself against me. I set the glasses at the bottom of the sink and turned off the water. Only then did I grip the edge of the counter and jerk back, sending Leo stumbling into the island behind him.

Without saying a word, I reached for a linen dish towel, polished each glass dry, and placed them both back in the cupboard while Leo watched. Slowly, I walked around the island so we faced each other once again, the block of cupboards and quartz between us.

Leo recovered quickly, making himself busy, wiping the counter down with a dry bar towel. He tossed the cloth back so it rested over his shoulder like a limp epaulet. "You seem to be doing much better," he said. I didn't know what he meant, at first. "I was worried about you."

He was talking about France. That all seemed so long ago.

"This summer, we'll go back. You'll be amazed. Warm weather, cicadas. Swimming in the Mediterranean. Sitting outside in cafés . . ."

"I'm not going back."

"We can go somewhere else next time. Italy or Croatia—"

"One last dinner. You *promised*."

Leo grinned a devious little grin and shrugged, palms up. "I changed my mind."

Once again, I struggled to pry the diamond ring from my finger. It wouldn't budge. I kept pulling, twisting my swollen skin, jutting the metal against my knuckle. "I just want to leave." My voice came out cracked, like a sob. "I want this to be over."

"You can't leave."

"Watch me." I pivoted and strode across the room. It was a triumphant moment. I was seconds away from freedom. I would grab my coat from the hook and dash down the emergency stairs. Wendy and I would pack our bags and disappear. We'd cut our hair and dye it in a gas station bathroom and take a Greyhound bus to the Mexican border. We'd ride on the back of a pickup with some friendly farm workers who would take us to the next town, and eventually we'd end up in some small fishing village, some little place where no one spoke English and no one even had the internet, let alone a Lookinglass account. We'd learn Spanish and rent out a little hut covered in dried palm fronds.

"What about Wendy?" Leo shot out.

I should have kept walking. I shouldn't have listened. I froze in place, deliberating with myself. Then I turned around. "Don't." I pointed a finger straight at Leo, a warning.

"She needs help. Professional help."

The hairs on my arms bristled with energy, stood straight up.

Leo was still talking. "When she first moved in, she was—how should I put it—full-figured, right?" He cupped his hands in front of his chest. "Buxom."

"Stop talking," I said.

"She just started shrinking, didn't she?" Leo frowned, feigning perplexity. "Wearing all those baggy clothes. She stopped eating, for attention, maybe. Who knows. It didn't work. You didn't notice. She fainted in class, and still, you're like, sure, that's normal—"

"You've been *watching* my little sister? Creeping on her like some—some pervert?"

"She has a public account. Her friend, that woman, Hannah Westover? You know where Wendy met her?"

"On Lookinglass," I said flatly.

"In a pro-ana group. Ana Glass, they called it—you know, where girls get together and talk about starving themselves, brag about surviving on nothing but a head of iceberg lettuce. Hannah, she's like an old pro. In and out of facilities for years. She had to be tubed the last time. She was down to eighty-five pounds. She almost died."

"Wendy's not *anorexic*," I said, reeling. "She's vegan."

Leo raised his eyebrows as if to say, *You're sure about that?* "There's an in-patient eating-disorders clinic right here in town. Doctors, therapists, nutritionists. Wendy needs that."

My mind scrambled to make sense of everything. What Leo was telling me was true. It hit me all at once, a giant crashing wave, the truth of it. The baggy clothes, the empty containers in the sink, the fainting. I hadn't noticed. I hadn't paid attention. I'd let this happen, and Leo had watched everything, watched my sister dwindle down to skin and bones, and he hadn't said a word.

"Will they take her away from you, do you think?" Leo asked, as if this thought had just occurred to him. "When they find out? You're not even Wendy's legal guardian, and you're leaving her for weeks at a time with an unstable twenty-year-old. Your poor little sister is suffering, hurting herself. She could *die* from this. What's CPS going to say, I wonder?"

Leo wasn't going to give me a severance package. He wasn't going to let me walk away. I knew that. I had prepared for that, hadn't I? I'd been preparing since that day I held the steak knife to Jason's throat and told him to never touch me again.

After that time I *didn't* murder my stepfather, I thought about it a lot. I thought of how to get away with it. When other girls my age were fantasizing about weekend parties and boys and college applications, I was thinking about all the ways I could do it. I'd run over scenarios and weigh their pros and cons during class when I should have been learning how to graph a parabola or write a villanelle.

Drown him, push him from a great height. Shoot him, stab him, poison him, light the house on fire. Cut the brakes. There were so many ways to do it, but only three ways to get away with it. That's what I figured.

Make it look like an accident.

Make it look like self-defense.

Never get caught.

I didn't kill him, but I felt like I could, if it came to that again. It comforted me, knowing what was possible. It gave me the strength to keep going, to bide my time until I could leave home forever. He never did touch me again. I thought that was enough. I thought I had stopped him. I thought it was over, but it wasn't over. I had been a fool to think it was over. He didn't stop—he moved on to someone else. His own daughter. My little sister.

I could have saved her. That thought had haunted me, ever since she came to stay with me. And my mother, too. If I had taken care of Jason all those years ago, my mom would still be alive and Wendy would be okay and I wouldn't be standing here, in Leo's kitchen, right now.

The air between me and Leo quieted. Everything froze then. The island lights illuminated the dust floating through the air. Faint streaks became visible on the quartz countertops. The coils of his curls glistened. The light bounced off his skin, so smooth and tan, taut across the bones of his skull. Even from halfway across the room, I could make out the glacier blue of his eyes. I swear I could see a reflection of myself in the black pools of his pupils, like a hidden detail in an old Dutch painting.

Leo had a patient little smirk on his face, like he knew he had already won. Like he just needed me to calm down so we could sit on the couch and talk this out like adults. "You chose this," he said.

I yelled. I yelled a crazed, unleashed kind of yell, more animal than human. I backed up slowly, keeping my eyes trained on Leo. Then I ran, as fast as I could, back into the kitchen, and flung my whole body straight into the cabinets.

"Rosemary, what the hell—"

I yelled again and banged my face against the cupboards over and over again until I felt blood trickle down my nose. I didn't feel a thing—no pain—but I could smell it. I could taste it. The sharp, iron taste of blood.

"What are you doing?"

I turned to glare at him. I couldn't even feel my face, or whatever I'd done to it. "Making it look like self-defense," I said.

He looked confused and then like he was going to laugh. My hand shot out, reaching for the nearest knife on the magnetic rack. The boning knife. I raised it up over my head in one swift movement.

He was scared then, with the knife's pointy little edge so close to his pulse. His eyes pled with me. His lips curled back, revealing those straight gapped teeth. I wasn't looking at his face, but at his neck. His head was arched back, his neck wide open. Time slowed down, and my vision narrowed only to that part of his body. His Adam's apple bobbed up and down, once. His skin smooth, freshly shaven. Poreless. He hadn't missed a hair. I could almost feel it under my fingertips, just looking at it. Soft as a baby.

"Why are you doing this to me, Leo?" I hissed, pressing the tip of the knife against his throat, just enough to indent the skin without drawing blood. "Why won't you just *let me go*?"

Leo blinked at me. He no longer looked scared. He sensed an opening, a reprieve. The corners of his mouth turned up in a calm, placating smile, the kind of look you give a little kid or a dog. "You know why," he said. "Because I love you."

I plunged the blade deep into his throat, all the way down to the handle.

CHAPTER 26

I don't know how long I stood over his body. The knife was still in my hand. For however long it was—seconds, minutes—I couldn't move at all. My mind was empty and blank, a sky with no stars. I blinked down at Leo lying on the kitchen floor but couldn't make sense of it.

The knife had entered his throat so easily. It seemed like something that should have been harder to do, something that required more strength, more muscle. There was no give at all. Just—slip! My hand drew away from his neck, and my arm fell to my side. His eyes were round and scared and—surprised. He didn't think it would come to this. He didn't know—and how could he? I had never told him—that I had been preparing for this day for years, so long it felt like I'd been preparing for it my whole life.

He reached up and grasped his neck with both hands, and blood oozed out between his fingers. It didn't spurt out of him like a fountain. It came all at once, like lava gushing from the cracks in the earth, thick and hot. He tried to say something, but of course he couldn't, and then he crumpled to the ground.

It was very fast, or at least that was how it seemed to me then. I stood ready to fight, ready to plunge the knife in again and again until the job was finished, but that hadn't been necessary. He was dying all on his own, twitching once or twice and then lying still, his eyes open. He was dead.

His body was lying in an unnatural position, his legs twisted over to the side, his head resting in a pool of dark blood. The way his head was angled, you couldn't see the wound I'd made in him, the drain of his throat. The towel that he'd slung over his shoulder lay underneath him, soaked in blood, a bright-red flag.

The knife slipped from my fingers and clattered to the floor. The sound jarred me, and I snapped out of my trance. My mind went from blank to overloaded in the space of a second. I blinked my eyes and looked down at Leo Glass's body, and I understood what I had done. I took in a breath and covered my mouth with my hand, stifling a scream.

Then I did scream. I screamed for help.

When the echoes of my screams faded, I closed my eyes, trying to think.

This didn't look like any kind of accident I had ever heard of. It was too late for that. I would get caught—there was no question about that. They would find me. I'd be the first person any reasonable person would suspect. I had the three main criteria the police looked for in a killer. Motive, means, opportunity.

I couldn't dispose of the body. It would be impossible. My DNA was all over this place. My golden hairs threaded through the fibers of his clothes. My skin cells in the dust. I'd met his mother. Alejandro, Teddy, even Margorie. Everyone in La Cuisine. Everyone knew about me.

Calling the police was how I got out of this. It was the only way. That was the plan, I reminded myself. I scrambled across the loft, searching for my bag. Usually I set it down as soon as I came in, right by the door. Yes—there it was, on a small table. My hands shook as I opened it. My hands were clean. This struck me as strange. I turned them over in front of my eyes, inspected each side carefully. Not a drop of blood. The diamond on my left hand glinted, even in this unlit corner of the loft.

The Mirror wasn't there. I dropped my bag back on the table. Of course. I had destroyed it. Boiled it alive.

I would have to use Leo's. I made a mad dash through the loft with the hope that he had set it down somewhere. He hadn't. Back at the island of the kitchen, I positioned myself just right, so I could avoid looking at the body lying on the ground on the other side, wedged between the island and the stove. He kept the Mirror in his back pocket, usually. I could go over to the body, reach underneath him, dig it out.

You're never supposed to move a body. It would tamper with the evidence. Police needed to see exactly how someone died in order to solve the crime. I closed my eyes and tried to think. I couldn't think; I wasn't thinking straight at all. What did I care if the police solved this crime? It was self-defense. I wanted it to look like self-defense. If I dug out his Mirror to make the call, that would only support my story. Right? Yes. It would play. I needed to retrieve his device from his corpse, from a pool of his cold, sticky blood—

There was just no way. I couldn't bear to tiptoe around the island and look at him lying there, twisted up like a deer on the side of the road, a lump of bones and skin and blood that had moments before been alive, its heart beating madly, its lungs pumping air in and out, in and out.

I opened my eyes again. There was still a way to make this work, to call this in, to tell the story to the authorities, a story they might believe. There was still a chance.

"*Hola*, Consuela," I said out loud, in a weak, trembling little voice. I cleared my throat and tried again. "*Hola*, Consuela." This time my voice was strong, like a captain issuing orders to her crew. "Dial 911."

I stood still, listening. I waited to hear a dial tone, waited to hear someone at the other end of the line. It was silent, as silent as I'd ever heard it up here. Even the dishwasher made no sound. A blue light shone down from the machine onto the polished cement floors, refracted off the pool of blood.

I began to unravel. I lifted my hand to my face and felt my skin, broken and swollen. When I placed my hand in front of my eyes, I saw blood on my fingers and I reared back, afraid, for a moment believing that Leo's blood had appeared there spontaneously, burst from my hands like the stigmata of Christ. Then I laughed out loud. It was *my* blood. I'd hit my head against the cabinets. I had done this; I'd done it to myself. For the first time I felt the pain in my face, the skin swelling from the smacks I'd delivered against the surface of the cabinets. My sinuses tingled when I took in a breath.

"*Hola*, Consuela," I said again. When nothing happened, I yelled it into the apartment, over and over. "*HOLA*, CONSUELA! *HOLA*, CONSUELA! *HOLA*, please! *Por favor!* It's an EMERGENCY!"

After that I stopped thinking altogether. I moved like a robot around the island and lifted the knife from the floor. I stepped over to the sink, careful not to set foot in Leo's blood. It didn't disgust me. It interested me, in that moment. It was like I wasn't seeing it at all, but processing it in a clinical, dispassionate way.

I ran the knife under water and washed it with dish soap, using no sponge or cloth. I scrubbed the blade with my own fingers and then let the hot water rinse all the evidence down the drain. I dried the blade with the dishcloth and then, holding the blade with the cloth, hung it back on the magnetic rack. Every knife hung straight up and down, in descending order of size. The boning knife rested between the Santoku and a serrated utility knife. The sight of them assured me that everything was going to be okay. I stuffed the dishcloth down the front of my dress and went over to the table to collect my handbag. After surveying the loft one more time, I slipped my arms through the sleeves of my coat, and I walked out the door.

~

Out on the street, the air was cold and damp, but it wasn't raining. I pulled my hood up over my head and put on my sunglasses, glancing up and down the street. No one had seen me exit the building. I stood there for what must have been several minutes before I heard voices in the distance. The Park Blocks, a moment before dark and empty, now teemed with people, talking and laughing. I walked toward them, into the crowd, and stopped to wait in the shadows at the trunk of a giant ash tree.

I stood, waiting, holding my body completely still. If I stood like that, no one would notice me. No one would remember seeing me at all. It would be as if I didn't exist. I waited for a quarter of an hour, maybe longer. I wasn't even sure what I was waiting for until the first rush of the crowd faded away, down the streets, away from the dark Park Blocks and into late-night restaurants and bars.

The symphony players filed out of the concert hall last, out on Salmon Street, carrying their instruments in cases. Some of them were laughing, talking. Others walked quickly, heads down, in a rush to get back home, out of the chilled air. Maybe they had husbands or wives. Little children waiting to be kissed good night.

I didn't know how I would recognize Sam, dressed like all the others, but I did. I saw him right away, his hair messy, flopping as he walked. He was walking with a man and a woman, and I was afraid I'd have to call for him, to draw attention to myself. I imagined everyone—the entire symphony—stopping dead in their tracks to stare at me, to note the bruises blooming over my skin, the blood drying around my nostrils. They'd remember something like that. They'd know the exact time. They'd all be in perfect agreement.

I willed Sam to sense my presence under the tree, in the shadows, but he didn't look up as he and the others walked up the path. In a moment, they would pass me by, and I would be forced to slink after them, to yank him by the arm from the path like a masked villain. I had to get his attention now. Before he could slip past me, I stepped out of the shadows and onto the path.

"Excuse me," Sam said, almost crashing into me. Then his eyes opened wider, taking me in.

The other two in his group were still walking, absorbed in their conversation. I stepped back off the path and turned my face away from the light as Sam called after them. "Hey, guys," he called out. His voice sounded unnatural, like a bad actor trying to come off as casual and failing. "I'll meet up with you later."

A painful back-and-forth ensued. They wouldn't just let him go. They insisted that he join them. He had promised—one drink. Sam said no, he was tired. It had come over him suddenly, this fatigue. He didn't have it in him after all. He needed to get home. Finally they relented and walked away.

Sam watched as they proceeded down the path. He watched until they crossed the street and disappeared around a corner. I crept away over the grass, so when he turned back to find me, he had to jog into the park to catch up to me. I turned around to face him, and I could see him trying to absorb everything: me, my battered face, my trembling hands. He didn't say anything. He gathered me up in his arms and held me, squeezing me so tightly that I almost couldn't breathe. I rested my head against his chest and closed my eyes. I wrapped my arms around his waist. It was going to be okay.

After a minute, Sam placed his hands on my shoulders and held me at arm's length, inspecting me. He tried to pull the glasses from my face, but I wouldn't let him. "Glasseyes," I whispered. His fingers ran over my face, gently, feeling my bruised skin.

"I'm okay," I said, because the look in his eyes was killing me. Like he couldn't bear it, the sight of me. "I'm okay."

Gently, he removed the sunglasses, and I flinched, my eyes adjusting to the glare of the streetlights in the distance.

I could only shake my head at him, and I could see him taking it in, deciding. Deciding what to do. "We need to call the police," he said after a moment. "You need to file a report."

I should have agreed. It was what I wanted, what I had tried to do. I *had* tried, too. I had yelled for Consuela. I would call the police and they would see me, my bruised face. They would see Leo lying on the floor, the thin little slice in his neck, made with a knife so sharp they would hardly know it was there if it weren't for the pool of blood. They would conclude I had had to do it, that it was self-defense. They would send me in for questioning, and I would lie. I'd tell them that Leo had banged my head against the cabinets, and maybe they would believe it—because why wouldn't they? It would make sense to them. He banged my head against the cabinets, I grabbed the knife, I sank the knife into his throat. Just like that.

They might ask why I didn't call the police, not right away. Well, I didn't have a phone. I had destroyed my Mirror. That made sense. I'd explain that part. They might ask about the knife. If it was self-defense, they might ask, can you explain the knife? Can you explain, Miss Rabourne, why you picked the knife up off the floor and washed it? Why you dried it and polished it and hung it back on the rack? Why you took the towel you used to dry it off and stuffed it down the front of your dress?

I looked up at Sam. "I can't go to the police," I said.

His face changed. The concern in his eyes, the ridges in his forehead, all shifted. He had been concerned for my welfare, enraged on my behalf—and he still was. I knew he was. Now I could see something else in his features. Fear. "What did you do." He didn't phrase it as a question. His voice was calm, but he gripped my shoulders more tightly when he said it. "What the fuck did you do?"

He wasn't asking because he judged me. He was asking because, whatever it was, whatever I said next, he was going to help me. He would do anything for me.

When I closed my eyes, hot tears ran down my cheeks, all at once. I swiped them away with the back of my hand. My hands were trembling. I squeezed my left hand in my right, trying to stop them from shaking. A shiver ran through me, and then my whole body caught up with my hands. It wasn't that cold outside, but I was shivering as if the streets were slick with ice, as if I were buried in snow.

Sam took me in his arms again. He was whispering something in my ear, but whatever it was, it seemed like it was coming from very far away.

~

I don't remember the drive to my apartment, but there must have been one, because the next thing I knew, there we were.

"She won't stop shivering," I heard Sam say.

"What's going on?" Wendy asked. "What happened to her face?" She waved her hands in front of me. "Rosemary? Hey! Look at me! What's *wrong* with her?"

I felt a thick quilt wrapping around me, and then I was being lifted up and deposited on the couch. I didn't fall asleep. I didn't even close my eyes, but the next few hours passed by in a murky, distorted way, as if I were an extra in someone else's dream. Sam's and Wendy's footsteps thumped over the hardwood floors.

Sam came back to me. He placed a warm hand on my forehead. "We've got to go," he said.

I may have dozed off in the car. I don't know. They set me up in the back seat, fastened my seat belt, and arranged blankets around me like I was some dying child in a British historical drama. I had stopped shivering by then, but the chill hadn't left my bones. They felt frozen all the way through.

Sam drove us out of the city, away from the lights, and into the forest. They didn't turn on the radio. I could hear their voices, murmuring, but couldn't make out any of the words. I turned my head and watched out the window. We wound through the woods, the trees looming over on either side of the road. I couldn't see the sky at all.

Then we left the forest, and the road opened up before us, a black strip with a yellow line dotted down the middle. Wendy and Sam had stopped talking, and all I could hear was the sound of tires and the engine humming. We were the only car on the road at this hour, and I remember thinking that this was a good thing. I didn't know where we were going, where Sam was taking me. This was good, too. It was better not to know.

CHAPTER 27

I woke up in an unfamiliar bed, unsure whether it was day or night. I opened my eyes for just a split second and then closed them again. It seemed like several days had passed. Years, even. If I could drag myself out of bed and look at myself in the mirror, I'd see an old woman, gray hair down to the floor.

I'd had dreams, a confusing jumble of dreams, just flashes of sounds and pictures with no story at all. My throat was dry, completely desiccated. I opened my mouth, but I couldn't make a sound. The thirst was unbearable, but I was pinned to the bed by the sheets. I couldn't move.

I drifted off again, not quite into sleep, but into some twilight world where sleep and waking blurred together. I heard his voice, the voice of my stepfather. I could feel his hands over me, smoothing the sheets over my body, tucking them in under the mattress. I lay still. If I lay like this, I could sink down, through the bed. I could disappear. Snug as a bug in a rug, he whispered.

"No!" I yelled. And then I did what I had never done back then, back when I was a kid. I thrashed in that bed, kicking my legs, punching with my fists. "No!" I yelled, and my voice was dry and cracked, but it was loud all the same. The sheets ripped out from the mattress, loosening their hold on me, and still I kicked. My feet battled with the sheets until they were defeated, a damp and crumpled lump on the floor.

Someone murmuring. A door opening and closing. Rosemary, they were saying. It was just a dream. You were having a bad dream.

Someone held a glass of water to my lips, and I drank in sloppy gulps. "Slow down. It's okay." It was Wendy.

I opened my eyes and saw Wendy and Sam standing over me. Wendy put a cool hand on my forehead. "She's burning up," she said.

"Give her more water."

Wendy placed the glass to my lips again. I took it from her and tried to sit up. Wendy and Sam looked at each other.

"We should call a doctor," Wendy said.

"We can't." Sam's words came out clipped. Panicked. "We can't call anybody."

My eyes drifted closed again. Their voices sounded too loud. I wanted them to leave me alone, let me sleep. I tried to tell them, but my words came out as a grunt. "Okay, okay." I felt Sam's hand smoothing my hair. "Lie back down."

"I'll remake her bed," Wendy said.

"No!" My eyes opened, as wide as they would go. "No sheets." That was the last thing I remember before fading back out.

~

I woke up shivering. This time was different, as if I'd been stitched back together in my sleep. The shapes in the room wouldn't come into focus. I switched on a bedside lamp and squinted until my eyes adjusted to the light. The room was rustic, like a ski lodge. The bed was made out of logs. A hunter-green tapestry hung on the wall, something woven out of rough wool.

Someone had dressed me in a flannel nightgown. I didn't own a flannel nightgown, certainly nothing like this one, a navy-blue plaid like furniture upholstery from a boy's bedroom. Long, down to the floor, with a ruffle at the hem. Yoked collar with buttons up to the neck. I was wearing different underwear, too, a plain pair of cotton briefs.

I changed into some long underwear and an oversize sweater folded neatly on a chair next to the bed and crept down a hallway and into a bathroom. A tiny collection of travel toiletries lay arranged on a folded washcloth: new toothbrush, miniature tube of toothpaste, shampoo and conditioner.

I brushed my teeth with my eyes closed, avoiding looking at myself in the mirror. I splashed cold water on my face. The water stung, reopening tiny cuts on my skin. Everywhere we go, we leave traces of ourselves. Skin cells and hairs and molecules from our spit. At this very moment, detectives could be scraping my skin off the cupboards in Leo's kitchen. They would find the salt left from my tears mixed in with his blood.

There is no way I am getting away with this. The thought scrolled through my head, waved in front of me like a banner carried through the sky by an airplane. It didn't frighten me or send me into hysterics. It was, simply, the truth.

~

Sam and Wendy didn't see me emerge from the hallway. Sam was stirring something on the stove, and Wendy was sitting at a wooden farm table. She was talking, trying to impress him with some story. While she talked, she was peeling and slicing carrots. I watched them for a few minutes. The kitchen was filled with steam, with smells of baking bread and canned soup.

Wendy was telling Sam a story about our mother. I couldn't hear what it was about beyond that, but from the way she told it, it sounded like a happy memory. She couldn't talk and peel carrots at the same time. She would pause midsentence to peel one long curl of carrot skin and then resume, looking back up at Sam to make sure he was paying attention. He was. He chuckled softly while she talked, raised his eyebrows in anticipation during the pauses.

When I shuffled in on stocking feet, Wendy dropped her peeler onto the cutting board, and Sam let the spoon clang into the pot. They rushed to my side, each taking an arm, and they led me across the kitchen to the dining table, settled me into a chair.

"Where are we?" My voice sounded hoarse. I cleared my throat. "How long have we been here?"

"We're in the middle of nowhere," Wendy said. "No one will find us here."

In the kitchen window I saw my own reflection, this picture of me curled up on a dining chair, Sam and Wendy behind me, a hand on each shoulder, like we were about to pose for a portrait. Beyond that reflection, darkness. A forest and a night sky. "What is this place?"

"We're at my aunt and uncle's cabin," Sam said. "Outside La Pine."

"What are we doing here?"

Sam and Wendy exchanged looks.

"We thought it's what you wanted," Sam said after a pause.

"What you *needed*," Wendy clarified, and Sam nodded in agreement. "You weren't talking; we couldn't ask you—we tried but you were in shock—and Rosemary, you should have seen yourself. Your face. Your dress, it was—"

Sam shook his head at Wendy, and my sister clamped her mouth shut. She stared at me, biting her lip, her eyes bulging out.

"Maybe we should eat." Sam dished out bowls of soup and set one in front of each of us.

"There's bread, too." Wendy opened the oven door, unleashing a gust of acrid smoke. "It's burned." She frowned at the baguette cremains on the tray.

"We can't cook," Sam said.

My lips cracked as I broke into a smile; it seemed like it had been weeks since they had formed that shape, since I'd had anything to smile about. Sam and Wendy beamed back, and for a few moments we pretended nothing was wrong. We sat together and ate our soup. For the first time in a long time, I started to imagine that everything might work out, that the last several months had been nothing but a horrible dream, that my real life was here, in this A-frame cabin in the middle of the forest. This is where we belonged, in this place where no one would ever find us.

CHAPTER 28

I couldn't fall asleep that night, not after dozing all day. I'd been off schedule ever since my trip to France. It was dark inside the room, but I could make out the shape of Wendy on the twin bed next to mine, the blankets sighing up and down over her breathing body.

I padded down the dark hallway and into the living room. I told myself I'd go up to Sam if his light was still on in the loft. The light wasn't on, but I went up anyway. The moon shone through the skylight, illuminating his face. I'd never watched him sleep before. All those nights we'd slept, side by side in our separate beds, in our separate apartments, that wall between us. His face was twisted up, tortured. His eyeballs moved back and forth under the lids, faster and faster. I reached out my hand and let it hover over his face. I couldn't remember—were you supposed to wake someone from a bad dream or just let them work through it, ride it out?

His breath quickened. He was sucking air in quickly, in bursts. *Fft, fft, fft.*

"*Sam!*" I whispered. The moment my hand landed on his cheek, his eyes opened, two unseeing moons. His own hand lifted to his throat, like he was choking, and then he jerked straight up.

I shook his shoulders and said his name over and over until I felt him collapse onto me. Our arms cinched around each other, tighter and tighter, and I closed my eyes and buried my face in his shoulder. Into my ear he whispered, "What did you *do*, Rosemary?" Instead of answering, I placed my mouth on his. He tasted like buttered toast.

I wanted him to touch me everywhere, to erase all the places Leo had touched. When I was with Sam, I could forget everything that had happened, pretend to go back in time, before I'd made such a mess of things. As if being with Sam reversed it all. Everything could go backward: Leo in the pool of blood, the knife in his throat, the knife in my hand, my head on the cupboard, France, the symphony, Hawaii, San Francisco, Thai Lotus, Sebastian St. Doug, and just before that, when Leo didn't exist at all, not for me. When I was with Sam, I could forget that I'd ever met anyone named Leo Glass. I could pretend that I'd never heard of him, that he never existed at all.

And without Leo there was only Sam. We were naked, our bodies still wrapped up in each other. Holding on to each other in a way I didn't remember from before, like we were keeping each other from falling off a too-small life raft.

"You have to tell me what happened," he said into my hair.

"It's better if you don't know."

By the light of the moon streaming through the skylight, I could make out the features of Sam's face. His eyes were narrowed, his mouth set in a firm line. A determined look.

"What?" I asked. It seemed like he had something he wanted to tell me.

"I've been thinking," he said carefully. "You need to get out of here. *We* need to get out of here."

"Out of the cabin?"

"Out of the country."

"They aren't going to let me out of the country."

"They will if we do it now," Sam said. His eyes held mine, and I studied them, tried to memorize them. He pulled my body in closer to his, so every part of us touched, so I could feel his skin against mine. He kissed me hard on the mouth, cupping the back of my head with his hand.

When we broke apart, we were both gasping for air. "They will what?" I asked.

"Let you leave the country," he said. "We'll leave first thing in the morning. You, me, Wendy. I have our passports."

"They'll stop us. They won't let us out."

"It *will* work. And they won't stop us at the border because no one knows—whatever you did, no one knows. Not yet. I've been paying attention to the news, listening to police reports. Trust me: there's still time."

Sam told me he had worked it all out. We would drive to Redmond and take the first flight out—it didn't matter where. Then we'd make our way over to Europe. He knew people in Europe. He could get a symphony job. He had studied under Magdalene Heiss. That meant something. She was a friend of the family, she would help. We could go to a nonextradition country. Even if the police did find me, they couldn't arrest me. It would be too late.

"A nonextradition country?"

"Russia, maybe," Sam said. "Or Iceland."

"Russia? What would I do there? What about Wendy? She hasn't even graduated from high school."

Sam had thought about that, too. He had worked it all out. Wendy could get help. "I'm not saying it would be easy," he said. "I'm saying we could be together."

For a moment neither of us said anything. The silence rang out, demanding my response. All I had to do was say yes.

"I don't get it," I said at last, my voice so soft he had to press his ear to my mouth to hear the words. "Give up everything—your whole life. Live in Russia. And that's if we didn't get caught. You could go to jail. Aiding and abetting—what is that, a felony? How many years would they lock you up for that? You'd risk everything, and for what? For me? Why would you do it?"

Sam kissed me on the forehead and then worked his way down my face. The bridge of my nose. My cheeks. My lips. "You know why."

I wanted to tell him that I felt the same way, that I loved him, but I couldn't make myself say those words, and I wondered if saying those words so many times to the wrong person had altered me forever, cursed me somehow. Like some old fairy tale or Greek myth, saying the words to the wrong person could haunt me for life, unleash a box of evil spirits. Saying it to the right person, then, would have the potential to fix everything. My mouth opened and closed again, but the words didn't come.

We lay in silence, just looking at each other, for what must have been an entire minute before he spoke again. "Promise me you'll let me help you now," he said. "You have to promise me."

I thought about this new life he talked about, living in some snowy tundra. Wendy getting better by summiting mountains and lying on analysts' couches and soaking in geothermal mineral pools. Me and Sam, together. We'd live in an attic garret at first, with skylights. I was picturing the attic where Sara lived in *A Little Princess*, after she lost her fortune and Miss Minchin banished her upstairs to be the scullery maid. We'd start out somewhere like that, but Sam would rise up the ranks in the symphony and I—I didn't know what I would do. I couldn't envision it. I'd paint, maybe. I'd never painted before, but it seemed like something I could do, in my new life.

"I promise," I said.

I believed it when I said it. I remember it, that feeling. That feeling that he was going to save me and we'd run off together and everything would turn out all right.

~

I waited until Sam's eyelids dropped and his breathing slowed down before I untangled our limbs, pulled on my clothes, and crept back downstairs to the kitchen.

I pulled out pots and pans from the cupboards and food from the fridge. It was stocked full of food, as if they planned to hide out here for several weeks. Walnuts and spinach and tomatoes and kalamata olives and garlic and onions. I wasn't sure what I was doing at first. Mincing onions and boiling water and rinsing greens. A half hour later I'd created some sort of vegan pasta casserole I hoped Wendy would eat.

Next, a pie. Apple with a lattice top. I made the pastry from memory, unsure of how it would turn out with vegan butter. Everything came together in a trance. Sliced apples tossed with cinnamon and sugar and a squeeze of lemon. A lattice crust woven across the top. Pastry edges perfectly crimped. I covered everything with foil and wrote down some vague baking instructions. I couldn't remember how hot to bake a pie, or for how long.

I understood, then, what I was doing: preparing food for them to eat after I was gone. As if I would walk out of here, disappear, and they'd still be here, in this cabin in the middle of nowhere, together. It didn't make sense, but I liked to imagine it anyway. I liked to imagine that future for them.

When I was done, I slipped into the twin bed next to Wendy's. I couldn't get warm. Under the weight of blankets, all loose on top of me, nothing tucked in around me.

This time I dreamed of Leo. Lying on the bed, I could feel him, feel his fingers inside of me, the pinch of the tweezers. I felt something emerge from my body, like I was giving birth, and then I was empty and Leo was saying, Look, Rosemary. Look what I found in there. I looked up, and there he was, his dark, curly hair and pale-blue eyes with the pupils big and black as beetles. With the tweezers he was pinching the tiny legs of a bird, a brown bird with wet feathers and frightened, flapping wings. He closed both hands over the bird, and the bird disappeared into his cupped hands, but they weren't Leo's hands anymore. They weren't Leo's eyes. They were Jason's. You've killed him now, Jason said. You've killed him with your human scent.

I bolted upright. "No!" I yelled.

"*Shh.* It's okay. It was just a dream." Wendy bent over me, picking up blankets off the floor. She flapped them out over me, piling them back on, one by one. "Go back to sleep," she whispered, and I wrapped my arms around her, forcing her to climb in under the covers with me.

I felt her body stiffen and then relax. She put her arms around me, too. We hadn't nestled together like that since she was very young, maybe four or five years old, when she was the one waking up from a nightmare and I would be the one to straighten her covers and shush her back to sleep. Her body was so slight, slighter than it should be. I could feel the ridges of her ribs on her back.

I waited until her eyes drifted closed and her breathing slowed, and then I slipped out of her arms, out of the bed. She looked different lying there. So small, no makeup on. She reminded me of the little girl she had been. For the thousandth time since that trip to France, I tugged at the ring on my left hand. This time it came off—slipped right off my finger. Carefully, I placed it on Wendy's hand. It fit on her index finger. The huge diamond on her frail little hand struck me as one of the saddest sights I'd ever seen. I pulled the blankets up higher, covering her hand with the edge of the sheet.

~

The air outside was cold, like it wasn't springtime here, not yet. Patches of old snow still remained on the ground, over webs of grayed leaves and pine needles. The sky was just beginning to glow with light. The kind of morning that was so beautiful and perfect, it made me question why I slept through most of them. I should have risen before the sun every day and looked out at the sky, but I didn't. I'd just slept right through everything.

Only one road led out, twisting west through low hills. I followed it to the highway.

CHAPTER 29

During the entire bus ride back to Portland, I kept expecting to get pulled over by a fleet of police cars with sirens and megaphones. They would demand the bus pull to the side of the road, and then they'd storm on board, yank me out of my seat, and arrest me on the spot for the murder of Leo Glass.

I thought they would be waiting for me when the bus pulled into the downtown station, but I got off the bus with everyone else and walked out into a bright spring day. Trees swayed overhead, their leaves new and bright green. The sky was blue, spackled with fluffy white clouds that billowed into shapes that looked like animals. Like a poodle chasing a T. rex. Birds chirped. A man in filthy pajama pants pushing a shopping cart asked me for spare change. I gave him a dollar and kept walking. No one stopped me.

Life was going on as if nothing had happened. Sunshine felt warm on my skin. I lifted my face up to the sky and breathed.

~

"I want to confess to a crime," I announced to the woman sitting behind a desk at the downtown police station.

She was on the phone, listening intently and nodding her head.

"I want to confess to a crime." I made my voice strong, so the woman would pay attention, so everyone would pay attention. The police in the back rooms would hear it. I wanted everyone to know. "I killed Leo Glass."

~

I sat in an interrogation room for hours before anyone came by to question me. Finally a man came in and settled himself into the chair across from me. Sanders was his name, according to his badge. Middle-aged guy, soft around the middle. He didn't look like the city's top homicide detective or anything, but what did I know. I wanted someone more handsome, someone with hard edges and expressive eyebrows, someone who would reduce me to tears with one scathing look.

He handed me a candy bar. "You must be hungry, sitting in here all day. Can I get you anything? Coffee?"

I stared at him reproachfully. Like he was wasting my time.

He sat across from me and took out a notebook. "So what brings you here today?" he asked. He pointed to his own face, frowning. "Those are some pretty nasty bruises you got there."

If this was an interrogation strategy, I didn't understand it. "I *came* here to confess." I was annoyed. I'd walked into the police station and told them I'd committed felony murder, and no one was doing anything about it.

"All right then," he said. Poised a pencil on the notepad, eyebrows raised.

"I already did confess—*hours* ago."

"You have my undivided attention—oh, wait." He flipped around his notebook, searching for a blank page. "Can you state your name for the record?"

"Rosemary Rabourne."

"No middle name?"

"No."

"All right. Go for it."

"Leo Glass. I—I killed him." I tossed my hands up in the air, as if to say, *That's about it.* The confession had, in the hours that had ticked by, lost its power.

The detective didn't write anything down on his notepad. He stared at me, and I stared back. "Leo Glass," he said, breaking what must have been a five-minute silence. "Walk me through it."

"Walk you through what?"

"You killed him, didn't you? Tell me how it happened."

"What do you want to know?"

"Start from the beginning."

"The beginning of the day or—"

He waved his hand. "Before that. How'd you meet the guy."

I sighed. "Listen, I don't see how that's relevant."

Raised eyebrows. "Not relevant? Your relationship to the victim is irrelevant to the crime?" He made a fake *I'm confused* face.

"I'm saying I did it! I killed Leo Glass—I'm admitting it." I held both of my hands out in front of me, locked at the wrists. "Handcuff me. Read me my rights. I don't *want* to tell you the whole story. I don't want to go to trial. I want you to lock me up in a jail cell and leave me alone."

"That's not exactly how things work around here."

I laid my head down on the table. I was so tired. If I closed my eyes, I could fall asleep in an instant. I just wanted it to be over. I lifted my eyes up to Officer Sanders without moving my head. "Please, just arrest me."

For the first time, the officer dropped his jovial affect. I saw the switch happen right before my eyes. His face went from fake-confused to blank and then—soft. "All right."

At that moment, the door opened, and a woman walked in. She looked out of place, as if she'd accidentally stumbled in here on her way to the restroom. An officer held the door open for her. He nodded to Sanders and then pulled the door back closed.

She was young—about thirty, I guessed. "Priya Chandra," she said to me, extending her hand for me to shake. "I'll be representing you." She seemed to be out of breath.

She didn't look like a lawyer. Her long black hair was messy. She hadn't brushed it this morning or maybe even this week. The ends were dyed chartreuse. The whole bottom three inches of her hair, that bright neon green of a traffic safety vest. What kind of lawyer dyed the ends of her hair neon green? Her clothes, too, struck me as very unlawyerly. A black skirt over thick black tights, a vintage Iron Maiden T-shirt, and a thick cable-knit cardigan a few sizes too big. It was a strange color that clashed with her hair, a fusion of lavender and pink.

She straightened up and cleared her throat, slowly gaining her footing. She turned to Officer Sanders and asked in a firm, commanding voice, "Is my client under arrest?"

Sanders looked surprised, too. His eyebrows were pasted halfway up his forehead. "Nooo," he said slowly, "but not for lack of trying."

"Then I'm taking her out of here," she said. "Rosemary, don't say a thing."

"I've already confessed."

"Not one more word."

I gave the officer a pleading look. "Please, just do it now."

Officer Sanders stood up and frowned down at me. He gave me a strange look. He felt sorry for me, I guessed. Me with my black-and-blue face, the tragic vintage ski clothes I had put on in the cabin. "Rosemary Rabourne," he said. "I'm placing you under arrest for the murder of Leo Glass."

CHAPTER 30

The next few minutes were a jumble of confusion, with everyone talking over everyone else. The officer was reading me my rights. The lawyer was echoing everything the officer said: "You have the right to remain silent, Rosemary! You have the right to consult with an attorney!" I was saying, "I don't want a lawyer, I did it. I confessed!"

I don't know how she ended up getting her way, but she did. Officer Sanders left me alone with her in the room. She sat across from me, the stainless steel table between us. I was under arrest, but nothing felt any different. He hadn't even handcuffed me. I crossed my arms over my chest and frowned at this woman with the weird hair. She was ruining everything.

"Listen, I didn't have to come here today," she said, as if she could read my thoughts. "I'm *trying* to help you."

"I can take care of myself."

"Obviously you can't."

I narrowed my eyes at her, her tousled hair, her horrible granny sweater. "Are you a public defender or something?" It seemed like a public defender would at least be in a suit. A cheap suit, but a suit.

"No. I'm here as a favor. Don't do anything stupid." She pulled back her sweater sleeve, looked at her watch, and sighed heavily.

"A favor? Who would be doing me a favor? No one even knows I'm here."

"Trust me, Rosemary, everyone knows you're here."

"I came in hours ago, and they've just been ignoring me."

"It just broke on the news."

"What did?"

She gave me a strange look, as if she couldn't quite figure out what to tell me. "They found Leo Glass dead in his apartment." She looked at her watch again. "Oh, thirty minutes ago. Social media was all over it. They're saying you did it, and then some reporter claimed a young woman had turned herself in for this very crime, and—"

I sat there, stunned, taking it all in. Leo Glass, dead in his apartment. When she said it, I had winced, shocked. I wasn't acting. In a strange way, it had shocked me. The last couple of days had unspooled like a fever dream. Nothing had seemed real. I had tried to confess, and no one had cared.

"Stop crying," Priya was saying.

I reached my hand up to my face. It was covered in hot tears. I wasn't crying for Leo Glass. I was crying from exhaustion. Relief. This would be over soon. I would confess and they would lock me up and I would get what I deserved. I had been wrong, wrong about everything. I hadn't been able to save Wendy. I hadn't fixed anything. I'd made everything worse. Locking me up would be the best thing for her, really. They needed to keep me away from her for good.

"Listen, she's going to help you. Just sit tight, okay?"

I made an attempt to dry my face with my hands. The tears had stopped. "Who?"

"Another lawyer. She's flying in from LA. She jumped on the plane the minute she heard the news. She made me run over here before—I don't know. Before you did anything stupid. I ran here. Ten blocks."

"I don't need your help."

"Look, Rosemary. This doesn't look good for you. It looks like you're going down for this. Is that what you want?"

"Yes," I said without hesitating.

She flopped back in her chair, defeated. "Just wait until she gets here, okay? She'll talk to you. She might change your mind."

Once again I examined her. She gazed back at me calmly. Her face revealed nothing. "I doubt it," I said.

We sat there waiting for hours, until the door to the interrogation room finally opened again and another woman walked through. She came in breathless, as if she'd run miles to get here.

"Thank god," Priya said.

I straightened in my chair, staring in disbelief. My mind was having a difficult time processing the image before me. While we'd been waiting, I'd had plenty of time to imagine who would show up to save me, to rescue me from my own mess. Mira, maybe? She had started this whole thing. Maybe she knew, maybe she'd flown in from wherever she was now to sweep me away from here. It wasn't Mira.

"Rosemary." She held out her hand for me to shake. "Do you know who I am?"

I nodded and cleared my throat. I knew exactly who she was. "Jamila Heath-Jackson," I announced, unable to disguise the awe in my voice. She was older now, but she was instantly recognizable. Her hair natural, tight black curls that jutted out around her head. That same cool bohemian look she had in the pictures from her college days, back when she was Leo Glass's girlfriend. Narrow face and large hazel eyes. No makeup except for lipstick. She was wearing a suit but didn't look stuffy at all, with a colorful silk scarf tied around her neck.

She nodded back, opening her eyes a little wider, as if to say, *Right. Good.* "Priya and I, we're lawyers. We went to law school together, here in Portland. We know people, we have connections—we can help you. Whatever happened, we can get you out of this."

"She doesn't want to get out of this," Priya interjected.

Jamila leaned in and took both of my hands in hers. Her fingers felt warm and smooth. "Is that true?"

I hesitated this time, disconcerted. I opened my mouth, but nothing came out. She held up a hand. "Don't answer that," she said. "Let me tell you why I'm here."

She told me they met their first year of college, she and Leo Glass. "We fell in love," she said, lifting her hands up, like it was an admission. "Seventeen years old, two nerdy computer science majors. Leo knew about that international prize I'd won, back in high school, for this code I'd written. He said it was brilliant. I was brilliant."

"Jamila had *plans* for that code," Priya interjected. "She was going to develop it into a neighborhood watch program, keep people safe—"

"He said he could help. By our junior year, we had it all ready to go on campus. We had investors lined up. As soon as we graduated, we would be co-CEOs of our own company."

"He screwed her over," Priya said flatly. "To make a long story short."

Leo wanted to make changes, Jamila continued. He wanted to name the company Lookinglass. Lookinglass, for a neighborhood watch program? It didn't make sense. Jamila wanted to take a step back. It wasn't about money at all, not for her.

It had all happened right under Jamila's nose. He'd been taking the company in his own direction for months. He had even flown to Japan without her. The Japanese investors were old-school, he had told her. He knew how to handle them. "You know what he told me? That they didn't respond to women in power. Especially not Black women in power."

He said he hated it, how sexist—how sexist and racist—these businessmen were, but he knew that this was how they would get everything they'd been working for. By playing the game. Jamila said she didn't want to play the game. It was over. She was taking her code and striking off on her own.

Leo said she couldn't leave. Leaving was a sign of weakness, he told her. When you love someone, you don't leave. Ever.

"So I stayed," Jamila said. "I stayed with Leo for two more years."

"Because he blackmailed her," Priya said to me. "You know what he did? He installed cameras in Jamila's dorm room. He recorded them having sex. This sex tape, it wasn't just a bunch of raw footage. No. He *edited* the thing, like a best-of collection of every sexual encounter they'd ever had."

"Okay," Jamila said. "She gets it."

"He even set it to *music*."

Jamila focused her attention on me. "I'm on your side, Rosemary," she said, squeezing my hands in hers. "Whatever happened—"

"I'm not going to get away with this." I raised my fingers to my cheek, over the bruises. The skin felt strange, like it didn't belong to me at all. Warm and puffed with blood. "I killed him."

"There are men out there, right outside this police station, holding up signs," Jamila said. "You turned yourself in, what? Six, seven hours ago? And already they're lining up out there, demanding justice for Leo. I know these guys. All those gamer bros and tech dudes who don't like women playing a man's game. Leo Glass is a hero to them. They want you to pay for this—"

"Maybe I should."

Priya heaved an audible sigh. "Just let her go to jail, if that's what she wants."

Jamila ignored her friend and stared me down. It was impossible to break eye contact with her. "This is bigger than you, Rosemary. You have to let us help you. If you don't, Leo Glass will go down a hero. Is that what you want?"

"No." The word came out small, a wavering, pathetic little thing. "But I killed him. If you kill someone, you have to go to prison. It doesn't matter why you did it. It doesn't matter if he was following your fourteen-year-old sister around, it doesn't matter if he *knew* she was starving herself and never said a thing. They'll try me, convict me. That's the law. Justice." My little speech had started off quiet and gained momentum as it went along. By the time I arrived at the last word, I sat back in my chair, exhausted.

But then what? Jamila asked me. I would rot away in a cement block cell, and no one would know. No one would know what he did or why I did it.

If I went to prison, Leo would go down a hero, and my sister would go to foster care. She would wither away, down to nothing. She'd have no one. She'd be worse off than ever. Is that what I wanted, Jamila asked me. Was that the way I wanted this to go?

"Don't let him go down a hero," Jamila said.

"I already confessed." This time I wasn't resigned. The words came out high-pitched, laced with panic.

Jamila took both of my hands in hers and squeezed. "Just tell us what happened. Those bruises—he did that to you, right? And then you picked up the knife, in self-defense. You have a *right* to defend yourself—"

Tears streamed down my face. I couldn't tell her the truth. The truth wouldn't get me out of this. "I can't—" I started.

"Why did you do it, Rosemary?" Priya shot out. "Are you saying you killed him for no reason? You must have had a reason!"

"No," I said. This time it came out like a sob. "No."

"Tell us why you did it, goddamn it!" Priya shouted.

"Priya," Jamila warned, but I was already jumping out of my chair.

My hand slammed down on the table. "I did it because he fucking deserved it!" I yelled.

Jamila and Priya exchanged glances. Then Jamila nodded once, as if we had come to an agreement about something, and I guess we had.

Priya clapped her hands together, as if she had been struck with a brilliant idea. "Leo films everything, right?" she said quickly. "Puts cameras up everywhere?"

I slumped back down in my chair. "Not in his apartment."

"If they found some security footage, though, we could *prove*—" Priya started.

"It would be better if they didn't," I said quickly. A silence descended on the room then. "It would be better if they didn't," I repeated.

"Don't worry about that," Jamila said, her voice clipped.

"He filmed you," Priya said to Jamila. "He filmed you for years, without your knowing. He's got to have cameras all over the place. It's crazier to think he *didn't* have cameras—"

"Either way, don't worry about it." A preternatural calm had settled over Jamila's features. "If he doesn't have them, great," she continued. "If he does—I'll take care of it."

"Like hack his security system?" Priya widened her eyes comically.

Jamila turned to me, ignoring Priya. "I can fix this. All of it. You've just got to trust me."

I found myself nodding. I found myself saying, "I do."

CHAPTER 31

Half a year went by. The cherry blossoms bloomed up and down the riverfront, and then the pink flowers dried up and floated away in the breeze, the petals flying like snow through the air. It was so beautiful. It was always so beautiful, those cherry blossoms, but I wasn't there to witness them. I missed the summer, too, the entire season. No hot days and long nights and sipping cold drinks in sidewalk cafés. No sunbathing on the roof of my apartment building or road trips to the coast to cool off in the frigid Oregon coastal waters.

It was always the same temperature in jail, and the lights went off at the same time every night and flipped back on at the same time every morning. I didn't get beaten up or tormented by heartless guards. The food was terrible, just like you'd expect. Sometimes—most times—I struggled to identify the food at all. Soft mounds of a mushy meat mixture next to even softer mounds of vegetable matter, a hodgepodge of carrots and peas, perhaps, blended into a sickly grayish-green. I closed my eyes and swallowed each spoonful like medicine.

The worst part was the boredom. The way the days blended into each other, punctuated only by visiting hours.

I didn't see my sister at all for eight weeks. For eight weeks, I was tormented by her silence. She had to hate me, after everything I had done. Everything. Leaving her to fend for herself with her abusive father. Failing to take care of her when our mother died, and when she ran away to be with me, what did I do? Did I welcome her with open arms? I made her go back. She had to stab herself in the wrist to make me take notice, and even then I hadn't tried hard enough. And then she moved in and I was supposed to take care of her, but I didn't. She became best friends with a twenty-year-old who enabled her eating disorder. Wendy was wasting away before my eyes, and instead of doing anything about that, I went to France, murdered my boyfriend, and got locked up in jail. I really couldn't have done a worse job if I had tried.

She had been sent back to live with her grandmother, right back where she started. Maybe it would be different this time. Maybe living with her grandmother would be a welcome respite from life with me.

But then one Saturday she showed up for in-person visitation. I was so happy to see her that tears sprang to my eyes. I pressed my hand to the glass separating us, and she lifted her hand, too. "Oh my *god*!" was the first thing she said. She was smiling. A huge, ecstatic grin. All those weeks I had imagined her withering, shrinking further from herself. Her hair falling out in clumps. But she looked good. A flush to her cheeks, a little filled out since I had seen her last.

We talked through heavy black telephone receivers, and she told me she'd worked everything out. She was sorry it had taken her so long, but all this time she had been working her way back here, to Portland, to me. "And here I am!" she said, holding up her arms like a magician's assistant.

She'd sold the ring. This was a long, complicated story, but the salient detail was that she got $120,000 for it. She'd checked herself into a thirty-day program for girls with eating disorders. Her grandmother signed the paperwork. Hannah had gone there, too, at the same time. They'd done it together. "Look," she said, pulling up one of her sleeves to show me the creamy-white flesh of her arm.

"What am I looking at?" I leaned up to the glass and peered at the white expanse of skin stretched over bones. The arm was still thin.

"The lanugo," she said. "It's gone."

"I don't see anything."

"That's what I'm *showing* you." She brought her arm closer to the glass. "I *told* you I'd get better."

"Yeah." I attempted to lift the corners of my mouth. "You did." When I got back to my cell, I wanted to scream and punch my dirty little prison mattress with my fists, but I felt too worn out. I just stared up at the ceiling. My little sister had almost withered away, the fat dissolving from her bones. Her skin tried to protect her, sprouting almost invisible hairs, a fine veneer of fur. How did I miss that? It seemed impossible.

How long would she be in town, I asked her at the end of our visit. When could she visit again? She smiled her big smile and said she was here for good. She was living with Hannah now. Her grandmother was allowing this? I asked, incredulous. Wendy shrugged. She didn't have much of a choice. But, I protested, Hannah was an adult and Wendy was fourteen. (Fifteen! Wendy reminded me. Fifteen in May.) Fourteen, fifteen. What was the difference? Why did a twenty-year-old woman want to take care of a teenager? What was in it for her? What was *wrong* with her? It wasn't like that, Wendy insisted. They were friends. That was all.

I didn't get it. It haunted me, this idea that Hannah was using my sister somehow, taking advantage of her. Damaging her. I hated the idea of them living together, but what could I do? Nothing. I was in jail.

Margorie visited me a few times; even Steele came once. I should have told them, they both said. I should have let them help me. One person who never visited me, not once in the whole half year I spent locked up in that jail, was Sam. They had remote visitation now. Jamila dialed in from Los Angeles; reporters chatted with me from their Manhattan lofts. If he wanted to visit me, he didn't have to leave his apartment. He wouldn't even have to come downtown.

I tried to see things from his point of view: I had promised him I'd let him save me again. I was the damsel in distress, and he was the valiant knight, swooping in to rescue me. He liked that. He liked saving me. I promised to let him whisk me away to Iceland or Russia, let him give up his whole life for me. Hours later, I broke that promise. No wonder he was upset. He had to know, though, that I did it for him, for my sister. I couldn't let them live like that, as fugitives, covering up a crime I'd committed. What kind of person would let the people they love take the fall for them—with them—like that? I did it for you, I would tell him, if he ever gave me the chance. You have to understand that.

~

It was hard to fall asleep at night. All those noises from the other inmates. The clanking, empty sounds of jail. After the lights went out, I would lie on my cot and close my eyes and try to visualize my happy place. It was a technique Wendy had told me about, something she learned in her last round of therapy. Just imagine yourself somewhere beautiful, Wendy said. Remember the color I painted her room? That was the color of the sea, and she pictured herself floating in it, in the middle of the Caribbean. Warm water, salty breeze, faint sounds of strumming guitar. White sandy beaches, palm trees. You have to immerse yourself in it. Picture it all. It relaxes you, Wendy said.

I tried to picture it, the turquoise-blue water, the screech of tropical birds, Calypso music, the white sand, the palm trees swaying in the breeze—everything. I pretended I was out in the water, just floating, but I couldn't do it. I couldn't float. My body plunged underwater, like someone was pushing me, pushing my chest down so I couldn't breathe. I'd shot up in bed, gasping for air, like I was drowning, like I was dying.

The Caribbean was *her* place, Wendy said when I relayed this to her. I needed to come up with something else, a place of my own.

The next night I lay in bed and nothing appeared. Not at first. Then it came to me. That first day Alejandro showed me the apartment. It was October but it was sunny outside, and I'd thrown open the windows to let in a breeze. The wind rustled through the leaves on the trees below;

the leaves were yellow and flickering in the sun, a golden carpet. I could hear the viola play, a clear, haunting sound, a little melody.

In my jail cell, I couldn't hear the echoing sounds of guards' feet or the other inmates' coughs and grunts. I heard only the rustling of leaves, the viola's lingering refrain, and my own voice, humming along. I felt my arms lifting over my head, my bare feet tapping on the shiny wooden floors. I called over to Alejandro. Look at me, I said, who am I? I was the girl from the music video, the girl from the New Order song. That's where I wanted to be, the moment I wished I could relive again and again. Back in my own apartment, my hands raised above my head, dancing.

CHAPTER 32

My trial was the most awaited, most highly publicized, most politically charged murder case in Portland history. Buzzfeed put me in a list of our nation's top ten accused murderesses, along with Andrea Yates and Aileen Wuornos. I was only number seven.

Wendy had tried to tell me and so had Jamila—this was huge. I was huge. Blowing up Twitter. Features in *Willamette Week* and the *Oregonian*. The cover of *People* magazine. Even after they showed me, even after I read the whole spread—my life, dissected and examined on the page, a timeline and map of the "unthinkable act" I committed in Leo's "upscale urban hideaway"—I still couldn't believe it. I read the entire story with fascination, as if the woman in the story were a stranger. I almost didn't recognize the picture they used for the cover, my twelfth-grade yearbook photo. My cheeks still fat with youth, my eyes wide open. "Pretty Little Killer," they called me.

In a guarded bathroom, I changed into a brown tweed suit with a soft silk blouse that tied at the neck in a floppy bow. In the tweed suit I felt different. It was structured, holding the pieces of me together in a way the prison uniform didn't. I had brushed my hair into a severe ponytail and didn't wear any makeup. I looked young this way, sort of forlorn and innocent, like a kid dressing up in her mother's business suit. I wondered who had selected these clothes, how they had settled on my look for the trial. It was hard to imagine my lawyer doing it.

Jamila had promised to hire me the best criminal defense lawyer she could find. The best was Calvin Lewis. From the very first time I met him, in a windowless room at the jail, I'd been impressed by him. I was in my jail uniform—tube socks, rubber sandals, grungy sweats, and a faded-to-pink T-shirt with a stretched-out collar—and he strode in wearing a three-piece suit. He had the body of a marathon runner, tall and lean, and wore his wiry black hair buzzed close to his scalp, with a neatly manicured beard. He was serious, with large dark eyes that stayed trained on me the entire time we talked.

After meeting with him several times, I still didn't know anything else about him, while he knew everything about me. Almost everything. I didn't know how old he was, but I guessed midforties. If I squinted, I could see little white hairs poking out through his beard. He was handsome, in that severe, stern professor way of his, and he was married, judging by the ring on his left hand. That was all I knew about him.

In the courtroom, I stood beside Calvin Lewis, stunned. I had planned to bow my head before the judge, the audience. A nun heading to the altar to receive a benediction, eyes cast downward. Hands clasped together in prayer—no, that would be too much. Hands clasped at my chest.

In the hubbub, I forgot my nun impression entirely.

"Order!" the judge was saying, pounding his gavel.

Every seat in that courtroom was taken. Some people in the audience were holding signs, like they were marching through the streets or participating in a parade. They were demanding justice, one way or the other: LET HER FRY or SET HER FREE. Several of the signs had no words at all, just pink squares printed with an illustration of a raised fist gripping a knife. At the tip of the knife, fat cartoon drops rolling off it like tears.

"This is a courtroom, not a political rally," Judge Landsberger cried out, ordering a deputy to gather up the signs. We weren't happy about this judge. It would have been better to have a younger judge. A female judge. A not-so-white judge. Landsberger hadn't tried another case like mine, though—murders of tech gurus being fairly uncommon, even in

295

this day and age—so they held out hope he'd be fair. It was the jury we needed to convince, Calvin kept reminding me. I tried to believe that.

We took our seats, waiting for the courtroom to settle down. I began to make out familiar faces in the crowd. Margorie was there, and Steele. Jamila and Priya.

Hannah. Hannah Westover. I noticed her and her big brown anime eyes before I saw my own sister sitting next to her. When my gaze landed on them, they bounced in their seats and smiled broadly, waving. I was so happy to see her there, my sister. At the very sight of her, all the tension in my shoulders, in my neck, relaxed. My face broke out in a huge grin at the sight of her. My fingers lifted up in a wave.

The crowd was quieting. The deputy had collected the signs. Before I turned back around, I scanned the crowd one last time, hoping to spot Sam. Part of me had hoped he would show up, even to sit in the background and glower at me. He wasn't there.

~

"Here are some things you already know about Leo Glass," the prosecutor began. Her name was Linda Murray. While I tried my hardest to give the appearance of concentration, I was finding it difficult to focus on her words, mostly about what a great guy Leo Glass was, what a loss to the world. He built a company out of nothing in a few short years. Contributed to Portland's economy. Employed hundreds of people. Blah, blah, blah.

"Here are some things you may not know about Leo Glass." Her voice was very calm and soothing, as if she were talking to a small child, lulling him to sleep. She named some charitable organizations that flourished thanks to Leo's generous contributions. Think of all those that benefited from his largesse, like the children in sub-Saharan Africa who wouldn't contract malaria, all because of Leo and the mosquito nets he provided them, she said. The way she talked you'd think

Leo had personally woven those nets and draped them over the bodies of dying kids.

She wrapped up her opening statements with a reflection on the future I'd denied Leo Glass. All the good he would never be able to do, life cut short, talent snuffed out.

Her tone shifted, right at the end. Went from soothing to a little regretful, a little angry. "It's easy to talk about what a great guy Leo Glass was." I didn't know why she kept repeating his first and last name like that. "But he was more than a vibrant citizen, a passionate patron of the arts, a generous benefactor. He was also a son. A beloved son."

As Linda talked about Leo's mother, I could see that they made the right choice, choosing this woman to prosecute. She was in her fifties, with fluffy brown hair. She wore a strange, bulky mauve skirt suit. She looked like a mom. She was there to remind the jury of that fact: Leo had a mom. "A mother lost her son," she said, her voice cracking, and she was done.

I resisted the temptation to turn around and find Leo's mother in the crowd, though I'd spotted her earlier, sitting by another woman, her sister, perhaps. Leo's aunt. I bowed my head and squeezed my eyes shut, trying to block out this image, this image I had of her in my mind's eye, crying over the death of her beloved only child. I wasn't acting this time. I was sorry. I wished—maybe for the first time—that I hadn't done it.

The next morning I sat up in the front row, alone, waiting for Calvin to join me. I twisted in my seat nervously, craning my neck around to look for him. The judge entered the courtroom, and we all stood up. When he took his seat, we sat down, and Calvin still wasn't there.

A moment later, he came bursting through the doors, then, apologizing to the court, demanded a minute to consult with his client. "*One minute*," Judge Landsberger said, raising his bushy eyebrows. Calvin took his place next to me and slapped a file folder in front of me. We leaned over the folder, and Calvin circled his arm around it, the way a kid leans over a test so no one can cheat off him. "What is this?" I asked.

"You tell me, Rosemary," he said.

I opened the folder, and my own face stared back at me, a picture of me from yesterday. I was turned around in my seat, my head tossed over my shoulder, my fingers lifted up in a wave. I was smiling—a huge, toothy grin, my eyes sparkling with what looked like either joy or mischief or some combination of both. The jaunty white silk bow tied at my chin.

Calvin flipped through the pages in the file. The same picture, over and over again, all of which looked like they'd been downloaded from the internet. Articles had been written, think pieces. My goofily grinning face was now a meme. "The better to eat you with, my dear," and "Who me?" and, straight to the point, "GUILTY."

"No," I whispered.

"You know who Diane Downs is?" Of course I knew. She was way up there on the Buzzfeed list of our nation's maddest murderesses. She drove her kids out to a secluded place and shot them while Duran Duran's "Hungry Like the Wolf" bopped along on the radio. A wild-haired bogeyman did it, she said. No one believed her. When the prosecution played "Hungry Like the Wolf" in the courtroom, she didn't break down and burst into tears. She snapped her fingers and sang along. "You know where Diane Downs is now?" Calvin didn't wait for me to respond. "She's in prison."

"The jury won't see the pictures. It's the jury that—"

"They saw it," Calvin said. "They were sitting right over there." He jerked his head in their direction.

"Is everything okay, Counsel?" Judge Landsberger asked.

Calvin swept the folder up and rapped it against the table as if we'd settled something. "Everything's fine, Your Honor," he said.

~

Over the next several days, the prosecution made its case against me. No surveillance footage was admitted into evidence. Whether this was because Leo had told the truth about not keeping Glasseyes in his loft, or because Jamila had somehow worked her magic and made the evidence disappear, I didn't know. I would never know.

The prosecution had to piece its case together the old-fashioned way, by inundating the jury with witness after witness. "This is a cut-and-dried murder case," Linda Murray intoned.

We had seen Leo's business manager, Douglas Hemper—otherwise known as Sebastian St. Doug—on the prosecution's witness list, so when he took the stand, it was no surprise. Calvin had fought it. Whatever Doug had to say about me, it wouldn't be favorable. Linda would get the whole story out of him, and after that, I'd no longer be the innocent little girlfriend who lashed out at her domineering boyfriend—I'd be the fiery hussy who stabbed a famous tech innovator just for the hell of it. Doug's testimony would be prejudicial, Calvin had tried to argue to the judge. Linda had insisted his testimony would be essential in understanding the nature of my relationship with Leo. If I was in it for the money, not for love; it could establish my motive for murder. The judge allowed it.

Sebastian St. Doug did not want to be in a courtroom talking about hiring prostitutes. Throughout his testimony, he kept his head down. He talked about getting a referral from a "friend" and setting up a date with me. He talked about meeting me in the Valerie Hotel and taking the photograph he would later show Leo Glass. Why did he show him the photo? He was bragging, he supposed. She got him to admit that he had hoped to hire me, that he expected to pay me in exchange for sexual favors.

She asked him about the monthly transfers from Leo's bank account to mine. Did Doug know the amount?

"Six thousand dollars."

"Did Leo Glass tell you the purpose of these transfers?"

"No."

"Would it be fair to infer that Leo Glass was paying Rosemary Rabourne for sexual services?"

"*Objection*, Your Honor!" Calvin shot out, offended.

"Sustained." Judge Landsberger cut Linda Murray a stern look, like a disappointed father. "You know better than that, Counsel."

Linda Murray went back to her seat, smirking.

Calvin got up to cross-examine him. "Mr. Hemper," he started. Doug's eyes lifted, slowly, to meet Calvin's. Like a dog who had just been scolded for peeing on the living room floor. "Did the defendant perform a sexual act with you on the night she met you at the Valerie Hotel?"

His eyes opened wider, and his lips parted as he ran his mind over the question. "No."

Linda Murray looked like she wanted to object, but she thought better of it and zipped her mouth into a tight line.

"Did Rosemary Rabourne take any money from you on that night?"

"No."

I'd gone over the night with Calvin, every detail. I remembered very clearly: I hadn't gone through with the act, and I'd left the envelope stuffed with bills in the hotel. It shouldn't matter if I had, I had insisted. Calvin didn't bother responding to that.

"Thank you," Calvin said. "No further questions." And that was that.

A steady parade of expert witnesses followed. The prosecution tried to bring up the fact that the absence of fingerprints on the knife handle was suspect. Why would the knife—only that knife—show no evidence that anyone had ever touched it? It was a fair point, and I glanced sideways at the jury, to see how they were taking it. They looked bored out of their minds.

The prosecution brought in another expert who, based on photographs of my bruising and the DNA found on the cupboards, said it was "certainly possible" that I'd inflicted the wounds myself.

The funny thing is . . . the prosecution got everything exactly right. I *had* banged my face against the cabinets. I had swiped the boning knife from the rack and plunged it into his throat. I had picked up that knife, washed it off, and hung it back on the rack. They said I didn't call the police. That was true, too. But I'd tried. At least I'd tried.

~

After what seemed like weeks, it was our turn. We didn't need to prove that I hadn't killed him. I had confessed as much. We needed to make the jury believe that I'd been justified in doing it, that I feared for my own life when I picked up that knife. That I had killed him not in cold blood but in self-defense. Calvin Lewis was convinced we could win. During his opening statements, he had talked about me and the sad little life I'd lived, the tragic death of my mother, my selfless act of taking in my orphaned sister. He alluded to my twisted arrangement with Leo Glass.

There was one detail Calvin Lewis didn't add to my life story, and it was a crucial one for our case: he didn't tell them about the IUD. The prosecution had ruled it inadmissible during pretrial proceedings. It was prejudicial, Linda Murray had argued: "Leo Glass is not the one on trial here." The only way for the jury to hear it, to hear the whole gruesome tale, would be for me to go on the stand and testify, something Calvin Lewis refused to let me do. It never ends well, he insisted, and I was inclined to agree. If they didn't put me on the stand, I couldn't lie.

Instead he brought in forensic specialists, psychiatrists, a medical doctor who specialized in post-traumatic stress disorder with a possible explanation for my behavior after the stabbing. I'd been operating under a fugue state when I'd washed that knife, hung it back on the rack. My conscious mind had shut down, and my subconscious mind was working overtime, trying to put order to the chaos. Calvin also brought in an entire team of tech guys who worked on Consuela, the smart-speaker prototype Leo had designed to respond only to his voice. They were able to corroborate the statement I had made to the police: I had tried to call for help.

Our star witness? Alejandro Navarez. Alive and well! Calvin got Alejandro to tell him everything—how Leo had asked him to show me an apartment, to arrange private meetings with me, to escort me to mysterious doctor appointments, to monitor my movements on Lookinglass, to pluck me away from an evening out with old friends. Did Leo Glass tell Alejandro why he was so interested in me? He never said, Alejandro answered. "But I was pretty sure it wasn't for her coding skills." The crowd tittered at that. "No offense," Alejandro added, looking straight at me. I could have almost sworn I saw him wink.

Alejandro testified that Leo had hired him to follow me around, like some sort of low-rent private dick, for two weeks. I sat up in my seat, paying close attention. I hadn't known that. "I didn't want to follow her," he said. He did it halfheartedly. If he saw me doing anything Leo would disapprove of—flirting with another guy, for example—he was supposed to report me immediately.

Did Alejandro witness any suspicious behavior during that two-week period? Calvin asked. "She spent all day walking in and out of coffee shops," Alejandro answered. "She led the most boring life of anyone I'd ever met." Another titter from the crowd. "The next time he asked me to do it, I said no. No way. Not going down that road again."

"The next time he asked? When was this?"

"January," Alejandro answered. "Leo's birthday. He summoned me to pick Rosemary up, and she was standing out in the rain wearing a hideous version of Leo-leisurewear—sweats and a navy-blue hoodie." The crowd laughed, and Alejandro smiled at them. He was enjoying this.

"And Leo Glass asked you to follow Miss Rabourne around again?"

"No, that was the thing. He wanted me to follow her sister."

My entire body went cold.

"What was your response to his request?"

"I quit. I quit on the spot." Alejandro looked straight at me when he said it. Then he turned back to Calvin. "I wasn't going to stalk some little teenager like a pervert. I could go to *jail*. Plus it's just—distasteful."

Linda didn't bother cross-examining him.

Teddy testified for me, too. Teddy, who had had the great misfortune of finding Leo's corpse in a sticky pool of blood. He mumbled so much during his testimony that the judge had to keep advising him to speak up. He admitted to placing the Glasseye over the elevator on the fourth floor of my apartment building, under Leo's orders. "He was weird," Teddy said, raising his eyes to the judge, as if he needed approval. "Possibly mentally unstable."

Linda cried, "Objection!" but Teddy acted like he didn't hear.

He looked straight at me. "I didn't want to do what he asked me, I swear!" he choked out, tears streaming down his face.

It was going well. Better than I could have expected. A stream of witnesses followed: Wendy's school nurse, who reported that I'd been acting odd on the day we picked her up at the school, that she had feared for my safety. The two musicians who had overheard me whispering with Sam in the hallway at the gala after the symphony. They heard Sam ask me if I was safe, if Leo was hurting me.

Our next witness should have been no surprise, but when Sam Ferguson's name came from Calvin's mouth, I shivered the way you do sometimes, that someone-must-have-walked-over-my-grave feeling. He must have been sitting there, in the crowd, watching the proceedings. The first few days of the trial, I'd looked for him, scanned the crowd for his face. Now he was here, and I hadn't even known.

I took in a slow, steady breath through my nose and sat up straighter. It took all my self-control not to twist around and catch Jamila's eye. I hadn't told Calvin about me and Sam. Jamila had told me not to. It wasn't relevant, she said. Not really. Why complicate things?

Calvin's questions were routine. He had brought Sam in to testify about the conversation we'd had after the symphony. I focused all my energy on Sam the entire time he was up there, trying to figure out what he was thinking, what he felt about me. He never so much as glanced my way.

When Linda Murray got up for the cross-examination, I must have visibly tensed, because Calvin turned his body slowly toward me and then looked back at Sam with renewed interest.

She started out easy, thanking him for coming in today and complimenting him on his work with the symphony. She was attempting to banter with him—gushing over one of the guest conductors last season, cracking some joke about the viola section's hilarious Twitter feed. She laughed, but Sam didn't. He narrowed his eyes at her, as if he'd grown impatient and was bracing himself for the real questions. "How did you know Rosemary Rabourne?" she asked him.

"She lived next door in my apartment building."

"So you were neighbors," Linda said, raising her eyebrows as if to suggest that this was a very interesting development indeed, although Calvin had gone over this during his questioning just a few minutes earlier. "You were neighbors," she said. "So you must have seen each other a lot."

Sam frowned. "Not really."

"And her sister? You knew Wendy, too?"

"Objection," Calvin shot out. "Relevance."

The judge sustained the objection, and Linda Murray waved her hands, impatient. She was wearing a navy suit with gold buttons on this day, a strangely nautical look. It wasn't quite as matronly as her previous ensembles, and I wondered if this was an intentional move on her part. She looked like a naval officer in an old movie, one from the 1980s. *Top Gun*, maybe.

"Mr. Ferguson," she cried out a few decibels louder than before. "Did you and Rosemary Rabourne have a sexual relationship?"

Calvin slapped his hand on the table in front of us. "Objection, Your Honor!" This was a startled, angry objection. Not his style at all. I knew he was seething.

I didn't register what Linda Murray had to say—I just heard the high-pitched, whiny cadence to her voice. The judge overruled the objection and told Sam to answer the question.

Sam didn't shift in his seat or look the least bit uncomfortable. He said yes in such a curt, matter-of-fact way that Linda Murray looked momentarily off-kilter. She shuffled through her notes. She hadn't been expecting him to admit it so readily, perhaps. She had wanted to beat the answer out of him in a cinematic courtroom moment.

She asked him when and for how long, and Sam said it had been about a year ago, for just a few days. She asked what the exact dates of our "affair" were, and Calvin objected to the term "affair," and finally after Linda rephrased the question, Sam said he couldn't recall the exact dates.

"And why did the affair—excuse me—the sexual relationship with Miss Rabourne end?"

"She ended it," Sam said. Again, he showed no emotion whatsoever. I sat in my seat and mirrored him. No emotions. I wasn't sure if Sam was truly over me, if he'd turned off the switch, snuffed out any shred of feeling for me, or if he was acting this way because he loved me, because he was, once again, trying to save me.

"Did she say why she wanted to end it?" Linda Murray asked.

"She said she wanted to be with Leo Glass instead," said Sam, and the courtroom rumbled. The judge shot the crowd a warning look.

"She said—what?" Good old Linda was off her game again.

Had Sam perjured himself for me? No—he was telling the truth. I had told him I had a boyfriend. That was true.

"Asked and answered," Calvin said, and I relaxed. He was back to his old self. We'd won this round—she hadn't been able to prove that I'd cheated on Leo.

Right as Ms. Murray said, "No further questions," I thought of something. I shot up in my seat and grabbed the pen right out of Calvin's hand so I could scribble him a note: "I told him about the

IUD." I underlined it twice, ripping the page, and I gave Calvin an intense, begging look to make sure he understood the importance of this. He was already out of his seat, asking the judge for permission to approach the witness again.

"Mr. Ferguson, did you see Ms. Rabourne after her return from France?"

"Yes, I did." Calvin got him to explain how I'd pounded on his door, beseeched him to help me. I'd dragged him up to the roof of our apartment.

"Why did she drag you there? Why not talk in the hallway, or inside one of your apartments?"

Sam told him what I was like that day, my skin prickled with an angry rash. My hair, which had been cut since he'd last seen me, was lank and tangled. I wasn't acting like myself. I was afraid, Sam said. He could feel it radiating off me, the fear.

Linda Murray tried to object several times, but she was the one who had opened up the line of questioning in the first place, saying my relationship with Sam was relevant to establish a possible motive for the stabbing, so the judge let Calvin keep going.

The whole time Sam testified, I didn't breathe. I sat as still as a statue in my seat, watching him. He was coming unraveled, a bit, under Calvin's questioning. He was melting. His face had flushed, just slightly, and he ran his hands through his hair nervously.

"What was Rosemary so afraid of?" Calvin asked.

"Objection, speculation."

Calvin held up a hand. "I'll rephrase. What did Rosemary *tell you* she was afraid of?"

"She told me Leo was watching her," Sam said. He inhaled audibly, and the pink flush deepened. The cords in his neck tensed. "She said he'd been watching her, watching her sister. She told me he'd paid her to be with him—he wasn't her boyfriend, like I'd thought before. He was paying her." Sam was upset now. The words were tumbling out. Linda

Murray didn't object—the jury knew this already, or they had guessed, anyway, after Sebastian St. Doug's testimony.

Sam looked at me then, for the first time. Our eyes met, and I tried to telepathically communicate everything to him, that I didn't want to break my promise but I had to, for his sake, but now that he was here, I needed him to help me. Please, Sam. I couldn't go back to jail. A life sentence in prison—I couldn't face it. I'd committed a crime, yes, a horrific crime, but locking me up forever wouldn't undo any of it. If I got out of this, if Sam helped me get out of this, I would devote the rest of my life to—

"She told me he hurt her." Sam's voice shot out, carried over the courtroom. "Leo Glass hurt her. He watched her and he manipulated her and he made her get an IUD, and then, while they were in France, he tore it out." Sam looked at the jury when he said it. "Leo Glass ripped the IUD out of her body with a pair of *tweezers*," he said, and the jury, the audience, everyone seemed to gasp. I could feel it, the shock of it, ringing out.

"Thank you," Calvin said. "No further questions."

~

Our little victory didn't stop Calvin Lewis from chewing me out afterward, as we exited the courtroom. "Never surprise me like that again," he said into my ear. I told him I didn't think my relationship with Sam was relevant to my case. It wasn't an affair—hadn't we proven that in court? And even if it was, cheating on your boyfriend isn't a crime. I wasn't on trial for being a slut. That's what I said to Calvin.

He said that was where I was wrong. That was exactly what I was on trial for. We need the jury to walk away thinking Leo was an abusive psychopath and I was as pure as the driven snow. If I didn't get that, well—Calvin didn't complete the sentence. He let it sit there as I got carted away by a deputy, shuffled back into my cell for the evening.

~

I had hoped Sam might appear in the courtroom again on the last day, to hear the verdict. I had held out hope, just a shred. He wasn't there. Everyone else—my haters with their angry scowls, my advocates wearing pink T-shirts emblazoned with the now-ubiquitous raised-fist design—filled the seats. Wendy smiled and gave me an enthusiastic thumbs-up. This time I had the sense not to return the gesture. Jamila was there, sitting next to Priya. When I caught Jamila's eye, she opened her blazer jacket, revealing her pink raised-fist T-shirt.

Jamila had become a bit of a celebrity herself. A journalist had spotted her in the courtroom audience and asked to interview her for the *New York Times*. It hadn't been clear—not at first—why Leo Glass's ex-girlfriend was there, watching my murder trial. When it came out that she was there for me, because she believed in me, because she wanted me to win, it became huge news. Jamila appeared on the *Today* show. She gave a TED Talk about women in tech, how vital they were, how important it was for them to rise up and let their voices—their ideas—be heard over the "persistent chatter of men."

I was winning in the court of public opinion once again. But the jury didn't see any of that. They wouldn't have seen Jamila on the *Today* show or read about her in the *New York Times*.

"You should put her on the stand," I told Calvin in a desperate phone call. "This could be huge for us." Jamila, Leo's successful, brilliant ex-girlfriend, was in my corner. The jury had no clue! This could cinch a win for me.

I heard Calvin sigh on the other end of the line. "We've been over this," he said. Putting Jamila on the stand could backfire for the same reasons putting me on the stand could backfire. We wanted the jury to understand how Leo hurt me, how he manipulated me—but he never beat me. He never beat Jamila. He never left a mark on either of us. "The prosecution will get that out of you and they'll run with it. It could sink us."

Linda Murray stood up at her podium and faced the judge to deliver her closing statements. She was wearing the same mauve suit she wore on the very first day. It must be her lucky suit. Her hair was blow dried and puffed out to perfection. She was wearing copper earrings, two shiny disks, like blank pennies. She smiled calmly at the judge and at the jury and fed them a few lines about how important their role in this process was, how it made them a part of the judicial system that guarantees each citizen a right to a fair trial, etc., etc. I sneaked a look at the members of the jury. Their faces were impassive. Tired, even. That was good. They weren't getting puffed up on the idea of the power they wielded over me, my fate.

She talked again about Leo Glass, what a great guy he was, quite the humanitarian. They looked unimpressed by this as well. When Linda Murray gestured to Leo's mother, Christine, who sat in the audience, dabbing her eyes with a tattered tissue, I looked down at my hands, contrite. "The defense is arguing that Rosemary Rabourne brutally stabbed Leo Glass to death in an act of self-defense," Ms. Murray said, her voice rising now. "They say Leo Glass used his power and influence to manipulate the defendant. He paid her. He gave her and her sister the ability to stay in a nice, safe apartment. Yes, he watched her. He scheduled doctor appointments for her. He bought them matching outfits." Linda laughed a little here. "Who are we to judge what goes on behind closed doors, in a relationship between two consenting adults?" Linda gestured over to me and Calvin. "If Mr. Glass was making Ms. Rabourne uncomfortable, she could have told him to stop. She could have"—Linda widened her eyes—"walked out the door."

The jury was paying attention now. Some jurors were leaning forward in their seats. "Did Leo Glass slam Rosemary Rabourne's head against the cupboards?" She shrugged in an exaggerated way, the shoulder pads of her suit rising up to her ears. "We don't know. What we do

309

know—what both sides agree on, what Rosemary Rabourne confessed to—is that she killed Leo Glass on that cold, rainy night last April.

"I'll leave you with this," Linda Murray said. "If being with Leo Glass was so awful, why didn't she leave? Rosemary Rabourne stayed of her own volition. We don't know how she got the bruises on her face. The defense wants you to believe Leo Glass did it. We have no evidence to corroborate that. She could have tripped and fallen into the cupboard. She could have banged her own face against them in frustration. We don't know. We do know she stayed even after she knew the relationship wasn't working. That was her choice. It was also her choice to pick up a knife and brutally stab it into his throat, severing the carotid artery. Leo Glass died within minutes. 'Exsanguination' is the technical term. I call it cold-blooded murder."

The crowd shifted and murmured as Linda Murray took her seat. Calvin Lewis unfolded his long limbs and rose to standing. He didn't approach the podium immediately. He had an amused smile on his face, as if he were arranging his thoughts, as if everything the prosecution had just said was too comical, too much to take in.

The crowd went silent, watching him, anticipating his next move. By the time he approached the podium, the room was completely silent. Calvin adjusted his lapels and smoothed down his tie. Still wearing that smile, he looked up at the judge and then at the jury. Then he began his closing statements. "Let me tell you a little something about Rosemary Rabourne," he said. He talked about what a selfless person I was, going to such extremes to help out my troubled, orphaned little half sister. He talked about Leo Glass and reminded the jury of the testimony from various witnesses that painted a picture of what the last several months had been like for me. "Now, is any of this justification for taking his life? No. But it sets the scene. It provides *context*. Rosemary Rabourne is not a 'cold-blooded murderer.'" Calvin said "cold-blooded murderer" in a mocking tone, as if it were the most preposterous accusation anyone could hurl at me, the person who confessed to stabbing Leo Glass in the throat. The audience tittered. "She's a young woman who has endured extremely difficult circumstances."

Calvin paused here and leveled his gaze once again at the judge, then at each member of the jury. He laughed a bit, as if he had at that moment recalled a private joke. His head shook back and forth. Courtroom theatrics, reporters would call it later. When he spoke again, his voice was louder and more urgent than before. "The prosecution asks why she didn't leave." He jerked his head once, disgusted by the very question. "Why didn't she leave?" He was almost shouting now. His words echoed through the courtroom. He looked again at the jury, at the entire courtroom audience.

I looked back, too. Jamila caught my eye and nodded once. Wendy and Hannah sat together, so mesmerized by Calvin's performance that they didn't notice me. I turned to the jury. Calvin had them spellbound. They were leaning in, toward him, like he was a magician onstage. Like he was a rock star. They didn't want to miss anything. This was good, I thought. They liked him. They bought into him.

"Leo Glass manipulated my client from the start. He spied on her, by his own admission. He spied on her sister, a minor. Fourteen years old. Leo Glass isolated Miss Rabourne from her friends. He paid her for her friendship, for her companionship. He *insisted* she get an IUD and then what did he do? He yanked it out of her body with his bare hands. So why didn't she leave?" he asked again, incredulous. Dramatic pause. He surveyed the audience. His face wide open. Eyes big. The courtroom was silent. He had them—the judge, the jury, everyone, in his thrall. His voice rose for the finish. "She didn't leave because she FOUGHT BACK." His voice boomed out and the courtroom erupted. His words were met with whoops and claps and, yes, a few boos, too. Some people in the audience stood up, their hands furiously clapping.

It was epic, really, and ridiculous. Even I had to admit that, how ridiculous it was. I realized I was smiling, that my smile was huge, spreading across my whole face. I might have exclaimed something,

something like "Ha!" and bounced in my seat. I got caught up in it. We all did.

The judge pounded the gavel, over and over, demanding order in his courtroom.

~

The jury deliberated for forty-five minutes. They filed back in, one after the other, and took their seats. A young woman on the jury raised her eyebrows at me, and the corners of her mouth turned up. Her eyes sparked. That's when I knew they were going to let me go.

PART THREE

CHAPTER 33

We had to move away from Portland after the trial. We tried several places, each one farther and farther away, until we wound up here, in this city, this city in a whole new country, on a whole new continent. I don't want to name it, this city, but it wouldn't be difficult to figure it out.

By the time we got here, it had died down a bit, the media circus. They had turned me into a feminist icon. You couldn't go anywhere without seeing that image of the fist holding up the bloody knife. The country—the world—flocked to social media to tell their stories. The hashtags #whyIdidntleave, #howIleft, and #Ifoughtback all went viral. A photograph of me, raising my fist in triumph as the verdict was read, appeared on the cover of every newspaper and magazine in the country.

The most famous one was digitally altered to turn the subdued gray skirt suit I'd been wearing that day into bubble-gum pink. In my raised fist, they'd added a carving knife slick with blood. That was how I was being immortalized, dressed in pink, raising a knife in the air, a gigantic, full-toothed grin on my face. People stopped me on the street. I never knew if they were going to throw their arms around me or spit in my face. Wherever I went, I braced myself for either, or both.

We had to get away. First to Seattle, then to New York City. Now here. It had been Wendy's idea, moving here, across the Atlantic, in the middle of a whole new continent. Why there? I had asked her when she proposed it. I thought she'd suggest an island, somewhere hot where we could lie on white sandy beaches all day, drinking piña coladas out of pineapples.

But no, Wendy had insisted we move to this place, to this exact city. After eight weeks it already felt like home, like we could settle in here for good, make a life for ourselves. No one recognized me, or if they did, no one bothered me, running up to snap my picture or demand an autograph. Wendy started going to an international high school, and I was taking language lessons in the morning. After the lessons, I went to a coffee shop and sat on velvet benches with my classmates, a menagerie of students ranging from age eighteen to seventy-six, hailing from Eastern Europe, Africa, and Asia. We drank espresso out of little white cups.

I spent the late-fall afternoons in our attic apartment that looked out over the rooftops and spires of the city, this beautiful old-world city with its gardens and churches. I went upstairs and sat at a little desk under the sloped ceiling and looked out at the darkening sky and wrote. I started with the fires, the smoke that had choked out Portland that day when Wendy showed up at my doorstep, begging for me to take her in. That seemed like the right place to begin.

I wrote most of it in a rush. Hundreds of pages, thousands of words tumbling out. I couldn't get them out fast enough, the words, to cover everything I'd been through, everything that had happened. I was tempted to make Leo worse than he was. I considered turning him into a more sinister character. He could have humiliated me, threatened me. I could have had him cup the back of my head in his palm and slam my head against the cupboards that night. I could write that and they'd publish it, and everyone would believe it. It fit in nicely with the narrative they created. The story everyone wanted to believe.

Instead I tried to get to the truth of it. Do any of us understand the truth of our own lives, of the very best and worst that we've been through? Probably not. We all have our own filters, our own perceptions and misperceptions.

After they read this, they'll lose faith in me. Some of them will. They'll feel betrayed, perhaps. They'll demand a retrial. They can't try me again, though. I know that. And even if they wanted to, they'd have to find me first.

I walked around my new city, and I felt grateful for it, for the freedom. Lying in that cell all those nights, it was all I ever wanted: freedom. Mornings in language class, afternoons writing. In the evenings, Wendy was home and we cooked dinners together. I was trying to teach her to cook, and maybe it was helping her.

I kept a close eye on her, but I tried not to let her know I was doing it. I would weigh her daily if I could, record her progress in a chart. Examine her skin for signs of sprouting hair, sniff her breath. I would root out those telltale signs of regression, any little sign that she was just faking her way back to health. But you can't love someone by watching them. I should know that better than anyone.

Did I deserve it, this new life, this freedom? Probably not. I tried to be grateful. I got away with murder. When I think about it, my mind uses those words exactly: I got away with murder. I wanted to spend the rest of my life *trying* to deserve it. Someday, after the hubbub died down and everyone was wrapped up in the next scandal, the next hashtag craze, I'd go home. I'd slip back into my old life, go to law school. I wanted to follow in Jamila's footsteps. Pay it forward. So many others just like me—or nothing like me—went through what I went through, or worse. Not everyone got away with it. Jamila reminded me of this every single day, forwarding me articles. A girl, sixteen years old, sentenced to life in prison for shooting her captor, who had kidnapped and raped her for two years. Women held for years in ICE camps after getting smuggled over the border by sex traffickers. A girl who had killed her own father with an axe. No one knew why. I could guess.

I wanted to help them. I promised myself I would, someday. It would make a suitable ending to this story, wouldn't it?

The book needed an ending before they would send me the second half of my advance. I needed the second half of the advance before I could go back home, go to law school, and swoop in to save all those women, deliver them from a system that was designed to keep them down. If I had my ending, I could do it. I could save them all.

I couldn't write the ending of this book because I refused to end it this way, with me depressed and lonely in the drafty attic apartment. Sometimes when I was sitting in the attic, a blanket wrapped around me, my hands gripped around a mug of tea to keep my fingers warm enough for typing, I closed my eyes and pictured myself dancing by the open window of my old apartment. I tried to summon the sound of Sam's viola. I knew I'd never hear it again except dimly, warped through my mind's ear. My punishment. My life sentence.

I was tempted to simply invent something. How would anyone ever know? I tried endings out, drafting pages and pages of possible futures. None of them felt believable.

I tried to think of all the women wearing the pink T-shirts with the fists holding knives. Of all the women crawling out from the hashtags, telling their stories. I wanted to give them a happy ending, show them that it was possible. I could give them that.

CHAPTER 34

"We're going out tonight," Wendy announced. "Put on something nice."

"I don't have anything nice." I didn't look up from my manuscript. I'd been staring at it for days, weeks, reading and rereading. Editing for errant commas. I had written it all out longhand, in a notebook. Then I bought a computer and typed it all myself. That had taken a few weeks. My editor kept hounding me for pages. Just send the first chapter. Just send me what you've got. I told her it wasn't ready. I wasn't ready. She was acting panicked, like if the book didn't get done, the world as we knew it would end. She would hire me a ghostwriter, she said. The world needed this story, and they needed it now, while it was still hot.

I had started to ignore her. Maybe I'd never finish it. Maybe I'd never get the second half of that advance and never go back to law school and never help any other women the way Jamila had helped me. Maybe I could live with that.

Wendy threw an outfit on my bed. A simple black dress, a pair of tights, a bright-red scarf. "Put this on," she said. "The concert starts at eight."

"Concert?" I turned to look at her, standing with her hands on her hips. She was already dressed up in her own teenage way, in a too-short skirt and a bulky cable-knit sweater. Her eyes were clear and bright, the lids sparkling with some sort of glitter eye shadow.

"Why did we even move here if we weren't going to take advantage of all the culture. The art, the music?"

"I don't know," I grumbled. "It was your idea, remember?"

We took the subway to the city center, and then Wendy led me through the streets, weaving us through dark cobblestone sidewalks as if she had been there a million times, as if she knew exactly where we were going. We entered an old church. It was so dark inside I could barely see anything at first. It had no electric lights at all, just candles. It smelled strongly of must and melted wax. "What is this place?" I whispered.

A small crowd of forty or fifty people had gathered in the pews. Wendy tugged my arm and led us to a spot in the middle. She was squirming in her seat next to me. "It's almost time," she said, pointing to the altar. Four empty chairs sat surrounded by more pillar candles on spindly stands.

At eight o'clock exactly, four musicians walked onstage, and at that moment, Wendy took my hand and squeezed it so tightly I thought she'd crush my bones. They bowed in unison and stood back up as the audience delivered a polite smattering of applause. Wendy let go and we clapped, too, but it was as if my body were acting of its own accord because my mind was having trouble catching up. I turned to Wendy, my mouth open.

Her eyes flickered in the candlelight. "Surprise!" she whispered.

I directed my attention back to the musicians. I knew them. Imogene Wu—I'd recognize her anywhere, with that jet-black hair down past her waist. Timothy Karr. Less recognizable than Imogene, perhaps, especially in those new glasses, but it was definitely him. Standing next to him was a short, stocky guy I'd never seen before. And on the far left, Sam. It was definitely Sam, exactly the way I'd last seen him, exactly the way I always pictured him. His hair was a little longer in the front, perhaps. That was the only thing that had changed. He brushed it aside with his free hand and bowed slightly to the audience.

Ferguson—that was what they were, after all, the old band, together again—took their seats and looked to Sam, who nodded and then counted them off. Their bows touched their strings all at once, sound filling the church. I sat through the entire performance without breathing, my heart thrumming in my chest. I felt like I was going to pass out from the sheer excitement of it. The air crackled. It was every-thing—the city, this city where no one knew us, no one knew who we were. Where no one rushed to snap pictures of us or hurl wet clods of moss at our coats. We were here and *he* was here at the same time. It seemed unbelievable.

The acoustics were odd, echoey, the notes bouncing all over the place, but it was perfect, somehow, plaintive and haunting.

Maybe I was imagining it, but the music told me a story and it was his story, about his brother, his sadness, his loneliness. I felt like I was following the story as clearly as if he'd written it all out in words, and I sat in my seat, spellbound, waiting for the next part, for the chapter of him and me to begin. I'd know it when I heard it.

The music picked up and there it was—the quick, frantic, ecstatic refrain of the two of us, of our meeting. Then heartbreak, a jangling interlude. There was the bird trapped in my apartment and then flying out the window. There was Sam again, rescuing me from my doom. The cabin. Heartbreak again.

The piece lasted an entire hour without intermission. It ended on one loud, resonant note they all played together and held. They lifted their bows from the strings, and still the note rang out. The audience waited until it faded completely, and so did the musicians. Everyone hovered there, suspended.

Someone started clapping, and then someone else, and then the church erupted into an uproarious applause. People stood, one after the other, for a standing ovation. They don't give standing ovations easily here, in this city. It wasn't like it was at home.

Wendy and I stood, too, clapping our hands together. After the applause died down, we sat back on the pew, waiting for the crowd to clear out.

"How did you know?" I asked Wendy then. "How did you find him?"

"Instagram," she said.

"He's not on Instagram anymore." I should know. I checked constantly. Scoured the internet for any trace of him. He had disabled everything. Disappeared.

"It's not like this concert was a big mystery."

I wasn't sure what to do. Something was holding me back, preventing me from rushing up to the stage, chasing after him and begging him to forgive me. Part of me wanted to leave things as they were. I knew he was still thinking about me. I knew he had loved me, once. Maybe I should leave it at that. Maybe that was enough.

Wendy was still talking, explaining how she'd planned this whole thing. She'd been planning it for *months*, actually, and she had kept it from me because she knew I wouldn't agree to come here just for a concert—

I had to laugh, then, at my sister. "We moved here for one concert?"

Wendy laughed, too, as if it were all a delightful game. "Come on," she said. "They're leaving."

We rushed back to the stage, and Wendy took my hand then, tugging me. I followed her—what choice did I have?—as she barged out a side door and into a backstage area. Imogene, Timothy, and the stocky violinist were all back there, talking over each other in loud, animated voices. Sam wasn't there, and I wasn't sure whether to feel relieved or devastated. He was gone. It seemed like the worst kind of luck, that he could disappear so quickly. That was a sign. I should pay attention to signs.

Wendy ran up to Imogene. "Where is he?" she asked.

Imogene stopped midsentence, surprised by the interruption. She looked from Wendy to me. She knew who I was. I could see that flash of recognition in her eyes, but she didn't reintroduce herself to me or even say hi. She pointed and said, "Down the hall. Out the door. He just left."

"Thank you!" Wendy cried, already running. I chased after her. It was all so surreal, like a dream. Like the ending of a movie.

The door opened up to a dimly lit street, a pedestrian walkway that in the daytime would be lit with little shops and bakeries filled with rows and rows of meticulous cubes of layer cakes. The cobblestone street wound around the corner. If he had gone left, we would see his retreating form. We ran, and as soon as we turned around the corner, we saw him, the silhouette of him, the dark outline of a man carrying a viola case.

"Sam!" Wendy yelled. "Sam!" She ran ahead of me and I heard her screech. She jumped up and threw her arms around him. "I got him!" she yelled back at me.

I made my way to them, slowly, winding up the narrow walkway. I could see my breath when I exhaled into the cold night. A single snowflake floated above me and whipped behind my hair. I looked up to the sky, surprised. It hadn't snowed since we'd arrived here. Another flake appeared. They weren't soft, fluttery flakes but small white dots that darted through the air and scuttled across the sidewalk.

I stopped in front of both of them and tried to smile, though I was nervous. If he was still angry, I could accept that. I had already accepted that. "Hi," I said.

He looked the same. So much like Sam that my throat closed up, like I could cry just remembering everything about him. His floppy hair. His handsome, rumpled face. Our eyes met. He wasn't smiling, but he definitely wasn't angry. If I had to pin down his expression, I'd say it was a bit baffled, like the guest of honor at a surprise party, right after the lights switched on and everyone shouted "Surprise!" and the confetti was still floating through the air.

Wendy announced that she had to leave. She had somewhere to be, she said. Friends to meet.

Then Sam and I were alone in the narrow street. He reached toward me, slowly, the way you might reach out to touch a ghost, not sure whether your hand was going to land on flesh or air. His fingers hesitated before settling on my cheek. "Hi," he said.

Everything happened quickly after that, the way it did the first time. He set his instrument on the ground, and I flung my arms around his neck, and he grabbed my face in both hands and kissed me. We stumbled back against the stone wall of a shop and kissed until we ran out of breath.

"I can't believe it's you," I said when we finally broke apart. What were the odds, the two of us here, so far from Portland, after everything? Maybe we would have a night together, or two. Maybe we would have a week and I could show him the sights. We could drink coffees and eat cakes and listen to music and read books tangled up in the sheets on the wide-planked floor of my little attic room with its sloped windows looking out at the spires and rooftops. He could move here—why not? It would be perfect. The perfect place for him. A city full of music.

Sam laughed. His laugh was loud and deep, and it surprised me so much I jumped a little. It surprised me because I'd never heard it before, not really. I had never heard him laugh until that moment.

We stood there under the streetlight, with the snow falling thicker and thicker around us, and I thought that no matter what happened after this—whether we said goodbye or went up to my attic room, whether he stayed an hour or stayed forever—I'd end the story right here, exactly at this moment. It would be difficult to make up an ending any better than this one.

It was almost impossible to believe that I deserved it, this happy ending.

ACKNOWLEDGMENTS

In 2015 I wrote a listicle for Bustle called "These Novels Should've Had Female Main Characters." High on the list was *Crime and Punishment*. Women didn't murder people enough in literature, I mused, and a seed was planted for *No One Knows Us Here*. While my book later veered off in several very different directions, I'd like to thank everyone who said this was not a completely horrible idea.

My writing group The Whom carefully combed through the entire manuscript, seven pages at a time, and their advice and support kept me going. Mara Collins, Art Edwards, Christina Struyk-Bonn, and Michael Zeiss must have read dozens of versions of this book, and each time they helped make *No One Knows Us Here* better. Heather Arndt Anderson, Sarah Gilbert, Justin Gauthier, Gracey Nagle, and Brian Reid also encouraged me to keep going early on, as I stumbled through that first draft—thank you!

My sister, Gina Kelley, read an early draft of the manuscript and gave me very detailed, valuable feedback that I took very seriously. I tried to incorporate all of her suggestions and hope I did them justice.

Jen Chen Tran, my agent, saw a wish list by a new editor at Lake Union, Melissa Valentine, and immediately thought of *No One Knows Us Here*. Without Jen and Melissa, the book would be gathering dust on the proverbial shelf right now. Thank you, Jen, for sticking with me all these years, and thank you, Melissa, for believing so strongly in the book's potential. I'd also like to thank Danielle Marshall for filling in while Melissa was away, and Tiffany Yates Martin, whose edits forced me to dig deeper into character motivation, resulting in a much more satisfying finished product.

And finally I would like to thank my family, Andy and Audrey—my two biggest supporters and fans. I'm so happy I could do this with you by my side, cheering me on.

ABOUT THE AUTHOR

Rebecca Kelley is a fiction writer from Portland, Oregon. Her first novel, *Broken Homes & Gardens*, was published in 2015. She also coauthored *The Eco-nomical Baby Guide* with Joy Hatch. When Rebecca isn't writing, she is conducting elaborate baking experiments, designing book covers, and keeping up her thousand-plus-day streak in Duolingo. Find her at www.rebeccakelleywrites.com.